OF GODS
AND MEN

OF GODS AND MEN

DONAL O'NEILL

Macdonald
in association with Lilliput Press

A Macdonald Book

Copyright © Donal O'Neill 1987

First published in Great Britain in 1987 by
Macdonald & Co (Publishers) Ltd
London & Sydney
in association with Lilliput Press, Gigginstown, Ireland

British Library Cataloguing in Publication Data

O'Neill, Donal
    Of gods and men : march of a nation.
    Rn: Eoin Neeson   I. Title
    823′.914[F]   PR6064.E4/

ISBN 0–356–14336–8

ISBN 0-356-14336 8

Printed in Great Britain by
Redwood Burn Ltd, Trowbridge, Wiltshire,
Bound at The Dorstel Press

Macdonald & Co (Publishers) Ltd
Greater London House
Hampstead Road
London NW1 7QX

A BPCC plc Company

Contents

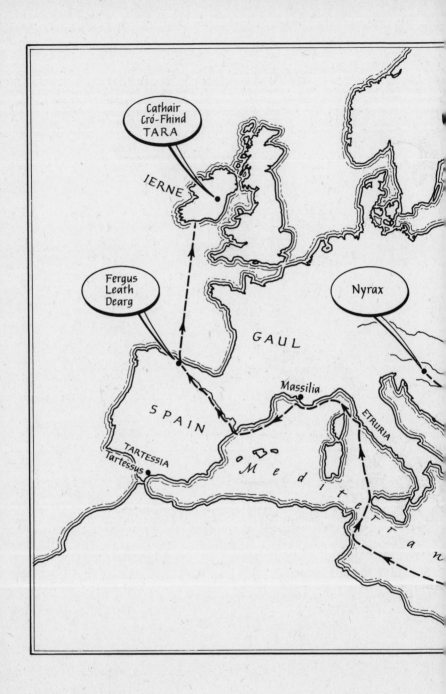

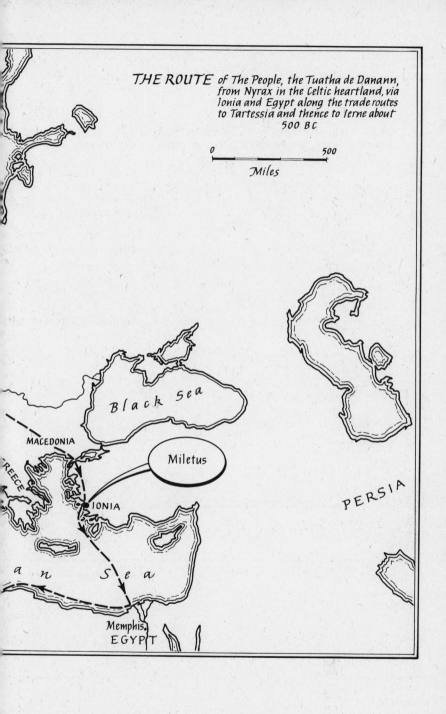

THE ROUTE of The People, the Tuatha de Danann,
from Nyrax in the Celtic heartland, via
Ionia and Egypt along the trade routes
to Tartessia and thence to Ierne about
500 BC

0   500

Miles

Black Sea

MACEDONIA

GREECE

Miletus

IONIA

PERSIA

an   Sea

Memphis
EGYPT

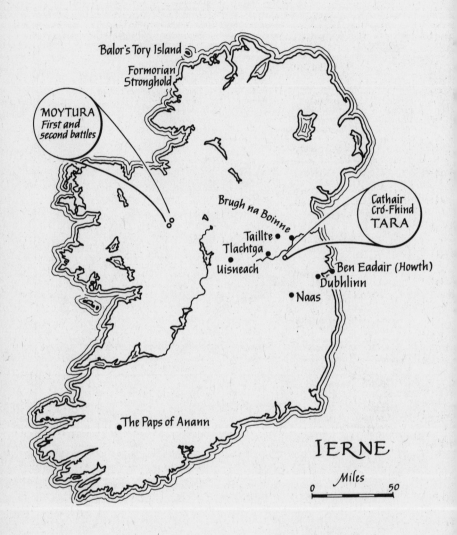

Balor's Tory Island

Formorian
Stronghold

MOYTURA
First and
second battles

Brugh na Boinne

Cathair
Cró-Fhind
TARA

Taillte
Tlachtga

Uisneach

Ben Eadair (Howth)
Dubhlinn

Naas

The Paps of Anann

IERNE

Miles

0   50

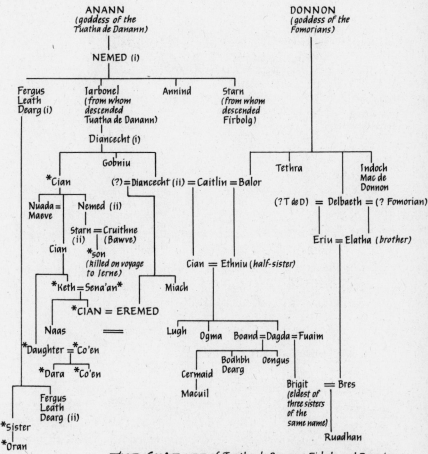

THE LINEAGE of *Tuatha de Danann, Firbolg and Fomorian showing the relationships between the principal characters in the tradition. The characters of the book have been woven into these genealogies, and they are, for convenience, identified either by *name or with (ii) following.*

Names of Characters
with biographical notes

*   Indicates that the character is traditional.

(ii)   Indicates that a character with a traditional name has been introduced into the narrative to simplify the complex relationships in the tradition.

Absence of either indicates a fictitious character.

ANNID*   One of the sons of Nemed*.

BALOR*   One of four brothers all kings of the Fomorians; demi-god. Has supranormal powers. Known as Balor of the Evil Eye. Fate decrees that he will name his grandson who will kill him. When the child is born arranges to have him killed (as with Astyages and Oedipus). But this is thwarted and events proceed as ordained. Killed by Lugh* at the Second Battle of Moytura. The other brothers are Delbaeth*, grandfather of Bres*, Tethra* and the Indoch Mac de Donnon*.

BARNEA   A dissolute effiminate who turns traitor.

BLANAID* Consort of Lugh*, a wanton.

BOAND* One of the Dagda's* consorts.

BOBHDH-DEARG* Favourite son of the Dagda* by Boand*.

BRES* Eochaidh Breas, Eochaidh the Handsome; Like Lugh* of mixed Fomorian and Tuatha de Danann parentage, also incestuous. But whereas Lugh's father was T.de D., Bres's father was Fomorian. Each supported his father's people. Fatally attractive to women, they persuaded their men to allow Bres to become regent of Ierne with disastrous results when he placed the T.de D. under an impossible tax-burden to the Fomorians, leading to the Second Battle of Moytura.

BRIAN Champion of Cian, grandfather of the principle character. Goes with him, to his death, to fight the God of the Ocean, Mananann Mac Lir*, when Cian is cast adrift for inadvertently betraying his geasa.

BRIGIT* Priestess, one of three daughters of the Dagda* all of the same name and all priestesses.

CAITLIN* Consort of Balor* (of the Fomorians) and sometime mistress of Diancecht* (of the Tuatha de Danann). Mother of both Cian* (father of Lugh*) and Ethniu* (mother of Lugh).

CERMAID* Son of the Dagda*, foster-brother of Lugh*, whom he cuckolds with Blanaid*. Killed by Lugh as a consequence.

CIAN Central character. Grandson of:

Cian* — brothers Nuada*, Diancecht* (ii) and Nemed* (ii) — sons of:

(i) *Cian*, son of:

Diancecht*, son of:

Iarbonel*, from whom the Tuatha de Danann descend. Also

(ii) *Cian** son of Diancecht*, father of Lugh*, Ogma*, and the Dagda* by his half sister Ethniu*. (For the purpose of the book he is son of Diancecht (ii). In tradition he was son of Diancecht* and Caitlin* and may be identified with (i) above.)

CO-EN   Cousin and friend of CIAN

CONAIRE   An old boat-builder.

CREDA*   King's (Nuada's*) champion.

CREIDNE*   The skilled silversmith. Maker of the silver arm for Nuada*.

CRUITHNE   (Bawve), consort of Starn* (ii). Becomes deranged.

DAGDA, the*   King of the Tuatha de Danann. One of three brothers of the incestuous relationship between Cian and Ethniu. The others were Ogma* and Lugh*.

DARA   Brother of Co-en, cousin of CIAN.

DELBAETH*   One of the four brother-kings of the Fomorians. Grandfather of Bres*.

DIANCECHT* (ii)   Chief physician and ancestor* of the Tuatha de Danann. Also (ii).

DRUIDS*   Of the Tuatha de Danann, in addition to Methger* and Mead*, Forgal*, Cairbre*, Ai* and Edan*. Of the Fomorians (?), Fathach*.

ELATHA*   Son of Delbaeth*, Father of Bres* by his half-sister, Eriu*.

EOCHAIDH*   King of the Firbolg.

EREMED*   Daughter of Diancecht* (here Diancecht (ii)), consort of CIAN. Skilled in healing with herbs.

ERIU*   Daughter of Delbaeth*. Mother of Bres* by her half-brother, Elatha*. Also Eriu (ii) daughter of CIAN. See Scota*.

ETHNIU*   Daughter of Balor* and Caitlin*. Mother of Lugh* by her half-brother, Cian*.

FERGUS LEATH DEARG* (ii)   Whose people settled in Spain. One of the four sons of Nemed*. The others are Iarbonel*, from whom descended the Tuatha de Danann, Starn*, from whom descended the Firbolg, and Annind* who died. Also (ii).

FUAIM*   One of the Dagda's* consorts.

GOBNIU*   The Smith of the Tuatha de Danann. Brother of Diancecht*. (Here brother of Diancecht (ii).)

GODS*   Some of the Tuatha de Danann gods referred to in the book; Anann*, the great goddess, Ishtar etc.;

(the gods and goddesses of war) Badhbh*, the Raven of the Battle-field; Macha*, the Hag of War; Calibh*, Death and Woe; Neit*, the Killer of Men and the Morrigu or Morrigan*, the Queen of the Dead in the shape of birds of ill-omen. Mananann Mac Lir, the Son of, or God of, the Sea.

of the Fomorians, the great goddess Donnon*.

IARBONEL   From whom descended the Tuatha de Danann. One of the four sons of Nemed*.

INDOCH MAC DE DONNON*   One of the four brother-kings of the Fomorians.

KETH   Father of CIAN.

KURUS*   Cyrus the Great of Persia.

LUGH*   Lugh Lamh Fada, the Ildanach (Samildanach), son of a T.de D. father and a Fomorian mother (the half-brother and sister, Cian* and Ethniu*). Adopts the heritage of his father. Principal protagonist for the Tuatha de Danann at the Second Battle of Moytura. Supranatural powers. The embodiment of wisdom and the sciences. Brothers the Dagda* and Ogma*.

MACUIL*   Son of Cermaid*. Killer of Lugh* in revenge for his father.

MAEVE   Consort of Nuada*.

MATHA*   Daughter of the Indoch Mac de Donnon*, king of the Fomorians, helps CIAN and the Dagda* to escape.

MEAD*   Ancient chief druid of Nemed's* people. Precedes the People to Ierne.

METHGER*   Chief druid of the Tuatha de Danann.

MIACH*   Son of Diancecht* in tradition. Killed by his father who was jealous of Miach's greater skill as a physician when he healed the arm of Nuada* (of the Silver Hand). His sister, Eremed*, planted the seeds of healing herbs on his grave from which they grew each from the position of that part of the body for which it was effective. Here son of Diancecht (ii).

NAAS*   Sister of CIAN, consort of Lugh*.

NEMED* Founder-father from whom Tuatha de Danann and Firbolg descend. Also (ii).

NUADA* (of the Silver Hand) One of the three brother-kings of the Tuatha de Danann, the others being Cian* (grandfather of CIAN) and Nemed*. Here transposed by three generations.

OENGUS* Son of the Dagda* and Boand*. Brother of Bodhbh Dearg*.

OGMA* Chief Poet and Seer of the Tuatha de Danann. Brother of Lugh* and the Dagda*.

ORIAN Nephew of Fergus Leath Dearg* whose people settled in Spain. The rival and peer of CIAN.

PYTHAGORAS* Greek philosopher and mathematician.

RUADHAN* Son of Bres* and Brigit*.

SCOTA* Milesian princess. Killed by accident having won a decisive horse-race against Eriu*, daughter of CIAN, on the outcome of which depended the future leadership of the people of Ierne.

SENA'AN Mother of CIAN.

SLAINGE FIONN* Firbolg king.

SONS OF MIL* Eber* and Eremon*, who divided Ierne between them after the invasion by the Milesians and the defeat of the Tuatha de Danann at Taillteann. Whether the defeat was actual or symbolic is traditionally unclear. For the purposes of the book it is both, in that a horse race involving a princess from each race, Scota* for the Milesians and Eriu* for the Tuatha de Danann, is substituted for actual battle. Traditionally such a race did occur between Scota and Eriu in a slightly different context, but with the same intent. Here both stories are combined for simplicity. The third son of Mil was Amergin*, the great poet and visionary of the Milesians. The fourth son was Ith*.

STARN* From whom descended the Firbolg. Also (ii).

SRENG* Firbolg emissary and chieftain who cut off Nuada's* arm during the First Battle of Moytura.

TAILLTE* Tuatha de Danann queen for whom the Taillteann Games were inaugurated as a memorial.

TETHRA* One of the four brother-kings of the Fomorians, the others being Balor* (of the Evil Eye), Delbaeth* and the Indoch Mac de Donnon*.

Part I
THE COMING

I am Cian. I took the name when I was initiated at the age of twelve because it was that of my grandfather and of his father before him. Before that I was called, simply, son of Keth. You will be surprised that I was initiated at twelve rather than at the customary sixteen and, in its proper place, I will relate how that occurred. I make this chronicle to record the coming of the people to Ierne, why we came, and of the two great battles we fought to establish ourselves, and I will also tell how, more recently, we were followed and joined by the Milesians, our kinsmen and cousins, and of what is now being done that will effect and guide the future of this island, now called Eire.

The people came to Ierne, most westernly of the two Iernides islands in the Northern Ocean, from Tartessia and Bregantia about sixty years after my great-grandfather brought them there in an exodus following the Ionian defeat by Kurus, the Great Persian. I remember how the after-affects of that decision still lingered on us many years later, so that we did not at times know whether to cling to it for reassurance as to a cloak in early spring weather or shed it and trust in what lay ahead.

The spirit that impelled my great-grandfather and many of the people of Miletus westward along the Phoenician trade routes, by Egypt and Sicily, clashed with feelings of envy of those who had remained under the rule of Kurus — or Cyrus as he is sometimes known nowadays. There were those among us who — even in my time — asked how bad was that? Had Kurus not been the most enlightened, the most powerful and peaceful ruler, as was Xerxes, his Achaemenidean kinsman, at the time I speak of? Was Persia not the greatest power in the world? And, of course, the wealthiest? This, especially, was often a silent — sometimes not so silent — irritant when they looked at the barren lands of Tartessia and thought of the well-cultivated, fertile soil of Ionia which Harpagus had taken for his master. Little use to be proud of our independent spirit, of the mingling of the roving blood of our Scythian land-locked cousins and that of the sea-roaming Phoenicians with our own Celtic fibre, when we lacked a proper place of our own. The people had been in Miletus for generations before the Medes or the Assyrians, even — for all I know — before the Sumerians, when the Carians lived in Ionia. They married with their neighbours, as is happening here in Ierne today. Thus the people acquired both a rich city and a richness of life, of belief, custom and dress — including, I might add, the fashion of the trousers some of us wear, which came down to us from the long-since vanished lords of Hattusa, the Hittites.

But in Tartessia our skills and sciences were diminished. It was not an appropriate place to settle and the sheer effort involved in trying to stay alive blunted their edge. For, in spite of what you might hear to the contrary, although the city of Tartessus itself away to the south-west is a wealthy commercial centre, Tartessia in general is a barren place of red earth and little water — what there is is unpleasant and occasional, and comes in rare and roaring torrents between dusty periods of drought. There was little copper to make bronze, and less tin. Further down the coast there are Phoenician iron mines, but they are secret and guarded by powerful troops from their strong settlement some distance inland, where a huge rock is split by a mighty cleft through which a mountain river bounces and flurries.

The land here was also better, but well defended. Where we settled the rock was porous and the earth infertile. Inland, beyond the mountains, it was said to be better but that was away from the sea and the rivers, such as they were, although it was the route taken by Nemed, one of my grandfather's brothers, and his people.

The kings of Tartessus are constantly seeking emigrants from the other end of the Mediterranean, luring them with promises which prove to be as worthless as the land they are offered when they arrive.

I was still very young when we lived on that arid plain backed by mountains and facing the sea, and at that time, above most things, I loved to listen to my grandfather's stories about the exodus in the year he was born and about the adventures of the people long before that. Even at an early age I knew a great deal about the people, for which I have always been grateful to Cian, my grandfather. We, the people of Anann, the Tuatha de Danaan, and our forebears, lived in Miletus in Carian Ionia (where some of our people then, as now, still lived), torn between the yoke of the Greek and that of the Persian until the city was finally overrun by Xerxes, murdered by his brother Sogdianus, also brother of Darius, the bastard and degenerate, who murdered his murderer!

Before Miletus we were a settled people of the country at the head of the Danube where our city was Nyrax and we were known by our family names, or simply by the name that the Greeks gave to all the people of the centre of Europe, Keltoi or Celts.

My grandfather was an ollamh (leader) and fille, or poet, having inherited the skills of one from my great-grandfather, the leader, and those of the other from my great-grandmother, the seer and fille who was killed in battle with the Samnian Greeks shortly after his birth. On summer evenings, under a sky full of stars, we often grouped around fires outdoors, but within the wattle fence that protected the village against wolves and bears. Ours was invariably the largest group, both because my grandfather was the leader and people liked to be close to him, and because he was such a good narrator. It is easy to recall the fire, the flames reflecting off faces and moustaches; the brown, grey and saffron of cloak and tunic, with the glitter of gold or some other rare metal here and there. The earth was reddish brown and I would sit beside my grandfather in a fold of his cloak, which he wore even on warm nights. To me, in those days, the Miletus he spoke of was a settlement of the kind we lived in, but with more and bigger houses. When he talked about its splendid streets and temples and storeys I had no idea what he meant.

I also learned how the people of long-dead generations came south and east with their horses and cattle, goats, sheep and swine, along trade and pasture routes from the heartland. Some, like the Tuatha, taking the easiest route, others going north and west. Few went south across the great mountains or north to the forests. Some went south-west by the mountainous land route to the plains and sea between Etruria and Spain, and some went eastwards into Cimmeria and Scythia.

Why did they leave, departing from strong homes and a bountiful homeland? The answer came in later years when I understood some of the pressures the people experienced — not the least the simple drive of conquest. In addition I began to understand that wealth is only wealth when it remains intact and grows. A pasture will feed only so many cattle; a river yield only so much gold, so many fish; land support only so many people. Moreover there is the exuberance of youth and ambition for power, which attracts leaders like honey attracts bears. But a settled community can have only a few leaders and this fact, too, led to migrations by the people.

When my ancestors set out they followed the route through Scythia, whither the young men of the people then, as now, often went to learn horsemanship and warfare. From there they went to Macedonia, a barren mountainy place and a poor, but hardy people, past the scattered cities of Thrace and across the narrow Greek sea to the broad lands of rich Phrygian Ionia and Miletus. Sometimes a Persian satrap slung an arm about the city — even the Assyrians at one time plagued its walls and the Sumerians once ruled there — and some-times Greek emissaries from one city or another persuaded the people to ally with the Hellenic Federation, but at all times it was a place of prosperity, of leadership — for our people were naturally resourceful among the fickle colonists of Phrygia — and, mostly, one of peace. But that was before the struggle between Kurus and his enemies, when control of the peninsular coast became vital to the growing empire.

They remained in Miletus for generations until, as I have said, following its conquest by Harpagus they moved west through Egypt and along the Mediterranean. They had many adventures, some of them brought about by the effects of the wars of the Shepherd and Anointed of Jehovah, as my cousin's mother still calls the Great Kurus. Our links with Egypt were also old and some of my grandfather's best stories were about the old wars with, and settlements in, Egypt: the wars in Cyprus in the time of Akhenaten, for example, and a great battle against the pharoah Ramses (the Third) in which the people, whom the Egyptians call the Danuna, together with our allies from Lycia, Tyrhennia, Etruria and Tartessia, lost more than 9000 swords. We had our victories also when the young pharoah Tutankhamon briefly ruled and the two Egypts were in disarray. But ... What with births and deaths, defections and acquisitions, the migrants' numbers rose and fell. The grandparents of my own mother, Sena'an, were Egyptian. Their wealth had been consumed by war and famine when they joined my grandfather's people with their only daughter. There were many others, such as the grandparents of my cousins Dara and Co-en, who joined us for different reasons that I'll tell you of later. The journey along the Mediterranean took time and my grandfather was six when they reached Tartessia where he grew up and was to spend most of his life. They were not, as they had hoped, welcomed either by those who had gone before them or by the king. They were too many and too powerful. Theirs was the biggest single migration in living memory along this route. Though they travelled in groups, they were nevertheless linked and homogenous. Poverty was not their driving force. Attacks on small groups by Phoenicians occurred too. They used to greet them from their ships with smiles, but if the people refused to bargain, they often attacked them. They also had a particularly unpleasant way of disposing of rival merchants, and our people have always been merchants. They would — for all I know they still do — take the chief men aboard and drop them overboard from their ships in deep water with large rocks tied to their feet. I remember, after a storm, a body tied in this way being washed ashore near the settlement, which is how I first learned about it.

The resentment of the people was understandable. Those who were there already had been lured there with all their possessions, by the promises of the settler-hungry king. They had arrived in small groups to carve their homes and homesteads from virgin land. They didn't want a host of newcomers, particularly not in numbers that would upset the local balance, and perhaps take over altogether. So the people were permitted to settle only provided they split up and took lands unwanted by earlier settlers. It was accept this or fight and, in justice, they chose to accept. But it was not what they had come to find and the idea of moving further on never died. Even then there was talk of the distant islands of the Iernedes.

In the second generation, when my grandfather was a young man, the people formed three groups each led by a brother, the three sons of Cian: Nemed, the eldest, Nuada the youngest and my grandfather, also Cian. Nemed took a third of the people and penetrated the mountains and the plains beyond to the northern coast where he founded a settlement in preparation for the journey across the sea to the westernmost of these islands, which journey about half of them later made. Another group, led by Nuada, the youngest brother, moved to the high midland plains, while some others, independently, went to the small, barren islands off the coast of Tartessia where they were welcomed by the Baleares. My grandfather's group remained where they were, with more breathing and living space. Although they were scattered the groups still maintained contact. That is until Nemed sailed for Ierne.

Things remained like that for many years, until, as I say, I was about ten, when they suddenly altered and the question of moving on revived in an unexpected and, for me, exciting way. Naturally I remember only what impressed my young mind, then hovering in the rebellious halfway stage between childhood and youth. They were not necessarily important things. But one incident — and it was important — is as clear to me now as if it happened yesterday. That was the coming of Nuada.

I was sitting by the main gate of the settlement whittling a shaft with the knife my father had given me when I was still very young and first went with the flocks. He had it from my grandfather and he from his father. It was neither bronze nor iron, nor any metal, but a very old blade of a black, glossy stone, much chipped and worn, a prized possession. My regret is that I have no son to pass it on to. My father told me it came from an island near Phrygia called Melos. He had made a new handle for it, a beautiful thing of walnut, carved with all the skill of the master harp-maker to fit the contours of my hand and be a thing of beauty in itself.

Concentrating on what I was doing, I did not hear them until, suddenly, a shadow moved in my range of vision and they were there. Rather *he* was there, for beside him the others were insignificant.

It was not only that he was big. A sense of power was evident in and around and about him. He led, others followed. To me then, looking up at him, he seemed the biggest, strongest man I had ever seen — although, in fact, he was neither as tall nor as broad as my grandfather. He was also the most richly dressed man I had ever seen. Gold and silver glittered from his chest and neck and arms and about his head, and his clothes were belted and clasped with bronze and coloured stones. But the magnificent sword, fully two cubits long, that hung from his hip in a painted and ornamented scabbard, rivetted my eyes. The hilt was a masterpiece, panelled with gold. The guard and the pommel formed glittering orbs, while the grip was bound with twisted silver and copper interwoven with crimson leather. The tang of iron protruded half a finger's length beyond the pommel and the teeth of sea-lion decorated it as well. He stood there, his hands on his hips, looking down at me and laughing.

'Are you the sentry?' he asked, replacing the smile with a scowl.

'Well?' he growled, bending his hairy, ugly face down towards me. I shook my head. Laughing again, he straightened up and turned to his companions.

'There you are you see,' he announced, 'no defences and an idiot boy as a sentry.' He glared at me again. 'Are you an idiot, boy?'

I found my tongue.

'No I'm not,' I said. 'And I'm not the sentry. Who are you? I'll call my grandfather.'

For an instant he looked down at me and, even yet, I wonder what persuaded him to contain his anger. Fortunately he contained it. If he had not I doubt if I'd be here to remember.

Quietly, with just the hint of a smile, he said, 'And who might your grandfather be?'

I stood up. What I had to say was of my genealogy. 'I am Cian,' I replied, 'grandson of Cian, father of his people.'

'Well,' he acknowledged, turning to his eight companions. 'Well!' he repeated. He turned back and bent towards me, smiling again, a hard smile.

'What you will do now, Cian O Cian,' he hissed, 'is take me straight to your grandfather ... quick!'

'Quick!' he shouted when I did not move fast enough. I ran as fast as I could through the gate to my grandfather's cave. Behind me I heard Nuada's laughter. Cian sat in the shade and appeared to be dozing. But I knew better. Little happened in the settlement that escaped his eye and before I had time to say anything he caught sight of the nine men coming through the gate.

'Nuada!' he breathed. He stood up staring at the approaching figures. 'Go and fetch Methger and the other leaders of the settlement,' he ordered, 'and tell your mother to come. We must prepare a feast. We have guests.'

He strode past me towards the men, his arms outstretched, and embraced his brother with cries of welcome.

And yet — there was something else. My own uneasiness was not dispelled as I expected. Perhaps it was that I sensed an uneasiness in him. I do not know. My mother says, in spite of my great bulk and awkwardness, that I am over-sensitive and inherited too much knowledge of the other world from my great-grandmother, and perhaps she is right.

The two brothers greeted each other with kisses and there was much general talk and preparation. The noblemen cleaned themselves and their weapons and when that was done the feast was ready. It continued during the following day and night, only us young children not being included.

Later, from my grandfather, I heard what Nuada's visit was about and even had some premonition of how it was to affect not only our own lives, but those of many generations of the people to come.

While the Iernides were remote they were not entirely unknown. They were reputed to be cold and icy, but we knew that they were very fertile. They were said to be inhabited by savages and wizards, but the south coast of the larger island had also been colonised by our cousins the Bretani, who had taken the north-west migration route rather than the one to Ionia taken by the people.

Some of the Bretani had penetrated to the east and south-eastern parts of Ierne, and it was they who had told us about Nemed. There was a rumour that Ierne was rich in gold … and if there was one thing the people understood it was gold. Men — and women — came from all over the civilized and barbarian worlds bringing gold with them for our smiths to fashion into beautiful decorated jewellery and ornaments. So that Nemed and his people went to seek a homeland and, besides, gold.

They settled for a time before their final journey on the northern coast of Spain, to build their ships, establish a base settlement (where many of his people still live today) and to assemble provisions. Many of the warriors and young men belonged to a newer generation, when at last forty and five boats were launched, each with the thirty people and some animals, and Nemed sailed for his goal.

Many ships were lost in the turbulent ocean. Some died on the journey and were confined to the foaming realm of the sea. Only three ships reached their destination and there were fifteen days between the arrival of the first and the third, and they were scattered on a wild, indented coastline. They searched the coast for a suitable river. Nemed led his followers up a broad river between wide rampart-like, round-topped cliffs and into a harbour, from where the river branched again and narrowed beween high wooded hills of tall pine on one hand and fistlike oaks on the other, until they came to a place where the hills receded from the river. There were fewer trees and a plain opened on the south bank and there was a broad, treacherous marsh on the other.

But on an edge of the marsh, like an island between it and the river, there was a span of firm land, perhaps thirty acres or so in extent. Here Nemed made camp. They brought timber from the forests and rock, plentiful dark red sandstone, and built a village and roofed it with rushes from the marsh.

On the plains on the far side of the river they ploughed and grazed their herds.

The feasting was nearly ended, Cian told me, when Nuada put down his drinking horn. In repose Nuada could be quiet, almost still. But with no lessening of power. There was something animal-like about him. He was like a lion — not one of those from the mountains that occasionally carried off a sheep or a goat, but one of those from Egypt or Carthage, such as I had once seen caged in a Phoenician ship that called for water. Nuada had the same bright, encompassing, cold eyes. The same indifference. And he could be brooding and sombre. He turned to my grandfather and said:

'Brother, I have bad news.'

Cian nodded. In the firelight his face became grave. The people sensed the change. Talk contracted, like the chattering of startlings before thunder. Faces turned to the two big men side by side, and eyes glistened. Nuada stood, held up his hand, and the talk ceased.

'I have bad news,' he said, 'and it concerns us all.' Again my grandfather nodded.

'It is of Nemed and his people,' went on Nuada, his shadow weaving into the darkness behind him.

'They are all dead.'

A gasp swept the people. My grandfather jumped to his feet. Nuada looked at him with hard eyes.

'Our brother and all his people are dead,' he repeated, 'slaughtered.'

'In the name of the god! How?'

'Treachery!'

'What treachery? Whose?' Nemed and my grandfather had been very close. Of the three brothers, Nuada, the youngest, even as a child had been a lone, powerful figure, who tended to halt gaiety by his presence. He held up both arms. They stretched up, like a supplication, into the night.

'Listen,' he commanded, 'listen to me, people of Cian, and I will tell you what treachery.'

He looked round the people and then spat one word like a curse.

'Firbolg.'

The Firbolg — the Bagmen or the Bellymen — had been slaves and the children of slaves, and had served the people long before Miletus existed. They got their name from the fact that they filled their bellies with the leavings from our cooking pots, for which they were also responsible and which they carried in leather bags. Some, but not many, came westward with the people, but the great majority had stayed in Miletus with those who remained behind.

When the first Xerxes later swallowed Miletus and it became a satrapy of his empire, in accordance with a quirk of Persian character, one of his first acts was to give these Firbolg their freedom! I have no doubt that Xerxes believed in the justice and wisdom of this; his empire was, after all, distinguished for method and efficiency, but, from what my grandfather told me, I also have no doubt that granting sudden and unexpected freedom to slaves such as the Firbolg, who neither expect it nor know anything of dignities and responsibilities of freedom, is imprudent. But that is what Xerxes did. He gave them the choice of their freedom, on the condition that they accept Persian citizenship with its requirement of military service, or, if not, that they leave the empire. To his surprise the Firbolg, almost to a man, chose to leave the empire.

Carefully avoiding settlements of the people as they did so, they went north and west taking with them herds and flocks. Eventually they reached the edge of the northern ocean, with its fertile islands.

I will not easily forget my grandfather when he spoke of the Firbolg.

'They crossed the small sea to the first island,' he told me, 'where they lived for a time with the Picts and other barbarians from the north, avoiding the Bretani, for they would not have allowed them to go free.'

He spat into the embers of the fire at his feet, sending up a shower of fine grey ash and making a black spot in it that quickly sank out of sight.

'Would to the gods they had met them,' he went on, 'and made of them again the slaves they are.'

He paused.

'They moved like a pestilence. Eventually they crossed to Ierne, where they fought a battle with some of the Bretani in the east. The Bretani were few and, though they fought bravely, were eventually overcome. Thanks be to Macha and to Cernunos,' he said lifting his hands, 'they all died, more than five hundred, rather than let themselves be taken by slaves and murderers.'

He looked so long into the dwindling fire that I thought he would not continue.

'Then what?' I asked.

'Eh?' he said. 'Oh ...'

'What happened then?'

'Listen,' he said, 'and do not forget. After they had beaten that group of the Bretani, they took over their settlement and began to spread out, moving across the island in small groups until they made contact with another people who had been there before them.'

'The giants?' I asked.

He smiled, but only with his mouth — and the only reason I knew that was because I saw the movement of his moustache and a gleam of teeth.

'No,' he said, and scratched his chin. 'They are not giants. But according to Nuada they are primitive, savage and very powerful. The Fomorians. They come, he says, from a land away to the north called Lochlann. And they also inhabit part of northern Albion, and the small islands in between. They have great strongholds and cities of stone, which they prefer to timber. Nuada knows little about them except that they are too strong for the Firbolg to trouble, and that they have powerful gods who lead them in battle. He also says they have only one eye and one leg and that the women fight in battle like the men in bands of their own.'

I quickly made the sign against the evil eye, turning east and spitting, and looking at my grandfather.

'Cichloiste?' I asked. 'Amazons!'

'I don't know,' he answered. 'Perhaps. But groups of women warriors for sure.'

'With one leg and one eye?'

'So Nuada says.'

'They should not be too difficult to beat so,' I said and he laughed.

'They say they are great warriors,' he went on.

In any case, the Firbolg did not make war against them, but tried to ally with them and win their favour.

'I don't need to tell you,' he went on, his face distorted with disgust, 'how they did so. In the only way they know how; by making slaves of themselves, their women and their children, and by doing the Fomorian bidding in everything. So they were permitted to live and form new settlements of their own. I can imagine the filth and squalor,' he added. He paused. 'They lived there for some years, hunting mostly and serving the Fomorians. Then came Nemed and his people. They made their settlement in the southern part, where were neither Fomorians nor Firbolg. For years they were undisturbed. Then they made contact with the Fomorians, according

31

to Nuada, and there was some exchange of hostages, even fosterage I believe. They traded a little, but neither bothered the other. Our people did not know about the Firbolg. One day they found a small hunting party of them half a night's journey from the settlement. They brought the Firbolg back to be slaves. Afterwards they escaped. Nothing more was seen of them or of any other Firbolg for some time, but it was a considerable loss as there had been both men and women, and Nemed's people hoped to breed additional slaves.'

My grandfather's voice hardened.

'At the beginning of Samhain, when the nights are long and the people resting, a huge party of Firbolg came through both the marsh and the river, and attacked the settlement as the sun rose – it was a slaughter. The male children were all killed', he said, 'and many of the older women. Most of the remaining women and children were carried off before they could kill themselves. Carried off', he went on, standing up in his distress and looking towards the roof of the cave where I could see nothing, 'into slavery by the Firbolg after they had mutilated and decapitated the bodies of the men whom they left lying in their blood and entrails. They took the heads to dangle from their belts and poles. They say ...', he faltered, '... the head of Nemed was used as a ball by them and kicked from goal to goal of piled bodies across the settlement before they left.'

I watched him as he sat again and leaned forward to put a root on the fire; mechanically, as if he didn't realize he was doing it. I can still see his face in the glimmer of that fire as he leaned forward. A long face, lined and creased between his nose and mouth and with similar strong lines in his cheeks and across his brows. They all disappeared into hair, into his great moustache that he trimmed and plucked out of vanity, and sometimes tied to his shoulders with leather thongs when he wished to appear most imposing, and into the fine, thick white hair kept in place by the seven-coloured headband of a chieftain. Only his eyebrows were still dark above hooded, hazel eyes that were often brooding and sleepy, but could also flash from an eagle face gone suddenly pale with passion. The picture is very clear, though he is long since dead.

32

'Cian,' I said, 'if they all died or were taken for slaves, how do you know? How does Nuada know?'

He neither turned nor moved the arm which still fingered the root he had placed in the embers. He looked up towards the door, but did not stand again. When he spoke he didn't seem to be speaking directly to me. It was as if he were voicing a thought to give it substance and force.

'We know', he said, 'because beneath one of those piles of bodies lay a youth who was not dead. Nemed's grandson Elchor. He lay under the pile of bodies of his brothers and his mother for a day and a night while they revelled in the settlement, took the women who were left — even children — lay there while they cooked and ate the flesh of our brothers and drank our wine. He lay there until they went and then escaped.'

'But ...' I blurted.

'He was right,' announced my grandfather. 'Elchor prayed to the gods to protect him from the savages so that he would survive to tell what had happened. The goddess took him under her protection and placed her shield between him and the Firbolg, even when they tore the body of his young sister from where she lay across his back and did unspeakable things with it, before dismembering it and roasting it on our own spits. Everything that happened, he saw it. And he lay there as if he were dead while it happened.

'When they had gone, taking with them all the women and children who survived, he pulled himself free. He was mortally hurt and had it not been for a further intervention by the goddess in the shape of her instrument the druid Mead, who had been absent from the settlement on some business of his own, then he would not have survived. But we know that Mead returned and saved him and helped him to make his way eastwards. Why he did not come too I do not know nor what has happened to him since. But, binding his wounds with herbs and animal dung and leaves, he directed Elchor to a small community of the Bretani. Elchor lived long enough to tell them what had happened and to put them under geasa — obligation — to carry word of it in every detail to myself or Nuada, whichever they

33

should first find.'

For an instant his eyes seemed to glow.

Mixed thoughts and feelings ran through me.

'Grandfather,' I asked, 'what will we do?'

Still looking straight ahead, he replied:

'We will avenge them.'

The following months became a period of one long preparation. Instead of the routine coping with one season passing to the next, our first concern was with the forthcoming migration, which is what had been decided. My principal job was herding. No longer the menial task of swine-herding, fit only for small children and slaves, but the cattle and sheep, which were fewer but more precious. I was particularly charged with ensuring that they did not scatter and that they grew fat, contradictory instructions if ever there were. So that, instead of bringing the flocks to fodder, I had to devise a method of bringing fodder to the flocks. So I organised every child I could under the age of ten and together we scoured the countryside, setting up and replenishing dumps of fodder at key spots near the few watering places, so that the herds could move from one to the other and remain under control.

Meantime the adults, that is everyone over sixteen summers, and those in between, had similar important preparatory tasks: weaving and sewing skins for tents; training pack animals; making arrowheads, spearheads and knives as well as shafts and hafts, shoes, clothing, food containers and water bottles; vessels were made from the abundant clay and fired by the hundred; smiths worked non-stop, milling and salting were continuous. The entire activity of the community, apart from that necessary for day-to-day existence, was concentrated on the forthcoming journey.

And it was the same in every other settlement, ashore and on the islands. There was much coming and going between them and our settlement, where my grandfather held the essential threads, pulling them ever closer and ever tighter as he directed all matters to the one purpose. And it was the same with the people of Nuada. In the weeks preceding the appointed time the people began to congregate around our settlement. The first to arrive came from the islands. To me they were in some subtle ways different, and yet they were the same; more colourful, perhaps, in their clothing; more lively in the songs they sang at night, and yet the clothes and the songs were familiar. It was curious to observe the sameness and the difference all at once, perhaps best seen in their burial chambers and monuments, which resemble ours, but are different. Much of what they know about building in stone, we brought with us to Ierne.

The departure date was decided by Nuada and my grandfather in consultation with the other ollamhs, or leaders: Methger the druid, the brothers Dagda the great seer and Ogma the warrior and historian, who knew the secrets of recording, and the Dagda's daughter Brigit who was high priestess of Anann. It was a night I well remember. Perhaps had I no special reason to do so, I would not now be recording this.

It was a high spring day when the warm sun had brought colour to the sparse land and little lizards lay upon the rocks. Towards evening I came back from minding the flocks after I had been relieved by one of the young warriors — a thing I much resented. It was supposed that a warrior, full grown, was needed to care for the flocks at night and protect them against wolves, wild dogs, bears and the occasional mountain lion.

Anyhow, on that particular evening I was relieved by a young cub with a spear and turned towards the settlement a little after sunset with the moon still hidden beneath the reddening sea. My knife, the one my father Keth gave me, was clasped in the belt of my tunic and I wore well-seasoned sheepskin sandals on my feet (I had made them myself and still preferred these to the more modern ones with thongs and thick soles, even though it meant putting them in water each night and putting them on wet each morning to shape them to my feet). The settlement was unusually quiet for the time of the evening when I arrived. Normally there would have been the activity of pre-paring the main evening meal, and the hum of talk mingled with the smells of the settlement would have reached me long before I reached it. This evening only smells greeted me, together with — a something. Something I couldn't place as I approached. Then I realized it was silence and an unaccustomed darkness. No fire glowed within the village wall, no warmth reflected off the mud and wicker. Nothing seemed alive and, for an instant, a shudder rippled my back.

When I passed through the gateway there was at first little sign of anyone. Only a hungry hound, his bent tail like an Egyptian sword behind him, foraged in the cess-pit near one of the huts on my right. He was so engrossed even he didn't hear my approach until I was quite close, when he started guiltily, lurched a light step sideways to where he could watch me from the corner of his eye, his tail drop-ping simultaneously so that it curved in between his hind legs and out again, while he momentarily turned his wary head in my direction. Out of habit I threw a kick in the air and his hind legs lurched further to one side, but he kept on foraging. There was no other sign of life.

But to the rear of the village, before the sacred pillared circle — called by the Greeks the temple — gathered in a great, dark, silent breathing mass, were all the people of the settlement and all those who had come to live among us these last weeks and months. Only when I saw that silent host did I realize what was happening. It was the five-year festival that was about to begin, which accounted for the silence and the absence of light and fire. The sun had dropped below the rim of the world but the symbol of the goddess had not, as yet, appeared, but a pale overspill from the unseen moon washed up and over from the underworld whence she was rising. Within the circle, in the clear space, was a smaller group. It formed two lines, one long, the other consisting of only five people. The longer line was of women only, wearing white, their painted breasts exposed in the old fashion of Crete. There was one exception: the leader and chief priestess, Brigit, who wore an Hellenic dress fastened round the waist with a broad Egyptian belt of papyrus and leather, with a bronze buckle bearing a curved image of the goddess depicted, arched and supporting the sky upon her back, with her fecund belly hanging richly above the world. The smaller group consisted of my grandfather, Cian, Nuada and three others, only one of whom I knew. That was the druid Methger, who stood in front beside my grandfather. The other three were in line behind them and at right angles to the priestesses so that the four mystic quarters of space were attended, male to the north and south and female to the east and west.

Both my father and Methger wore the feathered hoods — in my time to become the great full-length cloaks we now see — to signify the importance of their roles and Brigit had the symbolic swan's wing in her right hand. They stood still and silent, waiting, at the carefully appointed place for that time of year, for the moon of the goddess to rise precisely over the pillar stone beyond and in front of the sacred circle.

Who the other two men were I did not know until later, when I learned they were the great Dagda, ollamh and seer from the islands of the Balears, whose king had welcomed him and who became one of our own mightiest kings before he died not so very long ago in great old age, and his brother, the famous warrior and historian Ogma, who knew the secret of writing and recording events and who was to influence me so much in later years and pass these secrets on to me to hold in trust for the initiates of a later time. If my view was different — that the knowledge should be given to a greater number — it does not lessen the immense contribution to learning and to the history of our race by this noblest of men.

The entire crowd was silent, facing the men backed by the priestesses. They, in turn, faced the people and the sea from where the symbol of the goddess would rise into the night, to march the meadows of the heavenly river.

What had caused me to forget this important occasion — the five-year festival — I don't now remember. Perhaps it was because I'd been too young, then, to remember the previous one and had been absorbed in organizing the care and fattening of my flocks and the making of salt in the flat pans on the bitter land between the dunes by the shore. Whatever the reason, I had failed to distinguish the preparations that must have been going on all round me from those for our departure and had marched brazenly in on the most solemn moment of the five-year cycle.

For the benefit of strangers and barbarians, let me explain. I have already outlined, however briefly, the origins of the people as handed down to us from the time when gods still walked the earth. Now perhaps I should also give some account of our main beliefs. Of course, we know that there are many gods; they say that the Hittites — who were our cousins from the navel of the world — had a thousand gods: they gave us some. But we did not take — or want — all. Well may there be a god of day and a goddess of night; a god of the underworld and a goddess of the earth; one of the wind and of the sea; of battle and of peace; of want and of plenty; of war and of virility. But when you have a god or a goddess for every natural thing in the world, life becomes very complicated. That happened to the Hittites who had to summon their thousand gods to every important council they held — and look what happened? They vanished from the face of the world, together with their gods, before the Medes or the Sumerians. And the same thing is happening to the Greeks today. From the Persians, the mightiest of people and the wisest, we took the belief of a single great god — though, as you doubtless know, Kurus himself was a generous man, brought up to believe in many gods — and the love of Ishtar, which is another name for our own Anann or Danann, whom the Greeks or the Danae, as they term themselves, call Aphrodite (or so I'm told, for they are a people for whom we have little regard nowadays, having betrayed the Ionians, and who make a virtue of lies and deceit).

We are the people of Danann. By some, for example our cousins the Scythians, she is called Danu. She is the queen of the night and of the sky. And as each day is divided equally into darkness and light, so she rules the mysterious darkness and may be sometimes seen by day (yet the sun is never seen at night), though her fields and the rivers of stars, which are her own, are seen only by night.

She is the goddess of all rivers, which are the life-blood of nations and of nations of men, both. Just as there is light and darkness in each day, there is also summer and winter in the year: the period of light and that of darkness, the beginning of each remarked by its own festival.

Bealtaine at the beginning of summer and Samhain at the beginning of the bleak winter, when the world and men rest from their labours, and remember, in stillness and in the man-made warmth of their homes. This is the simple cycle. Yet is anything in life simple? Neither gods nor men are simple! In their own way each is subtle. To make a meeting place of subtlety so that there may be understanding between gods and men and due acknowledgement of one by the other, and an offsetting of any hurt that may befall one from the other (which is important to men), worship of and communication with the gods has been devized on an elaborate scale so that what is propitious to both may coincide and man may not offend, may not act capriciously when it is inauspicious to do so, and anger the gods, who are quick to be roused.

Therefore have we sixty months of two thirtys, each five years divided into two periods, each of thirty months and therefore in each year are there twelve months, six of them good months of thirty days each — a holy number given us by the Assyrians — and six of them bad of twenty-nine days each, a system the Greeks have stolen from us. There is a special month, a sacred month of adjustment, at the beginning of each sixty and yet another at the beginning of each thirty half-way through the cycle, which, thus, is also divided into the light and the dark, the right hand and the left, the good way and evil way. And yet we do not believe it is that simple, as many of our Scythian cousins do (having, like the Persians, learned from the Magus Zarathustra), who say that there are gods both good and evil. I do not wish to offend the gods of anyone, but who shall say that this is a good and that an evil man or deed? May not a man or, for that matter (and perhaps more often) a woman, distinguish right from wrong and appear to choose wrong? But who can judge their hearts or know their reasons? Do we all not know those who seem to do good, only to will and achieve the opposite? Is not the reverse also true? If it is so with man, can it be less with the gods? Therefore, we think of things being constructive and destructive, which seems a better way of putting it than good and evil. For, as sure as there are influences on men they will be towards construction or destruction. What are good or evil but a backward look at what has already happened?

Our cycle, and each of its months, begins on the sixth day of the moon and I arrived back at the settlement when the people were assembled and waiting for the coming of the symbol of the goddess on the most important date of all, the sixth night of the first sacred month of the new cycle of five years, about which I had forgotten.

When I realized what was happening I slowed. Then, as quietly as I could, I slipped quickly to the shadows on the right and climbed to the thatch of a hut from where I could see. One of the boys already there tried to prevent me and cried out when he fell.

But I hissed at him to shut up, which he did, before I helped him up again. At times being big and awkward has its advantages! He was my cousin Dara. We sat together and watched the moon start to rise and the celebrations for the new cycle of fives begin with the chanting by my grandfather of the Song of the World, with its great opening, that is now more popular and, for that reason, I believe, stronger than in those far-off days, when it belonged only to the privileged few.

'I am the Wind on the Sea; I am the Wave. I am the Roar of the Breakers; I am the Bull ...' It was taken up by the four other men, the chorus of priestesses intoning 'Aiee-ee' at the end of each couplet so that their voices rose like a wind from the circle of pillars, though no breeze stirred as my grandfather stepped foward full into the moonlight. He carried a short bow in his right hand, a shaft of hardwood and two pieces of softwood in his left. He stood above the place at the base of the pillar in the centre where the holy fire had, until tonight, continuously burned, tended night and day by the maiden priestesses, the swans of the sacred circle. Now the blackened earth was clean and bare.

I must describe the circle. Of its twelve pillars — some of them capped — within which the ceremony took place, a few were of stone, durable and upright, while others were still pillars of wood; trunks of trees carefully matched, cut and carried here to help complete the carefully aligned circle that followed a pattern handed down from one generation to another as long as can be remembered. The circle is the centre of our existence; of mysteries.

Within it, and with it, my grandfather and his fellow seers calculated the mysteries of night and day; the rising and the settling of the sun and of the moon and their places among the stars in the limitless sky throughout the years. And in the centre was the largest and most sacred pillar of all, at the navel of the circle, dedicated to the union between the goddess and the people.

Ours was a new circle, but the mysteries behind it were older than memory, their beginning long forgotten, so that the importance of the circle was not in itself, but in what it represented; that which was given us by the gods and expressed by our people in this manner wherever they are.

Sometimes the circle is small and impermanent, as with us in Tartessia. But where there is a strong settled community the sacred circle is permanent and a great physical presence among the people, as are the rituals great in the movement of their lives. This can be seen happening here at Tara today, where the ancient monuments of the Bretani remain wonders and holy places of the gods and are being incorporated within the greatest monument of all. The Bretani, so I'm told, have similar huge and ancient monuments in their eastern island of Albion.

While Dara and I watched my grandfather and the others begin the sacred mysteries, the dark mass of the crowd outside the circle exuded a sense of collective fear and fascination that I could almost feel. I have often noticed this thing since, but that was my first

41

experience of it. It is animal-like. Perhaps because of my perch on the roof I felt outside it, but none the less I shivered.

It got cold and yet there was no change. No movement at all except for the mass swaying, which was neither rhythmic nor responsive, but was more like the instinctive rippling of skin by some enormous creature that lurked in the shadows of the circle.

Then, as the moon rose higher, like a glowing ball in the night, having rested a full minute upon the pillar-stone from where she lit the countryside around with pale light until the night creatures acknowledged her with their voices (the cicadas and frogs loudest of all), the five solemn men turned to the people and raised their arms.

Holding the bow and pieces of wood, my grandfather lifted his arms above his head, which he threw back to look at the river of the night which was now becoming clear. Then he knelt down and placed what he carried carefully on the ground. From a pouch at his belt he took some things — I later learned they were dry wood, moss roots and fine deadwood, together with something else I am not likely to name.

He laid the larger piece of softwood on the ground. The shaft of hardwood had been previously pointed at both ends, and now he rubbed one of these points against the softwood to make an indentation. He took the little bow and, twisting the string twice around the centre of the stick, placed one end in the indentation and, taking the other piece of softwood in his left hand, fitted it over the other point so that the stick was held upright with the bow dangling by its string from it. He looked again into the night. Then his rich and solemn voice sang these words that seemed to hang in silence above the anointed place. 'I am the bringer of fire, who announces the ages of the moon.'

A sigh overswept us all, myself included. I was as spellbound by what was happening as everyone else and was no longer aware of my surroundings. The impending presence of some awful power filled the world.

With his large — often stiff — fingers the ollamh, Cian, my grandfather, placed the tinder at the point of the hardwood shaft. He took the bow in his right hand and moved it back and forth, rapidly turning the shaft. I had no idea what he was doing. I had never before seen the village without fire or torch that I could remember, and had never seen fire summoned. I saw him bend and appear to kiss the ground — though in fact he was blowing as I now know — continuing to work the bow. Then I saw a drift of something pass his feathered hood — smoke! and then the miracle. A spark, a flame, fire!

The host surged forward and a shout went up. But they had not passed the pillars when the ollamhs stopped them with raised hands. Methger came forward and added kindling. Soon a small flame burned where fire had done as long as I remembered. More wood was added and it grew and blazed until it was as big as it had ever been. Shouts of happy laughter rose from the people, clear now in the dancing firelight. I could see that almost all the men — and some of the women — had pitch-coated sticks and torches to catch the fire and bring it home.

My grandfather drew back and I followed him with my eyes. Now I could see that the little bow he still carried was very ornate, horned like the bows of the Scythians or the Cichloiste, the man-killers or women warriors whom the Thessalonians called Amazons. I learned more of that bow in later life.

Suddenly the people were silent. But now it was a different sort of silence. There was no brooding in it. Rather there was suppressed gaiety, excitement and anticipation. They had made a line which, I guessed, would file into the circle to collect the fire, which is exactly what happened. But first one more ritual took place before the revelries of that night — and the three nights to follow — started.

Everyone except Methger drew back from the fire. My grandfather and Brigit, the Dagda's daughter, stood at opposite poles facing each other.

Tension suddenly crackled across the circle from which the blazing fire now shouldered out the darkness that had come closer and more awesome.

Brigit's voice, low and rich, like a black fleece, flew into the night: 'Who am I?' she sang.

'Heaven, earth, sun, moon and sea,
I am the queen, the goddess, the night;
Mother, womb, giver, fruitful,
Where am I?
I am here.

Before the terrible power of what she said immobilized our blood
my grandfather's voice came loudly from the other side of the fire:
'Who am I?'

'I am father, son, brother,
Plougher and sower;
Hands, eyes, tongues.
Where am I?
I am here.'

The silence was intense, louder, even in recollection, than any
battle cry I ever heard roaring from a thousand throats.

Then Methger raised his hands and the head of the file passed
between the main pillars to take the fire. In no longer than it would
take to count a hundred a moving line of lights curved back among
the homes of the people from the great fire that would not go out
again for five more years even when it was moved — as it was — from
place to place. I saw people clearly now, including my father Keth
and Sena'an my mother, who was an Egyptian — or, more correctly,
whose father had been an Egyptian and came with my grandfather's
people from there. I looked for a long time although there was little
now in particular to see. In my lifetime I have taken part in many
five-year ceremonies, some of them lavish and splendid beyond
description. But this one made the most lasting impression on me
and has always remained in my mind as the greatest, though it was,
in truth, very humble.

When I looked again among the pillars I could see neither my
grandfather, nor Brigit. Perhaps I should have left then and gone
with my cousins Dara and Co-en to join the fun, but instead of

44

sliding down from the roof with them I stayed where I was, compelled, why I have no idea — perhaps by no more than a whim to be different — to stay behind. If I had not I might never have known what happened next nor precipitated the change that was to affect my future life as well as my relations with everyone around me, my parents and friends — even Dara and Co-en — and so might never have gained the privileged position among the people of my race I later came to possess. Though, in truth, my grandfather maintained that it would have happened anyway.

By now the moon was higher and the countryside, but especially the sea, was bathed in gentle light. I felt isolated. Yet simultaneously able to identify with everything I saw. I stayed on my perch for some time, just looking; turning my head now and again to absorb the atmosphere I felt. My senses responded strongly to everything. I could almost feel with my sight, my hearing, my sense of smell. The effect was like the first heightened awareness after eating the sacred mushroom or having taken strong wine.

I suddenly shivered, but not from cold. It was like coming out of a sleep in the open. In a sense, perhaps, that's what it was, an other-awareness which had nothing to do with activity. Everything I saw was normal, people rejoicing more than usual perhaps, but I no longer had the sense of being suspended between two realities. Yet — the awareness of power, of presence, remained. I didn't 'sense' it, I *knew* it and it seemed to me that none of those below, dancing and singing, drinking, eating and enjoying themselves as celebrating people ever had and, I suppose, as they ever will, knew it as I did. The only one who might was my grandfather whom I could not see anywhere.

Determined to find him I jumped from the roof, in my hurry falling over a youth and a girl, and ran towards the nearby hills with his curses behind me. It was clear that my grandfather had gone in that direction. In any case I circled the sacred pillars and, still running, took the path towards the bluff beyond. The fence was no problem and once on the far side I settled down to a steady lope that quickly brought me up and beyond the settlement and into the dwarf pines.

Ahead of me was a grove, forbidden to anyone but initiates such as my grandfather, and sacred to the goddess in her role as Ishtar, mother, goddess of love, who was Anann to us and before that Inanna of the Sumerians, mistress of heaven.

Ahead was a steep, dark outcrop of rock sparsely covered with the small trees through which my path wound. Still rising, it curved round the base of the outcrop and emerged again higher up, but now facing towards me and the sea. I reckoned I could save time by climbing straight up and over the rocks and drop down on the path as it curved past the forbidden grove.

So strong was the moonlight that the trees cast dark shadows and more than once I stumbled into thorn scrub. But, sticking mostly to bare rock and avoiding crevices where the vicious spiked shrubs clung, I clambered upwards as fast as I could.

Quite suddenly I emerged onto the bare top of the rock and into full moonlight. Behind and below me the sea glittered beyond the pale and shadowed, green globular tree tops. It was beautiful, wide and tranquil. But I had no time to pause or appreciate it. Hopping from one bare place to the next until the trees again overtopped me and my feet sensed earth and roots, I came down the other side of the outcrop. Now I faced the sea. Below was the path, turning back again on itself and disappearing inland between the breasts of two small hills. Below it, on the seaward side, was the grove, surrounded by trees on the land side, open to the sea so that it was washed in white light from the moon. I stopped. Something — a shadow — moved there. I strained my eyes but could not make it out. Because of excitement and the climb I felt a thumping in my chest, which seemed to have grown bigger. I held my breath until it burst from me in a gasp, and I moved downward again. Then I heard a voice — two voices — but I could not understand what was being said, except that the sound was in a low, rhythmic chant. First one voice, then the other; answering. A man's and a woman's. I recognised that of my grandfather.

Although I now knew where he was, I stopped. The feeling of presence was strong. It seemed to swell from the ground; to inhabit the dark trees, even the air around me. My heart hammered and my breathing was loud in my ears. I felt a profound awe. Stealthily I crept closer. At last I could distinguish the voices, but did not understand the language.

Just then my knee touched a thing that yielded. On other nights I might have stalked a marten or started a hare and captured them before they escaped, but that night I was so tense I all but gasped. I put out my hand and felt woven cloth. My grandfather's cloak! His sandals and belt nearby. Of the feathered headdress there was no sign and I assumed he still wore it, but these worldly things were forbidden within the precincts of the grove on such occasions, as I later learned.

I realised I was hungry, starving more like, for I had eaten nothing since morning and the hour of the meal was long past. From his belt hung my grandfather's pouch. In it he sometimes had food, if nothing else then some of the sacred mushrooms, though dried, that he was never without and used sparingly.

Stealth, hunger and awe; these bore on me. Which was the stronger I cannot say, any more than I can explain my sudden secrecy. That it had to do with the awe I felt for the place is certain. I could do something about the hunger. I untied the thong at the neck of the pouch and felt inside. Sure enough there were mushrooms, four of them, dried and strong-smelling, but food. I crammed them into my mouth one after another, terrified that my grandfather would appear out of the shadows and want to know what I was doing. Any answer in that forbidden place with my mouth full of forbidden food would have been, at least, interesting. Fortunately I wasn't called upon to make it. Swallowing the last of the mushrooms I slid through the myrtle trees towards the lip of the grove below me. As to what happened next, what can I say? Take into account the circumstances — my youth, my excitement, my weariness; the time and place, the effects of the sacred mushrooms — and who can tell between the spirit world and this or understand upon what shimmering ledge between the two Teutates stands?

I myself have performed the full ceremony of Ishtar only once and then — as you may hear — circumstances also hung so suspended by belief between the two worlds that truth, on that occasion too, faded from one to the other as I looked, for fear that I might see its face and die of knowledge.

I could see my grandfather clearly. He knelt in front of the small oratory built on the principles, so I'm told, from which the temples of the Greeks to Aphrodite derive, but closer to the realities of nature.

A tall, slender, pillar-stone stood before the half circle of trees, banked higher on the landward side. Its top was swollen under its tapering point. Two smaller stones stood beneath. It was from in front of it that I sensed rather than saw the movement which had first attracted me and it was from here that the woman's low, musical voice answered my grandfather's.

Though I lay in the shadow of the trees, and the space between it and myself was also in the shadow, moonlight flooded the front of the oratory and cast my grandfather's shadow upon the rough grass. Behind and above his head, the silver-golden moon was painted on the sky. My grandfather rose and I could see he was naked save for a gold belt and his feathered cap. There was another movement by the sacred pillar. He raised his arms and threw back his head. He opened his mouth ... and my senses swam! I shall never know if the howl I heard came from him or from some prowling wolf behind me in the hills.

Everything blurred. The moon rushed towards me and as quickly receded, leaving behind a great cloud of luminescence filling the oratory. From its centre came a tall and naked woman moving with the motion of the murmuring sea.

One moment there was the cloud of pale light, not strong or glaring like sunlight, which excluded in darkness everything else; and the next moment she was there, her back towards me, moving towards my grandfather.

Their images appeared to shimmer and merge, undulate and fade in the nimbus, at the centre of which they were. The moon grew large again, moved towards me and as it did so I became smaller and smaller until everything outside was huge ... huge ... Then it receded, turning now on its side this way, slowly, and now that. My head reeled. My breathing was harsh and rasping. The figures were one figure, horizontal ... I could hear a drumming ... voices ... the enormous light moved towards me again ... and then? Nothing! I saw no more.

The next thing I remember is looking up at my grandfather's anxious face bent over me, one great arm supporting my shoulders.

'Are you all right, boy?' he asked urgently. 'MacKeth.'

I coughed and tried to sit up, he pressed me down and I was glad to stay.

'Wake up, son. Are you all right?'

I looked up at him and blinked, shaking my head to clear it. Behind him the sky was streaked with the pink fingers of dawn.

The trees and the grove were washed with flat colourless light and there was dew everywhere. I felt very cold and shivered though, as I now noticed, I was wrapped in my grandfather's cloak. He was wearing his belt — with the pouch I had plundered — and, I guessed, his sandals. We were on the edge of the grove. There was no sign either of the goddess or of her aureole, nor of Brigit whom I had half expected to see.

Before the sun was truly warm I was fully recovered and sat up. In the meantime my grandfather questioned me and, without waiting for answers, talked on about something else. What it came down to was why had I come there; how long had I been there, what had I seen or heard and I shouldn't be there in any case. Each time he asked a question he looked at me with strong eyes before continuing without waiting for my reply. He talked of the goddess, of the people, of the journey we were about to make and, finally, that the goddess herself had told him it was propitious. It was a moment before the significance of this struck me. I sat upright.

'When?' I cried. 'When did she tell you?'

Gravely he looked at me.

'During the night,' he said. 'You have seen much — more than any but the druids and ollamhs ever see. I have no choice but to tell you more, yet I cannot reveal everything. That will come later. It is only through your own doing that I am forced to talk to you about it at all.'

I nodded. I knew he was glad as well as sad about it and, I sensed, a little uneasy as well.

'This is the festival of renewal,' he went on, 'All the things of the earth die and are reborn. A new birth ... of fire, of faith, of life itself, just as the winter is a death and spring a renewal of that life. Sometimes there is even death of old leadership and birth of a new one, as with some of the Greek kings. Above all there is the regeneration of life in the womb of the world. The goddess herself is responsible for all of this. She is the mother and the giver. The leader is her mate and sower. This part of the ceremony is most important and significant for our people. It must take place every five years. Without it we should have no security, no future.'

At first when he began to speak he had been looking at me, but when he finished he was gazing far out across the blue and gold, the red and glittering sea.

He paused.

'I am the leader here,' he said, 'the link between the people and the divine mistress ... just as you may well be one day.' He looked at me again. 'That is why you must know and understand these things. Tell me,' he asked, 'did you – did you yourself see the goddess, with your own eyes?' I could not be sure whether it was interest or anxiety which lay in his own.

'Ye-es,' I stammered, 'I don't know ...'

'You felt her presence?'

I nodded and my relief must have showed because he smiled and nodded himself. 'Yes. I understand. You are the one, all right.'

He stood and helped me up. Together we walked down to the settlement where all was quiet after the revelry of the previous night, and a hundred columns of smoke rose straight into the motionless sky.

There is little purpose in recounting details of our trek north — more accurately, north-west. It took many nights and several months to accomplish, during which, for the most part, we followed the course of a great river which emptied into the sea near Bregantia, having forged a path south and east from its source close to the northern coast. In this it differed, I should add, from most of the rivers in Spain which mainly flow exactly the other way, from north-east to south-west. Once we penetrated the hills behind the coast, a great dark green mass of trees, like a garment, covered much of the land until we reached a high plain that stretched as far as forty nights march, and where it was very cold. As we moved towards our goal it became colder.

Our tents of skins were warm, but they were burdensome and it was troublesome erecting them at each camp site. Those with covered wagons were the lucky ones as these were used at night for sleeping in.

I experienced deep snow for the first time in my life on that journey, and it was a dreadful trouble and hardship to those of us responsible for shepherding the flocks, made no easier because it also drove the wolves to roaming the edges of these even during the day. By night we had to bring our herds within makeshift pens and light fires to keep the wolves at bay. We were forced to carry much of the material for the pens with us in the more barren parts as there was nothing there from which to make them, and this added to our burdens.

However we were soon able to make reasonable progress along the shoulders and bottom of the river valley avoiding, as much as possible, the need to cross smaller rivers as we went. And as the summer approached the rivers grew easier to ford.

At times we were forced to detour in order to avoid the territory of savages who lived in the hills, but, since we were so large a group, this was occasional. We followed an established trade-route with two — or at most three — nights' journey between settlements, most of them small and insignificant. Naturally it took us much longer to cover these distances, but, although our progress was slow, it was reasonably steady and uneventful enough, save for what might be expected.

We moved in three camps or groups spread out during the day over about nine thousand paces from head to tail, with, perhaps, up to a thousand paces between the groups. But at night we closed up into three adjoining camps. Sometimes we stayed two or three nights in one place and at others were forced to make as much speed as possible to reach food or water.

We left in early spring. The last of the snow still layered the upper slopes of the mountains where the limestone and heather, so like what we came to know and love in this country, took over from the brown, lower hills. As we moved inland the growth of spring moved with us so that there was fodder and water for the animals for most of the journey except, as I say, in some of the arid places through which we had to pass. But we had timed our movement well and crossed the high flat plains to the accompaniment of the bleatings of animals which did not want to move from fresh young grass. Our horses, too, were strong and nourished, even after the end of our land journey came in sight, which was towards the end of summer. But no matter what the conditions, our rate of progress was limited to that of our powerful, plodding oxen without which we would not have transported a tenth of our belongings.

Occasionally one of the great wheels, made from three pieces of well-seasoned wood fastened together across the grain for strength, would break and cause delay. But delays had been anticipated and we maintained the progress we hoped for.

As the season began to change again and the nights fell earlier — though, to my surprise, not as suddenly as I was accustomed to in Tartessia, but colder — we reached the sea and set about occupying for the winter the settlement which Nuada had left.

I well remember our arrival. During that last, long journey from the head of the river to the coast, I was one of the lucky ones. As I have said, I was big for my age, tall and broad and, although I was at that time clumsy in much of what I did, I had keen eyes and could tell the ground and the sky as well as my grandfather could tell a story. For this reason as much as because I had organised and cared for the flocks reasonably well on the journey — instead of losing animals, we actually had more than we started with — my grandfather rewarded me by making me a scout.

Not that there was real need since the paths were clear enough, but it was a great relief to be unburdened of the task of managing straying beasts in the wooded country we were moving through. With some of the younger warriors — lightly armed with moulded leather shields and throwing javelins — I was part of a fan of scouts who moved ahead of the three main bodies. There was little fear of danger, as we had left alien territory well behind us in the mountains. In front of us, as was easy to guess from the height and lightness of the sky and the rolling manner of the clouds, was the sea, although we could not see it yet.

I carried my shield, with its round embossing with the traditional wedges on the left, in my own left hand which also gripped two spare javelins. In my right hand I carried my best javelin, poised and ready, a length of cord twisted round the shaft and ending in a loop for my finger, which was through it, holding it taut, so that the spear pointed backwards as I ran.

It may be interesting to know about this, for we were the first people to establish this custom in Ierne, although, of course, it had been brought here before us by Nemed and his people and, but to a lesser extent, by the Firbolg who had learned it from us … who learned it from the Phoenicians.

Indeed I remember Dara's grandfather at some time or another calling it the 'shuttle' or 'weaver's beam' spear and when Dara asked him why, he told us a story about his own people, the people of Isal or Isral, who were attacked by the Phoenicians, whom they call Philistines. That was when they first saw such a javelin, which can be thrown further and more accurately because of the twisted cord, which makes it spin, and it reminded them of a weaver's shuttle, hence the name. We also, of course, had spear-throwers, an acquisition from the Persians, but we scouts did not use them. They were a battle-weapon.

53

In addition I wore a bronze dagger in a wooden scabbard on my left hip, where it dangled from my belt and, opposite it, on the other hip, my short, black, wooden-hafted obsidian blade. It was useless as a weapon, of course. But, although the blade was clumsy and worn and I was often laughed at for it, I would not change it because my father — a gentle and retiring man — had made the beautiful haft for me, and I have not changed or parted with it since. Until now!

We scouted ahead at intervals of between two hundred and five hundred paces — sometimes closing up when the going became rougher — but because there was little danger, if any, there was strong competition between us to be first to see the sea and, above all, first to see the settlement.

As I loped out of a fringe of pines on a down slope — they were none too close together and looked as if they had been scattered there by some great god's hand (and perhaps they had) — I saw ahead of me and to my right another scout half running, half walking, up a steepish slope towards the summit of a rise ahead and about three bow shots distant. The slope was bare and some instinct warned me that to get to the top was important; to get there first! I began to run, hard, inclining to my left away from him in a direction which, although it was slightly longer, was less steep. The skyline sloped from my right to left. He was now labouring, slowly walking and picking his way upwards through the coarse undergrowth, while I was able to run. And run I did. Suddenly he looked in my direction. I saw him stop and straighten up, looking at me. He waved, expecting me to acknowledge him I suppose, but I kept going. He waved again. I sensed his hesitancy and smiled even as the breath whistled in my lungs, and increased my pace. Suddenly he turned away and started scrambling upwards. My urgency had reached him. It was a race now. I could see him clawing his way through scrub and thorn and I imagined his curses. I forgot about him and concentrated on the rounded summit that moved nearer with each aching pace. Then above the fringe of growth on top I saw it. The sea. Far off it glimmered, blue and gold and silver-white where the sun struck it, stretching from side to side as far as I could see on either hand. I stumbled another step or two and then sank to my knees in the thick scrub. I looked to where my companion was just pulling himself over the ridge some few hundred paces to my right, and waved my arm, before leaning forward with both fists on the ground between my knees, my head hanging, as I recovered my breath.

Below me the land fell away in smooth slopes that turned to green some distance off. There I could see cattle grazing and beyond ... beyond, but before the yellow strip of sand that skirted the sea, was a haze of what was surely smoke. I fell forward and rolled over on my shield, my right arm with the javelin in it outflung, and looked up. Above, against the blue sky, a harrier hung, its wingtips trembling in the air and otherwise motionless. I wondered what he saw that I could not; what he thought of me below him. And then a slight tilt of the wings and he slid sideways down the slope. Now weaving the other way and skimming low and fast with the curve of the land. And then he was gone, hidden against the hillside where it was the same colour as himself. And a bird sang.

I jumped to my feet and shouted. My companion shouted back and, together, we looked back towards the woods from where we had come and shouted at the other small figures – our companion scouts – who were strung out between the trees and the ridge on which we stood. At once they responded. Two of them turned and ran back towards the first main body. The others loped towards us, con-verging. For their sakes I was glad that neither my grandfather nor Nuada was there. They could have lost their freedom. In any case neither my companion nor myself waited for them. As fast as we could, leaping as only those who know the mountains can, from heel to heel, we raced downwards over the rough ground, careless of a fall or broken ankle, startling the larks and other little ground birds shrilly from their cover. Arms flung wide, we ran, down to where the scrub and thorn and bracken gave way to scattered bushes on a fringe of red earth and then onto thin grass, racing to where the cattle grazed upon the green and herdsmen from the settlement of Nemed stood them watch.

Perhaps they thought at first that we were cattle raiders, and who would wonder at it. For, as we raced through a scattering of black animals running head-down in every direction from us, suddenly a stone whistled over their backs and past my head so close that the noise it made was clear. Then I saw the herdsmen, three of them in short shaffron cloaks. One of them already had his sling taut behind his head in the Balearic fashion and ready to swing. I stopped with a skid and, holding up my arms, wide, shouted at the top of my voice:

'Friends. We are your cousins. Cian's people and Nuada's. Stop.'

They looked at me for a moment. Then one of them gestured to us to come forward – my companion, who was a little distance behind me, had also stopped running when I shouted – but the one with the sling still kept it cocked behind his head. Slowly we went forward through the now idling cattle, most of whom had moved off from between us and the herdsmen.

'Who are you?'

The celebrations which followed lasted several days, but did not begin until we had settled in with these new-found cousins, all that were left – so far as we then knew – of Nemed's people.

The festivities began on the sixth night after our arrival. In the interval our own people, numbering more than three thousand souls – some of whom had gone to the spirit world during the course of our journey, perhaps to have already returned as children – occupied the derelict homes of those who had gone with Nemed to Ierne, or built new ones or pitched their tents as we had been doing all these months. Later in this chronicle I will describe the building of houses and fortresses. Order came out of the chaos of reaching journey's end; pastures were found for our cattle and pens for our swine. Within a few days it seemed as if we had been there forever. The thing I remember most clearly from that period is the cold and I was thankful for the sheepskin coat my father, Keth, had thoughtfully made for me from one of the flock that had been used for making broth.

The new settlement, as I will call it, was now very substantial, accommodating nearly five thousand people. My father and mother, Keth and Sena'an, myself and my sister Naas occupied a stone house with a thatched roof — more correctly two stone houses under one roof, opening off one another — facing on to the great central community space, with the sacred circle at one end, the pillar of Aengus the Forever Virile at the other.

All round were buildings of one kind or another, some stone, some clay and wattle, some of mud and turf, some skin-covered tents, some round and some oblong, which was a local custom. They stretched far behind the open space in a semi-circle to a depth of about eight houses — sometimes five or six, sometimes nine or ten — and ten houses faced the open space. The largest of these, the king's house, was in the centre facing the sacred circle at the southern end of the settlement. That was where my grandfather and Nuada lived with the king of this settlement, Fergus Leathdearg (or Redside), so called because one half of his face was scarlet, and who was one of Nemed's sons and their nephew. Because of this he now relinquished leadership of the entire sept to my grandfather, his uncle. I saw very little of him these days.

My father Keth, who was a silent man, was a very different person to his own father. Indeed it was sometimes difficult to see the resemblance between my father and grandfather. My grandfather, whom I have already described, could never be mistaken for anything but the leader he was whereas my father was ... well, in those days I admit I sometimes felt ashamed of him and tried all the harder to resemble my grandfather whom I was already like in many respects. I know better now, of course, and realise that my father's strength and courage were no less, just different and harder to see.

He was also a tall man, as tall as my grandfather, but he did not look it. Indeed smaller men often looked bigger than him. He was lean, with a slight stoop to his shoulders, and unlike the rest of the family, he had blue eyes that could look into distances beyond your shoulder which were never there when you turned to see. He never that I can remember lost his temper — a thing that often seemed to exasperate other people, especially my mother, who was his only woman. I think this also annoyed her because, while she always did the work of our household and kept it better than many where there were two or three or even four women, I do believe that as she got older she resented the fact that she had no one to help her or to give orders to except my young sister who would soon leave. But my father who was a fille, or poet — and, thus, a member of the third rank only of the five levels of society, entitled to wear but three colours (unlike my grandfather who belonged to the first) — simply ignored her and made lyres and bows when he was not making epics. Of course he was a good story-teller, but he never managed to make them come to life in quite the same way as my grandfather. Another strange thing about him was that, while he was the quietest and gentlest of men, it was his ideas about war which were to give us victory in two important battles.

Our flocks were quartered out and, naturally, had to be taken to pastures further from the settlement than was normal. This fact led me to a new appreciation of Keth, my father, which we shall come to in a moment. Meantime there was feasting and rejoicing and the preparations for both.

My mother, as you may judge, was a strong-minded woman, very conscious of her position and, perhaps, a little goaded by the fact that position did not seem to trouble my father. I suspect it was a constant source of irritation to her that he never troubled to become an ollamh or even a druid and so of higher rank, entitled to wear more colours and to a greater fine-price.

In any case, in preparing for the great feast she was determined not to be outdone by anyone. I had the misfortune to be stretched on my back out of the wind in a patch of sun, between two houses, when suddenly a shadow fell on my face. I looked up. She stood above me, tall and with her arms folded under her bosom, and I didn't at all care for the expression on her face, which while very handsome and really beautiful when soft and smiling, was very far from being either just then.

'Well?' she snapped, 'And do you find the sun pleasant?'

I jumped to my feet feeling angry, ashamed and tongue-tied all together, and looked sullenly at her. Her face softened then in that wonderful manner and she put her hand on my arm.

'It's nothing, son. Sometimes I'm too hasty,' she said. Then briskly, 'I need three young boars for the feasting. Will you bring them?'

I looked at her with my mouth open. Three boars! We could hardly afford one.

'But ...' I began.

'Just go and get them, and don't but me.'

'Sena'an,' I said, very formally, because the enormity of what she intended demanded it, 'three boars?'

'Three boars!' she replied firmly, 'And I'd be glad if you went now.'

'Does my father know?' I felt bound to ask.

Her mouth tightened slightly as it always did when her mind was made up and argument loomed.

'Your father will agree with me.' That much I knew was true.

'Yes, but ...'

'There are no buts. Do as I say.'

I went. She was that sort of woman. I was deeply attached to her, but it was difficult to get close to her. I think she felt position and responsibilities more than love. It made her a powerful and dominant person, but not a very fond mother and wife. But I didn't understand any of this until much later when I came to find my own woman — for, like my father and contrary to custom, I never had but the one woman, and she was the greatest gift life held for me.

I went to get the boars that day with mixed feelings. I was excited at the prospect of the festivities, where my grandfather was sure to tell a story or two and where there would be much asking and answering of riddles, with prizes for the successful and penalties for those who failed, and feats and trials of strength and skill. But mostly because it was also initiation time when young candidates for warriorhood who had reached sixteen winters would be tested for their fitness to assume a new life. How I envied them and longed to be one of their company. I was also proud that our contribution to the festivities would be a noble one for, in addition to the boars — which were more than ample for a family of our standing — I knew that my mother had already prepared loaves and honey and had persuaded my grandfather to confine his contribution to wine alone, for which he was famous, owning many barrels and amphorae which he had brought with him. So the contribution from our family, not counting cousins and uncles, was impressive. But I was also smarting at the peremptory way my mother had ordered me to fetch the boars and this gnawed at me until I met my cousin Dara near the gate.

'Where are you going?'

'To fetch swine.'

He grimaced, and I remembered that his parents refused to eat the meat of a pig and would not allow their children to do so either. Something to do with the religion of his father's grandparents who had joined the people in my great grandfather's time in Egypt, having been expelled from their own tribe in the desert. It was a curious story that I heard about only much later. They belonged to a scattered and wandering tribe who worshipped a nameless god — only one — of great power. I have heard rumours that this great god speaks with their leaders on the mountain tops of the desert, but whether that is true or false I don't know. They call themselves by different names: Children of this prophet or of that piece of desert. In reality they are impoverished nomads of the desert east of Egypt, preoccupied with their desert god. And that is where this story begins because this god of theirs made life very hard for them. Their lives are governed by do's and dont's to an extraordinary extent. It's all very well to pay homage to the gods and do nothing to offend them, but it is, it seems to me, another matter altogether when the gods interfere in every last detail of man's everyday life. Their god forbids them to eat swine! Unwittingly, Dara's great-grandparents, newly married, infringed one of the strictest laws.

I'm not certain of the details. I think that she was an orphan, or for some other reason inadequately instructed by older women in the rights and wrongs of their law. The young couple loved one another, perhaps too much — if that is possible — and they lay with one another during the onset of her sickness, a thing expressly forbidden by their law. It was discovered — don't ask me how — and they were banished for it. It seems strange to us, perhaps, but each people has laws which must be obeyed. They fled to Egypt, which was less than hospitable to their people at the time, and there met my grandfather's people on their way to Tartessia and joined them. As you know they married into our family, but still kept faith with their own god to whom my uncle — by marriage that is — prays and whom he calls 'Lord'.

'Come with me instead,' said Dara. 'You can get them later.' I was tempted, but remembering the mood of my mother, I said no.

'I'll see you when I get back,' I said. 'Where will you be?'

'Down by the shore,' he replied. 'I want to see them making the boats.'

'I'll meet you there,' I called to him, and ran on.

Now, shall I tell you first about the feast or about the boats? The feast, I think. The boats were being built throughout the winter. And the feast gave birth to incidents which were greatly to shape the future. I found the swine and with the help of the herd cut out three young boars. Each was marked with yellow on its back, in the shape of a cross. That showed that they were ours. All the swine — and the other cattle — were marked, some with yellow like ours, crosses, crescents, lines and circles, others in red, blue or green. Those of my grandfather alone were marked white and black.

With the help of a dog and a leather thong about the hind leg of each, I brought them home and helped in the preparations. First they were strung up by the hind legs, all three together, on a cross-beam between two sets of triangular supports cut from straight, young trees. These were set up at a chosen place away from the main settlement where the flies and smell would not be too bad, but not too far away for convenience. Women brought large earthen pots — which had been baked fifty or sixty at a time in pits fired with timber and kept at great heat by many bellows — to catch the blood and intestines. They also brought straw and wooden trays for the meat. After butchering this was wrapped in the straw and two of us — for this was a job for us youngsters — would carry it on the trays by the pairs of handles at each end to where it was to be stored for cooking. I'm sure there were 200, perhaps even 250, animals for the slaughter that day besides countless numbers of chickens and 15 oxen.

It was a scene the like of which I would not see again for many years, food for over four thousand people for several days being prepared all at once. To simplify matters we had, of course, broken up into groups of between twenty and fifty. Otherwise we would never have managed. But the great number of extra cooking places that had to be prepared meant considerable work for my friends and myself.

Dara and I and three of our own age group were given the job of making a boiling pit. It took us most of two days. First we dug a pit as long as a man and nearly half as deep and wide. This we had to line with flat stones and seal with clay, straw and cow dung mixed. There was much rivalry and competition for suitable stones, but we got enough to manage and successfully lined our pit with slabs carefully mortared with the sealing mixture. Then came the worst part. We had to fill it — or as near enough fill it — with water and leave beside it enough timber and stones to complete the work; the timber to heat the stones, the stones to heat the water. It wasn't light work, but we eventually had it finished, and I was pleased with the look of satisfaction on my mother's face as she and my father came to inspect. Of the three boiling pits in our immediate area ours, while not the first to be finished, looked better than the others, as if it would last. Before she turned to the roasting house where Co-en and some of the others were making great spits and fire pits — a lighter job — she nodded (but not at me) and my father looked over his shoulder and winked. I winked back and he smiled.

All I can now recall of the next few days are, of course, occurrences isolated by some chance thing of significance to me at the time and pinned by it in my memory, but there is no continuity or sense of moving from one thing to another in the logical fashion of planned events.

Take the cooking, for example; I can't say why, but it is one of my great and abiding recollections of those days, possibly because it was on such a vast scale and was the biggest activity — well, one of them — during the period.

I had pleaded, with success, to be allowed to attend the cooking, although it is not normally considered a man's work. The occasion and the magnitude made this different and many uninitiated young men whose hair had not yet been cut or braided for battle, and who had not been daubed, were involved. But at first my status-conscious mother said: 'No.'

'But Sena'an ...' I pleaded.

'I have said no. Let that be an end of it.'

'Ah, now,' said my father from where he sat in a corner stringing a small-harp, 'the boy has done good work.'

'We must all work,' said my mother grimly, but I noticed that she had avoided an argument.

'And we must all get our rewards,' he said.

She flashed him a look as if she were about to reply, yet, I felt, in a different context. But she said nothing, concentrating harder on what she was doing — which was kneading flour, spices and blood together to help make a filling for pigs' intestines.

'I would say that he has deserved his reward,' said my father, flashing a smile at me, 'and, in any case, what reward will it be? He'll be working as hard as anyone ... be glad of the offer.'

'Huh,' grunted my mother. 'If it weren't for the other men I swear you'd ask to help yourself.'

My father leaned back and let the insult, deliberate and provocative, slide easily over him in a way I could not, would not, ever have done. He plucked a cadence from the harp while looking at the ceiling and, without taking his eyes from it and still running those strange, thin, fingers over the strings, replied:

'And why not, if the circumstances warranted?'

My mother grunted in exasperation. In a sense I understood her, for at times my father appeared to have no pride. After all this was really slave work, supervised by women like my mother. In another sense I understand him better now for he knew then, what even yet I sometimes do not hold my understanding of, which is that pride, like

63

everything else, is useful only so long as you can master it. It is a bitter bridle when it masters you. But none of these things were in my mind at that instant, and I seized my chance like a young child (which probably irritated my mother more than ever, for my own pride was gone before my desire to do what I wanted).

'May I, Sena'an,' I cried, 'may I?'

I took her non-committal answer to be accord and fled through the door before it could be shown to be otherwise. Thereafter I had no problem in that regard except with Dara whom I recruited as my helper. For some reason he was all thumbs when it came to twisting a straw rope. We had fourteen pieces of meat, mostly haunches with the bristles burnt off — at which he was good, I'll give him that, better than I was; he didn't seem to mind getting his hands burnt when I couldn't stand the heat. (That has always been a curious thing with me. Although thick, my skin is highly sensitive and could stand neither extremes of heat nor of cold ... and yet I loved the sun.) Anyway, there we were with these fourteen pieces of meat, six haunches and fore-ends from our own beasts, and we were trying to twist straw to make ropes to bind a straw wrapping around them.

Perhaps I should make that plainer.

He held one end of the double twist, a stick in the loop, and I the other — the difficult end — to which I was adding straw as I twisted. But instead of keeping it tight and firm, Dara let it loose. 'For the love of the gods, Dara,' I shouted at him, 'will you hold the cursed thing while I twist it?'

'I am.'

'You are in your arse. Hold it!'

He scowled and gripped tighter and for a moment things went all right. But then I had the same problem all over again.

'Dara!'

'Ah — !'

Afraid that he would walk off on me I mollified him and encouraged him to make the extra effort. Sweat was streaming off us and I didn't really blame him. We were close — too close — to a roaring fire which one or other of us fed from time to time with some of the timbers we had earlier collected. It was still light and other young-sters and slaves moved among us doing similar work under the supervision of my mother and others who directed things from what I can only describe as group centres.

Our task was to see that the meat was properly prepared and cooked. We took a piece of meat, some of it salted and precious having been soaked in brine for several days, and wrapped it in straw. Each bundle was about as large as a medium-sized dog. This was secured with straw rope or soogawn, and then laid by the side of the boiling pit.

Meantime stones were heated in the fire until they were white hot, with the lime peeling from their surfaces like white dust from a Persian road. These were raked from the fire and rolled into the pit with a great hissing and roaring of steam. In a short while the water itself was bubbling and then the meat was put in. By adding more stones we kept the water at the boil. The meat was retained by the straw, which also held the heat, and it was quickly cooked. Until you have eaten fresh-boiled young boar in this way you have not lived, and so much the better if there is wine and apple to go down with it.

Meantime the oxen and some of the other meats were cooking in the roasting houses, but this work was done by women — with the assistance of Barnea, who had the feminine affliction, and thought and behaved more like a woman than man. Later he proved to be vicious as well, not only more disloyal than any woman talking about her friends, but untrustworthy and treacherous besides.

Beyond the cooking place, inside the compound, they took their places in order of rank. My grandfather flanked by Nuada, Ogma, the Dagda, Fergus and the Gobniu at the head and centre of a great table, facing south, all wearing several coloured cloaks. My grandfather and the Dagda wearing in addition the feathered head-dress of druid and seer. The champions and ollamhs came next, then the druids, the filli and warriors, then the bards followed by skilled craftsmen — except for the gabhainn or smiths, who were with the warriors — and An Gobniu who knew the secret of iron, and who ranked with the kings. Below them were the last of the freemen, the farmers and traders.

Only the kings, ollamhs, champions and druids were allowed their women with them... one of the never-ending sources of anger to my mother ... except for those who, like Brigit, were there in their own right. The women of the filli, warriors and bards could attend, but not sit. The other free women had the privilege of serving. Because my mother was who she was she could have attended, but she was too proud to do so unless she could also sit, and that she could not then do. It was my pleasure many years later to justify it for her, when she not alone sat, but did so beside me at the head of a great feast, and it was both amusing and gratifying to see the accumulated satisfaction in her face as she gazed on that concourse with eyes which could no longer distinguish her friends if they were more than two spears' length away, yet nodding graciously in every direction as if they were known to her one and all.

It was a great assembly who sat at these tables set in the shape of a huge oval stone with the kings' table across the top, before Fergus's house. Seats of straw were around each table, which sat about forty, and there were more than a hundred tables. On each one were countless loaves, prepared by each household, huge sausages of offal, blood, grain and spices, mounds of precious salt fruit and, before each man — or woman — was a mether, or three-handled cup, for wine, his platter of wood or bronze, depending on rank (gold in the case of my grandfather and one or two of the others at his table), and his eating knife, stuck in the table now instead of lodged in its usual place in the small scabbard attached to the great one of his sword.

Now that the cooking was complete my companions and I joined the women standing behind the seated assembly since we, not yet having had our hair cut, greased, braided and fed with lime, and as yet uninitiated, could not sit with the men. But we could enjoy ourselves and we did!

As it happened I was standing behind Diancecht the physician, a remarkable and skilled man, but arrogant and bad tempered. He was large, almost gross, with a great head the most distinguishing features of which were cruel, fleshy lips, and a huge and shapeless nose which his arrogance had, on some occasion, caused to be violently and permanently changed … but it made no difference. He was as arrogant as ever. Now he turned it on me.

In his left hand he held most of the leg of a boar, a large portion of which was in his mouth. It seemed to me too much for any man to swallow. His eyes glared from above the meat with permanent anger.

He gripped with his teeth, held the leg out from him and, with his eating knife, sliced through the meat close to his mouth and began to chew. Grease ran down his chin and jowls and his cheeks bulged. I am not exactly fastidious and I have seen the Germans eat, but there was something particularly unpleasant about the way Diancecht did so. He reached for his mether and found it empty.

'Boy,' he roared through the food in his mouth and without turning round. 'You!'

He meant either Dara or myself. We were talking to his daughter, Eremed (as different to him as sunlight is to a cess-pit), who was a year or two younger than we were. Some distance away was her brother, Diancecht's son, Miach, older than we were, but also as yet a youth. He fell half-way between his father and his sister, for, while he had much of the gentleness and seriousness that made us forget the difference in our ages when he spoke to her, he also had something of his father's arrogance. We pretended to think it was to Miach that Diancecht was speaking, and we ignored his shout.

'Boy!' Diancecht swung round, grabbing me by the arm and spraying me with spatterings of pork and saliva. 'I called you.'

I struggled in his grip, but I might as well have struggled with a lion.

'Wine,' he roared. 'Get me more wine.'

My father was watching me from his table further down and I could see the anger spurt in his eyes. But there was nothing he could do. Diancecht outranked him and, in any case, he had done nothing he wasn't entitled to and had wounded nothing but my pride. I felt my grandfather's eye, too, upon me and looked at him, but his face might have been carved from the hard limestone in the hills behind us. Diancecht shook me and I rattled to and fro helplessly.

'Wine, boy; get me wine!' He handed me his mether and threw me away from him so that I stumbled against Eremed who looked at me with pleading eyes as if asking me not to blame her for her father. I smiled and walked over to where several large amphorae stood in holes specially dug for them. A ladle protuded from the wide neck of each, but uselessly, for they were empty. I knew where the wine was and walked — perhaps sauntered would be a better word, for I still smarted at my treatment and intended to show my independence — towards it. I was joined by Miach.

'He had no right,' he said.

'It's nothing,' I replied.

'He thought it was me.'

'You?'

'Yes. He saw me where you were a moment before.'

'We knew about Diancecht's treatment of Miach, having seen many examples, but I had never heard him speak about it before.

He thought it was me at first. But when he found out he couldn't change, so you got it instead.

I said nothing. Miach went on: 'I hate him. He can get away with it now, only let him wait ...' We neared the wine store and on this day no one guarded the open door. It was a shallow cave dug into the hillside. In front were roofed mud walls and within it was cool. Thousands of amphorae and large leather bottles of wine — all marked with similar brands to those on the sheep — were stored here and normally the oaken door was locked. We stood outside in the sun for a moment before entering.

'But why?' I asked. 'Why is he like that to you?'

Miach looked at me in that curious way I was to come to know well, half arrogance and half something else; self-assurance. I'm not sure. It wasn't confidence, he had no need of that. I think it was a sort of defiance, for I believe he truly missed the father's comradeship which was denied him and, for all his arrogance, was insecure for want of it. But there was nothing weak or indecisive about what he said.

'Because he's jealous. He knows that I will be a greater doctor than him.'

I looked at him open mouthed and then again, for a moment, to see if he was joking. He was speaking of Diancecht, the greatest physician of all our people, whom even Persian and Egyptian doctors consulted. Miach's face was cold and unsmiling. He was not joking. I said nothing further and led the way into the cave expecting him to follow, which he did.

Together we searched for and lifted down an amphora with Dianchect's brand, a red crescent, on it. There was no reason why he should have anyone else's wine although on that day he would not be begrudged and we both knew, since he had a reputation for great meanness, that he would be annoyed because we selected his own. But we would not give him that satisfaction.

We grunted as we lifted the heavy jar to the ground and knocked the beeswax from the neck — it was one of the narrow-necked variety.

'So that people can't dip a ladle in so easily,' grunted Miach. But, in reality, there were many like it. They were smaller and made for easier handling and carriage and, in truth, it is the wide-necked kind which is less common. We leaned it against the pile of stacked ones to recover our breath. Then I helped Miach incline it on its pointed base and held the mether. Just as we were about to pour, Miach pulled it upright again.

'Wait,' he said.

'Why?' I asked. 'What's wrong?'

He didn't answer. But he tilted it himself until he had spilled about a measure on the ground.

'What ...' I spluttered, but he looked at me and grinned, a cold sort of grin that didn't reach beyond his mouth.

'Here,' he said. 'Hold it,' straightening the amphora and pushing it towards me so that I had no choice. Then he lifted his tunic and, raising himself on his toes, placed his penis over the mouth-edge of the jar and began to make water into it.

'Now,' he said, 'I'll make sure the old bastard will never be my equal, if he ever could have been.'

'But ...' I said, and stopped. There was little point in argument. If he didn't do it then he would some other time.

I shuddered. I knew the power of what he was doing and of the accompanying imprecations to Belenus. I also knew that such deliberate invocations for authority over another often manifested themselves in strange ways, sometimes to the appellant's disadvantage. And so it proved. My immediate problem, however, was that it was I who had been told to fetch the wine. Shaking himself above the neck of the great wine-jar, Miach fell back on his heels and lowered his tunic.

'Now,' he said. 'A stick! The very thing.' He darted to the door where a number of reeds for testing the wine were racked (some of the lighter wines from young grapes tend to go bitter if they are kept overlong and are tested through small holes in the amphorae which can be plugged with wax, softened when it is necessary to pass the reed through). Taking one he came back and stuck it down the neck of his father's jar, stirring vigorously. After a while he withdrew it and broke it in bits, saying:

'We don't want anyone else affected,' and threw the pieces in a corner.

Then he took the handles of the amphora from me. 'Now,' he said 'you hold the mether. I'll pour.' He did so until the cup was brimful of a tawny liquid, some of which he spilled on the ground and I heard another muttering under his breath. I looked at him with some reluctance and distaste. If he handed me the mether now I would refuse to take it.

'That's that,' he said. 'Let me take it to him. It must be by my hand.' My relief was considerable. I wanted nothing to do with it for all that I disliked Diancecht. Nevertheless I followed Miach as he carried the overflowing mether to his father who took it from him with a snarl.

'What took you so long?'

'We had to open a new amphora.' Diancecht's head jerked up as his mouth was pursed to drink and he snarled again.

'One of mine?'

'Of course, who's else?'

With that he struck Miach a backhanded blow with his free hand that sent the boy sprawling in the dust beside where I stood. But all the time Maich never took his eyes from his father's face. Nor did I. I was fascinated as the surly physician put the mether to his mouth, almost in a continued complementary movement to that which had sent his son sprawling, and pursued those great, ugly, purple lips to receive it. And receive it, and its contents, they did. I saw his throat working and his other hand came from behind to take a second handle while he held the mether to his head and drank. He released his left hand, raised the half-empty mether forwards and upwards from his dripping face and wiped his mouth with the back of his left hand.

'Ah-ah-ah!' He belched. He looked round for his son, who stared stonily at him. Without so much as acknowledging him Diancecht turned back to the table and growled over his shoulder: 'More!'

'And ...' he turned back again this time searching out Miach's face with his eyes, and beckoned with his head. Once; twice when he did not come close enough or fast enough. When he saw him coming he turned back to the table. Miach knelt and when his head was beside his father's, from the side of his mouth concealed with the mether, Diancecht said:

'But get it from someone else's barrel. Mind now.' But Miach did not!

As he went towards the wine store I watched his face. His expression was unmoved. Nothing might have happened. There was no indication of the momentous thing which he had done and of which only he and I knew, or of the effect it must, surely, be having on him.

However, in the excitement of the rest of that day and those that immediately followed I quickly forgot. My principal job was to see that the huge, bronze cauldrons in which the stuffed intestines were cooked, were kept full. Other cauldrons held stew, oatmeal or hot wine. But mine were the ones with the sausages, and I kept them full. When I judged them to be cooked, myself and the slave who assisted me lifted them out with a long stick, forked at one end, and tied

71

them with double knots at intervals so that they could be cut into manageable lengths ... a task I carried out, need I say, with my obsidian knife.

Our cauldrons are the envy of many races who, while they make similar ones, cannot make them as well or as large, and the secret is one known to few of even our people. Of course any fool can see that they are made from plates of bronze rivetted together. But that is not the reason ours are so famous and are handed down from father to son as inheritances of great value. The secret lies in the size and positioning of the rivets and, consequently, in the size and positioning of the plates themselves. In a properly-made cauldron, round or flat bottomed and full bellied with a thick, reinforced vertical rim — which must not be too large, but must be large enough — and round handles attached to clasps which are part of that rim; in such a cauldron, I say, in which the plates have been carefully selected for size and uniformity and hammered by a master to the proper shape, the rivets and the rivetting are all-important. The master craftsman punches the bronze and fits his rivets — which have also been carefully made to purpose — so that when it is above the fire and cooking what is within, they deflect the direct heat from the bottom so that it flows evenly upwards and all around the cauldron and, not only is the cooking speedier, but the metal is not damaged by the fire as happens with the inferior cauldrons of other peoples.

I'm telling you this because the greatest of the cauldron-makers of the people was also one of the greatest of men and one I was privileged to know: the Dagda, who also made the largest cauldron ever made. Now at Tara and, as we all know, called the Dagda's Cauldron of Plenty, it is never empty and from it no man ever went empty handed ... a privilege he extended even to a slave, once, though there was a special reason for it.

While I was thus employed a young warrior, having had his hair cut only that day, swaggered up to me. Why he had left his seat I don't know, unless it was to relieve himself. I was cutting sausages with my knife and paid him no attention until he stopped behind me. I was conscious of him then and an irrational unease and aggressiveness went through me for no reason that I was aware of. The mere fact that he stood behind me perhaps, and that he could now call himself a warrior. I had no idea who he was except that, by his dress and the fact that I knew all of his age in our group, he was one of the initiates of Fergus Leathdearg's people. The annual initiation ceremony was postponed that year until we completed our journey and messengers had been despatched well ahead of us to Fergus informing him of this decision so that it would be a joint and major affair, symbolically reuniting our settlements, so the ritual — always of importance — had a particular significance and mystique on this occasion. As everyone knows, the initiates were required to be isolated for a month before the ceremony — which explained why I had not seen this one before — which had been very difficult for our seventeen aspirants during our journey.

'Woman's work and a savage's knife.' If the words weren't enough, the sneer in his voice settled it. I swung round, my knife in one hand and a sausage, which I kept swinging, in the other. It caught him on the chest and burst, the hot, sticky contents going all over his new saffron tunic, up to his face and into what was left of his precious hair. He was taller than I was, but the surprise was total and the blow considerable. He staggered back, his mouth open. He raised astonished hands to his face, to his matted hair, visible symbol of his manhood and only a moment before his pride and joy, and then held them unbelievingly in front of him. He looked down at his ruined tunic.

'I ... you ...' he managed. Then he closed his mouth and charged. We fell backwards, narrowly missing the fire and the boiling cauldron above it, and rolled, in the dust and straw, between the cooking tables. My slave screamed and others ran to watch. Quickly a circle formed around us, and shouts of encouragement and protest, which to me were merely a noise, sounded above us.

His charge had carried me backwards and off my feet so that I fell under him. But as we fell he opened his arms slightly to break his own fall and I twisted so that when we landed I was face down. Immediately his arm was round my neck and his free hand clawed at my face, as he straddled my back. I tucked my chin in and knelt up.

Then as powerfully as I could I heaved upwards with my back and my legs and sent him flying over my head. He landed with a thump and before he could move I was on him, one hand at his throat, glaring into grey eyes that glared back at me just as fiercely. I sat up the better to grip his throat and got a punch from his fist — delivered straight upwards like a Greek — that stunned me and forced me to let go. He, too, sat up and we struggled together exchanging blows for a moment until I felt myself being pulled irresistibly backwards by powerful arms. I struggled and kicked, but it was useless. Whoever held me now was an altogether different matter. I looked at my enemy and saw that he too was in the grip of a large warrior, Fergus himself, and that he was struggling to get at me just as much as I was to get at him, and just as uselessly.

'Now then,' said a well-known voice above me, 'what's this all about? We came here to make allies and friends, not murder each other.'

I twisted my head and saw the smiling face of Ogma. 'Now,' he said, 'calm down, both of you, and tell us what it's about.'

'It's him ...' we both said simultaneously, struggling again to get free to fight, in which neither of us was successful. But things were calmer all the same and the restraints protective only. Then in a welter of accusations and justifications the general outline of the incident emerged — two versions of it, of course, as different from each other as could be — at which point we looked at one another for the first time. And, for the first time I think, we each realised how inconclusive the incident was. He had received the greater insult, but he had also started it.

We were introduced — it seems humorous looking back at it — and forced to embrace which neither of us wanted. He was Fergus's nephew which explained why I hadn't seen him about the king's house and, together with some thirty other youths all aged sixteen, was taking part in the initiation ceremonies which would render him acceptable as a warrior. Some of these rites were already over; the ritual bathing and anointing, the hair-cutting and smearing of the heads with cattle-dung, and the examination in poetry. But the most important were still to come and I will recount these in some detail, for in doing so I shall tell how, by chance, I was myself initiated during this particular ceremony although still four years too young. My opponent's childhood name, which he was about to lose, was Tanasta, but it is a name I have never used or associated with the aloof, lone man who was soon to become Oran. As soon as we had formally embraced he turned his back and walked away, proud, straight and unbending, to clean away the mess I had caused. Looking at him I felt a pang of remorse through my satisfaction for I well understood the dreadful blow to his pride involved. I thought then that he would be my eternal enemy. But, while we were never friends, we became indebted to one another in unexpected ways, the first of which was to happen before two more nights had passed and without the second of which I would not be here to tell this tale.

The thirty-three initiates sat at a table by themselves almost opposite that of the king and therefore at the far end of the assembly place and on one side of the open end of the oval made by the tables. Opposite them were the lowest ranks, facing west and north while the initiates faced east and north. Opposite each three or four sat a senior warrior, a champion, whose responsibility it was to shepherd his charges through the rites; to prepare them for each in turn and to mark any signs of weakness or unsuitability. Of course the initiates were not permitted to join in the feasting, being allowed nothing but gruel and water once a day, but being present while everyone else ate and drank as much as they liked was part of their ordeal. So far none had failed. They all sat in their new saffron tunics — all except Oran, that is, who'd had to change to an unbleached one — their short hair newly cut and braided, bound about their foreheads with decorated straps. They were permitted no wine but were allowed to drink a little milk, cows', goats', or horses', which was much prized by some whose fathers had learned war from the Scythians. Up to this their trials had not been exceptional. They'd had the ceremonial bathing, as I mentioned, in the conical sweat houses and many, including myself, had gathered to see them come out and watch the fun. Sweat houses are small and round with a pointed roof, sometimes made of

75

stone, sometimes of earth and sods on a timber frame. They are always sunk within, about a cubit below the level of the ground outside, to help retain the heat. The method is simple and similar to that used in the boiling pits. Stones, heated in a fire (often begun in the house itself, but later, as more were needed, in a larger fire outside), are placed in the centre and water is poured over them. Steam fills the sweat house and the results are the same as nowadays. It is uncomfortable to stay within too long, but the ritual washing requires initiates to stay for an hour, during which they sometimes faint.

As nowadays, they were attended by women, priestesses, who went in with the water and one could hear them singing before they came out again. They were very beautiful, some of them particularly so, and I found it hard at times to take my eyes from their liquid-moving bodies as they went, naked but for their swan wings, between the fires and the sweat houses.

The fun did not really begin until the initiates came out, to the accompaniment of great cheering and shouting. They were herded — rushed is a better word for it — to baths of ice-cold water (sometimes, in winter, to the sea) and thrown in by the priestesses who then danced slowly and invitingly like a flock of the beautiful and graceful swans they were called for, about the edges, but ushered them back again if they tried to emerge.

I did not, at that time, know to what the priestesses were inviting the initiates with their sinuous movements and out-stretched arms, but their words and the movements of their breasts and bellies enticingly revealed and concealed by their wings, were explicit enough to excite the imagination — admittedly inaccurate — of a twelve-year-old boy whose ambition was for command and who thought all women (except his mother) were inferior weaklings.

Now and again one of the initiates would manage to get out of the water and run towards the sanctuary of the sacred pillars, but it usually took several attempts before success. The priestesses herded them back again and kept them there for as long as they could, while the initiates were obliged neither to resist the priestesses with any force nor to cry out, whether from the cold or the manhandling (perhaps I should say womanhandling).

Eventually they all reached sanctuary and were allowed to dress in their new tunics. Then their hair was cut and braided in front, shaved from the neck and ears to the crown and plastered with fresh cow dung by the most renowned champions of the settlement. The cuttings were burnt before the pillared archway, which was to figure later in the ceremonies as well, as Aengus the Forever Virile and Anann.

This haircutting marked the beginning of the serious and awe-inspiring secret ceremonies which faced them over the next three nights, during which the goddess, gods and demons would themselves participate and breathe upon the youths their breaths so that they would never be the same again and, through the mysteries, would move from the carefree world of children to the responsible one of men.

Their knowledge of poetry was tested first by bards, including my father, who took them at random through a prescribed twelve of the many hundreds of books of poetry known to the bards and filli. None of them failed in this test, which was completed before the feasting began.

Now the sun fell aslant the houses and threw long triangular shadows. Soon it would slip beneath the world and the storytelling would begin, carefully ordered to increase the atmosphere and tensions of the night's events.

The celebrations, the eating and drinking, the boasting and banter, riddles and singing and music-making, had already been in progress for about three hours when I had my encounter with Oran. But it served only to make me more disgruntled and resentful than ever that I was not having my own initiation. I knew poetry and I was confident I could cope with the feats and tests — even the mysteries of the Cave of Cruach and its Beasts — if I were allowed to do so. But I was laughed at when I suggested it and told I'd have my turn in four, or perhaps even three, years' time. The condescension in the hinted concession of a year only made me madder.

After my opponent stalked off I returned to my place supervising the sausages and remained there until it got dark. I returned to the assembly place in time to hear my grandfather finish an early story — for, of course, in his presence my father would not tell one anyway. It was a tale of a hero who overcame many difficulties and problems to reach his fairy bride and was proper to the occasion. It was the kind of story which has a meaning — but not one lightly read — having to do with everyday reality. It was not a story well liked or understood by women. No hero in his senses would marry any woman, much less a fairy woman, and elope with, and go through a multitude of dangers for her. If he did the marriage might not be accepted or, what would be worse, his caste might be diminished. Marriages, as everyone knows, are for agreement and arrangement between like kinds. But stories are for the allegorical telling of mysteries which are not to be too closely spoken of, and have a power of their own.

When he finished, with these words: 'That is my story. If there is a lie in it, so be it. It was not I who made it up,' there was some cheering and hand-clapping. Then he did an unusual thing. He stood up. At first I thought he was going to announce the trial of the initiates by unarmed combat, which was their next test. But he did not. Instead he looked round the assembly and, standing his tallest and speaking with his full voice so that it carried even beyond the confines of the assembly place, he said:

'My people — you are all my people now; people of Nuada —' he turned to Nuada sitting on his right, '— my own people —' his eyes swept round and he nodded here and there, '— people of Nemed,' and he turned to Fergus on his left, 'all my people as agreed between us, I have a question for you.'

A cheer greeted him then, for we knew it was a riddle, although it was most often that riddles were made by challenge between kings and champions or other contestants, and not put by the high king to the people. But it sometimes happened when the matter was important. When he did not respond to the cheer and his face remained grave, the sound died and an expectancy pervaded the following silence.

'We have a blood price to claim,' he cried looking about him. I felt a murmur swell around me. 'And we will claim it!' he shouted. The end of his statement was drowned in a roar of response which brought the entire throng to its feet, shouting, 'Yes, yes, yes!' Now I could not see him because of those who had risen, shouting, between us, but the multitude suddenly became quiet again, and resumed their seats and I could then see him standing with both hands raised to quieten them, waiting for them to sit. With his hands still high so as to control them, and lit from the flames of the many fires, torches and rushes, he said; 'Yes! we will avenge Nemed and the rest of your people. That is why I have come. We must decide when.'

Again a murmuring filled the square, but he subdued it.

'I have questions for you,' he said. 'Give me the answer.' He looked round as the crowd began to murmur, one to another.

'How many riddles?' shouted a voice.

'Three,' replied my grandfather.

'How many answers?' shouted another.

'One,' said the king, and there was silence. He looked over them. They were aware of the power in what he said. Three questions and one answer.

'Ask!' cried a voice.

The king, my grandfather, looked down, first at Nuada, then at Fergus, and out again over the throng.

'When', he asked, 'does a maiden burn without fire, with a heat not easily quenched?

'When does the earth move, but remain still?

'When does the first bird fly that is not the first bird?'

Nothing moved but the shadows. I heard an insect hum a full man's length from me and in the flickering light I saw face turn to face and lips silently question. Then from the far side of the assembly a man leaped to his feet shouting.

'Bealtaine,' he shouted. 'That is the answer. We go in the spring.'

I recognised him, a distinguished warrior named Creda. My grandfather smiled and the whole place erupted in a mass of shouting, cheering people who were not calm again for many minutes

79

until my grandfather nodded and said, 'Yes, we go in the springtime.'

Now, of course, the answer to the three questions was obvious. Everyone knows that girls are most attracted to youths in the spring and youths to girls in the autumn. Therefore the answer to the first question is Bealtaine. In spring everything is growing and stirring the earth, but the movement is unseen, therefore it is the same answer for that question. And in springtime the first migrant bird appears, but he is not the first bird, so the answer is also the same. It was a good riddle, perfectly tuned to the mood of the people.

But my grandfather, that great man whom I loved and revered so much, was never to touch the soil of Ierne or avenge the deaths of his brother Nemed and all his people.

When the noise died my grandfather announced the trials by unarmed combat, at which there was more cheering, for a night-time contest was an event.

The trials were not held in darkness after all. As night wore on the stories became more absorbing and more powerful and the people huddled together in groups, awe and fascination impelling them to ask for another when each was ended. Finally the Dagda ran his fingers across the strings of his harp so that a hush fell and the sweet, liquid music gentled them for a moment before he began, softly at first, a love epic which took four hours or more in the telling. Now and then, to give mood or emphasis to this or that part of the tale, he again rippled the strings of the harp with his nails, so effectively that, as the story progressed, one could feel its power and presence every-where. Of course, the harp he played so evocatively, was made by the most skilful of our harpmarkers — whose hands could woo a branch into a song curve or winnow the melodic heart of a boarded box as no other hand could — my father, Keth, who was much sought after on account of this gift and made and sold harps and lutes from our house — forever full of woodshavings, the pungent smell of resin and the unmelodic plangency of strings being tuned to new instruments — by which means he provided for us.

The stars were paling and the sickliness of the false dawn was past before the Dagda ended. By then the people were at a pitch of tension which was almost touchable. Although no signal was given, it was as if one were, and right across the assembly place they began to shake and stamp, to cut their arms to let blood and to run for the sweat houses so as to plunge and free themselves of the uncanny influences of the stories they had heard.

I went to the sweat house we usually used and cleansed myself well before running outside to roll first in the sacred dew and then wash the sweat from my body together with the power of the great tales. If I was over-thorough in the cleansing, perhaps it was because I had some intuition of what was going to happen. I've already told you that my mother held I was sensitive in this way, and I believe it.

By the time all was ready true dawn had broken and a gentle light had descended on the world. Birds sang and we all thronged to where the contests would be held. Because there were so many initiates they were to be tested seven at a time, and a great ring had been marked out with stones for the purpose. Within the ring were seven pits, waist high and fixed to the rim of each pit was a spear, its shaft buried in the ground and the point protruding inwards so that it would be very difficult for anyone to stand, much less move, in the pit without being wounded by the blade. Yet this was precisely what was required. A noviciate took his place in each of the pits. He stood so that the spear point touched his breast. Then he was handed a staff about a cubit long, and a leather shield of no great merit.

The people were gathered around the circle, outside the stones, and there had been some jostling for the best positions. Now all were settled as my grandfather and Methger entered the arena and stood in the centre. There they invoked the gods and goddesses to aid the initiates in their trial, Neit, god of battle and Macha goddess of war, and other gods and goddesses who might help and strengthen them.

Then Methger made a signal and eighteen warriors from the previous initiation (which required a mixture of Fergus's people and Nuada's as well as our own) marched in carrying javelins, but without the loop. Each man had five javelins. A cheer went up as they marched smartly in two files of nine. They divided and marched to the centre where they stood back to back and it was immediately seen that the eighteen men, between them, covered each of the seven pits with the initiates. These now raised their shields and staffs so as to defend themselves.

Co-en was beside me, with Eremed and her brother behind. Dara was somewhere close, but I could not see him.

'What's happening?' asked Co-en.

'Shut up,' I said, without irritation, and he did ... for a minute.

'What're they doing?' he demanded.

'Quiet,' I said, this time meaning it. He was spoiling my concentration. But Eremed answered him, putting her hand on his shoulder in that gentle way of hers, so that his expectant face swung in a full half loop from looking up at me over one shoulder to looking up at her over the other.

'They must defend themselves,' she said, 'without being hurt.'

'But what about the spears?' he asked. 'Those ones, I mean,' pointing to the nearest pit with the spear blade against the breast of one of the initiates.

'They must try not to be wounded by that,' she replied, 'or if they are they must not cry out.'

He looked up at her with something like awe on his face, and then looked back at the scene before him, his little mouth open. I could not help smiling to myself, and I winked at Eremed across his head. She smiled too, and patted his shoulder.

'One day you will be there,' she said, 'so watch closely.'

Suddenly, with a shout, one of the warriors whirled and hurled his javelin unexpectedly at one of the pits. It was not one he was facing directly and he might have taken the occupant by surprise, but the initiate warded the javelin off with his stick and received a round of applause and cries of encouragement. That started it. The warriors hurled their throwing spears, sometimes one at a single pit, sometimes three or four together. Blood began to flow and I saw one initiate's face turn white as the large blade in front of him bit home when he made a sudden turn to dodge a flying javelin.

Their chance came when the warriors had exhausted their five javelins, because they had to run beyond the pits, recover them, and return to the centre before they could throw again. Naturally they did not all expend their weapons together and there were normally some with a javelin or two at the ready for any attempted escape during the recovery period. But one youth, bleeding from the shoulder, tried to make it, covering his back with his shield. Before he had taken three strides one of the warriors launched a javelin at him and it pierced his shield, hanging like a lethal finger, and the acolyte halted, kneeling. Later it would be decided if he might proceed, and the decision was usually favourable if he had not run from cowardice.

Each aspirant was expected to sustain the attack of nine men, each man armed with five javelins, so that they defended themselves against forty-five casts. Sometimes it was difficult to keep count as the attacks were random, but the first seven were soon through. None had reached the perimeter, and three knelt within, spears – in one case three – protruding significantly from their shields. All the others were wounded, either by javelins or by the great blade in front of them. One, the one I had seen go white, had a bad wound in his chest. But not even he uttered a sound.

They were quickly relieved by the next seven and were given a substantial amount of applause for their performance, which wasn't bad. While the second seven were being positioned, something caught my attention, and I noticed nothing until Eremed said, 'Watch Tanasta!'

My head jerked up then and I searched for him among the initiates. I quickly saw him and a twinge of something, perhaps a combination of things, envy, anger, jealousy, went through me. I looked at Eremed and was far from reassured by her smile and the way her eyes were fixed on Fergus's nephew. I wondered how she had come to know him; it could only have happened that day. I scowled.

Already the javelins were flying, but it was a moment or two before I was able to watch with any awareness. Then a great roar grabbed my attention and forced it back to the spectacle before me.

'Did you see? Did you see?' from Eremed. 'Oh he was magnificent.'

'Who?' I asked, unnecessarily, for I already knew.

'Tanasta,' she said, giving me a strange look. 'Did you not see him? Weren't you watching?'

I shrugged, angry with myself.

'Not bad,' I said. Though I had no idea what I was talking about.

That angered her. 'Not bad! I hope you'll do as well.' And she turned back to watch, her hand suddenly firmer on Co-en's shoulder, so that he looked up at her in surprise.

Now I paid full attention, my eyes on him alone. And he was good. He was more than that. He was brilliant, bringing murmurs of appreciation from the crowd and shouts of acclaim now and again.

So far as I could see he was unscratched, although he was by now receiving almost the full attention of the nine young warriors on his side. Nor was he scarred by the large spear blade, the point of which, I could see even at that distance, was firmly pressed against his chest in a most honourable way. He made no attempt to ease back from it as many did. He stood there as calm and aloof as when he turned his back on me and walked away, and I could not but admire the way in which he conducted himself. Three spears came at him, two from one side and the third from the other. The single spear was on his shield side. But he did not, as one might expect, cross his shield to protect himself against the double threat and run the risk of being wounded by the single javelin.

Instead, with a grace and skill which brought those who were sitting to their feet in a spontaneous burst of applause, he blocked the single spear with his shield and, as specifically as if he had all the time in the world and there were no dangers — but so fast one could scarcely follow the motion — shifted his grip on his staff to the centre and, with a clean and fluid movement right and left, deflected the whistling javelins so that they fell harmlessly, one on either side of his pit, a few feet away.

His success seemed to enrage the attacking warriors, for singly and together now they hurled their javelins at him, determined that he would be blooded. But for a moment he held them off, his shield and staff flashing in the sun, the only movement for that space of time in

84

any of the pits. Then, suddenly, he did the totally unexpected.

Instead of waiting for the warriors who had cast all their spears to move, and without any apparent preparatory observation — and that, surely, was the secret of the move's success — he blocked a flock of javelins with his shield and, before anyone knew what was happening was out of the pit and rolling. Only then did I realise that he had anticipated the warriors' move for recovery, for he was still rolling several feet beyond his pit as three of them took their first steps towards getting back their spears.

'Look at that!' I exclaimed involuntarily, my eyes rivetted on him — so that I almost missed the gentle smile that spread across Eremed's face when she heard. I smiled in return. Whatever else he was, he was a magnificent warrior and there was no shame in acknowledging that. Those who still had spears cast them, but he suddenly stopped rolling and they overshot. Then he was on his feet running. At that the warriors shouted and some of those attacking the other side turned and cast at him, at which there was a roar of disapproval from the crowd. A javelin whipped above the rim of his shield and I thought it had wounded him the way it stayed.

'Oh no!' gasped Eremed.

But we were wrong. He had dropped his staff and grabbed the javelin instead. If they were going to break the rules, so could he. He turned, his shield on his left arm advanced, the javelin held like a heavy spear in both hands, the left forward and high, the right back and low. He swung the point in an arc and ran a few steps. The semi-circle of warriors retreated. He turned away again, but a javelin whistled from one of the other nine.

The shouts of the crowd warned him and he pivotted unbelievably fast, at the same time bending double so that he was almost entirely covered by the shield. Simultaneously he scooped from where they lay near his feet two fallen javelins with his right hand. Hardly had that aimed at him struck the ground beyond him than those he'd picked up were on their way. And his targets were without shield! He took the foot of one man and the arm of another, and both were grazed, but before the javelins struck he had run like the wind to the edge of the arena where the crowd parted with a cheer to swallow him in safety.

There is no doubt that this feat was the high-light of the celebrations so far, and he was welcomed as a hero who has already completed the full rite. But of course he had not. There was still the mystic and terrible rite of the Cave of Cruach and the Beasts, the open mouth of which gaped black and fearful beyond the temporary arena. Everyone stayed well away from it. Even Eremed shuddered visibly when Co-en asked her what it was.

She raised her fingers protectively in front of her face and turned her head away.

'You must not ask,' she whispered. 'You'll know in time enough.'

He turned to me then. 'What is it, Cian?'

I did not want to tell him, for at the time I knew no more than the women and children and they were terrified by any reference to it — a fear and terror which increased at times such as this and helped create a proper atmosphere of awe-inspiring tension, of which the initiates were the epicentre. They, of course, were isolated from everyone except their mentors, the champions who, in turn, impressed on them the terrors of the cave and the secret, sacred and supernatural mysteries they would encounter therein.

It was no wonder that some young men fainted before the ordeal, others during it and some, like the effeminate Barnea, were excused it completely because of their strangeness. I sometimes wonder if a few did not deliberately acquire this womanishness out of fear of the ordeal?

After Oran's great display — I can never think of him as other than Oran, though he did not acquire that name for another night — the remaining thirteen aspirants were tried in similar fashion, but the excitement had gone out of it at that stage and people had, in fact, begun to drift back to their homes.

'I'm tired,' grumbled Co-en and, although I was feeling tired myself, I told him to keep quiet and stop annoying us.

Eremed said nothing to me, but bending over Co-en she said: 'Come on, then. I'm tired too. We've seen enough here,' and taking his hand she turned away from the throng, ignoring me completely. Co-en looked back triumphantly over his shoulder at me and stuck his tongue out, which I pretended not to see. I don't know where small children pick up such practices, which have such a profound and different meaning in later life.

Having stayed only long enough for them to have reached home, I must confess my own tiredness overcame me and I left also, looking forward to some rest.

Before long the whole settlement, save for the initiates and their mentors and a few guards, was resting also.

Also the trials the initiates were taken for another bath — not involving the priestesses — which, while part of the ritual, was functional rather than symbolic. Most of them had wounds of one kind or another and all were filthy — except, of course, Oran who, even though he had rolled in the dust of the arena, still looked as groomed and immaculate as if he were a king's guard.

After their bath, somewhat refreshed, they were taken for a run through the surrounding countryside, harried from time to time by the same young warriors who had assaulted them in the trials. These were now armed with long hazel switches which they used mercilessly, given the opportunity. The thinking behind the operation was good. The young warriors had themselves endured the rites only a year before. This was their chance to have some counter-satisfaction. Moreover they were themselves tired and stretched and, therefore, more inclined to be harsh. Finally, of course, Oran's success had galled them and they were out for blood whenever they got the opportunity.

This run took until the late afternoon and, by the time they returned, few initiates lacked welts and stripes. They were then bathed again and given some time to rest before the greatest ordeal of all, the Cave of Cruach.

I had resumed my duties at the cauldrons, boiling and making the sausages. By the time I had an adequate quantity prepared the feasting had begun and I hurried to reach my place ... as much because Eremed would be there as for any other reason. And she was there before me and smiled when she saw me coming.

'Hello.'

I nodded and grinned.

'You're late,' she said. 'Here, help me with this.'

This — was a smallish amphora with a beautiful, slender neck, obviously Etruscan. Instead of carrying individual methers to the larger amphorae every time, Eremed was bringing this to the table and filling the methers as they became empty. But she was finding the amphora difficult to handle on her own, even though it was small and only half full.

Of course I helped her! In fact if she hadn't asked I'd have offered. Even then she had this great power over me, to which I was always happy to surrender, because of its gentle strength.

After it grew dark and the lights were flaring in the slight breeze that had sprung up with the setting of the sun, the story-telling began. First the lighter tales and the lesser adepts — who nevertheless were applauded — and then on to the larger works told by the masters of the craft. The atmosphere that night was quite different to that of the previous one. The applause was serious and expectancy hung upon the settlement. Overhead black-centred clouds with pale and whitened surfaces moved beneath the moon before the sea-wind. There was a sombreness and a solemnity upon us all, which could not fully conceal the fear and fascination that surged, almost as if it had life of its own, about the assembly and caused me more than once to shiver and glance behind me at the shadows, expecting to see what I dared not think. But one could sense their presence.

The initiates felt it too. You could see it in the way they sat, for the most part silent, with strained faces which were not the result of physical stress and tiredness alone.

They listened to the champions opposite them without, or at all events with little, argument or discussion, and ate little of their meal of gruel and water. Even Oran, in his very stillness, showed signs of the terrible tensions they were experiencing. As I now know, the champions, far from easing that tension, were deliberately adding to it, ever watchful for excessive weakness and fear.

Even earlier, I had, for reasons of my own which I will describe later, reached the conclusion that danger in the mind is nearly always worse than the reality, though paradoxically it is the imaginary dangers which seem to affect people most. I think this is one of the differences between men and women. While, on the whole, men seem to have greater imaginative powers, they also seem able to bring them more readily under control. Women's fear of the unknown often makes them unreliable about important facts. But, perhaps, I'm wrong and I am sure there are many women who would disagree with me, just as I am sure there are many women who are more reliable than the average man. But I think the generality is true.

The climax came when Methger, druid and seer, rose to his feet — in itself an unusual thing for the purpose — to tell a story. The story he began to tell was, appropriately, of the adventures of a young man, of caves and of gods and of demons.

Methger was a man who always made me feel uncomfortable, even in later years when he was old and I had become king. There was a secret, dark and sardonic thing forever lighting his deep-set eyes and he seemed to possess a power that was more than natural. He was always calm and controlled. He avoided confrontation, but there was never weakness in his way of doing so. Merely avoidance in the sure knowledge that, somehow, he remained in command. He had undoubted influence, more, I believe, than mortal, which caused him to smile. But not with humour or sympathy.

Before beginning his story he looked round the assembly. Solemnly he raised his hands high above his head and silence fell upon the multitude. He was tall and lean, his dark face sinister in the changing light under his cap of bird feathers. Then, fixing each of us with his piercing eyes (for he had that capacity), he lowered his arms to shoulder level and slowly turned a full circle to his left.

As I tell it I feel a shudder even as the whole assembly sighed and shuddered when he made the evil turn. For, although we knew it was part of the initiation ceremony, when the sorcerer must do the opposite of what is proper, we were aware that by it, even in such circumstances, he opened the gates between this world and the other and that we were vulnerable until the ceremonies were over and he closed them again. Twice more he turned.

Before beginning he said, 'Some things herein are poetic fancies; some are for the amusement of fools.' He paused.

His voice dropped. 'Some are the delusions of gods or of demons; some are like truth, some are not. Who —' he asked, and those strange eyes gripped us all '— who shall say which is what?'

Silence was his answer.

He then began this story. He told of the coming to manhood of Partholon, one of the old gods who visited Ierne. He told how Partholon, because he loved a king's daughter whom the king himself desired for wrongful reasons, was tricked into going through the Cave of Cruach to the Eastern World at the uttermost bounds of man to learn the arts of war. On the way he had to traverse the Plain of Sorrows and the Fearful Valley where men would freeze and be clutched by dead hands sprouting from the ground like weeds, or roast and be bathed in oil by faceless spectres. Finally he came to the fortress of his teacher, the smith, which could be reached only by a perilous causeway that moved between the feet of anyone who approached and tried to hurl them into an abyss. Partholon was successful in reaching the fortress and drove his spear through the door which was then opened by the master's daughter, Dubhnoll, who was loathsome and misshapen, but would not let him enter unless he loved her. Partholon refused her and she vowed her revenge, but Partholon ignored her and was accepted by her father. After some time he sent him on his way again to learn elsewhere and on this journey he met a maiden who said she was his foster-sister and welcomed him with the friendship of her thighs. Thereafter she helped him overcome many trials and hardships designed by her father, who would not meet him unless he was neither within a house or without one, so she taught him to meet her father with one foot inside and another outside the house. Between them they overcame the sorcerer by clever ruses, but not without cost, for her brother also attacked Partholon and scarred him with his teeth.

Partholon faced similar trials on his return journey, but success-

90

fully managed it and so became a hero and warrior who carried off the prize, the woman he coveted.

Of course I know now that the woman was the craft or trade or warriorship that young men aspire to and the perils the difficulties and tribulations that lie on the road to mastering a mystery, which is at the giving of a god and therefore is opposed by demons.

When Methger finished his story the fires had died down. The shadows seemed darker and there was a feeling of foreboding in the air. We were all aware of the Cave of Cruach gaping behind us in the darkness and the awful and terrible powers that were gathering there and to which the young initiates would very soon be exposed. Did I imagine it or did a moan issue from the black hole? A shiver ran through me and I looked intently the other way.

I should explain that the Cave of Cruach is not always a cave. It is the home of the gods and demons who attend for the rites and, often enough, there is no suitable real cave available as happened on this occasion. In such circumstances it is usual to build a tunnel of withies and clay mixed with dung, that twists and winds and has several compartments. Sometimes it ends in a natural cave which is too small for the purpose itself. And this was the case here. The tunnel had been built some time previously and was about ten spears long with bulges and swellings at intervals, so that it looked like a huge overfed snake lying in the dark with its mouth open.

The Gobniu rose. He was a huge man, round of head, shoulder and belly with arms as thick as another man's leg and the forearms knotted and twisted with muscle and sinew. He wore a wolfskin jerkin and a seven-coloured cloak and his forehead was banded by gold, his throat by bronze and his cloak clasped at his right shoulder with a ring-pin of iron. He said nothing. He merely raised one mighty arm, holding his sheathed sword aloft, waved it backwards and turned and walked away from the throng into the darkness behind him.

Quietly the initiates, ushered by the champions, stood up and followed. Singly they filed through the silent, sitting people – the standing women and children keeping well back from them as they passed — and disappeared gradually into the gloom, their pale cloaks slowly merging with the night.

That was the signal for the end of the festivities. A few more methers were swallowed, a few more anecdotes exchanged in hushed tones. But within minutes the king, my grandfather, stood up and called to the people to return to their homes as the powers of the night and the otherworld were abroad, and they did so — in many cases thankfully enough. Only some senior warriors and champions of the king's retinue remained behind, quietly talking among themselves at the top tables and acknowledging absently the goodnights of the rest of us, who shook ourselves, let blood, and bathed quickly and quietly before retiring.

I slept deeply, but woke before dawn, alert and refreshed. Unable to sleep more, I got up and went outside to relieve myself. Standing there in the cold I shivered as the heat left my body in a hot stream. There was no sound except that I made. I could see red embers glowing here and there in the dark. I could almost feel the stillness lying over the settlement. Everyone was exhausted in sleep. Everyone, that is, except me and those in the Cave, from where a sudden choked-off scream panicked me for an instant.

As I looked across the compound a shadow seemed to slip between me and some of the glowing embers. I could not be sure. Whatever it was was now gone. I felt my throat tighten. But my curiosity was roused. Perhaps it was just one of the dogs back from the flocks? I sat by the door and pulled on my sandals. I slipped on my belt and tucked my knife into it. Dog or demon, I was going to find out what prowled about the silent settlement before the dawn.

I had taken only a few steps in the direction I'd seen the movement when a child's cry came from in front. It wasn't a persistent wail like a small, hungry baby, but the frightened inarticulate semi-scream of a toddler afraid to cry and equally afraid not to. I quickened my step and as I did so the frightened cry came again, now with a touch of panic in it. No one else seemed to have heard.

Silently I turned the corner of a building — the people here sometimes made oblong houses like our cousins in Nyrax — and moved. There was no time to think, to consider the scene or a course of action. Backed into a corner between two houses so she had no escape was a child, barely able to walk, waving a stick at a large, grey wolf which sat on its haunches between me and the child, looking at her and waiting its moment to attack the helpless offering. It had obviously not heard me coming and turned its head just as I rounded the corner. We moved together, the wolf and I. I saw the gleam of its red eyes as it twisted and sprang, while I simultaneously dived for its throat. By the grace of the gods who were that night all about us, and of the goddess herself, I gripped it with both hands and managed to hold the beast from my face, though it twisted and writhed with great strength in spite of its emaciated body, snarling and snapping inches from me. If I ever thanked the gods for my size and strength I did so then and summoning all I could I concentrated on pouring power into my hands. The stench from the animal was foul and hot saliva dripped onto my fingers and chest, flung itself onto my face. I kicked with my legs and must have caught it in the testicles, for it twisted in pain and howled. But in kicking it I fell with the wolf on top of me, and my left hand lost its grip. Instantly it tore at my shoulder, biting into it. I felt the wrench, but no pain. I could hear the child screaming and, now, an uproar and commotion somewhere else. But I also understood, clearly and certainly, that unless I did something very quickly the wolf would tear out my throat. My left hand jerked the obsidian knife from my belt. The creature was above me, worrying my shoulder while I held it off with my right hand alone, my legs locked about its body, forcing its head backwards, my fingers clenched on its throat. With my left hand I stabbed again and again at its belly close to where my legs were until the knife stuck and I could not pull it out. I managed to force its head from my shoulder and, as it lifted, I lunged and fastened my own teeth to its throat. I was indifferent to the stink, to the fur, to anything except

93

killing the thing which was trying to kill me. The bite was great. My mouth had opened extraordinarily and I felt my lips actually curl back from my teeth. It was difficult to breathe, but I throttled, with both hands now, and wrenched, wrenched with my head until the throat — fur, skin and flesh — ripped and I was drenched in a gush of hot blood that splashed over my face and neck. I clung to the beast's body with legs, arms and teeth, awash in its gore. Then sudden strong arms lifted me. I carried the animal with me. Spear shafts prized my legs apart from round its body, and swords and spears pierced the carcass. But I knew it was already dead! Voices I barely understood called me, but it was a time before I distinguished them or heard what they said. Then one voice, that of my grandfather, came through.

'It's all right, son. The wolf is dead. You can let go now.'

I looked up through a red mist and saw his face, concern and pride, both, plain in it.

'Let go,' he repeated. 'You killed it. You did it. You can let go,' he said again, trying to loosen my hands. I unclenched my teeth. I gagged and spat out lumps of fur and skin, swallowing a mouthful of blood as I did so, and sat up choking. But it took three grown warriors several minutes to prize my fingers from the throat of the dead wolf.

I had been lucky. The animal was old and desperate, an outcast from the pack, and was weak from fatigue and hunger, which was clearly what had brought it into the settlement, a place it would normally avoid. As I now knew desperation does strange things to animals and to men. Had it been younger and stronger I would have been dead with *my* throat torn out and the wolf would have fled with the child into the dawn, grey as itself, from whence it came. But, thanks to Anann and the gods, it was the wolf that was dead. And I had killed it!

It was light now. As I struggled with the wolf, dawn had spilled over the sea from the east. I could see the anxious faces around me. I was supported by my grandfather and Ogma. My father, Keth, and my mother, Sena'an were in front. Round about were many people, men and women, but those I noticed first, after my own clan, were the king, Fergus Leathdearg, his arm about a woman who much resembled him — except for an absence of his redness — and who was holding in her arms the sobbing infant I had saved. While she comforted the child her eyes sought mine. She wore the most extraordinary expression; one I never saw before directed at myself — and I'm by no means sure, at that time, I'd seen it directed at anyone else either. Her face showed a mixture of such deep, barely controlled emotions that I can hardly describe them. There was gratitude; admiration; love; tenderness, and all were intensified and conflicting. She was clearly the child's mother and was overwrought and torn between her feelings for the child and for me. Tears filled her eyes and smiles and sobs fled one another across her generous mouth. I smiled back as best I could. But that was too much. She wailed and buried her head in her brother's shoulder. What struck me then was that beside her stood Oran, who, with the other initiates, had run from the Cave of Cruach when they heard the commotion, thinking we were under attack. He looked me full in the face with his deep grey eyes, nodded and simply turned away much as he had done after our encounter the day before. Fergus came to me, put his hands upon my shoulders, and said:

'Thank you, MacKeth. It is my niece you saved. You have the thanks of my clan and we are under obligation to you. You will be a great warrior.'

Was it his words? Or perhaps the detached grey eyes of Oran? I'll never know. Whatever inspired me, I suddenly leaped from the clutches of those who tended me, across the body of the wolf and, ignoring their cries, ran to the gaping maw of the Cave of Cruach, where I stood and looked back.

As I stopped there fell a silence and my grandfather stepped out from the group. I turned to the entrance and renewed shouting arose. Suddenly it stopped. I looked back again and saw that my grandfather had raised his hand. With that gesture alone he silenced them and they stood still. It was clear to all that he had come to a decision of great importance.

'Let him go,' he cried. 'The gods have called him. Let us see if we have a champion amongst us.'

I looked away. Before me was the black opening. Fear gripped at my throat and I could feel my eyes widen and strain. My stomach lifted against my ribs. Without looking back I plunged in. The only sound I heard above that of my heart was the wail of a woman – I was told afterwards it was my mother – the only time I ever knew her do such a thing.

For reasons you will understand I can not describe in detail all that took place during my initiation in the Cave of Cruach. You know already that I was under-age, that I had been neither shorn nor ritually cleansed; fasted or tried by endurance or for poetry. These came later. Yet I knew – as my grandfather accepted – that the gods had chosen me specially, for the killing of the wolf was a direct sign of this and a greater indication of my fitness than anything else.

When I started into the tunnel-like cave I moved slowly, looking around in the gloom. My wound was throbbing now under the poultice and bandage that had been put on it while I was still half dazed. I felt suddenly cold and my foot slipped in wetness. I found myself walking on ice where the whole floor had been excavated and filled with it. Some had melted, so that I stood in an inch or so of bitter water. I could see dimly that from the walls, floor and ceiling of the tunnel sharp, pointed staves protruded which, if one slipped and fell against them, could produce a nasty wound. Cautiously I moved ahead to where I could make out a source of faint light. I was concentrating on my movements and avoiding the staves when, suddenly, there was a moan. I jerked my head up and saw an outline darkly move against the light, but, beyond that it was large and monstrous in shape, I saw no more. The hair stood on my neck and my flesh went cold on my back and arms. Stealthily I took another step. Again the movement and the moan; a threatening gesture. Again it vanished.

I kept on going, my eyes searched the darkness, my heart thudded in my chest and my tongue was large in my dry mouth. The water and ice ended and I stood on firm ground. I understood. I had crossed the Plain of Ice, a fearful place of the Otherworld. With this knowledge came confidence and I moved forward with less caution than was required and almost tumbled into a pit that opened at my feet. Peering down I could just see that the bottom was covered — not with staves, which might prove fatal — but with rocks and lumps of wood which might injure and that dully reflected the dim light. I stepped backwards, remembering stories of heroes. I called to mind the trials they underwent in order to reach their goal and wed the bride, the prize of their dreams and I knew then that I was undergoing their trials as surely as if my journey was truly through the Otherworld. And perhaps it was, who knows?

I saw that midway across the pit a log spanned it from side to side. To reach it one had to jump — a longish hop for a sixteen-year-old; for me a jump of some magnitude. I also saw that its surface had been scraped clean of bark and was smooth, offering little purchase, so that one could not jump onto it, but had to use it as a platform from which to take another flying leap to the far side of the pit without pause. Otherwise one must surely fall. Beyond the pit was a door of hide-covered wicker, whence came the dim light and, now, sounds I had already registered. Protruding from the door was the haft of a spear. It was the only hold on the far side of the pit, and the footing in front of the door was just wide enough to stand on. If one missed the spear-haft the consequences would almost certainly be a fall backwards into the pit.

I stepped back as far as possible, to the edge of the ice and, measuring the distance to the gleaming log as best I could in the dimness, I ran forward and leaped. As I jumped I felt my foot scuff the rim of the pit and felt too, rather than saw, clods fall where I launched myself. But my eyes were on the log which I hit with my right foot, the leg flexed for a second leap. But I had landed too far on the near side. A moment of panic as my sandal slipped. But I threw my weight forward and thrust down and backwards with my left foot as my body passed over the log. I leaped again, reaching with my right and momentum carried me over. I grabbed for the spear-haft with both hands as my feet scrabbled on the ledge before the door. I raised myself with both arms and stood on it. Holding the haft in one hand I looked into the pit, but from where I was I could see only darkness. I pounded on the door with my left hand. Nothing happened. I could hear movement. I pounded again. Then a voice — a woman's voice, but distorted — asked:

'Who is it?'

'Let me in.'

'Who asks?'

'Let me in, curse it, before I fall.'

'Who curses in the Cave of Cruach?'

'Open the door,' I shouted angrily, 'or I'll kick it in.'

There was a laugh from inside and another, a man's voice, cried: 'Give us your name, O kicker.'

'The son of Keth,' I cried, 'Open!'

Instantly the door swung inwards and, as I was still hanging on to the spear-haft, I went with it. I stumbled into a smoky, poorly lighted chamber where there were two people — or, rather, two figures, for one wore a hideous mask above a naked woman's body, painted and daubed so that it seemed as ugly and misshapen as a human body could possibly be. This creature grabbed me and intoned: 'Ah! a nice boy. What a nice boy. Marry me, boy, and I'll make you happy.'

I looked at the wretch, and drew back.

'Marry me,' she intoned again, bending that awful mask down to my face. 'Stab me with your bright young spear.'

'Get off, you old hag,' I cried, scrambling to my feet. 'Leave me alone.'

She advanced on me, arms outstretched and mumbling.

'Live with me,' she cried, 'taste the sweetness of my belly.'

But a laugh from the other corner of the small chamber, followed by a command: 'That's enough,' stopped her.

I turned and saw Gobniu standing beside a dim fire which was one of the two sources of light, the other being a small boat-shaped lamp which gave off an unsteady and faint flame and an unpleasant smell.

He wore an unusual horned headdress, one I had not seen before, of antlers set in a beautifully-worked corona of gold and enamel. The antlers were clearly older than the crown, so old that they were worn short and thin in places and were blackened and yellowed with age. But I knew that he was depicting the god Cernunos.

I was relieved to see him. I smiled, but he did not smile back. The great laugh of a moment ago was an illusion of humour, or for his own benefit or that of the hag. Whichever, it was replaced now by an unsmiling visage which gave added dimension to his great size. For a moment he looked at me before asking:

'Are you the MacKeth?'

I was tempted to reply of course I was, hadn't he known me all his life?, but his expression stifled the temptation and, after a fractional hesitation, I answered him solemnly: 'I am.'

He nodded, seemingly satisfied.

'Are you here to learn the artfullness and skills of a full warrior of the people of Danann?'

'I am.'

'Will you faithfully learn, cherish and preserve them and offer them to no man or woman of this world or the other by treachery or by guile, in soberness or infirmity, through treachery or malice, in weakness or in strength, in rage or malediction?'

'I will.'

'Do you swear on the breast of the mother Anann —' and at this there was a titter from the hag in the corner who danced in front of me her hands beneath her dangling and empty breasts that somehow seemed unreal (as it proved), so that I looked away '— do you swear on her breast that you will be a true warrior, a faithful champion and the honourable spouse of your noble vocation?'

'I do.'

'Then come forward, MacKeth, and let us see if you are fitted to learn all that a warrior of the people of Danu, the goddess, Ishtar, Astarte, Anann; wife, mistress, mother, daughter, grandam and fount, must know.'

I spent three days with Gobniu, the mighty smith — and, incidentally, brother of the unpleasant Diancecht and as amiable a man as the physician was not — studying and absorbing much that would be put into practice during the following years. Then as now our initiation ceremonies marked the introduction to the mysteries, not an understanding of them. Even the greatest of us could not accomplish such a thing in so short a time, and even yet while my knowledge is as great as any man's, my understanding still grows. It came as a surprise to me that six of the other candidates, among them Oran, were also with us and that my battle with the wolf had interrupted their studies, which they now resumed. Each, as I had, had come singly to the door and was greeted by the hag. And each had been importuned by her to a greater or lesser degree. I had reason to be grateful that my limited years may have saved me from even more hideous and offensive advances than those I had experienced. We seven were instructed in a group and there were five similar groups elsewhere in the Cave, beyond Gobniu's particular cell, where the others were under instruction from skilled smiths and warriors. We were forbidden to speak and our food was water and gruel. Shortly after my arrival I felt sick and my shoulder throbbed, but Gobniu, noticing, put a fresh poultice on, together with some powder which he sprinkled on the wound, and made me drink something unpleasant, after which I felt better and able to continue.

There days passed speedily. So much occurred in that space, so well were our minds manipulated according to methods annealed by tradition, that we emerged with the heads of men instead of boys and certainly older if not wiser than when we went in. Singly we left Gobniu and proceeded through five similar cells where our fellows had received instruction. From now on our trials would, again, be faced alone. When it came to my turn to go I noticed that the other acolytes must have preceded us as the cells I passed through were all empty.

I will not — can not — recount the trials, except for one that I shall come to in a moment. First you should know that I was excused three — the initation scarring which usually followed the days of instruction, and which the others received after they left the cell. It was most often on the arm, between the shoulder and the elbow. I was excused on the grounds that the wound from the wolf was my scar. The second was the rite of Annan's arch and the pillar of Aengus the Forever Virile, which I was then considered too young to fulfill. (Afterwards some of the others began to laugh at me about this, telling me what I had missed with the priestesses and boasting of I knew not what, yet certainly belittling me. But it was after we had taken arms and I challenged any one of them to continue his laughter. None did!) And the third, for which I have ever since thanked the merciful dispensation of Providence in sending that wolf to me, was the unaccountable and horrible mystery of Cron, in which initiates are required to eat the flesh of a slain enemy — and thus acquire wisdom and strength through the portions of his brain, tongue and heart he swallows. In tearing out the throat of the wolf with my own teeth I was deemed to have acquired these things by divine ordinance and I was spared this inhuman and horrible ordeal.

As I have mentioned, there was a real cave at the end of the fabricated tunnel-like Cave of Cruach and in it took place the last of the trials — considered, in some ways, to be the most awful and to have the most profound influences. It was certainly one of the oldest and most mysterious and was known as the Trial of the Beasts. For obvious reasons it was not observed everywhere.

Save only for the trial of the arch of the goddess and the pillar of Aengus the Forever Virile, which in any case took place outside the Cave at night with the priestesses and, sometimes, with ribald and even participant onlookers — much as at the temples of Astarte, I'm told, in the eastern world — it was the last of the rites in the Cave of Cruach, but the two were directly connected. The remainder — the taking of arms, acquiring geasa, the exchange of family sureties and taking a name, all occurred afterwards, outside, and in public.

To enter the Cave I had to pass through a curtain at the end of the tunnel. I emerged into a high, narrow cavern lit by torches fixed at intervals to the walls. It was a shallow cave and turned a corner a short distance inside the entrance. Around it I could see more lights and grotesque and silent shadows. I walked forward, turned the corner and immediately halted in astonishment and not a little fear.

Terrible figures of great beasts were grafted on the walls where they seemed to dance in the fitful and smoky light, for here the torches were of a different sort that emitted pungent smoke as well as flame.

Some of the animals depicted were huge and of a sort I had never seen or imagined; many had spears protruding from, and what appeared to be wounds in, their flanks. The wall was covered with them and as I looked at them I was filled with an overpowering sense of cherished and accumulated mystery — even power — stretching backwards into the unknown past, and reaching out to embrace and absorb me; a feeling at once fascinating and repellent.

Afterwards I was told that these figures, painted and engraved, had been there longer than the memory of man and were fashioned by the ancient gods. But I doubt this. Young and inexperienced as I was, and in the half light of the lamps, I noted that the images conformed to natural shapes on the cave wall, incorporating here a hole and there a projection that resembled a little the animal in question — especially in the flickering lamplight. And the lines were drawn, fine or heavy as required, so as to accentuate the similiarity. It was well done, no doubt of that. But god or goddess would not have needed such devices. What they wanted they would have made. Moreover have we not seen similar techniques employed at Brugh na Boinne (where the ancients surely lived) and where now the gods are worshipped and the dead are honoured? Of course these works are designs and plans, rather than animals and beasts, but are on stone and have a shrouded sense of sorcery and the heartbeat of men. And are these ancient designs not also repeated in bronze and silver, aye and gold, by even our own metalworkers? I have myself seen men — and children — represent a scene or an animal upon a board and mark it out in clay. No! Although they are sacred now and used in some initiations, I do not believe, ancient as they are, that they were fashioned by gods, but rather by the hands of men so long ago that there is no memory of the doing of it, which may be why they are attributed to gods.

These beasts that plunged and lunged upon the cavern wall when I first saw them, shocked me. But my senses were so heightened by my ordeals, in spite of my loss of blood, that I was alert to any threat.

Suddenly from some hidden place figures leaped out; demons with strange heads and bodies that seemed to be half men or women and half animal. They danced so close to me that I was hard put not to cry out and run. But after an involuntary step back, I faced them as best I could, aware that a demon — or a god for that matter — could not harm me if my heart was honest.

Then they simulated congress with one another (but did not in fact) and while they enacted this incongruity so soon after terrifying me, they pointed, and attracted my attention, to the lances that seemed to pierce the beasts upon the wall and to the wounds they seemed to make.

And I felt, even if I did not understand, a sense of the profound and mysterious forces involved; of old relationships between men and women, male and female; of hunting and survival, hunter and hearthminder; of fear and courage, awesomeness and old, old powers in this and the other world among, between and about animals and men and gods.

Thereafter they circled me again in mock attack, demons from a nightmare, and vanished as suddenly as they came. A young priestess, little older than myself and dressed only in her swan wings, emerged and embraced me and led me from the cave into a moonless twilight beneath the first stars. And let me add that I enjoyed a sudden and powerful excitement, new and confusing, at her gentle embrace. This rite was even then very rare and, so far as I know, has been discontinued altogether in the civilized world.

I slept well that night. Next day the whole settlement assembled and with great ceremony we, the initiates, were formally pledged and given our new names.

The pledges were from our clansmen on both sides and absolved the community and the king from blood-price for us or any we harmed accidentally or otherwise. Sometimes we were free to choose our own names, more often we were given a name appropriate to our appearance or to some thing of renown we had accomplished. I was afraid of being called for the wolf I killed and I announced loudly and clearly that the name I wish to be known by henceforward was that of my grandfather, Cian. Contrary to what I expected there was a roar of approval when I said this, which, I think, reflected more the respect in which my grandfather was held than any acclaim I might have won by my victory over the wolf. In any case it was a popular choice.

Afterwards came the taking of arms.

For me this was the most important part. Consequently when I was informed by Ogma, who, as champion of champions was responsible for overseeing the choice by the initiates, that I would be last, because I was youngest, it didn't suit me at all.

It was a fine day with white, round-bellied clouds sailing an otherwise clear sky, the sun pleasantly warm as it often is in autumn. The thirty-three of us stood in a line in the centre of the arena where the unarmed combat trials had taken place, tallest at one end, smallest at the other. Young as I was I was not the smallest, nor by any means slightest. Ogma passed down the line telling each of us the order in which we would be called on to choose our weapons from the store made specially through the year for the purpose and now assembled at the far side of the arena. There were maces; swords, shields, halberds, heavy fighting spears, throwing discs, javelins and helmets. There were also some greaves and coats of mail, but these were supplied by wealthy clans for their own aspirants and, naturally, there was none for me.

'Wait!' I called after Ogma when he had given me my number, thirty-three. 'That's not fair.'

He stopped and turned and looked coldly at me.

I blushed, realising I had done something unheard of, but I did not intend to be the victim of an injustice. It was too important. The youth beside me hissed: 'Shut up, fool!'

But I stood my ground and looked levelly at Ogma. I had cried so loudly my remark had been heard by everyone and I could hear a murmur ripple round the assembly. From the corner of me eye I saw my grandfather and knew he was not pleased. But I kept my eyes fixed on Ogma. Having, with his glare, quelled my impertinence —

for so it seemed to him from my flushed face at the time, as he later told me — Ogma turned away to resume his march along the line.

'Ogma!' I called again, my voice this time ringing and the blood, I could tell, gone from my face (indeed it is a curious thing, but, while as a youth I sometimes flushed from embarrassment due to inexperience, in anger my face tends to become white). 'Ogma, I have complained.'

This time he turned back in a wheeling movement, his face grim and angry, and strode to stand and glare down at me.

'Cian,' he said, addressing me by my new name, the first time it was used outside the ceremony at which I'd received it, 'do not presume too much. We are all', he almost sneered, 'aware of your prowess with wolves. But that gives you no special privilege here.'

I was angered by his unjust attack. As he went to turn away I cried: 'Ogma I have no petty complaint, but one against injustice.'

He turned back.

'What injustice?'

'On what grounds', I asked, 'are initiates numbered for the selection of arms?'

'On their ...' he paused and caught my eye. I saw the light in his change as he realised what I was saying '... performance,' he ended.

I nodded.

'And was my performance the least?' I asked.

He looked at me for a moment and then, without replying, turned and marched to the centre of the arena. He faced my grandfather and cried out so that everyone could hear him:

'O king, Cian: We were about to perpetrate a wrong, and I was not alone in it, but none saw it. The champions are awarded arms by right of performance in the ordeal. Cian Ogue [meaning Young Cian] has shown further courage in demonstrating to me our error. In your grandson, O king, we have indeed a true champion. He will take arms first.'

I had not expected this much and again the blood rushed to my face. But I was not going to refuse the honour and, even if I'd had the thought, the cheer of approval from the crowd would have banished it. Ogma returned, smiled, gripped my forearm with his great fist while I tried to do the same to his arm with my hand (but could hardly span the half of it), and then he turned and resumed his march along the line.

I broke two spears, three swords and six javelins before I was satisfied, and would have broken more but Ogma stopped me with a laugh saying:

'If you go on at this rate there'll be nothing left for anyone else. Take that,' he added of the sword I had in my left hand, balancing it against a more ornate one in my right. 'It is the better of the two. Gobniu made it and there won't be another here to equal it.'

I took his advice. I also selected a strong, moulded ox-hide shield, wedged on the left side, and a round Phrygian-type bronze helmet, with a nose visor and ear pieces and three cunningly-hinged plates behind to protect the neck, but without the feathers favoured by my grandfather or the horns which adorned some of the more traditional type helmets which I might have chosen.

That evening the final feasting was inaugurated by a ceremony which later was to become an engine of corruption that, I'm afraid, is still with us. It is my hope that it will be purified before it gets worse. But that is a matter for the druids. I refer to the ceremony of the sorceress Tlachtga Bal, which was often observed — provided the occasions were auspicious — in a tributary way at the conclusion of the initiation rites, as well as on the formal occasion of Samhain which was yet more than six weeks off. Tlachtga — or as some of the Phoenicians call her, Tanit — is the dark aspect of the goddess and, because her dark side differs so greatly from the light side, she is worshipped under another name.

For such minor ceremonies some of the first fruits of the harvest are reserved. They are used to fill a misshapen mannikin made of wicker so that they might be seen within, and are then ceremoniously burned at the conclusion of the feasting to placate the sorceress-goddess and to show that we saved what was best for her and were freely offering it to her.

That is what occurred that night and, as the flames spouted skywards, vomiting through the wickerwork and consuming the produce within, there were those standing about who stared stony-eyed and unmoved, or who exchanged frightened glances, their hands resting on one another or caressing the features of their first-born, for the next Samhain was the one following the quinquenniel celebration! The opposite one, reserved for her honour. But for all the terror that this must have inspired in the breasts of some, no one there could imagine or foresee the manner in which the figurine we saw consumed would become a yet more awful thing to contemplate.

During the next few days I had more opportunity to study the settlement and get to know my companions though now, of course, I no longer lived with my parents, but in the hall of the youthful warriors. The settlement, which had time to grow and develop in a more secure and fruitful climate than in Tartessia or Bregantia, had been built more strongly and substantially. It was one of the largest I have ever seen. Even before our arrival it was larger than customary and accommodated up to three thousand people in Nemed's time. As you know, our present system is slightly different and we group half or less of this number in three adjacent settlements for sound economic and social reasons. Smaller outposts from one to five miles distant were also built here. Nemed's settlement was relatively new and therefore did not have the huge ditch all round it which — although I did not know it then — is a commonplace about the older sites of the people in many parts of the northern world. Instead they had built a great rampart of stone and earth, such as we now do also, strengthened by reinforcing timbers from front to back of the wall. Apart from the stone and earth, which was plentiful, a great deal of timber was required.

This — as you already know — was available not too far off and, indeed, I was shown an area of more than one hundred and fifty acres which had been cleared of young trees to provide timbers for the wall alone. As a matter of interest my calculation today is that a one-acre citadel will take more than ten thousand running feet of timber half a cubit square, and it will take a thousand trees from a hundred acres of woodland to provide it.

Within the settlement were the houses; some of them round and conical, some of them rectangular, built in rows with passages between them. I had never seen anything like them before and the style was to dominate my thinking when we later came to build at Tara. A great variety of materials had also been used, as I mentioned before. Many of the houses were built in the traditional way, by excavating a circular hole to an appropriate depth. The dug-out material was used to build walls outside the hole so that there is a platform between the wall and the hole. There is a passage entrance to these houses sealed with doors of skin or wicker, hung at each end for warmth, and the roof is framed with timber and covered with sods. This type is still quite common, especially in the south and east. Outside the walls of the settlement there was a shallow ditch from which the earth had been taken to provide a rampart butting up to the wall, and beyond were some two thousand acres of arable land and huge pastures for the various kinds of cattle. The settlement was set with its back to a slope, not so steep as to provide an enemy any opportunity of overseeing it, and, on both hands, by rolling land of considerable merit. Before it, lapping very close at one place, was the sea, a small stream joining it beneath the walls. Within there were two sources of water, ample cooking places, and the sacred circle of twelve pillars and one. The arena I mentioned lay outside the walls close to the bluff, or small cliff, which contained the forbidden entrance to the Cave of the Beasts.

The gentle understanding of people, so characteristic of my father, and which was to lay the foundations for an event which would affect us all so greatly in a few years, is typified for me by something that occurred at about this time. I was talking to some of my companions not too far from our house — I mean my parents' house — and keeping an eye on it hoping to see my mother or my sister, Naas, whom I hadn't seen since the ceremonies, when my father walked through the door, stooping in order to do so. He saw me, smiled, and to my embarrassment walked over and asked me if I'd like to go for a walk. I was so taken aback that I hesitated.

'Come on,' he said, 'unless you've something better to do.'

I had nothing better to do, nevertheless I was reluctant. My feelings for Keth were mixed. I've already mentioned how I despised — well, perhaps not despised — but failed to admire him, and yet how much I treasured the obsidian knife he had passed on to me with the handle so beautifully made by himself.

He saw my hesitation. It was not in his nature to display hurt feelings and he just turned and walked away. After a moment I went after him. When I caught up with him he didn't slow down, but looked sideways at me and smiled that slow smile of his. I grinned back and for a while we walked on not saying anything.

He was a surprising man. I thought my herder's legs would soon tire him out, but I quickly found that I had to maintain a half trot in order to keep up with him. His long legs seemed to reach for the ground without effort. We went like this for quite a while.

'You know,' he said suddenly, 'it's not always easy for me to know what is the best thing.'

'What do you mean?' I asked.

He stopped and turned to look across the bay beneath us to where a headland jutted brownly into the feathered sea. I looked up at him and then turned in the same direction.

'I'm not sure what I mean,' he said.

'You mean this —' I waved a generous arm towards the distant settlement '— our going to Ierne?'

'No,' he said. 'No, I mean about you.'

'Me?' I was astonished. We were not a close family. Even if we were, that a father should express such feelings openly was absurd. I had no idea what he meant.

'What about me?'

'One day', he said, 'you will be a great man among the people. Already it is being said that you will become Tanist or leader elect.'

My heart swelled with pride. I had heard this too. Something that could never have happened to my father.

'What's worrying about that?' I asked with a laugh. 'Isn't it something to be proud of?'

He didn't answer, just looked over the sea and then turned to look at me in the same way, with those blue eyes that saw things which were never there. It exasperated me.

'Wouldn't it please you if I became Tanist? Wouldn't you be proud?'

Still he didn't answer. Those eyes seemed to look right into me, penetrate me, but without harm. I was uncomfortable as well as rancoured, and it must have shown, for he put his hand out and ruffled my hair as if I was a small boy still. From anyone else it would have been a grievous insult, but from him? Well, I could only smile. Then he took me by the arm and led me to a tuft of hoar grass where we sat down.

'Naturally I'd be proud, as I was proud of you last week. But I was also anxious. Anxiety is the breath of caution that only a fool ignores. Any fool in the marketplace will be proud if a slave smiles at him.'

I could not follow and must have shown it.

He looked at me questioningly. Then his face relaxed into a smile. He leaned forward on the haft of his light hunting javelin and prodded the ground with it ... it always seemed to me incongruous to see a weapon in my father's hand, so much more suited to making and playing lyres and harps. Neither of us knew what to say next. Just before it became a barrier for the day, he said:

'Nothing is a more genuine cause for concern than being a leader of people.'

'Why?'

'Because the leader is responsible to them; for everything.'

'I thought it was the other way round.'

He looked away, then back again.

'Think!' was all he said.

I tried to think. Among the people there are kings and leaders, ollamhs, druids, champions and warriors. One man, the king of the tuath — of the settlement — is chosen to be the chief man of that community of the people, arbiter and final authority. He is elected by his peers and must be without a disfiguring blemish (in Fergus Leathdearg's case the blemish was not considered a disfigurement). He must be noble and just or he will be deposed. He nominates a

Tanist, who must also, of course, be a nobleman or of the warrior class, and if the king should become incapacitated, the Tanist rules in his stead and may well succeed him on his death. For all practical purposes he is the successor elect. Naturally he would have to be ratified by a formal election and pass the test of the Liath Fail, the Stone of Destiny. If a true king sits upon this stone — facing south, as all true kings must — and holds in his hand a plate of bronze with a finger of iron rivetted to it so that it can swivel, the finger will point directly towards him. Some say the stone cries out, but I have never heard it so and do not believe it. It came to us from the east where our learned men became versed in many mysteries.

It had been said of me that I would one day . . . Dimly I felt, rather than saw, what he meant; what could be involved. The price of such power was abnegation of a normal life. Slowly I nodded.

'You belong to them and not to yourself?' I asked.

He nodded back.

'Not to yourself, nor to yours. Duty and responsibility are the price a true leader has to pay for the so-called privilege of leadership,' he said. 'It takes much courage and enormous honour.'

Then he said a strange thing.

'Think', he said, 'of what your grandfather has told you of the Great Kurus. You need to be very sure that this is what you want.'

In a sense I began, then, to understand both my father's difficulty and his concern. He was not a leader, either by temperament or by choice. And he was concerned for me in case I didn't understand the implications as well as the temptations. But before we could talk further an arrow hit the tuft of grass between us and we rolled, simultaneously, to either side of it and slid back.

I looked at Keth. He looked at me, his eyes bright, and gestured with the palm of his hand to keep down.

'Do you see him?' I hissed. He shook his head. Keeping as flat as possible, and as quickly as I could, I indicated to him that he should roll to his right and take cover behind a boulder and that I would roll to the left and try to circle to see who had fired at us, and how many there were. We both knew it was a small party, probably one man as there had been only one arrow, but I wasn't taking any chances. Before Keth had time to prevent me I rolled away from him to my left and behind some heather. I saw him find the cover I indicated, and then I began to crawl. I was glad I hadn't my sword. It made crawling difficult, but I had two hunting javelins which, while they weren't much use against an armed and armoured warrior, were better than nothing if I could get close enough to aim and give them force. I thanked my stars I had kept the cord wound about each. I had them both in my right hand as I crawled, my index finger in the loop of one ready for a quick cast. I turned as I crawled and circled to what was now my right, towards the cover of a rise. I had no intention of climbing it, but if I could get behind it I might have enough cover to circle out more than a bowshot and, anyway, I didn't think he had been that far. The angle of the arrow was quite flat when it hit. So I reckoned he'd be low and within a hundred paces.

I came round, as I intended, under cover of the hillock, with the sun behind me, and found a suitable elevation for observation. At first I could see nothing. I had marked the boulder behind which Keth had taken cover and I was now about a hundred and fifty paces out from it, in the direction from which the arrow came. Gently I peered through the stems of the heather, careful not to disturb the top. Then I chanced edging to one side where it was lower and looking round it for a clearer view. Nothing! I reckoned it must have been an experienced warrior and, if he was alone, he had either made off once he realised he'd missed, or was lying low, waiting for a movement or the dark. In that case we were all in for a long wait! Then I saw a movement. To my left and closer to the boulder where Keth was, but quite a distance from where the arrow seemed to have originated. He'd moved, then. But it was no practised warrior who'd merely done the obvious and made for the left flank. All I saw was the heather moving, but that was enough. A lark leaped shrilly skywards and the movement stopped, but I had him pinned now. I chuckled like a grouse. Keth briefly showed himself on my side of the boulder. I waved to him to move to his right, and he vanished. I next saw him thirty paces beyond the boulder and, clearly, the attacker saw him too and suddenly rose above the heather, kneeling, his bow arm back, but Keth vanished again and the stalker sank out of sight.

But it was now the stalker stalked. I guessed what he would do next, and he did it. His head rose quickly over the heather cover for a quick glance behind, and then he moved off again at a tangent to intercept the line taken by Keth.

As soon as I saw the heather move I was on my feet and running. Twenty, thirty yards I covered before I dived flat again to a position from where I could observe. The gap between the stalker and myself was now much smaller. He was still crawling. Again Keth showed himself, this time unexpectedly to the stalker's right, and then vanished. The stalker did as he had before, but, as we had anticipated, he changed direction, so that he was now working towards us both, but closing on Keth. I could not afford the risk of another run so, watching the movement of the heather, I narrowed the angle between the stalker and myself and made for the point I calculated he'd go for to get a shot at Keth. But I also knew what Keth was doing. He was working towards, not away from, the stalker, so that, if all went well, the stalker would pass him and leave his back vulnerable. It was a maneouvre we were taught from childhood. I was within ten yards of the stalker when, suddenly, Keth leaped to his feet behind him, his spear raised. I was also up and running before there was time to think. I heard a shout, saw scrambling in the heather and an arrow fly into the air. But, instead of throwing his javelin, Keth stood still with it raised above his head.

In that tiny moment the stalker leaped to his feet and ran. Hardly breaking my stride I loosed my ready javelin after him, but — for once in my life — excitement overcame me and, instead of pinning his backbone to his breast as I intended, it took him in the fleshy part of his upper arm. The force of the strike pitched him forward and he stumbled in the heather. He was up again, the javelin dangling from his arm which he clutched with his other hand, and running lopsidedly quicker than it takes to tell. But there was little chance for him now. Past Keth I bounded after him like a hound. But before I reached him Keth passed me on those long legs of his and I slowed, a little irritated, I think, that he wanted the kill for himself. But, to my astonishment, instead of ramming his spear into the other, or taking his head with his dagger, he ran up behind him and placed his arm around his shoulders. I stopped in amazement when I heard his voice:

'Here, here! Sit down. Let me help you.'

The fugitive was terrified and looked incomprehensibly at Keth; as indeed, I did.

'It's all right,' said Keth, dropping his javelin, 'Here. Sit here, and let me have look at that.'

The other obviously didn't understand the words, but the sense was clear. And there was no doubting Keth's intention. He allowed himself to be led to a solid tussock where Keth sat him down and looked at the spear and the wounded arm from which it dangled. I stood by and watched. I could see the other plainly now. He was a wild-looking barbarian, dressed completely in skins. His wooden bow was still clutched in the hand of his wounded arm and he had two additional arrows with flint heads, stuck in his belt from which also hung a crude bronze short sword. I guessed he was one of the Vacce, a semi-barbaric people who lived in scattered settlements to the west of us. But what surprised me most was his age. He seemed little older than I was, and was certainly smaller.

I was brought back by my father's voice.

'Cian! Your water flask. And help hold him. This is going to hurt.'

I went over but not quickly enough, for my father frowned and clicked his fingers at me. I gave him my flask and he, in turn and to my anger, gave it to the wounded Vaccean to drink from.

'Hold his arm, Cian.' I took hold where my father indicated and, none too gently I must confess, held his arm and his shoulder braced back against my thighs. Keth took out his honed bronze hunting knife and our prisoner began to struggle, thinking, as I did for a moment, that Keth intended to take his head.

Of course we were both wrong as I immediately understood.

'It's all right, son,' said Keth, leaning over him and taking his arm

114

above the wound, with his left hand, 'but I've got to get the spear out for you. And it'll hurt.'

His voice must have reassured the other for he looked at Keth without anxiety, and calmly turned his face away.

Keth cut swiftly into the flesh around the javelin head, which was barbed. Luckily my enthusiasm was less affected by my excitement than my aim and it had gone almost completely through. Keth cut the flesh, broke the shaft and removed the head. By that time the youth was unconscious, but he'd made no sound.

'Why did you do that?' I asked.

Keth looked at me, briefly, as he worked.

'He's only a boy.'

'He tried to kill us.'

'He's a newly fledged warrior like yourself. He wanted to blood himself and go home a hero with two heads at his belt.'

I looked at him. The little fool, I thought.

'He wasn't ready for it.'

'No,' replied Keth, binding up the wound with moss and strips cut from the other's clothing, 'but we didn't need to kill him because he was a fool.'

We sat and talked a little until the prisoner stirred. I felt I had learned something of value, but I wasn't entirely certain what. When he opened his eyes and looked at us his expression remained unchanged. Keth and I helped him to his feet and Keth handed him his bow, but kept the arrows, stood back and waved at the other to go. I started to protest:

'Keth ...'

'It's all right, Cian. Let him go. Go! Go on.' He waved his arm. 'Off with you.' Suddenly understanding illuminated the other's face and with a smile that seemed to stretch from ear to ear – in spite of the pain I knew he must be suffering – he turned and ran. After a few steps he turned back, ran to Keth, went on his knees and, taking his hand in his own good one, brought it to his lips and kissed it. Then before either of us had time to react he was on his feet again and running. As I saw his back receding my index finger twitched.

115

'We shouldn't have let him go,' I said.

'Why not,' asked Keth. 'What harm can he do?'

'He can tell the rest of the Vacce.'

'What if he does? They already know we're here. We're far too strong for them to attack us. And ...'

'And you didn't want to kill him,' I said.

'No,' he replied, 'I did not.'

Although he didn't ask me not to mention the incident, I didn't tell my mother. Somehow I felt that her reaction to learning that we had let a perfectly good slave go free might not be entirely understanding.

But it was a lesson that stayed with me for many years until I myself understood it more thoroughly.

Before our journey to Ierne and the tragedy that befell my grandfather, something happened which bound my cousin Dara and myself even closer. Before that, though, I'll tell you about the ships and shipbuilding, which had already begun at the time of the incident with the young Vaccean.

One day, having finished our studies, a group of us went to the shore where the ships were being built. Most were of timber, brought in from the woods and dried in the sun and in long, low buildings, where the planks were stacked while fires of green timber produced much smoke and controlled heat. The shore was full of activity centred on the largest ship of all, which would carry my grandfather (and, I hoped, myself!). One of my companions nudged me and nodded.

'Look.'

A plank was being bent and warped to curve into position of ribs and stretchers to strengthen it. It would become like part of the skin on a body, supported and prevented from collapsing inwards by the bones of the back and rib-cage. A group of men, some of them slaves, strained at the timber. Others poured boiling water onto cloths which were wrapped round it where they wanted it to bend, and more men strained at ropes to haul it into position. There was a strong frame along its entire length and wedges and baulks were pounded in to hold it in position as the curve developed.

'Now,' cried the overseer, 'Together! Go!'

Simultaneously the water-pourers, the men at the boat and those with the ropes, acted. The plank moved a little. The wedges were driven further home. Then one of the men moved ... a lot. Boiling water from a cauldron above him fell on his arm and he jumped back with a cry. Swearing furiously as he rubbed his arm he proceeded to miscall both the man who had splashed him and his parents, with remarkable offensiveness. I couldn't help laughing, especially when the water-pourer leaped from his perch to defend his honour. As both were slaves it was ridiculous, and added to the fun. Eventually the overseer got them back to work with a few flicks of his bullwhip (an interesting implement fashioned from the twisted and dried penis of a bull; very discouraging).

The great ship they were working on was more than fifty cubits long, or about a great spear's case (without using a thrower). It would have accommodated forty or more paddlers and seventy additional men or women, more than one hundred and ten people plus cargo altogether. Many of the other ships would carry fewer people and more animals and cargo. In all there was to be a fleet of forty-five boats. (For those who may be interested in such things that is nine times five ships, forty-five, and five and four, nine.) The fleet was to sail on the sixth night of Bealtaine the following year. Since most of the ships, down even to the smaller ones of only twenty cubits or so, were built on the same principle, I will describe it. I speak of wooden, planked ships, of course, not ocean-going canoes of hide fitted over a frame, of which we also had a number. They, of course, were limited in size, the largest being about twenty cubits or ten paces long.

The method of building the larger ships was one that developed to suit our own requirements and was based on traditional methods and modifications of one kind or another, as I learned that day.

117

Near to where we were an old man sat warming his bones in the sun and leaning on a stick that he grasped with both hands folded one on the other and on which he rested his chin, while he watched the work with intense familiarity. Now, as I well knew, it was more from respect for my ability with arms and my short temper than from friendliness on their part that my older comrades tolerated me, and I often sensed they would have been much happier without someone four years younger than themselves at their heels when they talked about those things interesting to sixteen-year-olds, even if my curiosity was strong. I saw, having cursorily inspected the ship-building, that they were anxious to be off, so I excused myself and went and stood beside the old man as the others went laughing to the hills (and, I suspected, to some of the girls of the settlement). He didn't look at me, but said in a conversational kind of way:

'Are you not going with your friends, Cian?'

It wasn't surprising that he knew my name.

'No,' I said and leaned beside him. 'I want to watch.'

'Aye,' he said 'aye. You made the wise choice.' He glanced at me, with a sly and humorous expression, from the corner of his eye, 'which is what I'd expect.'

Before I could answer he continued.

'That was my job for many years, before the cold came into my bones. And the fire with it,' he added. 'I can't move now like I used to.' 'What?' I asked, 'watching boat making?'

'No, young man,' he said, 'making the boats themselves. Don't play games with me. You knew well what I meant.' Though he said it kindly, it had force and I had the grace to blush. For, of course, he was right. I knew what he meant.

'I'm sorry,' I said, 'I was thoughtless.'

It was no shame for me to apologize. My birth geasa, or obligation which I dare not break without sacrificing honour, included that I should not wilfully or knowingly offend or insult a man not an enemy, or if I did, unintentionally, then I could apologise without loss of honour.

'Thank you,' he said, 'you don't need to say it. Look at that,' he went on, 'ten of them straining at one plank when half of them would do if they did it right. They should strain more gently and further back. Ah-ah!' He sighed and spat contemplatively — or maybe it was contemptuously, I couldn't be sure — in the dust at his feet, where it made a little globe of dusty liquid, with a tail to it.

'It is a fine ship,' I said.

'Aye,' he said, 'a fine ship — it will be a fine ship. And a finer one if they'd listen to me.'

'Why don't you tell them?'

'Do you think they —' he nodded with definite contempt now '— would listen to, much less ask, advice from the likes of me? Let them make their own mistakes. It will only mean the difference between a fine ship and a masterpiece.'

And the time was to come when I wished, with all my heart, that I had persuaded him to intervene and offer his advice that day instead of listening to his stories of boats and boatbuilding, and that we had built a masterpiece instead of the fine ship she truly became; the *Cu-Feasa*, the Hound of the Sea.

She was long and the bow and stern curved upwards to a raking point fore and aft, raised in the bow and rough-carved into the likeness of a beast's head with staring eyes. Later this carving was refined and painted. I had seen large ships before, of course, mostly Phoenician, but never one of ours of such proportions and never one being built, for the boats that we had used in Tartessia were small fishing boats.

'How do they make them?' I demanded.

He turned towards me at this and a smile lit up his face.

'Well,' he said, 'your manner matches your reputation, Cian. You come straight to the point, don't you?'

I smiled at him and he smiled in return. He leaned back, lifting his chin for the first time from his hands and looked at me and at the great panorama of activity taking place in the harbour.

'How do they make them?' he mused. 'As simple as that,' he laughed. 'I suppose if anyone is entitled to an answer you are, but remember I'd tell anyone else "I spent my life learning how to make ships and now you want me to tell you how to do it in five minutes".'

I just stared at him and waited. After a moment he looked again at what was going on in front of us and said:

'That ship there is a ship of the people, built on traditional lines by traditional ways.'

I nodded.

'Ships like that,' he said, 'carried our ancestors when they fought against the Egyptians — who called them the Danuna. In ships like that our forefathers, with their Mycenean allies from Etruria and Sardinia and Sicily, battled against and were defeated by, the Pharoah Ramses centuries ago. With one difference,' he went on, and paused, 'and we learned from that difference, for in that battle the Egyptian boats had long paddles while ours had not. Ships like that brought your great-grandfather and ourselves along the Mediterranean, back to Egypt and from there to Bregantia and Tartessia; and ships like that brought Nemed and his tuath to Ierne, where you will follow.'

He paused again and looked at me with those wise, wrinkled eyes, before he seemed satisfied.

'There were some changes made', he said, 'in the basic design from time to time. We borrowed the paddles and one method of planking from the Egyptians, the rams and the deep wells fore and aft are like those on Phoenician vessels, but the centre platform for storage, both above and below, are ours and they borrowed that from us and the method of planking called clinker-building.'

'What platform?' I asked, for there was no evidence of anything of the kind. 'What rams? Do you mean where it curves up in front?'

Patiently he explained.

'No,' he said. 'Do you see the step at each end of the keel, below the curve and back towards the hull proper?'

I nodded.

'Under the rake, the rams will be fitted on those steps,' he said. 'Look. Over there. Do you see those men working at the copper forge? Look at what they're doing.'

I saw four men working on what looked like a cylinder, or cone of oak on to which they were fitting thick copper reinforcements.

'That is one of the rams,' he said. 'It will go on to the step on the keel and will project below the water-line beyond the curve of the bow.' He laughed. 'That, among other things, was one of our gifts from the Phoenicians.'

Even as he finished there was an almighty cheer from the men working on the boat as the plank was warped into place and lashed to the high stem. Immediately several artificers, who had been waiting close by with fanned braziers, moved into place with red hot metal rods, curiously curved. These were used to bore through the plank in a number of places and it was then firmly attached and held in position.

I looked first at the ship, then at the sea beyond, trying to imagine her moving across it with the sun beating on her bellied sail, and then I looked again at the old man. He looked at nothing I could see with dim eyes; but there was little doubt that they reflected far more than my own keen-sighted ones did.

'It will be a fine ship,' I said to raise his spirits.

He turned and looked at me and there was no smile upon his lean face this time, nothing but earnestness in his eyes.

'You will see Cian,' he said, 'what I have never seen; the Ceremony of the Bird, the Boat and the Sun when she is launched, which has not been celebrated by our people since Nemed left, when I was sick for dying. Never before that had I the opportunity, for all the boats we built were fishing boats not boats of war and adventure. Not boats like this. But I will see it now.'

Yet he never did. For he was dead before the *Cu-Feasa* was launched on the sixth night of Bealtaine in the next year. Much more, Conaire — for that was his name — told me about boats and boatbuilding; how the planks were fashioned with adze and axe, from larch and cedar and, sometimes, beech; how the ribs were fashioned, width after width, to a predetermined and careful calculation from ash or oak or yew and were fitted to the inner keel and the planking of the skin without nail or rivet, as, indeed, were the interlocking sections of the hog fitted to them. He told me about the making of the steering oar and the mast; about the sails and the ropes and the long paddles or bladeless sweeps fastened with twisted ropes to the sides. I left when it was time to return to our hall for the meal, thanking him for his kindness and arranging to meet him again — which I did on more than one occasion. As I left, for some reason a small incongruity caught my eye; it was a woman and a child, of about two and a half or three years old, standing between the boat and the sea looking now at one and now at the other with great intensity, a look of strain upon her face which, even to my eyes, was off-putting and which, equally clearly, indicated her anxiety for someone to talk to. There was something vaguely familiar about her, I couldn't quite say what. I carefully avoided her and made my way back to the hall.

My route back took me past some sheds in various stages of erection, where the stores and fittings for the fleet were to be kept. Most of them were close to the waterside but some old ones, hidden behind the new works, were further back and I passed close by one, now dilapidated and used only as a byre for milch goats.

As I did so I heard a muffled sound. I might have paid no attention, had it not continued. There was something unanimal about it that caused me to stop and turn back. The door was a lattice of rough boughs bound to transverse pieces, themselves tied to an upright sunk in the ground and swivelled at the top from a fork in a cross-beam. I lifted this door with both hands to clear the ground and pushed it inwards. As I did so there was a scuffle in the corner and Dara stumbled towards me looking frightened and anxious. With him came a cloud of dry straw-dust, dancing in sunbeams that glanced through the tattered roof, and the singular aroma of a disturbed earth, dung and straw flooring. In a shadowy corner, hidden behind bars of slanting light, there was a movement. A figure, which had been crouched, now stood, hesitantly. As Dara reached me and turned defiantly back, this figure moved quickly towards us so that involuntarily I stepped back to allow it to pass through the door. It was Barnea, the effeminate, with whom I had few dealings until then, but whom I instinctively disliked ... which had nothing to do with his nature, for I have known other men, similarly afflicted, who were as upright and honourable as any. But this man looked, and behaved, untrustworthily.

'What's up?' I asked Dara, 'what's going on?'

'That old shit,' he said with vehemence, which both took the humour out of what he said and shocked me, for Dara was noted for a reserve amounting almost to prudery.

'What?' I asked.

'Do you know what …? He tried to take my clothes off.'

'What?'

'I came in for a crap. Just as I was started he came in and stared at me.'

Doubtfully I said, 'Maybe he only wanted a crap too …'

Dara looked at me in disgust. He was, in any case, oddly sensitive about privacy in such things.

'I told him to go. Do you know what he said?'

'"Why would I go away when I can look at a lovely little bottom like yours?' I didn't know what to do. One thing I couldn't do was what I came in for. My ass tightened up like a twisted cloth …"'

I couldn't help laughing.

He rounded on me furiously.

'Maybe you think it's funny. I'm telling you, it wasn't one bit. The rotten old fart had his tunic up and was showing himself in front of me like a goat. I felt … I didn't know what to do. I tried to get past but he … he grabbed me and tried to … tried to …'

Suddenly I was shocked; sickened!

'He didn't!'

'He dam' did, I'm telling you …'

'Then what?'

'You came … I'm glad to say.'

I turned to the door.

'Come on.'

'What for?'

'We're going to report this to the king. He'll do something about it …'

'No, Cian, no.'

'Why not?'

'Because I ... I don't want it known.'

I understood. Whatever the real circumstances they could, very likely would, be later misrepresented to Dara's discredit.

'All right,' I said. 'We'll do it ourselves. Come on.' And I led the way from the shed with Dara at my heels. But, by the time we got out and looked round, Barnea had vanished and our 'revenge' did not materialise. But I never forgot the incident, nor did he, for, though it remained unspoken, I believe that it had a great deal to do with later events. As for Dara, he soon forgot about it and when I next saw him and Barnea in the same company it was as if nothing had ever happened. Perhaps it is a fault in me, but I am always far readier to take umbrage at an offence against a member of my family or clan than at one against myself, which strikes others as strange. To me it is not so strange. I measure an insult by the worth of the person offering it and by the ability of the insulted to withstand it. And if that is arrogance, so be it.

Samhain came and went and, with it, sadness and heartbreak for families whose first-born were claimed by the priests of Tlachtga, Baal, or Tanit, in her name. Some of the children were nearly five years old and understood what was happening. For them, and their families, the terrible ceremony was especially distressing. It was the first one that I remember attending – though my horror of it may well have been due to an earlier attendance which I had mercifully forgotten when my brother, older by two years than myself, was among the victims. It was also my last. Ever since I have managed, by one means or another, to absent myself from a ritual which, however placating to the goddess, is to me an exercise in human misery and degradation. Nor am I alone in that view nor have I suffered from the wrath of the goddess for holding it. I do not intend to describe the ceremony, which is well understood. All I will say is that the sacrificing of young children by fire to the goddess in this fashion seems to be to be merely the worship of Baal and Marduk, whom we have rejected, under another name. I believe that our priests — for reasons of power they would probably refuse to acknowledge (as is ever the way with priests) — rejected these gods but retained the ceremony in order to maintain a hold upon the people.

The year advanced and became colder, the nights shorter and the stars brighter. The river of the goddess stood out in the heavens as a glittering pathway through the night and from time to time the spirit of a man or of a god traversed the sky in a streak of white light.

Then the cold settled on the world in mid-winter and the work in the fields stopped. But not the work of preparation. All through the dark days, beginning in the morning before there was light in the sky and with ice and sometimes snow still thick on the ground, the sounds of activity rang upon the frosted air.

And then, before we knew it — certainly before we were ready — spring leaped at us. Ever earlier the morning veil drew back and later and later drew in the night. Suddenly there were buds upon the trees, corn thrust greenly through the cultivated land and nesting birds sang. In the sheds and shelters which had been specially built by the waterside, where piers and launching ramps now fingered the breakers, a huge accumulation of fittings and storage vessels assembled. Ropes, hides to make sails and the finished sails themselves, masts, booms, blocks, paddles and tier on tier of pots of all sizes ready and waiting to be filled with grain, beans, lentils, dried and salted meat and fish, honey and foodstuffs of all kinds, were gathered here. Cloth to make clothing had been woven, craftsman's tools, weapons — think of a thing and it was there a thousandfold. And, of course, our forty-five ships, some of them now riding at anchor close in, the magnificent *Cu-Feasa* among them, standing on a slipway with her back to the tide and her rearing prow with the head of a snarling beast turned towards the land.

As it happened I was with my grandfather, whom I now seldom saw, about a week or so — I'm not sure — before departure when that strange woman, the one I had seen by the boat-yards in the autumn with a child, approached him.

'Cian?'

'Yes. What is it?'

'You don't know me. I am Cruithne, wife of Starn, Nemed's son.' My grandfather did not smile. In fact, his expression was not even welcoming — surprising, isn't it, how such things can influence or confirm one's own attitudes towards people? My grandfather's face was difficult to read; if it were possible, it was expressionless. But that is a negative thing. What is positive is that there was no welcome in his normally expressive face, and that was clear to me. This time she was not accompanied by her child.

'I know you, Cruithne,' said my grandfather. 'What do you want with me?'

'Take me to Ierne,' she demanded. 'Take me to Starn, my husband.'

'Your husband is dead.'

'No!' she shrieked, the loudness and intensity of her voice startling me.

'Starn is not dead. He's not!'

My grandfather was unmoved.

'They are all dead, Cruithne. You have taken the role we know of in the rites on that understanding. And you know it. You have been told so many times. What good will it do you to go to Ierne only to hear it again?'

The demented look on her face softened, brought under control by an almost visible effort of will. I believe she could have hurled herself on my grandfather in a frenzy if some vestigial spark of reason — or perhaps it was cunning — had not held her back and guided her on a more persuasive course. She threw herself on her knees in front of him and her dark, lean face searched his.

'Please, O Cian. Listen to me. I know in my heart that Starn lives. What you say is not true. He is alive. I know it. I have the gift ...' Suddenly she swung her dark, intense eyes from my grandfather to me, and I felt my bowels surge as they locked with mine. And what she said next was far from reassuring, '... as he has. Your grandson

too has the gift. He knows that when I speak I speak a truth known to me.'
At that moment recognition came to me. In spite of her totally different appearance there was that about her that undeniably told of
the Cave of Cruach and the hag with Gobniu. I shuddered
involuntarily.

She turned back to my grandfather who had not moved and looked
down at her as impassively as ever.

'Please, Cian, take me to my husband, me and the child.'

'I cannot,' he said.

'You will not.'

As if he had not heard he continued in the same level voice which
was as full of command as when he addressed an assembly with all
the power of his lungs.

'I cannot!' He leaned towards her. 'Get up, Cruithne. I know you
believe what you say. But we have reports from the Bretani. These
reports come in all the time. Except for the women and children they
took as slaves, they are all dead. What would you do in Ierne, you
and your child, without a man to care for you?'

'What am I doing here?' she almost snarled, her lips turning down
and her mouth wet with saliva. 'Listen to me, Cian: I am a woman of
the south. I live in my own right ...' he would have interrupted her
but she rose and raised her hand to stop him, a thing few have done
'... and I know what you are going to say. I *will* go. I shall go where
Starn is, and take his son with me.'

He looked at her but said nothing. How she thought she could go
when he had refused to take her seemed odd to me, of a sort with
women's eternal logic — 'it *is* because I *say* it is'. But her next words
hung my breath.

'I put it on you, Cian,' she said, 'to take me. You cannot refuse me
since I ask your help!'

She stared brazenly at him for a moment and he stared back with
cold, debating eyes. I wondered what he would say. He seemed
caught, for part of Cian's geasa was that he must not refuse a virtuous
woman when she asked him for help.

At length he said: 'Very well, Cruithne, you and your son may come with us. You will be my responsibility, but only for the journey,' he added as she fell about his knees again in an outburst of gratitude. 'Do not thank me, woman,' he went on. 'I believe you are wrong in what you do. If you do not Starn alive in Ierne, you will have no resources there. You will be alone. An outcast. And your son will bear the burden of your folly.'

'Starn will be there; he *is* there,' she cried, rising to her feet. 'Thank you, Cian, I am in your debt.'

She turned and half ran, half walked away, carrying about her that invisible cloak of emotional intensity that had made me uneasy the first time I saw her at the shore, and anxious to get away from her as quickly as possible.

'She should not have put geasa on me,' growled my grandfather.

'You could not refuse her when she did,' I said.

He looked at me for a moment and then said: 'No. My geasa is that I must not refuse a virtuous woman when she asks for help.' And he put the slightest possible emphasis on the word virtuous.

'Oh!' I said, as if I understood, but I did not, or at all events, only in the vaguest manner. But, as clarity can blindly penetrate obscurity in a sudden remark from the least expected source when men are discussing the meaning of this and that, so did his remark, though imperfectly understood by me, forever illuminate the meaning of the word virtuous so that I understood virtuousness of intent no less then virtuousness of action and, more importantly, morality in the same way.

'You need not have agreed?'

'I believe not.'

'Then why did you?'

'I'm not sure,' he mused, 'perhaps because I know it is going to happen, as she said, and because I believe she carries fate with her like a shroud or the wings of the bawve — the hag.' I shuddered as he said it. He meant the Morrigu, and I quickly made the sign before my face and spat over my shoulder. Again a memory stirred in my head of my initiation in the Cave of Cruach and of the horrible female who had assailed me, and I wondered. Although she did not trouble my grandfather again until the day before we sailed, she was to be seen from time to time so that while it could not be said she was pestering him, she became a continual reminder of his obligation. Always she had the child with her, a curly-headed, attractive-looking boy with red cheeks and blue eyes and a full mouth who, in fact, was one of the most obnoxious infants I have ever encountered ... and I am noted for my liking of children and how well I get on with them.

Finally, on the fifth day of the moon all our preparations for the voyage were complete, and we waited for sunset and the ceremony of the Bird, the Boat and the Sun. Throughout the day there was a rejoicing mixed with trepidation, for on this day, as at Samhain, the passageway between the two worlds was wide and open, but, yet, at this time the prospect was of growth and the future and not of bleak, dark winter and death. So in the early morning the people began to celebrate by gathering dew on the hillside in which to wash in the sunrise, having first slaked our morning thirst in pure well water before the dawn. We symbolically plucked flowers and greenery and scattered dead straw in the wind as the sun approached us from the east and no family parted with food or fire or water on this day so that the prosperity of the new year might be well and truly safe-guarded. Rowan branches with berries were brought and attached to the houses, to sheds and cattle byres and to the ships of the fleet.

As the day wore on, a sort of quietness fell over everything. The ocean itself rippled on the beach with a susurration barely audible a stone's throw back. The sun hung immobile in the heavens, seemingly stationary above us, as if experiencing the same anticipation. The hot afternoon crept on until, at last, the shadows lengthened and began to point again to where the sun had risen and the entire population trooped to the waterfront, warriors in their red and saffron tunics; the greens and blues, browns and orange; the white of the druids and ollamhs and the purple and multi-colours of the kings mingled and interspersed with the unbleached of the children and the skins and coarse stuff of slaves. Finery was much in evidence and gold and jewels flashed everywhere, more than I ever remembered seeing together before — throats, arms, fingers, foreheads, legs — the golden wealth of our people was all assembled and it did not end there. Scabbards blazed with it and carbuncle and cornelian; ceremonial shields and helmets; belts and drinking vessels were all adorned with it, worked and sculpted by our finest craftsmen with a skill that was the envy of the known world. And where there was not gold there was bronze and silver and, here and there, an iron blade caught the light and added to the ostentatious panoply the colder gleam of unyielding power.

Dara was with me, none the worse for his adventure, but staying near enough to be within earshot all the same — but not too near to annoy me until I deliberately joined him, for which I was rewarded with a smile that went from ear to ear. We had managed to wriggle our way to the front of the slipway from which the *Cu-Feasa* would be launched and we slid over the side and stood on a ledge above the water which was just big enough to accommodate us. From here we could see everything. Above us and to one side reared the up-curved carven prows. All the boats were to be dedicated, even those already launched and at anchor, and all were bedecked with flowers and leaves, laurel and rowan, while the druids, in that strange forbidding way they have, produced young oak-leaf garlands spaced with the white gelatinous berries of the mistletoe, preserved by I know not what means for the occasion. Beside each ship was its commander and a druid. Those that lay at anchor were approached by boat, those on the slips lay there; waiting it seemed for life and that they would breathe; with a commander on one side of the bow and a druid on the other ... all except our ship, the *Cu-Feasa*, for both my grandfather and Methger stood on the same side, looking westward across the ship. The crowd was ranged around the harbour in a long semicircle, thicker at the centre than at the extremities.

Suddenly Methger threw up his hands. The descending sun had touched the top of the mast of the *Cu-Feasa*. Instantly a song burst forth from the throats of all the druids and the priestesses who, suddenly, appeared on each of the ships where they had been concealed. They wore nothing but their swan wings and head-dresses and they moved to either end of the ships, two to each. They too sang and, as the sun climbed down the mast and coloured the waters of the bay a dappled pink and blue, their voices rose all around in a hymn to safety and prosperity in the coming enterprise. As the sun disappeared the ships were manhandled down the slipways so that all were afloat, and all the time the song continued, now the voices of the priests and druids, now the answering chant of the swan maidens. Quicker and more exciting grew the rhythm as the sun went beneath the sea. More excited and restless grew the people on shore. Then the druids reached for the sides of the craft and pulled themselves aboard. Then the commanders. I saw my grandfather reach for the gunwale on his ship, but just then an unexpected swell lifted her and he missed and stumbled and a great gasp went up from those watching while my own fear stuck in my throat. We all knew that it was also a geasa of his that he should never immerse his head in the tide and, for a moment, it looked as if he was going under which would have been an appalling omen. But he clung to the side of the boat with terrible strength — ripping four nails from his fingers as he did so — and saved himself. (I may as well add here that his geasa included the following, and you will see why I do so shortly: That he must never permit another the use of his weapons and that he must never permit a child to be hurt or injured in his presence.)

Cian hauled himself aboard the *Cu-Feasa*, turned to the expectant crowd and waved, for which he received a cheer, and then joined the priestess in the bow — Brigit, whom he first embraced and then began with her the dance of the swan. He was wearing his cap of feathers and a golden lunula which I had not seen before. Then I understood. He, the king, was the embodiment of the sun. She, Brigit, was the swan — a creature of earth, air and water — and they danced upon the ship. They danced and the people watched until their dance became a living thing of itself in which they were intermingling elements. They dropped lower and lower like the sinking sun and then — and all the other commanders and their priestesses in the bows and all the other druids and their priestesses in the sterns — they sank, like the resplendent sun to the belly of the world, to the fortunate belly of their boats and made a union and a compact of symbolic power to protect their voyages upon the tumultuous and uncertain sea. Many of those on shore, excited beyond control or endurance by the ceremony and the impending journey into what would become their destiny, gave themselves to one another in a collective frenzy in the fading light there upon the beach and the pier, regardless both of age or relationship, as if Astarte and Dionysus had fled the Pheonicians and the Greeks and, hand in hand, strolled lustfully among us. But, in all likelihood, it was merely emotion breaking out in the greatest of all releases and if Tanit, or Ishtar or any of the other aspects of the goddess encouraged it, I saw no evidence of her immortal presence in that very mortal scene.

Mere hours later the loading was underway, first the baggage and stores for the voyage, then the animals and, lastly, the men, women and children who were to make the journey; in all more than two and a half thousand people and sundry cattle in this first wave. Another would follow with less people and more cattle, and a third and, finally, a fourth with the remnant, so that all the people would be in Ierne before Lunasa, or mid-summer, with the help of the gods. By dawn we were at sea and when the sun rose the land was a dark line behind us across the glittering waves.

The leave-taking was unnaturally quiet and uneventful after the compulsive scenes earlier. Those who remained included the elderly, slaves to care for them and enough warriors and craftsmen to secure and guard them and the herds until the ships returned.

Cruithne and her son were in our ship and I stayed away from them. They had come aboard at the very last and, because they were under my grandfather's protection, occupied the stern near him. I went well forward and stayed there with the rows of paddlers and the cargo platforms between us. There was much to see and to learn. So much that I could not take all of it in at first and it was not until I had seen a thing done several times, perhaps, or asked, that the apparent chaos became order.

Near where I and four of my companions were stationed, between two sets of paddlers on the western side, was a rest bench for the paddlers, who were relieved every two hours. Half way through the first spell there was a command and a sudden bustle amidships and at the stern, and the sail was hoisted against the sky. Immediately the ship lifted in the water and began to surge forward in a way it had not done under the power of the paddles. I looked up at the leather belly of the filled sail and saw that it was canted sideways and, indeed, tilted the ship sideways too, as it cut through the wave tops.

Behind and on each side of us the other ships had their sails up also and it was a fine sight to see the great fleet hurdling the swell, each one flying through the sea like a living beast. One of the paddlers near me looked over the raised side of our ship and said aloud: 'It's a brave sight.'

As if he had spoken to me, I quickly asked the question in my mind.

'How does the wind know the direction we want to go in?'

He smiled slightly, then turned a serious face to me, pointing straight over the side of the ship.

'At this time of the year — at most times, maybe — the constant wind is from the west, coming from the endless ocean.'

'Then why does it not blow us that way?' I asked, pointing to the east.

'Look,' he gazed up at the sail, turned away from us and bellying sideways from the ship, restrained only by the boom at the top of the mast and the ropes restraining it, 'look at the way the sail is turned. That is the way the wind is pushing ...'

'But ...'

'Now look at where your grandfather stands.' I looked back to see him standing on the small platform at the stern (which had a wicker fence on either side and curved round back, for safety), beside a huge man who grasped what looked like a handle protruding inwards from the side of the ship.

'That is the steering paddle,' said my companion. 'It goes deep into the belly of the sea and, by turning this way and that, we can point the bow of the boat in any direction within three-quarters of a circle and the wind will drive us that way. This wind is a good wind from the west and it will drive us straight to Ierne.'

133

Even as he spoke I felt a thump, thump, thump beneath me and the ship bounded like a steed and dipped her bow so that water splashed in on the other side and there were sudden cries of fear from the women. Already some — men included — were pale and I could hear retching and children crying.

My companion shook his head a little, but said nothing. I think he didn't want to swallow his words about the wind being a good wind — for it was so far as direction is concerned. But each of us knew that the other had seen the clouds, round-bellied clouds a bit like sails themselves, running in from the west, and both of us had noticed the sudden chill in the air as the boat lurched. 'It's nothing,' he muttered, 'just the breathe of Lir.' But I noticed Methger in the bows slice the throat of a cockerel with his knife, and let the blood drip into the troublesome waves.

Throughout the day the wind rose and the sea with it. Before nightfall the sail was taken down on all the ships, many now scattered and out of sight, but the paddlers maintained a rhythm and we made progress. Some even slept and there was food — cold to be sure, but food — for those who, like myself, could stomach it. I was ravenous after my spell at the paddles, and slept and ate when my eyes weren't filling themselves with the wonder of it all.

By morning the sea was grey and sullen, the sky overcast and sullen too. The wind had not died. If anything it was getting stronger and was now accompanied by rain squalls which marched towards us like dark curtains between growling sea and sky. Many of the other ships were out of sight, but a system of lanterns throughout the night, save for one or two, prevented them from scattering too far — and by a relay of signals all were eventually accounted for. By mid-afternoon it was as dark as mid-winter, and nearly as cold. Many of the people were openly praying for help from the gods of the elements, but, from my — admittedly limited — knowledge of storms on land I was sure that what we experienced was merely boisterousness, seeming worse because of the unaccustomed circumstances. But I kept my opinion to myself when I observed the wretchedness of many around me. My paddler companion reassured me greatly by

134

winking when he saw a warrior trying to bring up his ankles, it seemed, from the bottom of his stomach, and by whispering to me, 'There's nothing wrong with you, young king,' the first time anyone ever called it to me, and I was terrible proud. Too soon I regretted it!

That night was worse, yet we still made progress. But as light dawned next morning we could see that the mood of the sea and sky was darker. Anger tipped the billows and beetled the brows of scowling clouds. Gust after gust rocked the boat, and we had trouble keeping it from being swamped. Where the other ships were we had little idea. Now and again one might appear for an instant, riding like a twig on a wind-whipped swell of the sea, only to disappear in the valleys and crags of water that threatened all of us.

Some of us gathered food from the stores and shared it among the paddlers. Carefully I made my way the length of the ship bringing smoked meat and wine to my grandfather who had remained at his post for most of the two nights.

The woman, Cruithne, and her child crouched close to my grandfather. They looked as if they had not moved since we sailed. Just as I reached them a frightful crack above my head made me look up in time to see the great wooden and metal master-block plunging towards me from the mast top which had splintered and broken about ten feet fom the top. The block carried the main sheet for the sail, which had been coiled near my grandfather's feet. As the block fell it brought with it the free-running end of the rope which also passed through a smaller block at the masthead, now hanging beyond the ship's side. I jumped back to avoid the block, but it suddenly jerked to a halt at shoulder height, just above the heads of the paddlers, pulled up by a reef that clogged the smaller block … though how it took the strain I can't understand. But, as it was whipped from the deck, the running line snagged a foot of Cruithne's child and quicker than I can tell it, snatched him with it, up, screaming, past my grandfather who, try though he did, dared not let go the steering oar and was too late to save him. As the child passed him he grabbed to save himself and snatched the dagger in the king's belt. He was torn upwards and outwards. My grandfather bent to grab him and as he did so his own dagger pierced his eye and ripped it from its socket.

Before anyone had time to move, the child was carried over the side to hang, suspended by one leg, his handsome head being swallowed and regorged by the bellowing sea. The surge of the waves, the momentum of the boat and the rope trailing behind in the water, lifted the body now and then from the waves, only for it to lurch beneath the next instant.

His distraught mother turned wide-eyed and screaming to Cian and pounded his chest, oblivious of the bloody eye that hung from its torn socket upon his cheek.

'Save him; save him,' she shrieked.

The resting helmsman leaped at the steering oar and grabbed it from the king, who turned to the woman and covered his face with one hand, almost in surprise, as if he felt no pain.

Several paddlers tried to rush back to see what had happened, but were ordered to stay where they were for fear of endangering the ship. Two tried to reach the trailing line with the child's body attached, but could not. And all the time Cruithne shouted and screamed in frenzy at the king to save her son.

I still had not moved and still clutched the food and drink I'd brought for Cian in both hands. Now I dropped them and went to the woman to take her shoulders. But strong as I am, and though I exerted some strength, she shrugged me away as if I was a nothing, and made me feel the same.

'Save him, Cian. Save him. He is under your protection.'

My grandfather took his hand from his face and looked at it, then at her and at the child. I gasped when I saw the damage. The blemish was terrible. Terrible in itself and in its implications, for it was his left eye that dangled on his cheek from the bloody hole. Without question he could no longer be king. But, worse, the omen itself was serious for it was caused by his own weapon in the hand of another. His geasa was broken. And, with an inexorability that might have been written, even worse was to follow. The fatefulness was clear. That woman — the hag or the bawve as I will ever think of her, a

136

creature of the Fates — screamed and ranted at him to save her child. Three things: it was his geasa never to see a child hurt in his presence; it was his geasa never to refuse a virtuous woman's request — I remembered his cynical comment of half a year ago; and it was his geasa never to immerse his head in the tide.

He ignored the hag; he ignored the child; he seemed to ignore everything except myself and he locked my eyes with his single one which I could hardly see for my tears. But what I did see in that well-loved face was the same knowledge that had just illuminated me and along with — and because of — it, a typical resolve. Divesting himself of his great sword which, without a word, he handed to me, he lashed a rope's end, attached to a cleat, to his belt, and leaped into the raging tide towards and dangling — now truly dead — the body of the bawve's child.

For the only time in my life that I can remember I screamed when I saw my grandfather's head vanish beneath the waves. Thrusting the frantic woman aside I ran to the side of the ship and peered over, but all I could see was the heaving sea and the ropes and the swaying body of the child who had caused it all. Then my grandfather's head, ugly and distorted, rose from the sea and he struggled to reach up and grasp the small corpse, his blood all the while running from the empty eye socket. Everyone who watched him struggle in the water to retrieve the body knew that he was a destroyed man, as he certainly did himself. Then I saw something I will never forget. He clung with one hand to the rope that trailed from the child's foot and in a gesture of anger and frustration he brought the other to his face and ripped the dangling eye from where it rolled on is cheek, and threw it from him into the depths. What the pain must have been I cannot think. But he hardly paused. His hair and beard were wet and matted and clung to his head.

Pulling on the rope he tried to haul the body to him, but he could not. I saw how to help him.

'Quick,' I cried, 'you men. Here!' I ran to where the master-block still swayed by the mast where it had fallen and stood beneath it. Three men from the paddling area joined me and together we got our shoulders under it.

'Now … Lift!' We lifted together and it rose near a cubit. My grandfather drew in the rope. Again we lifted, and again he drew the rope towards him until he could reach the snag about the little foot.

Unfortunately as he drew the rope down to him, the body plunged deeper in the water and the woman, Cruithne, became near demented in her shrieking and crying. Nothing could convince her that the child was already dead.

Eventually Cian freed the body and both were pulled aboard by the rope tied to his belt.

The woman snatched the body of her child and crouched with it in the same place as before, madly and maliciously glaring at anyone who approached her. My grandfather was laid on the narrow deck by the steering oar while Methger and some others, myself included, tended him as best we could. It was clear that the pain struck at him now, and he had difficulty in keeping control of himself. But Methger gave him a mixture of strong wine, sacred mushrooms and other medicines and he went to sleep quite quickly. I wished that Diancecht, much as I disliked him, was on our ship. But he was not. However Methger did well, filled the socket with warm wine, cleaned it and padded it with moss, and then covered it with a leather patch. My grandfather, too, was stripped and covered with furs and left to sleep as comfortably as possible. But while the storm abated and the swell lessened, a dread and sadness hung upon our ship and men spoke in whispers.

That night the storm died and with it the rain. Next day the skies were blue and the ocean, though heaving, was not wild or distressed. As the morning grew the surface of the sea also calmed and by afternoon we paddled upon a glittering stillness. At first there were no signs of the other ships, but with the calm came cries from the lookouts and before long twenty were in sight and some signalled that they had others in view.

The council meeting, or Aireacht, took place on the *Cu-Feasa*. The other leaders — Nuada, Methger, Ogma, the Dagda, Fergus Red Side, Diancecht, Brigit and the rest — drew their ships alongside and came aboard. A platform large enough to accommodate them was rigged between the mast and the steering oar and the principal ships bobbed together like a great raft, the others drifting on the calm sea, while the council began. There were two important things to be decided. First, who was to succeed my grandfather as king and, second — and of more concern to me — what was going to be his fate. The inexorable, almost preordained, violations of his geasa would require some great penalty.

The hag, Cruithne, still clutching the pallid body of her drowned child, crouched close to the ship's side, her dark eyes moving, a mixture of fear and defiance in their unblinking gaze, from one leader to the next. None had been able to persuade her to part with the body and it was felt that it should be left until after the Aireacht, but besides offending the law, it was already becoming physically offensive. My grandfather lay against some sheepskin-covered cushions filled with straw, his vacant eye-socket covered with a poultice and bandages. He looked weak and drawn.

As each leader came aboard he acknowledged him before sitting on the platform. As the group became larger it fell into murmuring huddles from which my grandfather was excluded. If he knew what was happening he did not show it, but leaned against his props glaring straight ahead from his single eye. His weapons were beside him, his great sword — the one he had handed to me when he leaped overboard — was in his hand. When they were all assembled and had been talking among themselves for a while, he suddenly rapped on the platform with the shoe of the scabbard and attracted their attention.

'Let us begin,' he said.

To my surprise the first business concerned myself.

'It is my wish,' said my grandfather, 'that my grandson, Cian, be Tanist or king-elect until such time as the future kingship is decided and until such time as he is properly and duly elected or defeated.'

I said nothing; nor did anyone else, while those sitting about nodded. Then Nuada replied: 'Very good, Cian. Your grandson is a Tanist.' He placed a slight inflection on the article and it was clear that he reserved the right to nominate another if, as we expected, he became the new king. Cian nodded in return.

'The next matter', he said, 'is the kingship, since I can no longer be king.' Involuntarily his hand began to rise as if to touch his eye, but he halted it almost before the movement started. A murmur of protest rose from the gathering.

'Would you not continue ...' began Fergus. Nuada cut in.

'The situation is clear, brother. There is no point wasting words in meaningless politeness. You cannot continue as king. You have been blemished and ...' He stopped. Even he felt that it was going too far to remind Cian that he had torn his sacred geasa asunder or, more correctly, that Fate, or the goddess in whatever guise, had so ordained matters that he was pitched upon conflicting currents of prohibition and like a prisoner of the Scythians tied to four horses, torn between them. From the moment he first acknowledged the bawve's right to ask him for aid there was no escape. How right he had been when he scorned her virtuousness — how wrong to ignore the knowledge!

Cian nodded.

'I am blemished,' he confirmed, for many of them had not seen the blemish, only the bandages. 'I have lost my left eye.' At this there was a gasp. Even those who knew the facts looked stern.

Not only is it the law among the people that a blemished man may not be king, but, as you also know, among us, among the Egyptians and other people of the east, it is understood that a one-eyed man — particularly if it is the left eye that is missing — is a vehicle of evil over which he has no control.

Cian continued: 'The next question is who shall be my successor. We can not use the Stone of Destiny here, but the official ceremony can take place when we reach Ierne. I have already consulted with Methger and he tells me that would be the most auspicious time and place to offset ...' he stopped.

'It would not be a proper king if we hold an election now without the Stone,' said Fergus.

'We need a leader until we get to Ierne,' said Nuada.

They both looked round. Unless there was a compromise candidate there were only two real contestants, Nuada and the Dagda, and both knew it. Fergus Red Side might have had some expectations, but it was obvious that he wasn't in it unless there was a tie between the other two. The Dagda was the older, by far, and the more experienced. From Ogma, his brother, who now sat beside me as if he had already taken over the role of mentor he was to adopt shortly, I learned that the Dagda reasoned as follows: if he took the leadership then it would, in any case, have to be ratified when we got to Ierne. Moreover he knew as little about sailing as any of the others and if mistakes were to be made, then it was better that someone else should make them, preferably his nearest rival. On the other hand when they reached Ierne and held a full and proper election of the king, a carefully selected nominee might be proposed who would spilt Nuada's vote. Accordingly he said: 'I withdraw myself as a candidate at this time.'

Nuada's face lit up from inside, without appearing to change at all on the surface.

Diancecht, an old crony who was to be suitably rewarded for his support, growled from where he slouched against the side of the ship: 'I propose Nuada.'

There was silence, broken by a mutter from among Nuada's supporters. It was immediately clear that less than half of those present supported him and that the Dagda would get it, probably, if he could be persuaded to go.

'What about you, Dagda? Won't you change your mind?' asked Fergus.

The Dagda shook his head. 'No. I have decided ... for now!' he added.

Whether Nuada saw the trap or not I don't know. If he did he ignored it and looked round the gathering with confidence.

'Fergus?' said my grandfather from his corner, almost in appeal ... and, to this day, I would need to be convinced that it was not this remark alone which contributed most to the severity of his penalty.

Fergus nodded, reluctantly. I think, even then, he knew he would be defeated and already looked beaten and lacking in confidence.

'Anyone else?' asked Cian. He looked round. There were no further nominees. 'Very well,' he said. 'Since this is not a formal election of a king we do not need to spend the prescribed three days considering the candidate. In any case,' he added wryly, we hardly have the opportunity. Those who support Fergus raise their hands.' And few hands went up. It was obvious that if all the others voted for Nuada that he must get it, and he did!

'I declare Nuada to be the leath-ri, or half king, of this fleet and of the people, to lead them until an election is formally held when we reach Ierne,' said my grandfather. 'Nuada, will you take command of the Aireacht?'

Nuada stood up. He looked more imposing than ever.

'I swear', he said, 'to faithfully fulfil ...'

Methger interrupted him. 'There is no need to swear the oath of a king, Nuada,' he said. 'That won't become necessary until we elect one ... in Ierne.'

Nuada looked at him, turning his head slightly to do so, and said nothing. Then he turned back to face the way he had been and went on: 'Quite right, Methger. Nevertheless I swear to faithfully fulfil the duties and obligations placed on me by this Aireacht – as if I were a king,' he added, carefully distorting the oath to his own purpose and glancing at Methger as he did so.

There was a general murmur of assent and acceptance. Nuada sat down.

'The next business', he said, 'is that of Cian. Will you advise us, Methger?'

Before Methger could answer there was a scream and the spare black figure of the hag hurtled across the ship and stood beside the platform, looking up at those in session.

'Murderer!' she screamed. 'He killed my child. He should be killed himself ...'

'Silence, woman,' ordered Nuada, 'or you will find yourself on trial. Take her away,' he said to two warriors, who dragged her, and the dead child she still clutched, back to her place and muffled her shouts. They guarded her throughout the remainder of the council meeting.

'Methger ...?'

Methger looked round, his eyes finally resting, with something like compassion in them, on Cian. But that was the nearest he came — or, I believe, could come — to such a human emotion.

'Cian', he began, as if my grandfather were not there, 'has violated his geasa; he broke the first geis when he aided a woman who was not virtuous ...' he was interrupted for a moment by an unintelligible scream from Cruithne. Then he went on as if nothing had happened; 'he broke his second geis by being wounded by his own weapon in the hands of another; he broke a third geis by immersing his head in the tide ...'

'But', I could not help crying, 'he was trying to help the child under his fourth geis.'

'It makes no matter,' said Methger, 'and, anyway, the child was dead. And', he went on, no longer answering me but addressing himself to the others, 'he has lost his left eye in consequence and is a source of evil and a danger to us all.'

He looked round at the group. His sardonic face, for once, appeared to be immobile. My eyes followed his from face to face, but I could read nothing, except agreement and distress, in any.

'What must we do?' asked Fergus at last.

Before answering, Methger turned to my grandfather, with whom he had shared leadership of our people. Between them, they were the authority in political, spiritual and military matters. Besides they controlled much, although not all, or even a majority, of wealth of the community. Now they were opposed in fundamental law. My father was guilty and Methger was ollamh — not the law-enforcer, not the judge (both these functions now rested in Nuada) — but the reasoner, the one who presented the facts in context. He looked into my grandfather's face and a great deal passed between them, I swear, in those moments.

Still looking at Cian, Methger said: 'He must answer for what he has done.'

A sort of sigh seemed to rise from the ship. That was all. Not even the bawve was heard. 'How will he answer?' asked Ogma from over my head, and his hand pressed lightly on my shoulder.

'It is not alone that he has broken his geasa,' went on Methger. Raising his voice he displayed the facts. He recounted what had happened, and why, since the hag had asked Cian to take her with him.

'Any one of these things,' said Methger, 'violated his honour and requires satisfaction. Violation of them all requires greater satisfaction. But that is not all. Cian has become anathema.'

The terrible words hung over us.

'No!' I shouted. Although I had little idea what was involved, I knew it was something dreadful (and I must confess that I had kept my gaze away from my grandfather's empty eye-socket whenever it was uncovered by Methger for dressing). Ogma tightened his grip on my shoulder.

'Hush boy,' he said, and I was so distressed that I did not even notice the insult to my manhood.

Nuada stood. He looked about him, at the leaders, at Methger — even at me — and finally at Cian.

'I have little choice,' he began and I noticed, for the first time since the meeting started, a smile on Cian's lips, but it is impossible for me to say what it was that prompted it. Nuada saw it too and I think it made him angry; more determined to do what he intended, if, indeed, he ever doubted his own intention.

If we were on land Cian might become an outcast,' Nuada went on. 'We are not on land. We are nowhere near land. It is not possible that we can risk destruction by permitting Cian to remain among us.'

I could hardly hear him for the blood pounding in my head. Ogma's hand on my shoulder kept me silent and I remained silent until the end. It was hard to credit that Nuada was speaking about his brother. Perhaps it was that that helped keep me quiet.

'Cian can be executed,' he said, 'or — and I personally favour this alternative – he can be given a chance to survive, but so that his doom will not affect us.'

I hated Nuada then. Hypocrisy, I thought. I saw the others nod. But I knew – felt – that Nuada played a deeper game than it seemed. He could have influenced the others to save Cian had he wanted. But he wanted rid of Cian's power which, even if Cian were not king, could be used against him. So I did not believe in his apparent solicitude. I don't doubt he could have saved him. But he went on as if he were being greatly magnanimous.

'When the fates have speared a champion on the prongs of honour he no longer belongs to the mortal world. He hangs in suspense between the worlds, a danger and threat to each, and is rejected by both until he turns to one or to the other to accept what the Fates decree without hovering, an omen of evil, between both. I judge that Cian shall be made to answer for these violations as one who is guilty – but as one whose guilt is not unqualified.'

The shock of his pronouncement of guilt was softened for the members of the Aireacht by his qualification – as Nuada intended – so that when he resumed it sounded like a kindness and not the doom he intened. 'He shall be set adrift,' he said. At that time I had not heard of this punishment. Now I was to see it inflicted on the person I loved and venerated more than anyone else. As Nuada finished I leaped up and ran towards him, blind, neither knowing nor caring what I did, and struck at him with my fist. He made no attempt that I know of to stop me. Then, still blind, I turned and ran to my grandfather as if I were a child and threw my arms about him.

I will be brief about what happened after. A small, round boat of skins was provided, but without oars or paddles. My grandfather was stripped of all his finery and all his weapons – save one. He was given a bowl of gruel and a flask of water and towed behind a small boat far out on the ocean. The only weapon he was allowed to keep was a halberd, the short-shafted striking weapon of the ordinary warrior, with a bronze blade shaped like a wedge or a goose's beak. This was to keep voracious sea-birds at bay.

Nuada and the others watched carefully from the *Cu-Feasa* while he was being taken away and signalled when it was the appointed distance, measured by the men in the boat placing a white shield afloat beside them. When the men in the ship could no longer see it, the coracle with my grandfather in it was set adrift.

The two boats merged as the tow rope was unhitched. Then we saw them separate and move further and further apart, the larger coming purposefully back towards us, the smaller — in which the figure of my grandfather could plainly be seen — bobbing like a cork.

My grandfather's champion, the aire-eachta, a man called Brian, insisted on being one of the paddlers in the tow-boat. As it left the ship's side his eyes never left my grandfather's face. He was a huge man, old now, but still formidable, with white hair that hung in braids to his shoulders, like a Scythian. He had been my grandfather's champion ever since he had become the young king many years ago. He wore an iron helmet and carried a huge, two-handled sword, also of iron, that never rested in a scabbard, but was smooth with polishing and gleamed in the sun. It had been known to cut a man in two with one blow. Now Brian wore his full fighting regalia. As the boat pulled away from the coracle a remarkable thing happened. We saw a figure rise in it, saw it leap in the air and vanish, long before we heard the great battle-cry across the water.

Later the other paddlers told us that, just after the coracle was cut adrift, Brian turned his face to the west for a moment, and then, with his battle-cry on his lips and his great sword in his hands, the king's champion leaped for the ocean to do battle for the last time with the enemy who threatened his lord, the mighty god of the sea.

I watched as long as I could. When the paddlers began their rhythmic stroke and the sail bellied on the repaired mast before the light evening breeze, I clung to the stern platform rail and stared over the sea. For a long time I could see the small, black dot that marked the coracle of Cian as it rose on the back of the rolling swell. Then it disappeared for longer and longer intervals until, at last, I could not be sure. But I kept looking, looking, until the sun sank into the red and empty sea. That was the last that was ever seen of my grandfather, Cian, who had been such a great influence in my life and in the lives of the people. Nuada was now our leader and was a very different man.

As night crept on us I still clutched the rail. When Ogma came and stood beside me on the moving deck I shivered and he placed a hand, again, on my shoulder where I was to feel its comforting presence from time to time for many years to come, 'Come, Cian,' he said. 'He is gone. That is the end. There is nothing to be done.'

I remember nodding, and turned with him from the rail. As I did so another figure, crouched in the lee of the rail, also moved and I saw it was the hag, her face lit with a furious glee as her luminous eyes sought mine. She said nothing, but her lips drew back from her teeth in a fearful grimace that followed me as I clambered the length of the ship to my station. I had eaten nothing and they offered me meat and wine which I swallowed without tasting. Suddenly I dropped a mether, still half full of wine, in my lap and fell back against the side of the ship. I could hear someone sobbing and felt warmth and wetness on my face, but I didn't know it was I, myself, who was crying. During that night someone disposed of the body of the bawve's child, but she said no more about it.

Part II
THE BATTLES OF MOYTURA

O ur first sight of Ierne was not of Ierne at all, but of a great bank of fog which stretched across the sea before us, a grey-brown cloud on the blue water. Soon eddies swirled about us and then we were engulfed. It was dangerous and we were fortunate the sea was calm. Sails were taken down. Only four paddlers on each side barely kept the ship on course, and Nuada ordered a man to the bow turrent to blow regular blasts on a trumpet, and the same on every other ship.

We glided through the fog in a dead sea and everyone was quiet. It was as if we had entered the Other World, where all that is is inverted. (Perhaps this explains why the Milesians, who followed after us, believed — as many still do — that we came from the north.) The mast-top could not be seen and figures faded from sight a few feet away so that one sat alone in muffled silence. Each face was strained when you glimpsed it, but if one caught the owner's eye a quick, flashing grin was exchanged. We were listening; almost listening with our eyes, if you understand me. Then we heard it. Muffled to a deceptive softness by the fog it was nevertheless unmistakable. Surf breaking on rocks.

Long lines with weights attached were now used to measure the water and more paddlers were ordered to stand by in case we had to change direction quickly. The noise was clearer and suddenly there was a shout from in front and a grinding, jarring, as the ship slid on a half-submerged rock. Mercifully it was smooth and the sea was calm. The ship rode up on the rock and wallowed, but was soon warped off again and we moved ahead. Then the fog thinned in front. Blue appeared above us and I could see the mast. We sailed out of the rolls of brown rolling on the sea, into clear sunshine with a wide bay in front, low cliffs, a shingle beach and forest and grassland beyond. We had reached Ierne. Some of the other ships penetrated the fog abreast of us and now as we moved onwards the others followed and a great cheer resounded across the glassy sea while the paddlers set to work furiously to be first to reach the shore.

Now I must move my story sideways, for a moment, because even as we prepared for and undertook the journey to Ierne, matters of importance were also happening there.

There was much activity in the weeks following our landing, and the ships returned thrice to Spain and brought the remainder of our people who wished to come, together with our cattle and belongings. Then we moved inland until we reached a mountainous territory, well timbered and watered with rich grazing land and land suitable for the plough all about, where we made our first settlement — which, as it proved, was to be temporary. This place came to be called Sliabh an Iarainn, or the Mountain of Iron, by the native inhabitants who had never seen so many iron weapons and ploughs as we had … though in fact, as the goddess knows, we had little enough.

But before that, on the day after our first arrival, I was with Ogma, when, suddenly, an unusual disturbance agitated the air. We looked up together, and around, but could not see anything. But others had felt it too. I could see many people gazing around uneasily.

'What is it?' I asked.

Ogma didn't answer and shook his head. Then, simultaneously, we looked up, but not at each other, and said: 'Listen!'

Birds, which normally call to one another or coo or croak in the distance in these summer months, and wait for a reply, were now calling; calling without pause and wheeling in the sky. Then they all stopped. They went from the sky and fell silent, save for a gentle twittering, and the world was still. It became dark in the midday sun, and a cold wind passed our faces. I looked up again and saw a frightening thing.

'Ogma,' I cried, 'the sun is dying.'

All around us people were looking and pointing upwards and crying in fear. Even the giant Ogma must have felt something for his face paled and he said nothing.

Then Nuada and Methger strode into the centre of the encampment, the druid silent and with his hands raised above this head. Nuada was dark with anger. He drew himself up and shouted, 'Quiet. Quiet all of you, and listen to Methger. Quiet!'

'Do not be alarmed,' came the sharp voice of the druid. 'There is nothing to be afraid of. The goddess protects her children. Listen to me.' He stood for a moment while silence spread outwards in widening waves from the centre where he stood, like ripples from the place in a pond where a pebble has vanished. In some extraordinary way his voice carried clearly even to the very edges of the assembly and brought with it the force and power of his personality. Beside him Nuada exuded physical command.

'Look,' cried Methger, 'what do you see? The mighty hand of the great goddess protecting her people. She has turned day into night to hide us from Firbolg eyes and as a sign to show the people of Ierne that she is with us in our great enterprise. Of what are you afraid? Look! See for yourselves. She folds her cloak about us.'

As he spoke the sun grew completely black and a darkness swept over us like sudden nightfall. From the people came a sigh out of the profundity of their souls and a child cried.

'Look,' whispered Ogma, glancing up. I followed his eyes and saw an extraordinary thing.

The sun had, indeed, turned black, but all round its edge there was a dancing skirt of flame as if it were being consumed by fire. In spite of myself and of Methger's words, I shuddered. What if it were truly consumed? Were we destined to live our lives forever in darkness? Then through the darkness Methger's voice came again.

'It is a sign. It has been seen before. It will not last. Be reassured. Nothing could be more auspicious. The will of the goddess has the freedom of the heavens.'

There was no more to be said. And anyway I don't think anyone wanted his voice to be heard aloud in that strange night-in-day. The Other World, in all its power, had come upon us at the height of noon, and the world was inside out. What spectres now, I wondered, walked over the land … and had all that we knew and understood suddenly become what it was not? There was no answer. With the birds we waited in silence for the passing of the goddess.

Then — how much time had passed I could not say even now, but it cannot have been too long — a sliver of light showed along one edge of the blackened sun and gradually the veil was pushed aside and another sigh — of plain and unsuppressed relief — arose.

'Don't look,' cried Methger. 'Do not look at the passing of the goddess.' But many people were blinded that day by her going and, for some, it lasted a long while.

The next occurrence was the celebration of the Festival of Bealtaine, the first major festival of the new year, to celebrate which we journeyed to a sacred place in the centre of Ierne, called Usna, where we made another temporary encampment. The occasion was marked by two things of significance. The first was the election of the king, which had been postponed, and the other was a surprise which changed our thinking on many matters, and greatly affected our future. But our first surprise was to find a fire blazing in an established ceremonial place when we got there.

The explanation followed shortly. Everyone knew that the election would take place at the festival and a great deal of lobbying was going on while the slaves and lower orders cleared and prepared a temporary site for the sacred circle, and brought great boulders and

154

tree trunks to substitute for pillars. By a curious coincidence — perhaps it had something to do with the atmosphere of the country itself which was rich but also strong and rugged — we found that the use of boulders and uncut stone slabs was commonplace among those who inhabited the country before us ... of course it may also have been that the granite and limestone was harder to work than the sandstone we were accustomed to use ... to all events Usna, the centre, was already a sacred place with stones and pillars of worship abounding, which our druids had only to modify.

Ogma and I were active on the Dagda's behalf, even promoting a third candidate, as Ogma mentioned, to split the Dagda's vote. But it was too late. Nuada had established himself as a forceful and competent leader and the voters saw no reason to relegate him in favour of someone else. Nuada was elected king by fourteen votes to eight. After three days and three nights of discussion and determination of his physical and genealogical fitness, the inauguration took place on a temporary site beneath a venerable oak tree of billa, as it is called, for want of any traditional place of inauguration at that time, such as Tara.

The Stone of Destiny was placed under the tree and Nuada first sat upon it with the pointer in his hand and, when Methger indicated that it pointed towards him, a great roar went up from the assembly. Then Nuada stood on the stone, fitting his feet to the foot-marks in it which are said to be those of the first king of our people. He was unarmed and divested of all his finery. Methger handed him a white wand, symbol both of his authority and of the justice which was expected of him, straight and without a stain. Then Ogma the historian and recorder recited for Nuada the laws which would regulate his conduct and Nuada swore — 'na dea thungas mo thuath — to the gods what my people swear' — and then he turned three times, and the ceremony ended. It was followed by a great feast the centrepiece of which was a white mare, which had been sacrificially killed for the purpose. But before this feast began a most extraordinary thing happened. Preparations similar to those of the initiation feast in Spain were taking place (except that this time I was with the young warriors instead of making sausages). The camp was a mixture of activity and inactivity; the nobles congregated in and around Nuada's tent talking, riddling and drinking wine; the warriors cleaned themselves and their weapons — this included us — and the freemen kept to themselves and played games and counted their money or their cattle. The women and children and slaves prepared the feast. It was late evening and rain that had drifted in during the afternoon was gone and the countryside seemed fresh and clean. The sun sparkled through a thin haze as it dropped towards the hills in the west — it is a strange thing about this country, but the sky is not so blue as the sky in Spain, but the vegetation is greener and the colours subtler.

I was talking to Ogma who was my mentor when I saw a movement on one of those hills.

'Look,' I said and pointed.

He followed my hand and after a while we could make out people, four of them, and a horse or ox, coming towards us and making no effort at concealment.

Ogma looked for a moment.

'Tell the Aire-echta, the king's champion,' he said, and I ran to find Creda — the same who had correctly answered my grandfather's riddle the year before — in the king's tent.

When I told him what I had seen he nodded, put down his cup and stood up. I expected him to summon a troop of warriors. But, without saying anything, he turned and strode to the door-flap. There he turned back, sought my eye, and jerked his head at me to follow, and went out without waiting to see if I did. Creda was a huge man. His thighs were as thick as another man's waist. From his neck to his knees he was covered with a huge apron of hide. He wore an iron helmet, carried a great leather shield and a Lia Laimhe Laich, or champion's hand-stone, in his left hand, and a huge mace in his right. When I caught up with him he was running — galloping seems more correct — towards the approaching group who were now in plain sight. When they saw us coming they stopped and waited for us to come up.

An old, old man dressed in white sat on an ox that must have been near as old as himself. It was led by a boy a few years younger than I and two slaves, natives from the look of them, walked behind carrying staves and bundles, which they put down when they stopped. The old man was clearly a druid, although his head was covered and it was not possible to see his druid's tonsure. The boy was dressed as an acolyte and wore four colours, indicating that he was an orphan and nobleman in his own right. The other two wore the single drab garment of their station.

When Creda saw them clearly, he stopped running and relaxed and we walked towards them easily. Creda went up to the druid and bent his knee, slightly, before him.

'Who are you, noble druid?' he asked.

'I am Mead,' came the astonishing reply, 'Chief Druid of the king Nemed.'

That night he told his story to the assembly before the king's tent, and there was hardly a sound during the hours that he spoke. But first we brought him to Nuada, who rose to greet him and kissed him, thrice, on the cheek. So great was his emotion, indeed, that he would have laid his head on his breast, I believe, had he not been Nuada. Mead's story was most extraordinary.

'When we came here more than twenty-five years ago', he said, 'our ships were frail and useless after the voyage.'

He said no more about the ships after that, and I thought it was a strange way to begin the tale. He then expanded on what little we already knew, much of it wrong. For example I had not realised that they had been so long in Ierne, nor had I known that they established relations with the Fomorians, who lived in the northern part of the country for part of each year, nor that they paid them tribute nor, above all, that any had survived the Firbolg attack. But some had, including Mead and Starn, husband of the bawve — who was proved right after all — son of Nemed and Fergus's half brother. I looked at Ogma as Mead said this, but his face was impassive. And I could not help recalling bitterly what had happened as a result of that woman's forcing herself on my grandfather's honour. Had we known that

Starn lived there would have been no problem and she would have travelled in one of the other ships. Starn, after all, had followed Nemed many years after the first migration and his ties with Fergus's people were more recent. But one remarkable exploit of Mead's must be mentioned, above all the others.

'When we arrived here', the old druid said, addressing himself to the king, but we could all hear him, so clear was his voice even in old age, and so silent were the listening people, 'we found many groups here before us, mostly barbarians or primitive people who had not been able to establish themselves in Albion or Gaul. But, besides these scattered tribes, there was one powerful race who came down from the north and roved the sea in strong, fighting ships. The Fomorians, from Lochlann. We have never warred with the Fomorians,' he said, looking first at the king and then round about, 'although they are a fearsome people — yet! They are the one-eyed, one-legged, one-armed giants we have heard so much about in the past.'

A murmur of apprehension rose from all of us and we glanced uneasily around. Mead enjoyed his surprise for a moment before continuing.

'They are not really giants, though as a race they are big-boned and large and hairy,' he added in disgust. 'And they have strange and bizarre ways and customs. For example,' he went on 'their women fight alongside the men in battle and have regiments of their own.

'Like the Cichloiste — the Amazons,' whispered Ogma in my ear. I nodded, rapt by Mead's story.

'One of the reasons they come here — where they also have large settlements and stone weapon factories in the north of the country — is to fatten their cattle, mainly sheep. They have great herds of these which roam the northern and midland plains. While guarding them — which warriors themselves do —' There was a murmur of amazement at this. 'Do not be surprised,' said Mead, 'these sheep are their wealth and they guard them jealously.' He looked around for a moment before turning his attention back to the king. 'While they are guarding their herds the warriors do a strange — and for us a woeful – thing. They stand on one leg, resting the foot of the other against the calf of the one they stand on, and lean upon their spears, so that they seem to have but one leg, and –' he paused again for drama, 'but one long arm.' He had everyone's attention.

'Moreover,' he went on, 'they carry with them a certain drink to which they are addicted which produces an effect not unlike too much wine, including double vision.'

'Very often, in order to offset this,' he said, 'they cover one eye with one hand, or close one eye and squint so as to see clearly.'

A gasp went up from the assembly. Behind me Ogma said: 'The gods defend us, we are among the corrguinecht, wizards and men of power.'

But Mead held up his hand for silence. And, almost as if he had heard Ogma, said: 'But they are not wizards. These things are the result of custom and natural circumstances.'

From the throng a voice growled, 'That doesn't alter the fact that they adopt the evil postures.'

What was meant is that among the people it is the custom for druids, who in such ceremonies are themselves called corrguineach or wizard, when they are making a curse or malediction, a glam dichenn, against someone or something, to solemnise it and give it effect and venom, adopting the hideous, monstrous and unnatural posture of one leg, one hand and one eye while chanting their incantations aloud in a great voice, so that they have a oneness which is not a unity.

Mead nodded in agreement.

'No,' he said, 'it does not.' He raised his voice. 'There has never been a doubt in my mind that the Fomorians and the people will war with one another one day,' he said. 'And it will be a war of conquest, for the supremacy of this land.'

'But not yet. They are too powerful now ... and first we have to deal with the Firbolg.'

At this there was a great cheer and I looked at Ogma who was clapping his hands above my head. I caught Dara's eye where he stood behind one of the warriors at a higher table, and nodded and winked. He winked back. Then I saw Oran sitting just a little way from me. His face was impassive. Only his eyes betrayed his alertness and they were cool and bright at the same time, like the eyes of a hunting animal.

'Shortly after we arrived,' went on Mead, 'Nemed led his kingly retinue and the royal guard here to the centre of the island to celebrate the festival of Bel —' which is the druidic manner of saying Bealtaine.

'— When we got to this central place, the navel of the land, called Usna,' said Mead, 'the druids of the local barbarian inhabitants came to see what Nemed wanted, for, as you can judge, it is a holy place for them too.'

'Nemed ordered me to light the sacred fires so that the offering of calves might be made and the herd driven between them for safety from disease in the forthcoming year.'

He turned to Nuada.

'You will remember, O king, that it was for us, as it is for you,' he said, looking beyond the king to where the great fires of Bealtaine — one of which would remain alight for a year — glowed even in the fine evening light, 'a festival of great significance for our herds were small, smaller than yours, and we could not afford to run the risk of disease.'

Nuada nodded.

'With much solemnity', said Mead, 'I prepared large fires. As I did so the native druids muttered against me so that I had to summon Bel himself, and the mother of the gods, to help and assist me. When these druids saw what I was doing and that I was about to light a fire they brought up their people as if to attack us, but they were afraid when they saw our warriors.

'As the flames and smoke rose up they began to cry and lament and make incantations against me, making a curse upon me that was strong by the use of my name: "Mi-de," they called, "Mi-de!" (which is a play on his name and means evil, evil). 'And I was afraid, for they had power too. But the king was their equal and together we defeated them. Nemed stood when he heard them and raised his hand and looking over all the land from the eminence we stood on he cried: "Yes, Mi-de indeed. All this land as far as can be seen in every direction, is Mi-de, but not evil. It is fair and rich and from henceforth it is named Mead and will be called that from now and let this fire never cease." That is what he said and that is the name of this land even yet.' And it is true for, though the druid Mead is long since dead, the name of that territory will always bear his name.

'When he had done that,' said Mead, 'I made the soldiers capture those druids who had cursed us and my work and assemble them together in one of their own houses and, for their affrontery, had their tongues cut out, which I buried and sat upon them before their eyes.' He looked round, an old man, but a powerful one. 'That silenced them,' he said, and there was a roar of laughter.

Mead stayed with us from then until he died. He remained close to the king, who had known him of old. But he never became close to Methger, the king's druid, even though he did not interfere with him.

Mead also brought us word of the Firbolg, but before coming to that or how we established relationships with the Fomorians, let me say something about the country. The climate was quite different to what might be expected so far north. Indeed it was milder and more fruitful than many places further south. But we did not broadcast this, nor did any of those who went before us, for if it were known many other peoples would have come to colonize and there would have been continuous warfare for such a bountiful place. Instead we maintained the lie that it was a harsh, icy land of frugal and hard-won benefit, nor worthy of the attention of civilized and sophisticated people.

For some strange reason snow is very rare here, having fallen only twice in my lifetime. The summers are warm — with very long days and short nights — but seldom searing, and winters are mild. The climate is sufficiently moist to ensure two crops a year in many cases. There is an abundance of natural foods, berries and roots as well as grain crops which grow extraordinarily well — if somewhat slower to dry than elsewhere and so more inclined to rot — and there is pasture, immense pasture, for every kind of beast. These pastures and the great forests that border them are among the most prominent features. The forests are, in the main, of two kinds: oak and giant pine, far bigger than those we knew in Spain.

They provide excellent timber for building and reinforcing and, in addition, there is an abundance of other useful timbers as well; the rowan, or quicken, tree, sacred to the gods, among them and its cousin the ash which was to play an important role for us later on, as did the yew and the elm.

The rivers are the other great glory of the land. Plentiful, broad and deep, they were alive with the most wonderful fish we had ever seen or tasted — the bradawn, or salmon — as they still are today. How often, as a young warrior, I stood in wonder on the bank of a river and watched thousands upon thousands of these powerful and attractive fish, veritable monarchs of the water, thresh across the shoals or leap in their multitudes athwart the tumbling rapids? Their flesh is pink and succulent and as you well know there are enough and more than enough of them to feed us all if we never tasted anything else. They are one of the miraculous blessings of Ierne and where they go or whence they come, each year, to and from the endless ocean, is a mystery to man.

There is also plenty of game for hunting, especially fine, strong boar, and deer of two kinds, besides hare, badger, otter and other beasts. And multitudes of fowl, geese and duck, swan and pigeon. Of dangerous predators there are few — wolves and wild cat being the commonest. And, most strange, there are no snakes.

Ever since the incident with the Vaccean the previous year Keth and I had grown closer to one another in a strange sort of way, based, I think, on a mutual respect and tolerance rather than on any forced or artificial sense of relationship.

We were fishing together — though it is hard to call it fishing when we had to make the catching difficult for ourselves in order to enjoy it — on a river-bank about two miles from the first settlement (to which we had returned and had strengthened), when I saw the boy who was with Mead coming towards us. We were using fishing

162

poles with gut line on the end of which was a hook (of bone in my father's case; I peferred bronze) baited with rowan berries. For some perverse reason I resented the sight of the boy — perhaps simply because I didn't want him to see me, a warrior youth, with Keth, indulging in anything so tranquil as fishing with my father. Whatever the reason I pretended not to see him and deliberately flicked my line back for a cast as he approached, so that it would miss him — but by very little.

What happened then was so fast I could not follow it, and I was left with an empty line waving in the breeze, while the boy stood still, a long knife in his hand and my hook with a short length of line attached at his feet.

'You! — Look what you did!'

My father turned and surveyed us mildly.

'What?' he asked. Then he saw the line, the knife and the boy. He understood immediately what had happened. He said nothing, but looked at me with one eyebrow raised in a way he had, and said to the boy: 'What's your name, son?'

The youngster looked back at him from under even brows with eyes as blue as his own under a crown of red-gold hair. He wore his four-coloured tunic — very skilfully dyed so that one could not tell where one colour ended and another began.

'As yet,' he said, 'I have no name.'

It was a strange thing — well, perhaps, not such a strange thing; but a strange way of expressing it — for one so young. There was a dignity about him and a power that, young as he was, were very compelling and which even I could not but acknowledge in spite of my anger.

'You cut my line,' I blurted.

'You tried to hook me,' he replied calmly.

I couldn't deny it.

'Come and join us,' said Keth, and thus began something which was to have the most momentous consequences. The boy told us little and I can't remember how or from whom I heard the full story. Most likely I put it together in pieces from different sources before I

163

ever discussed it with him whom we eventually called Lugh, after a strange incident which occurred shortly thereafter and also after the great god Lug because it happened at the time of his midsummer festival, Lugnasa.

Now there is something I must explain, as best I can, about our family, and it concerns both what had happened previous to our discovering Lugh, and what happened thereafter.

My great-grandfather, Cian, who led our people from Miletus through Egypt and Tyrrhenia (so called after Tyrhennius who settled there with some of his people earlier on), had a brother named after their father — Diancecht. But he was a brother he never knew, for he was born when my great-grandfather was thirty-five years old, long after he had gone on his journey, and when his father was fifty-nine. After Diancecht took valour, or knighthood, he studied with the Persian magi and became a physician of great skill and learning. Then, together with a small company, he too left Miletus.

As you already know he was a proud and vain man, and he did not want to appear to follow his older brother's traces. Accordingly he took a northern route, via the Danube and Gaul to the coast east of Albion. From there he moved north until he reached, in winter, an icy and land-locked sea that became warm and pleasant in summer. It lies to the south of Lochlann. There he fell in with the Fomorians. After much voyaging they brought him to the northern islands where he lived in their company for many years, studying their medical wisdom and lore and adding to what he had already accumulated. The years he spent with the Fomorians probably account for his rough and uncouth ways. But then the desire to be with the people again overwhelmed him and although it was against their wishes, he left the Fomorians and moved south through Albion, thence to Gaul and Spain and so to Tartessia, where he lived with Nuada's people until our exodus. Although he was my grandfather's uncle he was five years younger, and only twenty-five years older than Keth, my own father.

You know the custom of the Fomorians of offering distinguished guests the hospitality of their wives. Well, when Diancecht left the

Fomorians they would not allow him to take his Fomorian son with him. The son was Cian — yet another, which made four of us in three generations — and his Fomorian mother was Caitlin, who was married to a powerful, but hideous, Fomorian champion called Balor, or Balor of the Evil Eye as he became known to us because — the gods protect us — of the white, blind, left eye he had since birth. And evil he surely was.

I have already indicated the kind of man Diancecht was and, since the woman Caitlin was content to take one such as he besides Balor one can imagine the kind she was ... as rough and as violent as the men she took up with, but then, the Fomorian women fight along-side their men, as you have heard. Perhaps one reason why they would not let him take his son was that they wanted a hold on him. Balor and Caitlin had a daughter called Eithne and, in the fullness of time and before ever she achieved the single pillared tower, she lay with her brother, Cian, and was brought to bed of triplet sons.

I heard some of the story from Keth and Sena'an my mother one evening when I was free from my warrior duties, and had been sum-moned to a family council for an important decision which required to be taken. They were already talking when I came in. 'I can't understand all the fuss,' said my mother. 'Marriage between a brother and sister isn't that uncommon. In my father's country it was obli-gatory in certain cases.' She always referred to Egypt as 'my father's country' and with pride in her voice.

'Aye,' said Keth, thoughtfully, 'for the pharoahs.'

My mother didn't answer. Like many women who tend to argue a general case to prove a point they believe in — however irrational — she had no defence except silence when the irrationality was demon-strated. Keth frowned. 'Unless there is a proper reason,' he said, 'it is a mockery of nature.'

Sena'an looked away as strong-willed women do when they do not accept what is stated, yet will not — or can not — argue.

'If it is a destined birth, then it is at the hand of the gods,' said Keth.

'Like the great Kurus,' said my mother.

'What about him?' I asked, and they both looked at me astonished that I should ask. Then they laughed, realizing they had forgotten how young I had become a warrior.

'I'll tell you later,' said Keth, the smile fading. 'First there is this other matter.'

'What other matter?'

'This child — this boy who Mead brought.'

'Who cut my line?' I couldn't help asking, although I knew perfectly well.

Keth wasn't in the mood for my pettiness.

'Yes,' he said. 'He is the one surviving son of those three.'

For a moment I didn't understand and when I did all I could do was ask, 'How?'

Nobody answered me for a moment. Then Sena'an, whose impatience showed, snapped: 'There's far too much talk about nothing.'

Keth did what, for him, was an astonishing thing.

'Silence woman!' he said, quietly. But it had such force coming from him, that she did not interrupt again while he continued. 'If it has meaning, then it has meaning that will shake the world, and it marks the birth of a hero. Let me tell you,' he went on, 'as Mead has put it to us. For much of the year Balor lives on an island to the north. Long since it was prophesied that he would be killed by his grandson and so when any of his children gave birth to sons these were immediately destroyed. When Eithne's three sons were born Balor had them taken from her and gave them to a servant to drown in the manner customary in such cases ...' which is identical to that used on my grandfather. They are cast adrift on the ocean as far off as a white shield can be seen floating on the surface ... 'But', went on Keth, 'the coracle came ashore on the mainland. Two of the children were dead, but the third was alive. A fisherman whose wife had produced a stillborn child and was mad of grief found the coracle and substituted the dead child for the living one. He and his woman reared the child for four years until the woman died. By chance the druid Mead was forced to shelter in the fisherman's house and heard the story. He recognised its significance and has had the boy with him ever since.' He paused. 'It is also foretold', he went on after a moment, 'that the child will be named by its grandfather.'

There he stopped and looked at the fire. Sena'an, sitting upright, sniffed loudly, but said nothing.

'But I don't see how that is likely to happen,' said Keth, as if in agreement with her disdain.

'I see,' I said. But I didn't.

'You asked about the great Kurus,' said my father after a moment, but without looking up from the fire.

I nodded.

'Well. Astyages, who was king of the Medes ...'

'But Kurus was king of the Persians,' I interrupted. Keth looked at me silently for a moment, in a way that made me feel uncomfortable, before going on. And this was one of the differences between his story-telling and that of my grandfather. Cian never made one feel uncomfortable, whereas Keth became another man when he was telling a story, and could look at one very coldly indeed if his story was interrupted for, as he saw it, no good reason.

'Astyages's daughter, Mandane, was married to a minor Persian noble called Cambyses. In those days Persia was a Medean territory and the people were thought to be very inferior by their conquerors. After they were married Astyages dreamed that his daughter's fruitfullness would cover all Asia and this was interpreted for him by his magi, or druids, as meaning that Mandane's son would take over his throne. So Astyages told Harpagus to take the child and kill it. Harpagus brought the child home, but would not kill the royal infant. He gave it to a shepherd called Mitradates to dispose of ...'

'And his wife had a still-born child,' I broke in, unable to contain myself.

This time Keth smiled. 'Yes,' he said, 'and it was buried instead of the prince. But the story emerged years later when the child was about twelve, and Astyages took a fearful revenge on Harpagus — but one in accordance with all the signs of preordained destiny.'

'What was that?' I asked.

167

'He invited him to attend a banquet with the new prince and to send his only son ahead to be with them. When the banquet took place all the guests except Harpagus were served mutton and pork, but Harpagus was given meat from the body of his son to eat, with the head, hands and feet missing. When he was asked by Astyages if he had liked his meal and said yes, these were brought in under a cover and he lifted this and saw his son's head.'

I understood the vastness of the mystery.

Keth went on to tell me how Kurus, with the help of Harpagus, eventually became king of the Persians, defeated the Medes, and extended his empire beyond anything Astyages and his Medes had known.

'... and so you see the similarity.' he finished. 'In this case we have the further mystery of an incestuous birth.'

'Huh,' sniffed my mother, 'mystery!' But that was all.

'The question is,' said Keth, 'what shall we do?'

'What do you mean?' I asked.

'Well,' he said, 'you know that we must establish friendly relations with the Fomorians — at least until we have settled with the Firbolg.'

I nodded.

'What has that got to do with it?' I asked.

'There is a fear', he said, 'that if Balor were to find out that his grandson were here he might ally with the Firbolg to destroy us.'

'We can't turn them away,' I said.

'No,' went on Keth, 'which is why we are holding this meeting. It has been suggested that, until the time is right, the youngster should be concealed here as a member of a minor noble family...'

'Ours?' I asked in astonishment.

They looked at one another. Keth nodded. I could see agreement as well as the customary fire in my mother's eyes. I was dumbfounded. I had not expected such a thing.

'You have a say,' said Keth. 'Your voice should be heard. Unless we all agree it can not happen.' By all he meant me as, of course my young sister, Naas, would not have a say.

My feelings were in conflict. Spite or vengeance inclined me to say 'no' forthwith. But I struggled with these emotions. I tried to think what my grandfather would say. I looked at Sena'an's face: impassive, but committed for herself. She would not try to influence me. In my father's face I saw anxiety that the right thing be done ... but he was by no means sure as to what was right, sure only of his own compassion. Was that enough? I did not think so. I forced myself to be calm. I listened hard with my inner ear to the recollected voice of my grandfather giving judgements.

'The Law', he used to say, 'is the fabric on which the community is built. Justice is what illuminates the law.'

'If what you say is true,' I said, 'this boy is the son of a de Danann king and a Fomorian queen, who were brother and sister.'

Keth nodded.

'If it was willed by the gods, it is a mystery which can only have an ordained end,' I said. They were listening to me carefully. 'That end must be a hero's end,' I said. 'It can only mean the destruction or the protection of our people.' A shadow moved behind me, but I did not look back.

'If it is his destiny to kill his grandfather, a Fomorian king, and if it is accomplished in justice, then it must be on behalf of the Fomorian people; or on behalf of some other people.'

Keth looked me full in the face.

'Have you decided?' he asked.

Instead of answering him straight off I continued; 'If it is on behalf of the Fomorians it might well mean our destruction.' Keth said nothing.

'On the other hand,' I said, 'it seems to me improbable that he would act to benefit the Fomorians or that such an act could benefit them. Yet if he stays with us we are those most likely to benefit. I am Tanist designate, unless Nuada says otherwise, which he has not done yet.' I went on, 'If this boy kills his grandfather on our behalf, where does that leave me?'

Nobody answered.

'Your story about the great Kurus ... I remember your words, Keth, the day we met the Vaccean ...' I saw interest glow for an instant in my mother's eye and realised I had not been wise, but I had more important things to consider now than her attitude towards my father because of a slave she never had. 'Remembering these things, and that Kurus, son of a Persian father and a Medean mother, raised the Persian people up, I ask who am I to stand in the way of the gods?'

A voice behind me said: 'Spoken like a true king'. For the second time in my life I had been called — even obliquely — king. I turned and saw the druid Mead behind me.

'I believe you have made the right decision,' he said.

And that is how Lugh became a member of our family and met my sister, who was one day to be his wife.

Mead also brought us word of the Firbolg. They had established themselves across the centre of the country, their principal settlement at a place called Druim Cain — the same Cathair Cro Fhind, which later became Tara, where we ruled and prospered for so many years. There their 'king' Eochaid held court. They had increased in numbers, said Mead, and could put ten or more battalions of three thousand men each into the field of battle. Naturally we were anxious to attack them as soon as we could, but this information put a different complexion on things.

'What do you advise?' asked Nuada at a council meeting.

'My advice is to do what your brother Nemed did before you.'

'What is that?'

'Send heralds, ambassadors, to the Fomorians. Make a treaty with them.'

'The barbarians?'

Mead nodded. 'They may be barbarians, but they are stronger than you and the Firbolg put together.'

'Will they help us against the Firbolg?'

Mead shook his head. 'I doubt it. Why should they? They have no

170

need, and so long as you and the Firbolg are enemies they will have little trouble, he said. 'But an alliance might give time and might keep the Firbolg from attacking before you are ready. They still have the minds of slaves. They don't want to offend the Fomorians. A Fomorian treaty might hold them off, long enough for us to gain strength.'

Nuada looked at his counsellors, the Dagda, Ogma, Diancecht — the paternal grandfather of the boy who was to become Lugh (I wondered why he hadn't been asked to care for the child and then I looked at him and stopped wondering) — Fergus and Methger and some others. 'What do you say?' he growled. One by one they answered and, with few exceptions, they agreed with Mead.

'Then who shall we send?' he asked.

They looked at one another, for this was a strange and dangerous mission. No one knew if these horrendous barbarians would respect and safeguard the inviolability of a herald as civilized people do.

'You, Diancecht!' said Nuada, 'you lived with them.'

Diancecht looked at him from small eyes sunk in his great head, and spat. 'No!' he growled. 'Not if you want success. They would strip my skin and hang my head from a doorpost and send my balls back to you in a fishskin.'

'May I make a suggestion?' asked Mead.

Nuada nodded. 'Please do.'

'The Fomorian attitude to women is not the same as ours,' he said.

'They respect them and also disrespect them. They don't treat women as people, to be judged on their merits. Unlike us they make a distinction between the sexes over and above what is required by physical circumstances — of which they take no account. They treat women little better than slaves, and at the same time send them into battle in battalions alongside their male warriors. The women don't seem to mind.'

Nuada nodded. We had heard this before. 'Well?' he said. 'If there is a high-ranking woman of dignity among you who is also a person of judgement and ability, the wonder and respect she would create in the Fomorians might be greatly to our advantage, for they would be both curious and envious. But she would run a great risk.'

There was such a woman. Nuada looked at the Dagda who stared back at him, then nodded.

'You will have to ask herself,' he said.

We all knew that he meant his daughter, Brigit, the chief priestess and poet of our people, renowned for her wisdom, and the one woman who might possibly undertake such a mission.

'She must not go alone,' said Nuada. 'You and Ogma will go with her.'

This was decided and preparations were made. Meantime Nuada took another far-reaching action; all the ships, including the noble *Cu-Feasa*, which had brought the people, or as many as wanted to, to Ierne, were burned where they stood on the beaches of the southern shore.

When the preparations of the emissaries were complete, and they were fully instructed in what to say, they were given presents of gold and precious stones with a purple roll of royal cloth for the Fomorian king, Delbaeth. A fine, four-wheeled cart drawn by four oxen was fashioned for them and they were provided with the distinctive red and white garb of ambassadors. They were given the symbolic white wands and stylised swords, symbols of their office, to carry, one in either hand, indicating the alternatives they had to offer – war or peace.

Before leaving for the far north where the Fomorians ruled, they were given a blessing from the gods through Methger. Mead, the druid of Nemed, was to guide them. Because I was the disciple of Ogma I persuaded Nuada to allow me to accompany him – in truth I think he may have been glad to see me go, in the hope I might not return, since at that time I was his nominated successor. But more significantly I persuaded my parents that, since Mead was going, it would be considered strange, and increase suspicion and the danger to the envoys, if the acolyte he had had with him for many years was absent on such an important mission. For that reason the boy – now a member of our family and known, simply, by the pet-name Dalta, or foster – accompanied us.

On a clear evening on the sixth day of July we set off, and all the nobles and distinguished people assembled to wish us well. As we left the settlement a chorus of brazen music followed us from a rank of trumpeters playing on their great, curved instruments, and stayed with us until it faded, and rose, and faded again in the distance as we moved north along the clear path that cut across the plain.

Besides the decorated wagon, which had decorated curtains and an elaborate, coloured canopy supported on four worked posts of bronze-covered ash above it, Mead rode ahead on a white ox led by Dalta, while I brought up the rear on a horse, having been made a marcach, or horse-soldier, for the occasion. There was also a small company of nine warriors on foot and a number of slaves to attend to the work of our camps.

I saw my first Fomorian three nights later, in the early dawn. We were camped in a sheltered place under a hill not far from a stream. In front the plain rolled up and down over a number of small, rounded hills of a very singular kind. To the left the edge of a tall pine forest followed the plain in, around and over these little hills and, away to the north-west — although I could not see them for the morning mist — were the blue mountains we had first noticed the previous evening. Standing on top of one of these small hills with the rising sun full upon it was a figure to strike horror in the breast of any man. It was in silhouette. What I saw was the figure of a grotesque man apparently looking towards us, for he shielded his face with one hand so that one of his eyes was obscured. The other hand, so far as I could tell, seemed to reach to the ground from his shoulder. And, between neck and thigh, the creature was square and from that square one leg only descended to the ground.

'Ogma!' I shouted.

He came from his tent at a run followed, from theirs, by the Dagda, Brigit, and Mead. I said nothing, only pointed.

'A Fomorian!' said Mead.

Ogma nodded.

'Quickly,' said the Dagda, 'show him what we are.'

The red and white banner of emmissaries was furled in the wagon.

I ran to get it.

'Never mind,' said Mead. 'He will not come. But from now on we will be watched night and day, so conduct yourselves accordingly.' Afterwards I recalled that Dalta had not come running with the others.

Next day, just before noon, they came to meet us, a company of warriors led by a chieftain of some sort whom we never saw again. We were fording a river. We moved the wagon down the sandy bank onto a small bed of shingle and stones. On the other side a similar — but far larger — place gave access to the opposite bank. The ford was marked with boulders. For the crossing some of our escort went ahead while the others stayed with the wagon urging on the oxen. At a shout from one of our men I looked up and there they were, silently standing in a half circle drawn up against us with this chieftain in the centre on the far bank. Some of those on the wings adopted the traditional resting pose and I might as well describe this, which explains the image I had seen the day before.

It was much as Mead had said, but he did not convey the real feeling, for it is a pose at once restful for the adopter of it and threatening to the observer. These warriors wear their hair long and tangled and have great shaggy beards. Some of them wear helmets, mostly of leather, but with one or two metal ones among them. On their bodies they wear tunics and aprons of rough stuff, sometimes entirely of leather, which fall to their knees. Over this they sometimes wear a sheepskin against the cold, but there were none evident that day. Their favourite weapons are a great, heavy spear about the height of a man with a strong, broad blade of flint or bronze and stone axes of very fine make. While resting they lean on the spear, holding it firmly with one hand at the shoulder — some of their spears have a small fitting below the blade to go beneath the arm — and fix the butt of the spear at an angle in the ground. They then raise the leg nearest the spear and rest the foot against the opposite knee. From a distance, as with me the previous day, this creates the impression of a one-legged man with a very long arm. They also use their free hand to shade their eyes when looking afar — which they can do for prodigious distances — and, since this tends to cover or shade one eye more than the other, the evil aspect is extended.

Apart from its unnaturalness and universal evil quality, we are in natural awe and fear of this pose because it is the one adopted by druids when they practise sorcery and wish evil on a person or thing. When they do this, they too are called corrguineach and they shout their maledictions or curses aloud while standing on one foot, with one arm outstretched and with one eye closed, and it is accordingly a posture of great power and dread. All that may be said in its favour is that when used as the Fomorians do it is — I believe — extremely restful for those who must stand still in the open for long periods. As Mead already told us, they do not permit their unattended slaves to guard their sheep, their only source of wealth.

The silent company — there were about a hundred of them — stood looking at us across the river. We had stopped when we became aware of them and now, at the Dagda's command, we started forward again. The Fomorians did not try to impede us, nor did they offer us any help when the wagon stalled in mid-stream. But we managed to get it moving again, several men working at each wheel — which left only myself and their leader on guard — and reached the far bank in a continuous rush. The centre of the Fomorians drew back as we came up the pebbled bank, to let us pass. Once we reached the solid surface of the plain again we halted and the Fomorian leader approached the wagon. I could not understand what he said, of course, but he spoke through Mead, asking us who we were and what we wanted.

The Dagda answered, again through Mead.

'Tell him,' he said, 'that we are the heralds and ambassadors of the people of Annan and that we bring gifts and a treaty of peace and friendship to Delbaeth, the great Fomorian king.'

This seemed to satisfy the chief, distinguished solely by the fact that he wore a bronze bracelet on his upper arm and had a great copper sun-disc on his breast.

For the rest of that day they escorted us until, at length, as the sun declined on our left hands, the Fomorian settlement came in sight. If

I had been surprised at the appearance of the men, the stronghold surprised me more. A strong, central citadel — a fortress — perched on a hilltop. It was surrounded by numerous dwellings of one kind or another, many of them dug into the hill itself and roofed with the same turf that covered it. But by far the majority were tents of skin stretched over wooden frames, held in place by large stones and other weights. Outside most of these were a pair of poles linked by a cross-bar. These archways were decorated with the heads, fresh and weatherbeaten, of men and women, some reduced almost to skulls. I learned later that it is their custom to preserve the skull of a par-ticularly brave or noble enemy and, when the elements have done their work, convert it into a drinking vessel for their potent drink — a thick, brown stuff which they drink in great quantities — and wine when they get it. Ragged and unkempt childen were everywhere and it is another curious custom of these people that very few children know their own father, for they exchange their women more fre-quently than their clothing, which accounts both for the numerous children and their unwholesome appearance.

We went directly to the citadel, which I will describe. The walls were uneven, between ten and fifteen cubits high, and they leaned inwards slightly. Unlike our strongholds they were built of unmortared stone alone, but they were immensely thick and strong, being perhaps five or six cubits thick at the base and four at the top, which had also a low rampart. The gate was small. Less than the height of a man and just a little wider than his shoulders so that it was, in effect, a stone tunnel running through the wall. No wagon or mounted horseman could get through it. The approach to the gate was aslant the hill on which it stood and so passed among the tents and huts of the settlement whose people crowded around in a most oppressive and barbaric fashion as we made our way upwards. Luck-ily we were surrounded by the warriors who met us at the ford, otherwise I doubt if we would have reached the gate unhindered. The walls of the citadel, too, were lined with people, all warriors — among them, I was interested to see, many women warriors, distin-guishable only by the fact that they had not beards ... at least, most of them had not! ... otherwise they were armed and equipped, and in bulk and stature, resembled the men. We were conducted through the narrow passage entrance to the circular enclosure within. We stood in this arena for a moment, unsure which way to turn, looked down upon by a circle of hostile eyes and faces.

The space within was occupied by buildings and enclosures of various kinds, some of them built into the mighty wall of the fortress itself. Others similar to those outside stood in the centre. One building, larger than the rest, occupied the very centre and around it was a stockade divided into sections in which were domestic cattle of several kinds — mostly sheep, with a few goats and oxen (no swine) and domestic fowl.

Before we had time to take it all in a voice hailed us and we looked up to see a large man standing on the rampart above and behind us.

'I am Delbaeth,' he shouted. 'What do you want with the king of the mighty Fomoire?'

The three emissaries turned, the Dagda in the centre, and raised their arms, holding in their hands the wands and ritual swords.

'We come in peace from Nuada, king of the Tuatha de Danann, brother of Nemed, son of Cian.'

The hairy brute above us looked down for a moment and then throwing back his great head he laughed aloud, so that it was like a signal and laughter rippled through the throng upon the ramparts all around us. Then, to my astonishment — for he was old and white-haired — the king leaped from where he was, landing on his feet in front of us.

'Ambassadors!' he cried. 'Heralds, with wands of peace and swords of war?' He laughed again. 'I spit on your fineries.' And he did. I thought the Dagda would burst. His huge body seemed to swell and his face turned the colour of the sunset. Beside him Ogma, his equally gigantic brother, gripped the stylised sword so tightly that I could see blood spurt from between his fingers. This wild king suddenly stopped laughing and looked levelly into the Dagda's eyes. As he did so the ring of laughter died above us and a sort of hush took its place, with all eyes in the arena focused on the little group.

Unexpectedly Delbaeth snorted like a horse, stepped forward and threw an arm around the Dagda's shoulders, looking keenly into his face all the while.

'Huh?' he grunted, and gave the Dagda a little shake. Some of the colour went out of the Dagda's face.

'Huh?' said the king again, and the Dagda's head nodded very slightly, whereupon the king, his arm still around the other's shoulder, threw back his head and laughed again, and kept on laughing until all joined with him. Then turning, and turning the Dagda with him, he walked, his arm still round the Dagda's shoulders, towards the large house in the centre of the enclosure.

There is little point in labouring over the details of our negotiations. The Fomorians accepted our proposals for a treaty, but at a price. They insisted on an annual tribute from us, which we had little choice but to accept; they insisted on hostages from the families of all the Tuatha de Danann kings and, lastly, they insisted that we accept what they called 'friendly helpers' who would live in the king's household.

These negotiations took several days and this final demand was one our envoys felt they could not accept on their own responsibility.

Delbaeth pressed them.

'Are you ambassadors or not?' he asked. 'Do you have to defer about everything?'

Under such insults the one who kept her head best was Brigit.

'It is not a question of deferring,' she answered, 'we speak for the whole people. Therefore in a matter as radical as this the people have a right to a voice in the decision reached.'

Now while this debate was going on one of the handsomest young men I have ever seen came one afternoon to the settlement. A grey, summer mist hung upon the hill and he strode out of it by himself like a young god ... and woe to us that he did so. He was so unlike the Fomorians that at first I thought he must be one of the Bretani or from some other overseas place. And I was partly right, but in the most surprising way. He was tall, as tall as Ogma or the Dagda, but

178

slender hipped and broad shouldered, and with the clear, beardless face of ideal youth. He was dressed in a black tunic with scarlet borders and a scarlet cloak hung from his shoulders where it was retained by a golden brooch that stretched from shoulder to shoulder.

His name was Eochaid Bres, or Bres the Handsome and Proud. Like our Dalta he was born of an incestuous liaison between Elatha, Delbaeth's son, and his sister, Eiriu, whose mother was one of Nemed's people — an emissary, like ourselves, sent by Nemed to the Fomorians and taken by Delbaeth for his own. She no longer lived among the Fomorians, but, as I discovered, with a small group of Nemed's people who had escaped the Firbolg slaughter.

Bres had been visiting his grandmother and, on his return, as grandson of the king immediately took part in the negotiations.

Meanwhile the Dagda had sent word by horseman — using my steed — to Nuada telling him what Delbaeth proposed and we could do nothing but wait a message in return.

The weather was fine and we were free to go where we liked — in any case there was always a Fomorian within ear if not eye-shot, and what could we do, even if it were in our interests to do anything? They entertained us as well as possible in their rough way, with food and drink in plenty and entertainment every night. Some of their entertainments were far from amusing. For example one night they brought in a young girl of little more than my own age, who had been a hostage but was no longer safe. They tied her to a post and then vied with each other to see how close they could throw their knives and darts to her without touching her. All the while they drank more and more of their potent liquor. When the girl eventually died — as much of fright, I believe, as from her many wounds — her body was left where it hung while the feasting continued and they turned their attention to something else.

Ogma, I'm glad to say, appealed to Delbaeth that he might remove the body, saying it was geasa on him to sit and eat in the same room as a dead body. Delbaeth, scornfully enough, gave him permission and Ogma, Mead, my foster-brother and myself took her and buried her as best we could in the alley and rolled a large boulder over the grave.

During this time it was noticeable that Bres and Brigit spent a great deal of time together, even at night. Although she was older than him by several years, she was a beautiful woman — the fairest of the three sisters, all of them called Brigit — and therefore one of the most beautiful women anywhere, as they were all exceptional. She was a seer and poet and, as a child, had spent some time on an island in the eastern Mediterranean where a company of women poets lived without men. For some reason this experience, besides sharpening her poetic skill to remarkable heights, also gave her a singular dignity which many powerful men found irresistible. But she responded to few, my grandfather being one. Bres, now, apparently, another. Women tended to dislike her, and she them.

One morning Ogma and I watched them stroll together down the valley towards the sea a couple of miles distant.

'Doesn't that worry you?' I asked, forgetting for a moment that she was his niece.

He smiled. 'On the contrary,' he said. 'Bres is the grandson of the king and has great influence over him. We have discussed this, the Dagda, Brigit and myself. She knows what she is doing.'

'I see,' I said.

Later that same day Dalta and myself also went to the shore, more because we had nothing better to do than anything else. The sun was hot and it seemed a good idea. At one end of a great sandy beach was a small spit of rock fingering the tide and at the base of it was a cluster of fishermen's huts. As we approached a boat was being launched. What we saw first was the black bottom of a hide boat, like a huge daol, or beetle, walking to the sea on ten legs. The men who were launching it had upturned it over their heads and in that fashion carried it down.

These fishermen were serfs and stopped their launching preparations as we approached. From my dress they could see I was a warrior. 'Where are you going?' I asked, but got no reply. I glared at them and repeated the question and then, simultaneously, as one of them began to speak, realised that they very likely didn't understand me. I certainly couldn't understand the gibberish this weather-beaten creature mouthed at me and I held up my hand to stop him. But I had picked up a few words of the Fomorian tongue, so I waved my hand towards the sea and said: 'Where?'

At once they all tried to reply and from their gestures, if not their chatter, I understood that they were going to an island about six miles distant which we could plainly see.

'Come on,' I said on the spur of the moment to my companion, 'we'll go too.'

The journey didn't take long as they hoisted a sail as soon as we were clear of the shore and the boat skidded across the wavelets very fast. It was evident that they were bringing provisions of some sort to the island, for there were several rush sacks and baskets of grain and seeds on board which had been loaded before we left. I waved my hand towards the island.

'Who?' I said.

The man I addressed, who held the steering oar, grinned at me toothlessly and replied with a lengthy sentence of which I caught only one word: 'Balor!'

We were going to the stronghold of the most infamous of all the Fomorian leaders and the grandfather of my foster-brother, who now sat beside me staring ahead as if he heard nothing, and whom Balor thought was dead. I caught his eye and he smiled as if nothing was the matter. But I grew uneasy as we drew towards the island and put in at a little cove fronted by a stone wall and with buildings behind. As we did so the braying note of a horn rose from the cliffs, causing the sea gulls to wheeze and answer in kind. Many great ships, something like our own, but narrower and with a higher prow, were beached in this cove and it was clear, not only from this but also because of the numerous warriors who were everywhere, that the island was a powerful stronghold. There was an alert atmosphere about the place that bespoke power if not discipline, which was not evident on the mainland. I later accounted for this when I learned that the island was where the main body of fighting men stayed. They had to be kept under control, and the only way to do so was by terror.

As we landed Dalta turned to me and said: 'I must see him.'

I nodded. I wanted to see him too. Dalta turned to the fisherman who was tying up the craft and, to my surprise, spoke to him in his own tongue. The man looked a little surprised, even frightened, but pointed ahead along a path that followed a contour of the cliff face to the top some distance away. As we went he called something after us and Dalta answered.

'What did he say?' I asked.

'He said to be careful,' he replied, and showed his teeth in a smile almost too angelic for a boy. Indeed I have heard it said that no boy had the right to be as beautiful as he surely was; that he was shrewd and had a head beyond his years was as evident ... but I run ahead of myself.

Topping the cliff we saw in front of us the scattered encampments of the Fomorian warriors, both male and female. Perhaps the thing which most distinguished this camp from the one we had left on the mainland was the absence of children. This was a battle-camp which could put ten or more battalions of men and women on the march in battle order within hours. Behind the clumps of tents and shelters, in a commanding position, was a larger structure of timber, sod roofed, and shaped exactly like an upturned boat. All around it and behind it stretched an arable of several hundred acres, with, closer in, a smaller area where beans and lentils and similar crops were grown. The corn in the distance waved yellow and ripe under the sun, the sea winds brushing the surface this way and now that, changing its colour with waves that were gold to ones of a darker saffron as it brushed a broad hand across the seeded tips. In front of this building stood a solitary figure staring towards us. His hands were on his mighty hips and, even at a distance, we could see that he was old and strong and I sensed his malevolence. Clearly the horn blast had been for his benefit. Motionless he watched us walk towards him. When we came closer I could see that his left eye was covered with a leather patch held in place by a broad strap that went over the crown of his head and round again below his ear, so that it fitted him like a cap.

He scowled as we approached and, when we were about thirty cubits from him, shouted, 'Be off. Get away with you,' and waved an arm.

I confess my heart was beating faster than I liked. But nevertheless I said, 'I am one of the Tuatha de Danann heralds.'

For a moment he looked me up and down from his horrible single eye and said, 'I don't care who you are. Be off.'

'I am under the protection of Delbaeth,' I said.

'Then go back to him,' was the reply. 'You have no business here!'

'We just wish to see the stronghold of the greatest warrior of all the Fomoire,' said Dalta beside me.

'And who might that be?' asked the other.

'Why, the mighty Balor, of course,' said Dalta. Balor looked at him for a moment. Then gestured towards the house behind him.

'Get me some apples,' he growled. Dalta's flattery had achieved what he wanted. I hesitated before following him towards the house and it was almost my undoing. For an instant I caught Balor's single eye and saw something suddenly stir within it. The expression on his face altered. I knew he was about to cancel his instruction and order us off and so I hurried after Dalta before Balor could speak. But he turned and with a thoughtful expression stared after us. I half expected him to shout, but he did not.

Dalta was already at the house, which seemed at first sight to be full of women at work of one kind or another. But right inside facing the door, sitting along on his hero seat (a raised platform), was a man who, for all that he was a Fomorian, was distinguished looking and richly dressed in gold and purple-edged, many-coloured robes to show that he was a high king.

'Ah,' he said, 'the young hero Cian of the Tuatha de Danann and —' he paused, looking Dalta up and down '— and who?' He asked directly, locking commanding eyes with the boy to force an answer from him. If I was surprised that he knew who I was I hope I did not show it. Obviously their communications were good. Dalta was not one to be intimidated, even at that age.

183

'I am Cian's foster-brother, sir,' he replied. 'Who have we the honour of addressing?'

The king smiled. But his eyes were hard and he paused.

'Well spoken, young man,' he said. 'Cian's foster-brother! I see. As for me, I am the Indoch Mac de Donnonn, one of the three high kings of the Fomoire. You have already met one of my brothers, Delbaeth, whose hospitality you enjoy. I trust you do not meet Tethra as yet. His profession and his pleasure is to kill ... but he is abroad in the Western Isles,' he said to my relief. 'What do you want here and how did you pass by Balor?'

'It was he who sent us,' I answered. 'For apples,' I finished lamely.

The Indoch looked at me and suddenly laughed. 'For apples?' He looked down at the reed basket at his side in which were clustered many. 'Apples,' he repeated, 'at this time of the year when they are still small and green on the trees? Where does he expect you to get them?' He was playing with me. My eyes followed his to the basket, while he smiled tauntingly.

'Those? Oh those are my apples, preserved by me for myself alone since last autumn.'

'And are there no others?' asked Dalta. The king shook his head, still smiling.

'And you will not give us some for Balor?' Again he shook his head.

'Well,' I said, 'will you give us some for ourselves?'

'Ah,' said the king, 'that is a different matter. These apples are the apples of a champion and only a true champion may have any.'

He looked down at me and though, as I have said, I was big for my age, at fourteen I was small beside him.

'Test me with a feat,' I snapped impolitely, and quickly modified it with, 'if you wish.'

'A feat?' he said. 'For my apples?'

'Yes,' I said.

'And what will you forfeit if you fail?'

I hesitated. I had little that I could offer which would be of interest to a king such as this — my sword, perhaps, but my geasa prohibited that. Gold I had none as yet. Then I snatched at my belt with inspiration.

'This,' I cried, holding up the black-bladed obsidian knife with the magnificent handle Keth had made. The king took it and turned it over slowly in his hands.

'Mmmm. I see,' he said. 'Beautiful. Very old, I would say?'

'It's been in my family longer than anyone remembers, passed on from father to son.'

'And you would wager this against my feat?'

'Yes.'

He stood up. 'Very well,' he said. 'Matha,' he called.

A large, full-bodied – and, for a Fomorian, surprisingly fair – woman approached from where she had been listening to the exchange.

'My daughter, Matha,' said the king. She smiled, and for the first time I understood how some of our men could find the women of these people attractive enough to mate with. She was strong and shapely and had good teeth and clear eyes.

'I will be fair with you,' said the king, in the manner of someone conscious of his superiority and excellence at some skill or another when they invite someone less skilled to compete with them. 'I will not ask you to do what I do not do myself. If you can equal me, you have won. Matha!' he commanded.

She looked sympathetically at me for an instant, and I felt suddenly happy, and then she went to the basket and took out an apple.

'Right,' said the king. Matha tossed the apple into the air and the king, with a sweep of his arm, drew his sword from its leather scabbard and cut it in half before it had fallen as far as his head. 'Now you,' he said with a grin.

It was a good feat, but not excessively difficult. I did not think that was all there was in it.

I nodded and looked at Matha, whose eyes were compassionate. Inwardly I was calm. Ogma had polished a natural gift until it was honed sharp. I could do it with either hand! I stepped back a pace and nodded to Matha. She tossed another apple in the air and, before it reached the top of its upward flight, my sword leaped to my hand and sliced it in two. Matha's face showed her surprise and, perhaps, relief. As I sheathed my sword again the Indoch snapped: 'Matha!' Now his smile was gone. She looked at him. 'Two!' he said.

The apples flew into the air and again he cut them. He looked me, full in the face this time, a sneer rather than a smile on his lips as he sheathed his sword.

I looked at Matha and nodded. Two apples were more difficult, but I had done it before often enough to know I stood a fair chance. Right, left, and they fell in four halves at my feet. This time the Indoch scowled. He said nothing, but nodded at his daughter who smiled at my success. When she did not move he snapped: 'Martha!'

'But . . .' she started.

'Three!' he said. Almost reluctantly, she turned and picked up three apples. One after another they arced into the air perfectly spaced. If he could do it he would never have a better chance than this, but it is a very difficult feat. One two . . . and he missed! The third apple fell to the floor and rolled away. His face thunderous the Indoch looked at me and snarled: 'You have not won yet. You must equal that . . . if you can.'

Then he looked at his daughter and said, 'and make sure you give him the same foul throw you gave me, bitch.'

It had been a perfect throw and we all knew it. She looked helplessly at me and I knew that she was going to − had to − spoil the throw. I also knew it would be the third apple. It had to be. One, two and − yes, the third went off to one side a little. I took it after the first and, as the other apple fell, I bent and put my sword upright under it to catch it gently on the point, where it stuck. Then I could not resist. Turning to the Indoch I presented it on my sword. Fuming he strode from his hero's seat and, as he passed Matha, caught her with a back-handed blow across the cheek that sent her sprawling to the floor.

'Take what you want,' he snarled. 'You have too much luck for one man.'

186

I sheathed my sword and jerked my head at Dalta. We filled our arms with apples and turned towards the door. As we did my eye caught that of Matha who had raised herself to a sitting position on the floor.

'I'm sorry,' I said quietly. 'I didn't know ...'

She smiled and shook her head, but put her finger to her lips. I did not see her again for many years.

We returned to Balor, our arms full of apples. When he saw us coming he glared first and then roared unintelligibly. Clearly he had not expected us to return to him, certainly not with the apples.

'Where did you get those? Did you steal them? If you did ...'

'I won them by feat,' I replied and, as I did so, two of the apples fell from my arms and rolled towards him. With similar speed to that he showed when he cut my fishing line, Dalta — still holding his own apples in the nest of his arms, bent forward and scooped them up before they were damaged against a stone.

Balor, perhaps at a loss for anything else to say, growled: 'Off with you lui lamh fada [small long-hand]. Away off with the pair of ye.'

We put the apples down and left, with as much dignity as possible.

Later that evening, when I told this story to the others and came to what Balor had said, Mead cried out:

'So is the prophecy filled. Lui he called him, and this is the month of Lugnasa. He has a name from his grandfather, as was foretold. Lugh it is and Lugh it shall be. Lugh Lamh Fada, Lugh of the Long Hand.'

It was certain that Dalta would take this name on his initiation. Meantime he continued to be known as Dalta MacKeth.

Two days later the messenger returned from Nuada. The Fomorian conditions were to be accepted but we were instructed to concede as little as possible in regard to the tribute. The number of 'advisors' the Fomorians wanted to send was to be limited to three.

On the question of hostages, it was agreed, there was little to be done. Negotiations became deadlocked, oddly enough, not on the question of the tribute — which, we had argued successfully, must of necessity be limited until we had time to establish ourselves — but regarding the number of people the Fomorians wished to send as advisors. They demanded that ten people be sent who would have the right to sit in on all important decisions. We held that two were enough and that their position be that of advisors only and only on matters on which they were consulted, which would be confined to those which might affect Fomorian interests.

Delbaeth called in Balor, whose attitude was, concede or we break off negotiations. This would not suit us, but we did not want to make that obvious. We indicated that we were informed by our messenger that our emissaries were even then preparing to go to Tara with offers of a treaty to the Firbolg. This was not true, of course, and the Fomorian leaders were very sceptical, stating to our faces that they knew we had come to Ireland to be revenged on the Firbolg.

'Of course,' said the Dagda, without blinking. 'But we did not then know the circumstances in this country. Wars there will always be between men and nations. But,' he went on, 'do you think, now that we have been able to judge the position here, that we are so foolish as to weaken ourselves by a war with the Firbolg, when there is land and enough for all?'

'You came for vengeance,' growled Delbaeth.

'Perhaps,' said the Dagda, 'but obviously circumstances change. The Firbolg might be more useful to us as allies than as enemies, especially if we had to face any major joint threat.'

Balor and Delbaeth stared at him in silence.

'What threat would that be?' asked Elatha smoothly.

Ogma looked at him blandly.

'Who knows? In a situation as fluid as this, one does not know where there is danger and where there is not unless the matter is sealed by a treaty.'

'You have our conditions.' Delbaeth was uncompromising.

'A *fair* treaty,' went on Ogma. 'A treaty of friendship cannot be one-sided, or it is not a treaty, It is an imposition.'

Balor scowled. 'Well that's it ...' he began, but Bres having exchanged a glance with his father Elatha, broke in.

'I have a suggestion. We are already allied to our friends, the Tuatha de Danann, by ties of blood, as my own family demonstrates. Those ties', he said, looking at Brigit, 'might be made stronger. In the meantime we need a solution that embraces justice and dignity for both sides. I am slow to put myself forward, but, perhaps, if I, the king's grandson' — and here he looked directly at Delbaeth, 'were to attend the Tuatha de Danann court it would be an acceptable compromise. I have the blood of both people equally in my veins. As the grandson of the king I would be no hostage; but I would be an advisor with the vulnerability of a hostage ...'

Delbaeth started to interrupt, but Elatha laid a hand on his arm and nodded at Bres, who continued.

'I know the people of Annan. I should, after all ... my mother is one of them.' He smiled again. 'They are an honourable race. I think I would stand in this regard in the place of several advisors and if — perhaps with one other — I was to represent the Fomorians, but I, and I alone, could attend Tuatha de Danann councils, with discretion as to what did and what did not affect the Fomorians, it might provide a basis for a solution.'

It was a compelling speech.

'It still wouldn't give us what we want ...' broke in Balor.

Delbaeth was quick.

'Perhaps we could break now and resume in an hour?' he said.

To cut a long story short, that is what happened. At the time we congratulated Brigit for we were sure that she had mesmerised Bres and persuaded him to propose this compromise and she said nothing to disillusion us. We didn't know — nor, I am convinced, did she — that the situation was very much the reverse and that Bres and his father had foreseen a possible advantage which they persuaded Delbaeth and Balor to pursue.

At that night's feast, the last we were to have at this Fomorian camp, Delbaeth concluded the treaty with the Dagda, Ogma and

Brigit in blood – a simple ceremony involving a small cut in the little finger and the mixing of a drop or two of blood with water which is then drunk. At the same time Elatha, Bres's father, proclaimed them foster-children and members of his clan. Thus it was that they became the sister and brother of Bres and his two brothers, Alla and Delbaeth the younger.

We returned to the people at Sliabh an Iarrain where we spent the next five years consolidating our position and building up our strength. Insofar as we could we avoided contact with the Firbolg although, twice, Eochaidh sent emmissaries to us with overtures of friendship. Each time we prevaricated without rejecting his offer outright, not because we did not wish to do so, but because it was vital that Bres believe we would turn to them if our treaty with the Fomorians failed. In this our hand was somewhat strengthened – if we were also a little confounded and dismayed – to learn that the Firbolg had begun to emerge as a people in their own right with reasonable laws and good government, instead of the chaos we expected. Much of this was due to Eochaidh – not, of course, one of their original leaders – who was wise and just. It was said of him later that there was never a year without plenty and that he executed the law with justice.

Towards the end of that period everyone, including Bres, knew that war between ourselves and the Firbolg was close and unavoidable.

In the meantime ... what is there to tell? Of how we and our settlements grew and strengthened? How we made or imported and accumulated weapons? Horses? Cattle ... people, if it comes to that, for many of those who were young matured as warriors, and there were few so old that they could not fight? Nevertheless we were still much weaker than the Firbolg. We cleared the land; felling trees, building, ploughing, sowing and reaping. We milled and reaped the abundant and glittering harvest of the sea. Perhaps I should begin by telling how the Dagda's wife, step-mother of Brigit and her three sisters — a handsome, sly woman called Fuaim — lost her real name and was named by Nuada, and became known throughout the land by three other names, Breg, Meng and Meabal; which mean Lie, Guile and Disgrace. That story will make all the rest clear.

Bres and Brigit were married long since. But that was no barrier to his indulgence with other women, and Brigit did not seem to mind. In fact she seemed amused — even proud — of his copious virility and the ample evidence of it. Nor did other marriage bonds trouble Bres. His attentions were devoted more often to dominant matrons than to young or unmarried girls ... although he did not neglect them entirely. In fact this was the cause of a near quarrel between us.

Eremed had grown into the living embodiment of the woman who had lived in my mind's eye as long as I can remember. She was tall and straight, with a beautiful full figure. Copper-golden hair that, in summer, glinted redly bronze, coursed over her shoulders and her level green eyes — wherein always lurked a secret smile — could soften my whole inside with a glance, and she walked like a queen. I was hesitant about approaching her for two reasons. The first was that I was sure she wouldn't have me and the second was that even if she would, I knew her father would not!

One blustery evening when the sky was filled with hurrying, white-rimmed, dark stretches of cloud separated by strips and patches of blue, I hunted with Ogma in the lee of a rolling hill and told him my problem. I was half-afraid he might laugh, but I had to tell someone. And he did not laugh. We crouched under an oak that grew from a bank, eroded by time and weather, so that it had an overhang where we could shelter from a squall.

Ogma listened and then mused:

'There are two pains which kill a man that no physician can heal.'

'What?' I asked.

'The pain of jealousy and the pain of love.'

'But what can I do? To run away with her would solve nothing. We would be outcasts or lose our station. Yet we are well matched and suitable for one another.'

Ogma nodded.

'You must wait. Diancecht cannot withhold his consent unreasonably forever. In the meantime,' he added, 'you have not yet performed the ceremony of the Arch of the goddess and Aengus.'

I looked away. Now I knew in more detail what the ceremony entailed I hoped my mentor would have forgotten. It was strange, and I knew if I mentioned it to anyone else I would have been derided, but my reluctance for the ceremony was because, when I contemplated what it involved, one person, and only one, came to my mind; Eremed.

'No,' I admitted.

We looked out from our shelter at where the path round the bank where the tree grew ran with thick, muddy rivulets, which the thunderous rain swelled.

'You must do it soon. You will not be accepted finally until you have.'

I knew and did not relish the thought.

'I will arrange it,' he said. I did not reply.

The squall tapered off quickly and we resumed our hunt through the dripping underbush and wet grass. I stopped and held up my arm signalling a halt, which Ogma did instantly. My own left foot was in the air when I stopped and I couldn't move it. My head was turned to the right and, through a tunnel of brush, I thought I had seen something about a spear-cast away. Those of you who have hunted in woods will know what I mean. Long grass carpeted the floor of the tunnel which was, perhaps, a little wider than my outstretched arms. On either side green-dappled brush and small trees reached leafy branches to the grass. Darker shadows heightened the effect. I strained my eyes, but could see nothing. I scanned above and below the spot, and, gradually, in the patchwork of green and grey, I distinguished the outline of a roe, perhaps a yearling, facing three-quarters flank to us. I flicked an eye at Ogma, but he flickered his eyes to indicate that he could not see her. A movement or a sound now and we would lose her. For a long time we watched and waited without moving. Satisfied, the roe turned its head to the left and at once her outline leaped at us. Delicately she stepped forward and leaned her neck to crop the grass — only to lift it immediately and scan again in our direction. Then she bent to crop and chew. By that time I was poised and as she bent her neck I let go my hunting javelin with all my strength. It flashed from my hand, the linen cord whipping it into a spin before I pulled it back. It pierced her neck with a solid 'thump'. Even before Ogma's javelin could leave his hand she was gone and we were both running. We crashed through the brush to the left, following the broken twigs and splashes of blood. Not far ahead we found her on the ground, legs folded beneath her body, looking at us; the spear, broken at one side, transfixing her neck. Quickly I straddled her back, grabbed her muzzle, pulled back her head and cut her throat with a long, sharp hunting blade.

We field-dressed it to save weight and slung the carcass by the legs on a pole between us. I was silent part of the way back. Some odd thing about the incident reminded me of the bawve and her child, of my grandfather — dead these six years or more — and of how she was reunited with her husband, Starn, whom we had all believed dead.

Shortly after our return from the Fomorian mission three riders rode into the settlement one day. Together with several other young warriors I was practising at spear-casting and the liath laoich, or warrior's battle-stone, on the exercise park outside the settlement when we first saw them. More for practice than anything else I aimed a cast at them as they approached, though they were still much too far off to be reached. Nevertheless I fitted the butt of a javelin into the socket of the caster, hooked my fingers round the grips and hurled it in the direction of the oncoming horsemen. It is curious how I can still see the beautiful, curved flight of that javelin — like a well-hit leather ball — in a perfectly straight arc, glinting as the light changed along its length. My cast was better than I expected, but was still a long way ahead of the riders. Some of my companions followed suit, and suddenly, there was a small fence of leaning javelins before the newcomers. They ignored it. They were led by a dark, grim-visaged man. They ignored us and rode to the gate of the settlement where they demanded entrance and audience with Nuada.

That was my first sight of Starn — but by no means my last. He was brought to Nuada who received his nephew with surprise and delight, that quickly changed to caution and then to anger and distrust. There was a feast that night in his honour at which the champion's portion became a matter for what was at first jovial contention, Creda, the king's huge champion, contesting yet again Ogma's acknowledged supremacy.

They boasted and bantered at one another for a bit and wrestled with their arms until, slowly, Ogma forced the mighty arm of Creda down until the back of his hand touched a burning ember and he leaped up with a laugh, conceding to Ogma. Smiling, Ogma was about to reach for the great haunch of the champion when a cold, snarling voice broke in:

'The champion's portion is mine!' Everyone looked in astonishment at Starn who, as guest, was entitled to eat first and from the most succulent portions.

'But ...' began Nuada.

'I claim it!' Starn looked around the king's hall with a cold face, immobile even in the flickering light from the rushes and lamps. 'There is no man here my equal.'

The king smiled and half opened his mouth to say something with a laugh, but Starn's eye halted him and his face became grave.

'You are serious?' he asked.

'I do not make jokes,' was the reply.

'But ...' Nuada tailed off and looked at his nephew.

Starn was dark: dark of skin, of hair and of brow and he had a cold, scowling countenance. He was big, powerful looking ... but certainly no obvious match for the giant Ogma, whose fair head was half a hand again higher than his dark one and who was both broader and heavier.

Ogma looked at him good-humouredly.

'Very well,' he said, 'Come on and we'll see.' And he set his elbow on the table and held up his hand for the other to grasp.

'Don't be absurd,' sneered Starn. 'I do not play childish games to

194

prove my worth, I do it a man's way.'

Ogma blushed to the roots of his hair and sat still for an instant while the shock of the insult reverberated round him. Then he stood up, slowly.

'I have no choice, O king,' he said. Nuada looked from one to the other, the towering Ogma and Starn who was still sitting on his other side. The hall was silent now. There was nothing Nuada could say to prevent what was about to happen. He nodded.

'Very well.'

Surrounded by his twelve chief men Nuada sat facing south, towards the white wind; behind them sat the warriors and facing them the bards and musicians. The druids, ollamhs, seers and men of learning were on the king's right and bo-aires or wealthy farmers and tradesmen on his left. In the centre of the nine-fold plan of the banqueting hall — like all the nine-fold buildings — was a sacred centre. This was cleared and the assembly drew back from the perimeter as the two men faced each other across it.

'You have the right of challenge,' said Ogma.

Starn looked back with that bleak, bitter expression.

'I am the son of Nemed,' he said. 'I have made myself a champion by my own might. I have Firbolg heads on my tent poles and Firbolg women when I want. You have done nothing against them. I will put your head where it belongs — on my tent-pole too.'

Ogma's face had grown whiter during this. The hush in the hall was such that when he spoke in a near whisper it was heard by everyone.

'What weapons do you choose?'

For answer Starn picked up his sword from beside his place and drew it. It was a beautiful weapon of iron, the hilt studded and decorated with the teeth of sea-animals, a claideamh det, or sword of teeth. He stretched an arm from his side without taking his eyes from Ogma, snapped his fingers and pointed; and a warrior, one of the three riders, handed him a lime-covered shield, gleaming white in the yellow light. Ogma turned to the pillar post behind him and drew his own sword from its bronze scabbard. He took his bossed shield from where it hung and the two men began to circle to the left. Then, with a great cry from each, they leaped at one another. Their shields clashed and their swords locked before their faces. A white cloud of lime rose about them. They strained together and it was evident that Starn was more powerful than he appeared, for it was a moment or so before Ogma was able to move him back. Once, twice more they clashed, and as they were straining after the third pass a sudden scream splintered the air and a dark shape sprang the length of the hall and into the arena. It threw its dark-covered arms to the heavens and screamed again with such force that the combatants fell apart.

Only then did I recognise Cailbhe, the bawve, Starn's wife, now totally demented. He, too, recognised her and the shock was evident, even on his blank face. He dropped his arms to his sides and stared. Ogma was more cautious and still kept his shield raised and his sword ready.

'Cailbhe,' breathed Starn. 'How …? What …? He looked at her, then at the king. She stood silent now, in front of him.

'We … I was going to tell you …' stumbled Nuada.

'She's — she's astray …' said Starn, dropping his sword of teeth and reaching a hand to her shoulder, under which she did not move.

'Starn …' said Nuada.

'Tell me what happened.' Starn's voice was flat as he turned to the king.

'I'll tell you Starn,' cried the bawve. 'They murdered your child and mine. They believed you dead. But I knew … I knew. They killed your child because of it. Out of jealousy. They wanted you dead. You and your son.'

He wheeled on her.

'My son? Dead?'

'Dead!' she screamed, 'dead, dead, dead!'

Starn turned back to Nuada.

'Is is true?'

'Not in that way …'

'Is my son dead?'

196

'Yes, but ...'

'How?'

'They killed him. Cian killed him, and was set adrift,' her voice was shrill.

'Is that true?'

There was no point in trying to explain. Nuada saw that. No explanation would be heard; no explanation that might be heard would be complete.

Nuada nodded.

Starn bent and picked up his sword, and his bronze scabbard. He said one word only, looking at his companions.

'Come!'

He moved through the silent assembly and no one tried to stop him. His two companions followed and, bringing up the rear, the dark, ominous and chuckling figure of Cruithne went with her husband into the night.

'Ogma,' I called from where I carried the back-end of the pole from which the deer was slung.

'What?'

'What will Starn do?'

He knew what I meant. We all understood that when Starn left us he left for good. Moved by implacable hatred (a hatred, I believe, that was in the man's belly anyway, requiring only the focus the Cailleach gave it) he had, against all belief and understanding, gone straight to the Firbolg and allied himself with them and become one of their leaders.

'He will fight,' replied Ogma, 'with the Firbolg.'

We approached the settlement through pastures and cornfields that had been laboriously cross-ploughed over the years until the soil was workable and fertile. Fields of wheat and barley and grazing land for cattle of all kinds, sheep, swine and beef as well as horses spread out on all sides of the settlement, with paths — four of them large enough to be called roads and take ox-carts — coming straight through them from nine directions. In the distance, on two sides, we could see smoke from two of our nine other settlements. It was very peaceful and swifts and swallows flickered in the crystal evening sky now that the rain storm was past. In the distance a cuckoo yodelled and nearer at hand corn-crakes and wood-pigeons echoed one another, harsh and melodious notes in tandem across the fields.

A couple of days later Ogma found me practising with the crann-tabaill, or staff-sling. This is a very useful and formidable weapon for those who master it. It was brought by the people from Ionia whither it had been imported from the desert tribes — indeed the people of my cousin's grandparents — who were renowned for their use of it in their battles with the Phoenicians, whom they call Philistines, and it was to play a significant part in our second battle, against the Fomorians. It is operated on much the same principle as the spear-thrower except that instead of fitting a spear to the end of a wooden caster, a similar piece of wood has the thongs of a sling at one end — one longer than the other — with a leather cup to take the missile. Another form of staff-sling, the deilclis, has no thongs, just the cup, and is much longer, but it was the crann-tabaill I practised with that day, and gathered and made sling stones, which had to be rounded and polished if they were not already suitable. For practice we did not, of course, use feat-apples, ubhall-clis, or brain balls as they are sometimes called, tathlum, made of blood (usually of toads, bears and vipers) mixed with sand, or with the brains of an enemy mixed with lime. These are very potent and destructive missiles with a mystic force of their own, as you will presently hear.

'I have done it,' he announced baldly. 'You will complete your initiation to-morrow evening when you undergo the rite of the Arch of Anann and Aengus the Forever Virile.'

I looked silently at him for a moment — by now I was almost as tall as he was — and said, drily: 'Thanks!'

He smiled and changed the subject. Picking up a staff-sling he fitted a stone — one of mine! — to the cup.

'I'll wager I can hit that dead branch before you do,' he said indicating the lifeless limb of a withered tree that protruded from the cornfields behind us, and about a hundred paces away.

'What?'

In reply he dug his thumb and a couple of fingers into the pouch at his belt and drew something out. He tossed it in the air, still grinning, and watched it spin in an arc, before I involuntarily snapped out my free hand to catch it. I opened my fist and in it lay a beautiful, new buinne-d'at, or tiny, gold finger-ring fibula. I scowled.

'I have nothing to match it.'

'Not today,' he replied. 'If I win you can put it on the long finger.'

He raised the staff sling, turned away from the target and, with a quick wrench of his back, arm, wrist and fingers sent the stone flying low and accurately across the whispering corn. The dead branch snapped in two, leaving just a jagged end projecting into the sky.

If I hadn't been so angry I would probably not have made a serious attempt at it. But I was angry, very angry and upset at what he — my friend and mentor — had so unfeelingly done behind my back. Hardly pausing to think, I, too, half turned away. While he had the advantage of age, weight and experience, I had those of youthful suppleness to aid my angry purpose and I coiled and unleashed myself like a bent yew-bow. The stone flew true and the projecting sliver vanished as if it had never been there.

Ogma laughed openly.

'Well done,' he cried, walking off. 'See you tomorrow before the ceremony.'

I picked up the sling he had dropped and glowered after him. He seemed to think it a great joke.

My way back to the settlement took me under a shady copse of oaks standing along the bank of a small stream. As I entered the greeny gloom beneath them a movement and a sound attracted my attention and two people came into view on the path ahead. I recognised Eremed immediately, but it was a moment before I recognised the man who leaned towards and whispered to her, She leaned away from him and laughed softly as I came up and I could see it was Bres, whose face showed little concern at my approach. Eremed's, however, softened and seemed to light a little when she saw it was me. My own scowl was no suitable response. Bres whispered again to her, and stepped aside with a smile on his lips. Eremed merely looked at him with humorous dismissal, quite in control of the situation — even if I had not been there, which was no consolation whatever to me to see. She put her arm through mine and turned to face Bres.

'You're a lucky man,' he murmured. 'Lucky.'

'Did I interrupt something?' was my stiff and foolish response.

He laughed while Eremed looked at me with a smile and squeezed my arm.

'Regrettably,' said Bres, 'no.'

I was in no humour to be sensible and dismiss whatever it was he had overtured as merely part of his venal nature.

'Bres,' I said, and I know my voice had a hard edge, 'if you as much as look disrespectfully at Eremed you'll answer to me for it.'

His smile vanished.

He looked at me coldly from his full height. 'You forget who I am.'

Just as coldly I returned his stare. 'I don't care who you are. I swear, by the wind and the sea, by earth and by air, by fire and by water, that you will show respect to this woman.'

At the greatness of my oath Eremed's hand tightened on my arm but she said nothing. Bres glared at me. For an instant I thought he was going to challenge me, but he turned and strode away between the dark trunks of the overhanging trees.

'That was not wise,' is all she said.

I had no words to answer but felt my lips tighten while my eyes followed the shadowy back of the retreating envoy. My mind was on tomorrow's ceremony and the tormenting passion of longing I had for the girl on my arm. I could not tell her; I wanted to tell her, but I did not know how. I wanted her to know how I felt. Above all, I wanted her. But I could put words on none of it so I remained silent. And together we walked beside the stream back to the settlement.

Shortly after midday next day Ogma came. I'd spent the morning cleaning and polishing my weapons and now it was my own turn. First an hour having my hair trimmed by a slave woman, then an hour in a sweat-house, followed by muscle massage and liming of my hair until it stood back from my head, strong and spiked and like the mane of a galloping horse. I assembled my few bits of jewellery — which were few and inferior. I had already decided to donate my new finger fibula to the goddess. My, by no means confident, hope was that she might, in some miraculous way, intervene on my behalf and spare me what I thought of as my betrayal of Eremed. Perhaps I was foolish in thinking like this, but there it was. I put bronze bracelets on my arms, a narrow band of scarlet threaded with a single strand of yellow gold about my forehead, and fastened my blue cloak to my shoulders with a modest, but beautifully proportioned, bronze brooch which I had been given by Fergus after I had saved his niece from the wolf. Then I lay down on my couch in the young warriors' hall and slept. Ogma's hand on my shoulder wakened me at sunset.

It was a mixture of reluctance and an unavoidable feeling of anticipation — excitement — that made my blood pulse a little faster, not unlike what one experiences before battle, that I went with him to the sacred circle. But it was a mixed feeling itself. I did not know what I would do when the time came. My feelings of disloyalty were confronted by a powerful natural urge and I was confused before the event began. That evening the sky was streaked with ridged yellow and crimson clouds that turned to white overhead and showed a touch of grey in the east. As we approached the circle something stirred in a bush beside me and a wren twittered. I shuddered and Ogma looked gravely at me, for it was a powerful omen … but of what? Neither of us was schooled in divination by bird calls (though I later mastered the art). But we both knew that for the wren to chirp as I passed was, in the circumstances, of great significance. And so it proved.

Ogma left me by the pillar-stone on which the moon had rested when she rose on the fifth of the month and I went on alone towards the central stone that soared upwards, even as my body responded similarly without my willing it.

201

I sensed a presence on the other side of the pillar, whether because I saw a flutter of white in the evening breeze or not I have no idea. But when I rounded it I saw a priestess, holding her swan-wings demurely crossed before her and with her head cast down. She was tall and slender without being thin and her young breasts rose firm and high between her arms. The small nipples were pink and risen.

Her burnished hair cascaded forward so that for a moment I could not see her face and then she raised her head and laughed at my astonishment.

'Come,' said Eremed, holding out her swan-girt arms towards me so that I gazed at her full, beauteous form clad only in a golden belt that girdled her waist and fell about her rounded hips, 'I am your initiate ...' she looked at me, still smiling as she took my hand and added, more softly, '... as you are mine!'

'But,' I stuttered, 'how ...?'

'Ogma! He had Brigit induct me as a priestess two nights ago ... a novice, yes. But fitting to serve as your priestess tonight.' She looked mischievously at me with her green, sparkling eyes, and went on, 'Fitting — and willing!'

I smiled. Then I laughed and squeezed her hand.

'That Ogma,' I said.

'He's wonderful,' Eremed nodded. 'But come, Cian. Let's go from here to where we can be alone. Brigit and Ogma have agreed to keep it a secret until after the rite is over and your initiation is complete. She, too, was very kind ...' I said nothing, thinking of Bres, her husband. But then my Eremed tugged at my hand and we turned and ran through the sacred circle, beyond the settlement to where the glowing corn-fields gleamed golden in the setting sun against the green forest.

And of the first part of that night I will say no more, except that together we explored the mysteries of the rite, which were all the more wonderful since in doing so we found and explored each other.

Whenever I hear a blackbird salute the morning I remember that dawn. From where we lay wrapped in a great woollen cloak that I stole back to get in the dark hours, we could see the yellow furze begin to blaze on a westen hillside. The sky lightened as the blackbird sang and then darkened again as Eremed leaned over me and the curtain of her hair fell about my face to mask the morning.

We had slept and woke and slept again. Then we woke and turned once more to one another, after which we did not sleep but lay, in the most inexpressible contentment, in one another's arms. I think it is true to say that our thoughts wondered rapturously together with little need of words. But matters of fact thrust words upon us long before we heard the soaring note of the lively blackbird. We knew that we were one; we knew that we could never, would never, be sundered and that nothing would come between us. We also knew that Diancecht would try to prevent our fulfilment and, so, we had decided to go to Nuada and seek his protection. We realized the cost might be considerable, but if it meant our being together and no obligation on her to participate in rites as a priestess (which would not arise once we were married), there was no cost we were not prepared for. As the king would be up before the dawn, we waited to go and seek his help.

As we passed a clump of small trees on the northern outskirts of the settlement, a voice hissed my name:

'Cian!'

Eremed had wrapped the woollen cloak around her. We turned towards the voice and saw Dara peering from the leaves. I was inclined to laugh because he looked so comical, but felt angry as well because I thought he had been spying on us. He had been initiated over a year ago, and I knew that that lot were up to any tricks ... a fact that seemed even more plausible as he had completed the rite in full at the time. I said nothing.

Dara stepped out in front of us.

'Well?' I asked.

'Listen,' he said, 'there's something going on between Bres and Barnea ...'

My jaw dropped for a moment and then I looked at Eremed and we simultaneously burst out laughing.

'No,' Dara interrupted urgently, 'not that. Something else.'

Something else …?' I choked, and found my laughter infectious so that Eremed fell helplessly against me, the tears streaming in her eyes. 'What … what else?'

'Will you listen?' snapped Dara. 'I'm serious. About Barnea.'

He could hardly have said a more unfortunate thing. Eremed and I fell helpless to the ground and rolled together, clutching our diaphragms in paroxysms of painful and uncontrollable laughter. Dara kicked me, hard, in the side.

'Will you listen?'

In spite of his exasperation I could only howl, even at the kick, and turn away from the sight of his earnest face.

Then he deliberately knelt beside me and slapped my face with his open palm. I saw the hardness in his eyes and was instantly sober. Beside me Eremed's laughter, now unfed by mine, tapered into spasmodic giggling and stopped entirely as Dara went on.

'Just listen to me. I know that Bres and Barnea are up to something. I don't know what. But I have been watching them for a while now. Are you listening to me?' I nodded, and I also remembered Dara's very cogent reasons for disliking Barnea.

'Barnea has just gone north,' his voice was insistent. 'But he's supposed to be going east to buy gold in Wicklow.' Both Eremed and I knew that for, notwithstanding his personal idiosyncrasies, Barnea was an excellent goldsmith and it had been generally understood around the settlement that he was about to make such a journey.

'Wicklow', went on Dara, 'is that way,' pointing to where the sun was beginning to lift above the forest. 'Barnea went that way.' He swung his arm north. 'What's more,' he said, 'he and Bres were together half the night talking, as they have been many times recently.'

'What are you getting at?'

'I'm getting at', he snapped, 'that I believe Bres and Barnea are plotting with the Fomorians and Barnea is taking them messages from Bres that he won't trust to anyone else.'

'What?'

'What else could it be?'

'But why would Barnea do such a thing?'

'How do I know? Because he's a perverse bastard. He's bound to be getting something out of it — or going to.'

'Are you sure about this?'

'I'm here, aren't I? Of course I'm sure. I've been watching them for months. Every time Barnea disappears it's after a session with Bres and —'

He paused and I waited. 'What?'

'I think Bres gives him ogham sticks to take with him.'

'You think?'

'I'm sure!'

If this was true it was serious. Treason, perhaps treachery. We had experienced both in the past, and Barnea seemed the type, but Bres? Was the blood of his father's people stronger than that of his mother's? On the other hand how unprejudiced was Dara? There was only one answer to that: not at all.

'We're on our way to see Nuada,' I said. 'I'll tell him.'

Dara nodded and I saw in his relaxed features a satisfied gleam which did nothing to reassure me. I remembered not only his experience with Barnea, but something else; only talk perhaps ... But it was whispered, about a year before, that one of the women who had succumbed to the ruttish Bres was Dara's own mother, the dark granddaughter of those desert people who had been expelled by their tribe. How reliable was what he said about Barnea and Bres, I wondered, in the light of that?

'We'll tell Nuada when we see him,' I repeated. 'But we must hurry. We must get to him before Diancecht.'

For various reasons to do with his role as king and his special relationship with the goddess, it was geasa on the king to be abroad before sunrise. So Nuada was in the grianaan, the sun trap, which caught and held its warmth on its daily round, when Eremed and I approached the palace.

He reclined on an elevated couch, his Queen, Maeve, beside him when we arrived.

When he saw us his face went blank for an instant before lighting up in a practised smile of welcome.

'Ah,' he cried, 'Cian and Eremed. It is good to see you.' And he bent his knee on the couch in an excessive — and for that reason condescending — display of offhand courtesy.

We dropped our heads towards him and Maeve, the Queen of the land, and crossed to chairs close to his couch. He waved us into two of them and we sat.

'What can I do for you?'

'I have just completed my initiation rite,' I began. Then I glanced at Eremed and I noticed Maeve's eyes follow me and a smile cross her lips. Eremed flushed.

Nuada saw his wife's glance and he smiled also.

'I know,' his lips smiled, 'and my congratulations — to you both,' he added.

I swallowed my annoyance. It was more important — both to us and to him — that I made what I had to say clear to him unclouded by irritation.

'We want to marry,' I said.

'Is that so?' he smiled and raised his eyebrows. His head swivelled from one of us to the other. 'Is it so unusual in the circumstances?' he added, his smile widening.

It was obvious what he meant: that we were so overcome with the events of the night that we had become physically infatuated. It often happens, which is one of the reasons why initiating priestesses are nearly always older women.

'This is different,' I said.

'Of course it is,' said Maeve, with a look at once totally understanding, and totally misplaced. My frustration tied my tongue. Eremed intervened, to my great relief, and with impressive composure.

'Nuada,' she said, directly, 'king and cousin, please realise that this was no ordinary rite and it is no ordinary reaction that brings us here.'

Her calm words produced an instant effect. His eyes which had been wide open in amusement, hooded over and his face fell into immobile planes. He nodded very slightly.

'Please take us seriously,' Eremed continued. 'As you know Ogma and Brigit arranged that I be made a priestess especially for this occasion, but our feelings for one another are much older. We want to marry. We have wanted it for a long time.'

'I see, and Diancecht, your father, opposes it.' It was said as a statement, not as a question. We returned his stare.

'We want to place ourselves under your protection, O king,' Eremed said, coming directly to the point.

Nuada's expression showed nothing of the seriousness of what she said, but his hooded eyes seemed to darken a little.

'Can you not wait?'

'Not without dishonour,' I answered, looking him directly in the eye. He knew what I meant. If we waited, apart from Diancecht's opposition, Eremed might — very possibly would — be obliged to participate in other initiation ceremonies, and neither of us were prepared to face that prospect. 'We are pledged,' I said.

Nuada glared at me. 'You are very young', he snapped, 'to be so positive about such a thing with each other.'

Then Maeve bent towards him and whispered in his ear. While she did so he kept his eye fixed on me. He paused when she had finished and leaned back in his couch again, to look at us with heavy-lidded eyes.

'Your grandfather named you Tanist,' he said musingly. I did not reply, half guessing what was to come, but not the form of it. 'I have never changed that.' His eyes opened fully as he looked compellingly into my own.

'No, Nuada you have been most honourable.' He didn't like that, but I couldn't resist it.

'If', he went on, 'I were to agree to what you ask, I must tell you that there are reasons of State which make it desirable for me to want to change it now. It has been in my mind for some time to bring the matter up with you. Would you object?'

What could I say? 'Of course not,' I replied, 'if the reasons are sufficiently grave — I will withdraw.'

He sat up and clapped his hands. 'Well done,' he cried. 'I knew I could rely on you. Consider it done!'

'You will take us under your protection as king?' asked Eremed.

He nodded.

'Against my father?'

'I have said it,' he replied.

She turned to me, her face smiling, and I took her hand. But I looked at the king.

'One thing, Nuada,' I said, 'may I know who will be my successor, and why?'

He exchanged a rapid glance with Maeve. Then said: 'Well, it's not usual. Naturally you are bound to secrecy, but I don't see why not.'

He was smiling and I could sense his feeling of easy accomplishment.

'You know how important it is to ensure the Fomorians are not aligned with the Firbolg against us, especially in the immediate future?'

'Of course.'

He nodded abruptly.

'For some time I have been anxious to establish — if not their assistance — at least their neutrality. We went a good distance along the road already with the marriage of Bres and Brigit.'

'What has that got to do with my being Tanist?'

He stated it baldly, looking at me with those curious eyes that could change so easily. Now they were flat and expressionless.

'I intend to nominate Bres,' he said.

It was as if I had been stung. I leaped to my feet.

'What?'

'You seem surprised?' There was surprise — even contempt — in his own expression. I was to discover why in a moment.

'But Bres ...'

'What's wrong with Bres?' It was Maeve who spoke, and I understood. She had influenced Nuada who, without his knowledge, was being cuckolded beneath his palace roof. But what a risk she was running. She looked at me with brazen eyes. She knew that I — that

Eremed and I – knew. Then she pulled her master stroke.

'Or perhaps', she added with consummate guile, 'you think I am like the Dagda's wife, one of his playthings?'

I was silent. The only people who did not know the scandal that amused the settlements were Nuada and the Dagda, one blind of his arrogance, the other of his magnanimity.

There had been a bitter struggle for the favours of Bres between these two women in which Maeve had triumphed. The passions and jealousy aroused had provided entertainment for the settlement all through the winter and it was all the richer because of the spice of danger involved and the threat of terrible consequences should either Nuada or the Dagda learn the truth.

Nuada laughed at her sally:

'The Dagda's wife,' he cried. 'I've changed her name for her. Instead of one, Fuaim, she has now three – Lie, Envy and Deceit – to keep her husband from learning the truth. The poor fool,' he added. 'As for Bres, he can't help the way he is and if some women are stupid enough to be taken in by his fancy face and figure, more fool them. That's right, my dear?' He turned to Maeve, who smiled in return and swung a basilisk stare at me as he turned back.

'His nomination will secure the neutrality of the Fomorians. That is why I am grateful for your offer. You did well … and', he went on smiling at us both, 'of course you have what you wanted as well.'

'But …' I started, and halted.

'Moreover', he added, 'he is my cousin so there's no problem there.'

He could see the reluctance still in my face.

'I'm surprised at your silence, Cian. Is there something more?'

I did not know what to say and as I hesitated Maeve asked the question which made my dilemma worse, putting me in a precisely similar situation to that which caused me to doubt Dara.

'Did you not have an altercation with Bres a night or so ago?'

I nodded. 'Yes'.

'And for this you oppose him?' snapped Nuada. The situation was getting out of hand. I could feel Eremed's eyes on me.

209

'It's not that ...' I started.

'What is it then?'

'I believe ... I have been told', I stumbled, 'that he and Barnea ...' Nuada and Maeve exchanged a glance. Not the amused or sardonic one I might have expected, but a serious look as of some knowledge shared between them.

'What about Bres and Barnea?'

'I have been informed that Bres is using Barnea to contact the Fomorians. To pass information to them.' Nuada's expression didn't alter.

'What are you saying?'

'Why would he do that?' broke in Maeve. 'He is a most loyal servant. *He* has kept *us* informed of Fomorian plans.' She looked coldly at me and then turned her beautiful head towards her husband, who nodded.

'You fought with him a couple of nights ago,' she stated, deliberately twisting the fact.

Nuada stood. He placed large hands on my shoulders.

'Cian,' he said, 'I understand. You are in love with Eremed,' he looked at her and smiled, and for that won some respect. 'And she with you. But you are blind of it.' I understood that he was genuinely trying to reassure me, and at the same time trying to extract maximum benefit for himself from the situation — a common leadership characteristic.

'We heard about you and Bres,' he went on. 'And, while I do not condone what he did, it obviously colours your view of him to a great extent. I understand that too.'

'But it wasn't me,' I said. 'Dara saw them together and saw Barnea head north instead of east.'

Nuada shrugged. 'Perhaps. If so it is unfortunate. These are things that are not for you or him to be involved in. Perhaps it didn't occur to you that Barnea might be working for us?'

Instantly my images reversed. I clearly saw the advantages and plausibility of what he hinted at. Barnea was the ideal tool to foster in Bres what we wanted him to know. 'I ...' I started, and Eremed, quietly, intervened:

'We have our own problem,' she said. In this, as in so many other things, she was far quicker than I. She saw that it was time to be off.

Nuada smiled and nodded. 'I understand. I am sure, Eremed, you will forgive Bres his importunity now that you know — what you should not know. He is incorrigible — but useful.' He laughed and smiled towards his wife.

Of course it made sense and I felt foolish for having mentioned it, especially when I was asking no mean favour of the king. He must have noticed. He moved between Eremed and myself and put a hand on a shoulder of each of us.

'Never mind. You were right to voice your suspicions. Had they been right and I had not known ...' he didn't finish. 'Never be reluctant to bring important information to me. Let me deal with it then.' He squeezed our shoulders slightly and it was clearly time to go. The sun was warming the grianaan pleasantly and I had no doubt he wanted to be alone with Maeve. I caught her eye as the thought entered my mind and what I saw there quickly drove it out again. If she wanted to be alone with anyone it was certainly not her husband.

'And don't worry about the other thing,' he boomed as we stood up and were guided forward by his large hands still on our shoulders. 'I'll take care of that. You will have your wedding. In the meantime lie low for a few hours until I see Diancecht.'

We thanked him and left.

'Now what?' I asked Eremed.

'He is right. We don't want to attract attention. But I cannot go back to my father's house now.'

That much was obvious. Our dilemma solved itself just then when Miach, her brother, with one of the other three physicians of the settlement, Forus (the other two were Fir and Oll), emerged from the sick house.

'Miach,' Eremed cried. 'He'll help. Come on!' and she ran ahead calling him. Miach waited, which was about as near to expressing a welcome as he could get. He was a curious man. Not cold in the way that Oran is cold, with the bleakness of a predatory animal. He was

cold with controlled purpose. I believe it amounted to a fury stem-
ming from his treatment at the hands of his father and at the depri-
vation he felt as a result. He waited expressionlessly while Eremed
ran to him, took his arm and kissed him.

'Oh Miach,' she cried, 'we are so happy,' and she turned, smiling,
towards me as I came up.

And all he said was, 'Good.'

'Miach, we are to be married.'

'Our father will not allow it.'

It was time I had my say.

'There's nothing he can do about it. We put ourselves under the
protection of the king and he has guaranteed it.'

Something — interest, excitement, satisfaction? — stirred in Miach,
and his eyes gleamed as they had gleamed six years before in the
Spanish wine store.

'Does he know?'

'Not yet ...' Eremed stopped.

'I would like to be there when he hears.' Miach brought his hands
together with a slap and, I swear, almost smiled.

'We need somewhere to go in the meantime,' I said.

He grunted. Afer a moment he jerked his head. 'In here.'

There's little more to be told. Miach made us comfortable in the
sick house with the ill and wounded, many of whom were happy to
see visitors, the remainder being too sick to care. They were mostly
women, with a few men who had been wounded in minor skirmishes
or — as in the case of one poor fellow with a mortal belly-wound,
gored by a boar — while hunting. The cross-piece on his boar-spear
had broken as he struggled to hold the pierced animal on the end of
it until it died. The furious beast had charged up the shaft, which
went right through it to penetrate the ground, and gored and
trampled the man before it was netted and hauled off.

These sick and wounded were cared for by an elderly freeman who
was no longer any use for anything else and showed an inclination
for medicine. He had lost a foot in a fight with some of the natives
about four years earlier, and hobbled about his duties on a crutch of

ash. He was kindly, but garrulous and as he dished out bowls of broth he maintained a running commentary of criticism about the running of the sick house, the settlement, the world in general and his own miseries and misfortunes which were unimaginably worse than anybody else's, and which he bore with the fortitude of a holy mystic.

The hospital, of course, had four open doors — one on each of its sides — to admit the healing powers of fresh flowing air. This, naturally, caused us some anxiety as we were concerned in case Diancecht or one of his people might see one of us. But, as he seldom went near the hospital — it was too far beneath his dignity — we felt safe on his doorstep, so to speak. A stream of flowing water also ran through the centre of the building, as usual, and I must say that the cool and melodious music of its passage did much for our tense feelings.

Matters went off as we anticipated. Diancecht's rage at what he called our 'betrayal' was violent and unremitting, but we were formally wed under patronage of Nuada three days later. Diancecht never forgave Eremed; nor Miach for his part, but in that case it was just another excuse. For, as he prophesied, Miach was already showing signs of being a great physician and surgeon. There were those of his colleagues who, echoing himself, said that he was already better than his father.

Then, with astonishing abruptness, we were faced with what we had first come for six years earlier: war with the Firbolg.

One summer's morning, after a night of continuous rain, the sun rose but remained hidden behind a grey cloak of cloud that stretched from one corner to another of the world. On the fields and pastures, and brushing the upper branches of the wet and silent forest trees, rested a white mist. Out of it cattle and other objects seen at any distance seemed to grow. As the morning grew older the mist gave way to soft rain which seemed to disperse it and, when it did, an encampment that had not been there the night before was seen on a hillside two thousand paces or more away. A scarlet tent, an ox-cart, and the browsing beasts revealed themselves, and men could be seen moving.

213

Immediately the king's champion, Creda, and four of the king's Scythian bodyguards — Tolc, Garb, Teidm and Tescad — went at a fast run towards the camp. It was some time before they returned — alone. When they did they went straight to Nuada where, with the leaders of the settlement, he had been waiting their return.

'Well?'

Creda looked at him for an instant, plainly showing emotions Nuada could not fathom.

'Come on, come on. What is it? Who's is that camp?'

'It's — it's an emissary.'

'An emissary? What emissary? What's his name? Are there new invaders of Ierne?'

Creda shook his head. 'No, lord, his name is Sreng. He is an emissary of', he hesitated, '— of Eochaidh, king of the Firbolg.'

'What,' cried Nuada. 'Not again?'

Creda nodded. 'This time he comes as an ambassador. He has a sword and white wand ... and ogham sticks addressed to you.'

'Where are these sticks?'

Creda produced them from beneath his huge apron and handed them to Nuada, who took them with distaste. For a moment it looked as if he was going to throw them aside without reading them. But he turned to Methger and held the square-sided sticks out to him.

'Read!' he commanded.

Methger took the three sticks, which were quite short, about half a cubit each, and looked at them.

'It is addressed to you, Nuada, from Eochaidh who calls himself king of the Firbolg nation.'

'Huh!' snorted Nuada. 'The Firbolg nation!'

'He sends you greetings; he wishes to know your intentions; he wishes you and your people peace and prosperity ... elsewhere. He wants you to leave Ierne to him and his people, who, he says, were here first; or', and Methger turned to the third stick, 'he promises you war of extermination.'

Nuada looked round.

214

'It has come at last.' Grim faces nodded back at him. 'Are we ready?'

Ogma replied. 'I would have preferred more time to train and rear more warriors.'

'We have run out of time,' answered Nuada. 'How many battalions?'

'Five — perhaps six,' said Ogma, 'fifteen — sixteen thousand fighting men.'

'And they?'

'At least eleven battalions.'

'Two to one. We must get help.'

'We can get a battalion of Gaetanae — spear-men — from Europe.'

Nuada nodded. The fearsome Gaetanae were mercenary troops, débordantach, or frenzied fighters, who went singing into battle naked except for their weapons and a golden torc, which was every man's prized mark of independence.

'And perhaps some Scythians', again Nuada nodded, 'and', said Methger, 'your cousins the Bretani will undoubtedly assist us.'

'It still comes out at better than two to one,' said Nuada.

No one answered him. 'Nevertheless,' he said, 'we have no choice. This is why we came.'

'What will you do about Sreng?' asked Bres.

'Kill him,' said Nuada, nodding towards Creda and his Scythians who instantly turned to run and destroy the Firbolg emissary.

'Wait!' cried Bres, so that they stopped and looked uncertainly at the king. 'Killing him will not help at all. It will bring the Firbolg down on us before we are ready.'

'Do you suggest that I send him back to his master saying thank you very much, we are going?' Nuada snarled.

'No. But if we deal with him adroitly we can gain the time we need to bring in the troops from Europe and Albion.'

It was noticeable that Bres now spoke of 'we'. It was also noticeable that what he said impressed his listeners. Finally it was agreed that he would go and talk to Sreng. This was considered particularly appropriate for a number of reasons. Bres, being half Fomorian, would impress the Firbolg with his presence; more so if he negotiated on behalf of the people. Moreover, it was argued, he could negotiate all the better since he would be in no danger of provoking Sreng through his contempt for an ex-slave as the Firbolg had never been slaves of the Fomorians and, finally (although I don't think anyone actually put this in so many words), it was clearly understood that Bres could acknowledge kinship with the Firbolg on the Tuatha de Danann side without dishonour also, for none of us was so idiotic as to believe that after years of slavery the same blood did not run in their veins and ours.

When he returned from his meeting with Sreng — which lasted for an entire day — Bres had a strange story. He brought with him some strange weapons, particularly Firbolg battle-spears, the creeshagh and the fiarlann. The former, which is very strong and heavy, has a broad, thick blade of which the point is rounded and sharp edged, and it is — like our own spears — socketed. The fiarlann, on the other hand, has a long, curved blade, also rounded, but is mounted to the handle by rivetting. It is often used for close combat in preference to a sword. They also have a variety of javelins of one kind or another. They are all quite different to our own elegant and deadly spears — nor have they any iron. All their weapons are of copper and bronze.

It was night when Bres returned and he was brought straight to the king in the banquet hall where the feast had been delayed on his account. After he had eaten the king asked him to tell the assembly the outcome of his meeting with Sreng. Bres stood and, fitting to the occasion, my father's fingers strayed across the strings of his harp and a shiver of music wafted up the strong, carved beams supporting the great roof before Bres spoke.

'O king, this Sreng is a mighty warrior. He is a big, powerful, fierce man,' he said, 'with impressive weapons and having no fear or awe of any man that I could discover.'

When Bres had gone to meet Sreng the two warriors faced each other at first from behind their shields, for protection. 'But', Bres informed us, 'after we had exchanged the normal courtesies —' when he said that a murmur began in the assembly at the thought of extending courtesies to the Firbolg, but Bres held up his hand and continued and it died. 'After we had exchanged courtesies I asked him to remove his shield — a great reddish-brown one of wicker daubed with pitch and lime and having hooks of bronze at the corners to use it as a weapon — and he did so. I also asked him to let me examine his weapons, which he did, and I let him examine mine. Let me assure you, Nuada, that we were both impressed.' Bres looked round.

'Big as he was,' said Bres, 'my weapons impressed him, for I had taken spears of iron and my iron sword. I told him that the Firbolg should give us half Ierne for ourselves.' Another, louder, mutter began at this, but Bres spoke through it. 'And his reply was that he would prefer to do that than face our weapons.'

'You had no right to say such a thing,' said a voice.

'You must bear in mind that all this took time and we were gradually feeling one another out. It was late before I felt I could make a case to him that would be to our best advantage.'

'Why did you do so?' Nuada asked Bres, looking keenly at him.

'For this reason,' said Bres. 'They cannot do it and even if they could, they would not. For to give us half of Ierne would leave them without the land to survive on, for my people would not permit them to have half and you to have half for we would have to leave. And', he laughed, 'there is no danger of that. But it may buy us more time', and he went on, 'it means that they must make war and that we will not be the aggressors. That could be important from the Fomorian point of view.'

Nuada nodded. There was wisdom in what Bres said, and no harm had been done.

'He also told me a strange thing,' Bres continued. 'More than a week ago Eochaidh was troubled by a dream in which he saw a great flock of black birds settle in Ierne to bring confusion and destruction to the Firbolg. He asked his druid, Cesard, to interpret this for him and Cesard, it seems, told him that it meant our coming and our victory. I also convinced him,' he went on, 'that the people had come to Ierne in a magic mist wafted over the sea.' He smiled.

Cheering broke out in the hall at this and at the surprising news which Bres had managed to find out from Sreng. Bres did not join in the cheering, but looked all the time at Nuada. When the noise abated he said:

'There was something else in the dream, Nuada.'

'What?'

'According to Sreng, Eochaidh's dream also had in it that one of them struck the noblest of the black birds and cut off its wing.'

The hall fell silent and every face turned towards Nuada. He, too, was silent for a moment. Then he leaped to his feet. 'Come,' he cried, 'let us drink to our coming victory.'

The shouting and cheering and stamping of feet, crashing of chairs and tables as the warriors and champions leaped to their feet, drowned whatever else Bres might have been going to say. But next day a war council was formed and Bres attended that. And although my father, Keth, was not one of the leaders and belonged to a relatively low rank he, too, became a member in a short while in unusual circumstances.

The war council decided that it was important for the people to choose their own battle-ground and, accordingly, they planned to send the army north-west to a suitable small plain, at that time called Moynia. It provided an outnumbered army such as ours with some advantages of manoeuvre in a relatively confined space, with control of water and the most tactically important height to the first-comer. It became known as Moytura after the battle because of the great number of post-stones left on the plain, as I will relate.

The council also sent fast messengers for help to the Bretani, to Europe and to distant Scythia, but felt only certain of getting the Gaetanae, who would come for loot and gold. At Moytura the army built a battle-camp behind a great ditch which came to be called the

Fort of the Onsets because of the numerous attacks it was to withstand. Inside, the camp was laid out in the usual manner with tents, shelters and huts for the troops, together with cooking and washing places. Sharpening-stones for weapons were erected in various parts. Two wells of healing were dug and each was filled with water to which, with much ceremony and incantation, the druids Methger and Mead, and the lesser druids, Cairbre, Ai and Edan, added many herbs and balsams to ensure that wounds would be quickly healed and that the injured would quickly recover their strength. Eremed, who was specially gifted in her knowledge of herbal properties, insisted — much against my will — on supervising their selection.

Every night Methger and Mead also made difficult and dangerous rites of sorcery, invoking the furious gods and goddesses of war and battle; Badbh, the terrible raven of the battlefield; Macha, the sinister hag of war; Neit, the frenzied killer of men, and Cailbh, the evil and hideous personification of death, woe and destruction. And they called on the Morrigu, the queen of the dead, who haunted battlefields in the shape of carrion birds. At night and in secret, dressed in black rather than the customary druidic white, they made spells and invocations, calling on the power of these destructive ones to rise against the Firbolg.

The Firbolg, too, were assembling from the five settlements they had established; that of Slainge; that of Gann; that of Sengann; that of Genann, and that of Rory, each of which could muster more than six thousand fighting men. When they were assembled they, too, marched on the plain and made a battle camp. This camp became known as the Fort of the Packs, from the savage packs of wild dogs that preyed on the bodies of the dead after the battles (although, by some people, it was called the Camp of the Pools because of the pools of blood surrounding the dead and wounded).

But, as Bres had predicted, the Firbolg had eleven fighting battalions while the Tuatha de Danann could not muster a full seven. As the Firbolg moved westward towards Moynia the sorcery of the people inveighed against them. Storms of giant hail and lightning lashed them for three days, although it was midsummer.

'We must delay further,' said Nuada.

'Then let us send envoys,' Bres suggested.

'To the Firbolg?'

Bres became exasperated, and, in one sense, I can hardly criticize him for it.

'In the name of the goddess,' he cried, 'will you forget your pride for a moment and consider the facts? They outnumber you two to one, as you yourself pointed out. You must delay — at least until the Gaetanae and the Bretani get here. You might achieve that by sending envoys ... and no disgrace on you for doing so.'

'How do you make that out?'

'As I say, it is time to face facts, Nuada — you and your people.'

No one except my grandfather had ever talked to Nuada like that before and got away with it. His face darkened, but he nodded to Bres to continue.

'Whatever you may wish to think, these Firbolg are not slaves, they are a free people.'

A murmur arose from the council, but Bres (who seemed adept at it) silenced it with his hand and continued.

'Like it or not they have the same rights in Ierne as you have, and it would be well for you to recognise that.'

'They slaughtered Nemed, and his people.'

'If they did, he had made slaves of some of them.'

'Why not? They *are* slaves.'

'They are *not* slaves! Whatever their ancestors may have been — even their fathers — these people are as free as you are. And Eochaidh has proved himself a wise king and a just one. You lose no face negotiating with such a man.'

'We lose face by talking as if they were our equals, to people who have slaughtered our brothers.'

'You will have the opportunity to avenge that. But if you do not act wisely, delay and build up your strength, they will slaughter you too. Is that what you want?'

'You think we cannot defeat an army of slaves?'

'I don't think your chances of defeating an army that outnumbers you two to one and has weapons such as these are very high,' said Bres, displaying again the fearsome, heavy spears of the Firbolg which, while not as good as our weapons, were nonetheless fearful and formidable.

Nuada didn't answer, but looked round the war council: at Ogma, the Dagda, Diancecht, Fergus, and twenty-seven others. Then he looked at Bres.

'Very well. We will send envoys. The ultimatum will be your own; that the Firbolg must surrender half of Ierne to us and we will divide the land between us.'

Bres stared back at him for a long moment before nodding slightly. No man there but remembered that his father was Fomorian and that Nuada's proposal was a direct challenge to their power. Should the Firbolg accept it, it meant alliance with them and inevitable war against the northern barbarians by the combined forces now on the plain. But it was virtually certain that the Firbolg would not accept and, I believe, it was for that reason that Nuada made the suggestion. The Firbolg would no more relinquish their hold in Ierne, ally themselves with the people and face inevitable war with the Fomorians than, I believe, the people would ally with them. But Nuada's strategy was that Bres could not be sure of that.

'Who will we send?' asked Ogma.

Again Nuada looked at Bres, who had gone to meet Sreng.

'Our sages,' he replied after a moment, 'our druids and poets and wise men — of the second rank,' by which he meant Cairbre, Ai and Edan.

These three were summoned and briefed and then were accoutred with the finest of weapons and armour; chain mail and greaves, iron helmets with ear flaps and nose pieces with tall plumes nodding from the crowns. They were provided with strong, socketed spears with the graceful and venomous points we have developed, and with leather shields of new-moulded hide plated with bronze. They were each given a sword of teeth in bronze scabbards and two javelins and they were sent on their mission.

When they returned they went straight to Nuada who was still with the war council in the centre of the camp.

'Well?'

Cairbre, their leader, seemed to find it difficult to control his excitement.

'There are many, Nuada,' he began.

'We know that,' snapped the king. 'How did you get on?'

Cairbre had not been informed of the underlying purpose of the mission.

'We failed. They would not agree to share the land with us,' he said. 'It is going to be war.'

The way in which he made this announcement made it clear that he, at any rate, was pleased with the result.

'But', he went on, 'they have put a geasa on us.'

Nuada leaped to his feet.

'What?' he roared.

'They want time to improve their armoury. When they saw our equipment they were worried at its excellence and demanded time to harness themselves as strongly. I told them I didn't think you would agree.'

Nuada stood with his hands on his hips and looked at his envoys, then at the council. He put his head back and started to laugh. To the bemusement of the envoys, who looked at them as if they had lost their senses, the councillors joined in.

'What ...' began Cairbre.

'It's all right,' said Nuada, still laughing. 'Go back. Tell them the people have ever — and will always — honour a geasa and they can have the time they ask for.' Cairbre looked at his fellow envoys and for an instant it seemed as if he might protest, but Nuada cut him off.

'Go,' he commanded. 'Quickly.' Cairbre and the others turned to move off.

'Wait,' cried Nuada. 'Tell them — tell their king; tell Eochaidh that while they are making their weapons, we would *welcome*', he emphasised the word with a grimace 'a game of hurling between picked teams from our two armies. That should keep them guessing,' he added, turning to the council. 'If we are going to honour them at all we may as well go all the way!' The envoys left convinced, I believe, that he at any rate had lost his reason. I have long since held the view that it is unwise — except, perhaps, on rare occasions — not to take an envoy or adviser into your full confidence. How otherwise can he act convincingly and with authority? What had happened here was a fortunate accident. One can not rely on luck. A leader should choose his envoys and advisers carefully, and then rely on them and on their judgement, which they cannot exercise if they are not properly informed.

As Nuada guessed, the Firbolg were surprised by his sham courtesy. They proposed that the match should be held the following day with teams of twenty-seven from each side, under a captain. Their proposing the mystic number of three nines plus one, making a unity, was their return tribute to us and we were surprised at the delicacy they showed in suggesting it. What we were not prepared for was that, instead of fielding a team of sportsmen — which no doubt was a problem for them since they did not play the game — they produced a team of powerful warriors who knew less about hitting the ball than about maiming men, with the result that many of our men were injured and three of them killed in the game, which began shortly after dawn and did not end until dusk. Their men were led by a giant called Rua who was personally responsible for two of the deaths among our men.

They were so elated by this apparent indication of our vulnerability that Eochaidh immediately sent his druid, Fathach, demanding to know on what terms Nuada wanted the battle fought next day; was it to be for one day or for several?

When Nuada heard this he asked Fathach to retire while the council considered the position.

'We must delay further,' said Ogma. 'The Gaetanae have landed in Wexford, but they won't be here for several days.'

'What do you suggest?' asked Nuada.

Ogma shrugged. The Bretani had arrived, good fighting men, but they numbered less than half a battalion, about a thousand men. We had to delay.

The Dagda, from where he sat huge and silent in a corner by him-self, growled, 'Why don't we put them under geasa?'

'To do what?' Nuada's voice was sharp.

'To battle with equal numbers on both sides'.

Nuada looked around. Every face at the council was suddenly alert.

'Why not?' asked Ogma, the Dagda's brother.

'It might work.'

'We have nothing to lose,' Fergus said. 'If they are as chivalrous as they pretend they won't deny us.'

So it was decided, and on this occasion they sent Methger to Eochaidh, as a mark of honour, to inform him of the geasa. Eochaidh was furious, but, being a man of honour, agreed and it was decided that four battalions would oppose each other on both sides. The first encounter to be next day.

For the remainder of that day and most of the night, under the watchful eyes of the deramaide, or sentries, hundreds of skilled slave-women ground the hammered blades of iron and the moulded blades of shining bronze on the cluiche-na-n'arm, or stones of weapons, until their venomous edges would cut in two a hair that was blown against them.

The swords, or claves; the calcs, rapiers; the claymores, the largest swords of all; the beautiful and deadly swords of teeth, even the golden-hilted swords of the king's hostages, and the scians or daggers — all were honed to a fearful sharpness. Likewise the spears and javelins and the deadly axes that could slice a leg or an arm off through the finest mail. As the weapons left the hands of the slave-women the warriors collected them, each his own, and stored them above their sleeping places ... but each man slept with his favourite weapon in his hand in case of sudden alarm.

All night, too, the tuithaiteanna, or shield-makers, worked on the sciaths and uibrachs. The sciath is a shield of wicker-covered hide and may be of any size, from a small buckler, to being large enough to cover a man from head to foot. The hide is seam-stitched over the wicker and is embossed and painted, usually with white or coloured lime. The uibrach, as the name suggests, is a shield of yew-wood, often covered with copper or bronze.

The standard-bearers, too, were at their work, so that when the morning broke the hundreds of banners and flags above the companies and battalions and on tall poles before the tents of cath mhilidh and the ceannfearthna, the battalion and company commanders, were like a stationary flock of many-coloured birds.

The armies rose on that first morning when the wailing notes of the curved trumpets sounded before a hint of light tinged the eastern skyline. Every fighting warrior prepared for battle, selecting his finest clothing and jewellery to wear; washing and cleansing himself elaborately, having his hair limed and shaped by slaves who also shaved him with his sharp bronze scraper.

I commanded a company of three fifties in Ogma's battalion and as I checked each man's weapons and equipment I noticed that now and again a surge of excitement rose inside me in a hard knot.

Presently, when the rising sun had cleared the mist from the plain, the tall, round-mouthed trumpets blared again, this time the call for the four thousand fighting troops to assemble. They did so and marched out of the camp towards the enemy, a great host of warriors. Followers and onlookers from either side formed a pair of semi-circles before each camp, separated by the wide plain, while the two bodies of men moved purposefully towards the centre.

As each of our men passed the gate of the fort he dropped a stone he had picked up for the purpose, on a pile that gradually rose to be a cairn of four thousand stones. On their return each man would remove a stone from the cairn and what was left would tell us the number of dead and missing. This was their order of battle. The heroes went in front to give encouragement and example. Behind them were ranged the noble fighting men in twos, each veteran attended by an older man, and behind them the young warriors leading the serving soldiers; bringing up the rear were the great champions and their personal retinues who would supervise the battle and guide its course.

The armies drew up facing one another slightly more than a spear-cast apart. The day was clear and bright and the sun glinted from the many metal points and surfaces that twinkled among the colourful banners and battle flags. The champions fixed pillar-stones in the field. These, as you know, serve three purposes. They make a fence behind which to retire when strongly pressed; which can also impede panic-stricken troops and help prevent a rout. And they are the anchors to which the champions, when the occasion demands, some-times attach themselves with iron chains for single combat or when standing fast, or when formin a cró, or protective circle, around the king.

The Bretani were to the right of my company, led by Aengaba of Norway. They were steady, reliable warriors and some of the common soldiers were shackled to them, leg-to-leg with horse shackles, in case they broke, which the Bretani, being far from their own settlement, were less likely to do. But in fact there was no need.

The Dagda began the attack with a company of hand-picked men and cut through the Firbolg left flank. But Cirb, a Firbolg warrior of great strength, at the same time attacked our right — through the Bretani — and did terrible slaughter. The main bodies met in the centre in a bloody encounter and that day I killed my first man in battle. By mid-day both sides were exhausted from fighting. But neither side could retire or advance in spite of encouragement from the watching hosts, which became less and less frequent and more and more silent as the day wore on.

As the sun began to descend towards the western rim of the world, as if by agreement, the front ranks drew back and men, covered with blood and gore, let their weary arms fall to their sides as they stood on the slippery surface of the bloody plain. The only sounds were the cries of the wounded and the harsh calls of the carrion birds, Badbh and the Morrigu, as they feasted on the dead.

Then Aidleo of the people stood out in the space between the two armies and cried out in a loud voice:

'Bualim sciath — I strike the shield,' holding his scarred and painted shield aloft and striking it loudly with the butt of his battle-spear so that the sound roared in the exhausted silence and the crows took fright and flew aloft in a croaking handful of tossed black and stinking rags.

Nertcha of the Firbolg came out against him and they fought a gallant combat between the armies, circling and smiting one another until Aidleo fell, mortally wounded. That ended the first day's battle and the people retired to the Fort of the Onsets and the Firbolg to their camp without pursuit for they, too, were too weary.

The wounded were gathered up by serving men from both sides and herbs exchanged. Exchanged is hardly the correct word, for the Firbolg had little knowledge compared to us, but Fir and Eremed went to their camp to prepare the healing baths for their wounded. And heads were taken from the dead.

The second day might have brought us victory only for the courage and strength of a Firbolg champion whose name is unknown to me. The three druids, Oll, Forus and Fir, had left the fort very early to perform some rite or other when, on their way back, they surprised Eochaidh, the Firbolg king, bathing in a stream unattended by any of his bodyguard. Seizing the opportunity they immediately rushed to attack him, but a warrior interposed himself between them and the king and fought them. So well did he fight that all four were killed, the three druids of the people by his hand before he himself fell to a fatal thrust from the dying Forus.

It was also the day that Oran paid his debt. We heard the great roar from the Firbolg camp when Eochaidh returned and told how he had been nearly killed. Shortly afterwards there was another roar as their four thousand troops for that day poured from the camp and onto the plain.

We had suffered, and, before any man added a stone to it our cairn was almost half its size that morning. Aengaba and his Bretani rushed through the gate of the fort towards the oncoming Firbolg and worked fearful slaughter on them. A hideous noise rose above the battlefield through the cloud of lime that shot upwards from the contesting shields. Spears twisted and blunted and swords broke themselves on splintered bones in savage hand-to-hand encounters.

227

Ruad of the Firbolg charged to where Aengaba was furiously fighting and battled through the Bretani to the frenzied champion's side. The hosts drew back from the warriors and for an hour they fought with all their weapons until Ruad, striking from the dreadful ground, thrust beneath Aengaba's shield and killed him instantly. Then he rose and took his head.

When they saw what had happened to their leader the Bretani were discouraged and started to turn from the battle. I summoned my men and ran to the left to stall them, calling as I did so for them to turn and attack. I was successful for not more than a few passed me — and they were either turned or killed by the champions at the pillar-stones — and the rest resumed with new vigour and, with me and my company, charged the mass of the Firbolg centre. Seeing our head-long rush Ogma, with his whole force, came up behind us and cut through the Firbolg. I have no idea how that battle went. I can see blood and eyes and mouths; I can hear screaming and clashing and the thudding of weapons and shields, but who I killed or who I maimed I do not know, only that I fought and killed lest I be killed or maimed myself, and that the blood of many men was thick and stinking on my clothing, and on my body.

Then, incredibly, a path cleared — or seemed to clear — before me through the mass of struggling bodies, and at the end of it I saw that same Ruad who had killed Aengaba charging towards me, a mighty spiked mace raised in both hands above his head and aimed at my own. I dodged to the right instead of the left and took it on my shield. But the force of the blow numbed my arm so that I thought it was broken. He drew the mace back for a second blow and I slammed into him with the shield, seeking to bring my sword arm up. But he gripped my forearm with a strong hand and prevented that. But he could not effectively use the heavy mace with one hand, although his blows were strong enough. Then he shortened his grip and raised his arm, aiming the head of the mace straight into my face. I realised his intention and deflected the blow with my shield again, at the same time bringing my knee up to his groin. But the maneouvre was thwarted because he had pulled me close with the hand on my arm to add force to his own blow and I stumbled and slipped to my knees. The danger was great. I fell forward, but righted myself by catching the ground, with the bottom of my shield this time, so that I was ready to spring up when, right in front of me, I saw the gaping head of Aengaba, eyes wide and mouth open, dangling by the hair from Ruad's belt. The sight momentarily halted me and instead of rising or rolling I looked up to see Ruad's mace poised for the blow that would open my head like a burst apple. But it never came. He stood there, it seemed, for a great time, and then, slowly, toppled forward in the same posture, so that I had to twist to avoid him and the slender point of the iron javelin that protruded from his breast. When I looked beyond him Oran stood tall and straight against the blue sky not ten feet away. He looked at me with those cold, grey eyes; nodded, turned and walked into the battle which had grown quieter. He had repaid his sister's life. But I don't think he ever forgot — or forgave — the episode of the sausage six years earlier!

To conclude my account of that day's fighting, Cirb counter-attacked when he saw Ogma's thrust into the Firbolg centre, but was repulsed with severe losses ... as we had ourselves, again, suffered this day as well. The victory, such as it was, was ours, though it was with sadness we watched the Firbolg trail back to their camp, each man with a stone for their cairn in one hand and a Tuatha de Danann head in the other, while the dead lay in twisted and contorted heaps among which only the carrion moved and foraged.

Next day, the third day of the battle, the Tuatha de Danann forces were again led by the Dagda. No sooner were we assembled outside the fort to advance for battle when an astonishing sight — from which the plain had its name changed from that of Moynia to Moytura, the Plain of the Props — met our eyes. Advancing from the Firbolg Camp of the Packs, above which a continuous cloud of screaming birds circled and wheeled, diving and fluttering and fighting among themselves for the scattered human offal, came the Firbolg host, each man bearing besides his weapons two great pillars of wood. Behind them came the non-combatants, also carrying many thousands of these pillars, some of wood, some of stone. They began setting them in the plain very close together between their army and the camp so that a close-packed fence of upright pillars stretched from one side of the battle-field to the other and backwards for a depth of two man-lengths. It is surprising how quickly they erected it, which was many times bigger than the smaller defence fences — called zariba in Egypt whence this type of defence comes — which we had built two days before. At first we were not sure if it was a good or a bad sign. On the whole we felt it was an indication of increased caution on their part. That could mean they were more wary of us than they had been. But it could also mean that they would fight more cunningly. We agreed it had both positive and negative aspects.

The Dagda decided on a quick, mass attack, and advanced on a wide front with all our troops towards the flashing dome of shields and the thick forest of javelins of the enemy. When the Firbolg saw his thunderous approach they retired behind the thicket of props, their champions defending their retreat, But the Dagda bore on, a leader at the head of each fighting column, breaking their battalions and companies and forcing them from their positions. Cirb rallied the Firbolg and attacked the Dagda from the east. But he was felled, at the head of his men, by the Dagda's powerful, iron-bound mace. Then the powerful Sreng leaped into the breach caused by Cirb's death and the men of the people fell before him on every side. But Sreng, too, failed to stop the Dagda's restless attack and, although the Firbolg counter-attacks drove to the walls of the people's fort several times that day, they were eventually driven back to their own camp with severe losses. The heads taken that day by the people were more numerous than those taken by the Firbolg. We sent physicians to the Firbolg camp to tend the wounded when we heard that three of theirs had been killed.

But the people were dispirited for, in spite of the victory, it had been at a woeful loss and it was clear that if things continued like this the Firbolg would eventually win by weight of numbers, at the last being able to field four thousand men on a day when we could not.

But that night, under cover of darkness, five hundred Gaetanae arrived and many of us crowded about to see these renowned and furious warriors. They were all big men, mostly fair and, when they arrived, were wearing the usual clothing of the people. But each man wore around his neck a golden torc, some fashioned after the goddess in the shape of a sickle moon, some rounded and some twisted; all of the finest workmanship. They were such as only nobles wore as a general rule, but for the Gaetanae, the renowned spearmen of the heartland of Europe, they were the badge of their warrior trade. And each man carried a light, U-notched shield.

That night, too, Keth, my father, made the first of the two important suggestions which were to prove so important in gaining victory for us in two vital battles. The war council was in session with the leaders of the Gaetanae when he approached.

'What is it Keth? We are busy,' said Nuada, not unkindly, but obviously uninterested in what the harp-maker and story-teller might have to say.

'I have a suggestion ...' began Keth.

'Can't it wait?'

'It has to do with tomorrow's battle.'

Nuada leaned back. He knew that Keth's knowledge of battle tactics was, to say the least, theoretic. But he was no fool and was not going to ignore a possibly useful idea.

'What is your suggestion?'

I have already described Keth. He was a gentle — even diffident — man of peace, not given to thrusting himself forward. But when he was taken by an idea he could be very convincing, for then it was not himself he promoted but the idea. Once he got that far it was certain the idea had been thoroughly tested, taken, shaken, throttled, wrestled with, sundered and put together again until he understood it and was thoroughly satisfied with it.

'So far', he began, 'the battles have been mainly free-for-all, man-to-man combats.'

With those flat eyes Nuada gazed expressionlessly at him.

'Even when we win, such fighting wears us down faster than it wears down the enemy, simply because there are more of them than of us.'

'What do you suggest? We are killing as many as we can.'

'Different tactics! Instead of charging the way we do …' he paused. And then changed both his tone and his approach completely. 'Last night I watched a hedgehog,' he said.

He received looks of surprise and anger from the war council. I was standing behind Ogma and felt my heart sink. He had gone wrong. Whatever it was he was trying to explain was now completely ridiculed.

'A hedgehog?' Nuada's voice was so expressionless that the absence of inflection emphasised the contempt.

'Yes!' Keth seemed not to notice. 'It was being attacked by two dogs.'

'What are you getting at, Keth? We are busy.'

'The hedgehog rolled into a ball …'

'They always do.'

'A ball of spikes. The dogs could do nothing but bark. When they tried to attack, the spikes held them off.'

'Is this a joke, Keth? What is your point?'

'My point is that if we get our troops to lock shields like we do on ceremonial parades, and advance with spears at the ready so that each man defends the man beside him, we would do better.'

There was a moment's silence. I sensed the impatience of the council. Nuada, however, was his usual unemotional self.

'Thank you for the suggestion, Keth. If we want more advice about hedgehogs we'll ask you.'

'I …'

'Thank you, Keth.' The dismissal was final. Keth slumped and turned away. Although I felt humiliated myself, I knew it was not his pride that was hurt, but that he believed what he said. I fumed, how ridiculous to waste the time of the war council on hedgehogs!

But when Keth was out of earshot Ogma mused.

'You know, I wonder if there isn't something in that?'

'Hedgehogs? Don't you start. What do you think?' asked

232

Diancecht, turning to the Gaetanae.

'We fight as we always fight,' replied their leader.

'The goddess inspires our blood-frenzy. We will do our best for you. But this of the hedgehogs ...' he went on in his thick accent, 'I do not understand that man!'

Nuada nodded. 'That settles it. We hold the Gaetanae in reserve until we see how things go in the morning. But one way or another they must be committed by noon. Agreed?'

There were nods and yesses all round and the council started to break up.

'I still think', Ogma's voice was loud, 'there is something in this idea of Keth's. What he said made sense to me. Let the Firbolg do the work attacking a mobile fence of shields and spears ...' he trailed off.

Nuada turned. 'A what?'

'A cippe catha,' said Ogma, 'a walking battle-hedge.'

'I see!' Nuada was thoughtful. 'Well,' he decided, 'for now we'll stick to the original plan. We'll see ...' and he turned and walked off.

A grey veil of soft rain drifted before the wind across a dripping plain on what was to be the decisive day of battle. It was cold. Visibility was poor. We could not even see the Firbolg camp on the other side of Moytura where everything was hidden by mist. But the noises of an army preparing for battle came through and as our soldiers marched out the points of the spears of the Firbolg host began to appear above the mist like disembodied arrows aimed at the sky. They were followed by the heads and bodies of the advancing warriors who bore down on us with terrible determination. In the centre we could see a fold of valour, a cró, formed by the foremost Firbolg champions and it was clear that Eochaidh himself was there that day to lead his people.

The Gaetanae had spent the early part of the morning, like the rest of us, preparing for battle, but in their own way. Like with us they had washed and oiled themselves, had their hair done by slaves, had cleaned and polished their weapons and had them sharpened by the women. But instead of putting on their finest clothing – or, as in our case, what was left of it – they stripped themselves naked except for the gold collars and the ornamented belts they wore about their waists. Carrying their great spears and two javelins each, they took the centre of our line and faced on towards the mists which shrouded the enemy.

Before the sun was warm the battle had become a flaming mass with pitiless single combats taking place here and there. The Firbolg charged, driving the Tuatha de Danann backward, through the pillars, right to the ramparts of the fort where the battle raged for nearly two hours. It began to look as if the people would, at last, be overrun. Seeing what was happening, Keth ran to where Nuada and Ogma stood on the ramparts above the raging, ebbing and flowing, battle.

'Nuada,' he shouted, 'the hedgehog!'

Both leaders turned on him and then to each other. Without a word being spoken, Ogma caught something in Nuada's eye and leaped for the ground, bellowing orders as he did so. The gates were flung open and, surrounded by a hundred and fifty of his men, Ogma sallied out to the rear of the battle and started to group more men around him. When five hundred were assembled he issued rapid orders and they formed a great triangle, each man locking shields with the man in front and to one side of him, their slender-bladed, venomous spears projecting between them like a rim of fearful thorns. The men at the rear walked backwards with their shields turned out. In the centre more warriors marched, ready to relieve those on the edges and fill the gaps when a man was killed or severely wounded.

In this triangular formation they advanced steadily on the enemy, supported on the flanks by the Gaetanae and by the remainder of the forces, who now fought with new vigour.

The battle-hedge moved on and through the Firbolg, remorselessly beating off or slaying all in its way. When one man of it fell another moved immediately to take his place and nothing halted its deadly progress. The flanks and wings of the whole advance were filled by veteran warriors, experienced in battle, with the young warriors behind and the champions bringing up the rear behind the

234

common soldiers as on the first day of battle. Then the Firbolg began to break and fall back. The mist had rolled away with the passing of the morning and low clouds hung above the damp field of battle. The dark camp of the Firbolg could be seen again, round and formidable against the fresh green of the further off hills. Then seers and magicians took vantage points and called on the forces of the other world to come to our aid. Historians wrote with black strokes on ogham sticks and Nuada, surrounded by his Scythian bodyguard, came out to lead the people to victory.

Later it was said that the furies and the monsters and the hags of doom cried so loudly that their voices were heard in the rocks and waterfalls and in the hollows of the earth. But the only cries I heard were of the fighting warriors and the wounded and the dying. Warriors lunged at each other with their spears until the points twisted from the quivering of pierced bodies; swords became blunt and turned on scarred shields, bereft by now of lime; the curved blades of Firbolg fiarlanns lodged in the boiling blood of de Danann thighs. The stench was terrible. Then Sreng fought his way to Nuada, through the Scythians, and beat on his shield for single combat, and Nuada went against him.

The armies drew back and the champions circled before clashing together seeking a blow. The turf beneath their feet turned to a bloody bog from trampling as they fought and each was wounded many times. Then Sreng dealt a blow at Nuada which cut through the rim of his shield and severed his right arm between the elbow and the wrist. Both it and a third of the shield fell to the ground. Immediately the Dagda leaped across the intervening space and straddled the slumped body of the king. Several more of the thirty-two leaders came up and formed a defensive fold, or cró, around the fallen king until physicians, led by Diancecht, carried him from the field.

After that the Dagda raised the king's severed hand as a standard round which the people's army could rally. Suddenly Bres, who had taken no part in the battle up to this, leaped to the fore and charged the enemy, calling on everyone to follow him. So surprising was his move that the warriors reacted on impulse and charged behind him at the Firbolg army, the armoured battle-hedge advancing again with fearful effect.

Bres fought through to Eochaidh, the Firbolg king, but he escaped in the confusion to where Sreng and his son Sláinge Fionn were holding the attacking Tuatha with terrible slaughter. During this encounter Eochaidh had been wounded and Sreng prevailed on him to go and have his wounds dressed.

He was also consumed with thirst and when Sreng assured him that he would hold the Tuatha in check until his return, Eochaidh, with his personal guard of a hundred men, went to find a stream where he could bathe his wounds and slake his thirst. But all the available water was either dried up or fouled with dead bodies. So he made his way to a lake strand. But the three foster sons of Nemed, with three fifties of warriors, followed and a venemous battle took place between the two companies until the king and the three foster sons were killed. Two cairns were erected at the western end of the beach to commemorate them, and they are called Eochaidh's cairn and the gravestones of the sons of Nemed.

Sreng, meantime, continued fighting against the warriors of the people until, at last, neither side was capable of attacking the other. The leaders looked round in their weariness at the heaps of bodies that had fallen in the slaughter, and their hearts wept. Their spirits fell and their courage failed at sight of the vastness of the disaster, and both sides retired to their camps.

Thanks to Keth's battle-hedge tactics the Firbolg had suffered very heavy casualties that day (apart from the loss of their king), and there were great lamentations and reproaches in their camp that night, much of which was spent by friends and relatives burying their dead; raising mounds above brave serving men, gravestones over warriors, tombs above the heroes and hills above the great champions who had died. When that was done, Sreng summoned a council to decide what it was in their best interests to do in the light of their great losses. He put three alternatives to the council.

'We can', he said, 'leave Ierne altogether; we can offer the Tuatha de Danann regular battle or we can undertake to share the land with them as best we can.'

The council looked back at him silently for a moment. They were not as optimistic that night as they had been four nights earlier, or even the previous night.

'For myself,' he said, remembering his meeting with Bres and what he had said on that occasion, 'I recommend some attempt at compromise.'

At that he was shouted down by the other Firbolg leaders, remembering the dead they had just buried, who demanded that they give battle, once more, to the people.

'Very well,' said Sreng, 'we have already battled for four bloody days. Resistance has meant — and will mean — further destruction. We fought well, but we have lost too many men. This country is full of trouble and our best road is to find an accommodation. We both have rights here. But our own rights do not mean that we can deny others theirs in favour of our own and expect peace. We have already found disaster and terrible loss following that course.

'The council has decided,' said Semne. 'What are you suggesting?'

'That we offer to fight the Tuatha de Danann with reduced forces of three hundred on either side to settle the issue once and for all.'

That was agreed to.

Sreng led his three hundred men in a fierce assault against the people's battle-hedge and was repulsed with great loss. Seeing that he could not persevere and anxious to do the best he could by his own people, he stood out and again raised his shield:

'Bualim sciath!' The cry rang out over the exhausted plain. 'I strike my shield!'

'Against whom do you strike it?' cried a voice from our lines. 'Nuada!'

In spite of his terrible wound, Nuada came out from the fort and faced Sreng bravely and boldly.

'If you want single combat on fair terms then fasten your right hand behind you since I have lost mine,' he demanded.

'If you have lost your hand', replied Sreng, 'that puts me under no obligation. Our first combat was on equal terms. And we each made our own decision to fight.'

Nuada summoned the war council and, having consulted with them, again approached Sreng, this time with a more limited offer.

This was his choice of the provinces of Ierne, of which there were five — being the centre, which the Firbolg already held, the north, which was largely held by the Fomorians and which would have meant battle for the Firbolg with them, the two Munsters in the south, which were wild, uncultivated territories inhabited by semi-barbaric emigrants, Leinster, which was largely controlled by the Bretani, or Connacht which the people ruled and which was the royal province.

Sreng choose the royal province of Connacht and there was a treaty of peace and friendship between his Firbolg and the people from that out.

The people, led by the maimed Nuada, retired to Eochaidh's palace at Tara while Sreng and the Firbolg took possession of Connacht. When we reached our new courts we were amazed at the ancient magnificence with which we were surrounded, and I will tell you more about it shortly. But first there was the question of the new king, for Nuada could no longer reign, having a blemish — the loss of his arm — which rendered him unfit. The obvious choice was the Dagda, but no sooner was this voiced than complications developed.

Part III
WOMB OF KINGS

The Firbolg's choice of Connacht (so called because a great wizard called Conn who once lived there had, on an occasion when it suited him, raised bleak storm clouds in midsummer and covered the land — but nowhere else — with sneachta or snow, so that it has been called Conn's sneachta, or Connacht, ever since) had not prepared us for the magnificence, the richness and prosperity in and around what was to become Tara. The place itself, where the chiefs assembled, was remarkable. A tremendous banquet hall, over a thousand paces long and fifty wide with fourteen doors on it and able to seat more than three thousand people, stretched outwards from the king's palace. The palace and other royal buildings stood close to one of two circular citadels, one larger than the other, containing the halls and castles of nobles, kings, lords and warriors. Beyond were the homes, huts and houses, shops and markets, of a large community who now became our responsibility. We renamed it the Crimson City, Cathair Cró Fhind, rather than Druim Cáin (the Excellent Height) as the Firbolg called it. It was not for many years, after we had built and assembled it into a great city that it came to be called Teamhair or Tara, by the Milesians.

Close by were other places of great importance. Uisneach, that I have already mentioned, where Mead had lit the sacred fires for Nemed many years before; a place which became known epony-mously for the festival of Samhain as Tlachtga and, further north, another which I, myself was to be partly responsible for naming many years later. But greater and far more mysterious than any of them, a place of wonder and mystery so potent that it permeated the very air about it, was Brugh na Boinne, Newgrange, whose awesome monuments had stood upon the plain since they were fashioned by gods when they walked the earth. And this I do believe.

We had never seen – never envisaged – anything of the kind, either in our own travels or what we had heard of those of our fathers. Three huge, awesome, white and solemn hills rise from the plain beside a broad river. They form a triangle a thousand paces or so apart and were made by the ancient gods, of that there can be no doubt. Here is no mere scratching and painting on the walls of a cave. Each hill is covered in shining white quartz which glistens by night and day with countless points of light, and can hurt the eyes in bright sunshine. Around the base of each hill – and they are a hun-dred paces across – mighty boulders, taller than a man and sunk in the ground, stand shoulder to shoulder to retain the white mounds. But it is what lies within that is most wonderful. A stone-flanked entrance gives access into each shining hill and a dark passage leads to the inner womb. Above the entrance is an aperture, hardly a hand-width high and about a cubit long. True and straight, through the aperture, when it rises on the very morning of mid-winter when it is nearest to death and at no other time, the life-giving bar of the sun probes and penetrates to the very depths of the womb at the end of the long, stone-flanked passage, to illumine and fertilise again the swollen belly of the world for the forthcoming year. Carved in the rock, where that shaft of light first strikes, is the mysterious symbol of the five-fold circle of life, and on many of the slabs that wall and roof this earthy vaginal passage are similar mystic carvings. Thus did the old gods guarantee fertility in the world and ensure the survival of men and the continued holiness of Ierne, the western island. And, in their bizarre and enigmatic fashion, in doing so they also bequeathed a formula for strife, not infrequently in their very name, which, as may be judged, can often convulse the people of this island.

I have had little to say about chariots until now and for good reason. Up to this time they were little used among us in Ierne for battle — although, of course, the people had used them in battle elsewhere for generations. But now they became important in two separate and singular ways, one of which has to do with Cathair Cró Fhind itself and the hill on which it stands. There is a fine plain on the hilltop bounded at one end by a tall pillar-stone, older than even Brugh na Boinne. It is the Cloch Gréine, the Stone of the Sun; the Member of the King of the World, and that ancient emblem is to the whitened belly of the earth beyond in Newgrange what the penis of a mortal king is to the warm and welcoming belly of his queen. In my time this hallowed pillar has come to be called as well the Liath Fail, the Stone of Destiny — although it is not the stone we brought with us across the ocean. But it has superseded that stone and is greater than it in that it is more powerful, more ancient and more befitting. I am satisfied that the transfer of supernatural authority from the one we brought (which was interred with great solemnity at the feet of the pillar-stone of Tara) was proper and accorded with the wishes and desires of the powers involved. That it could not be otherwise is obvious to anyone who has eyes to see and senses with which to inform himself.

Opposite the pillar-stone stand two other stones, Blocc and Bluicne. Between them and it runs the chariot-course of the king. And I must take a moment to elaborate on this before returning to my narrative. For what I am about to reveal is a great mystery which has but recently illuminated the spirit of the people and provided us with a focus for the mystic power that conjoins the minds of men and those of gods.

Blocc and Bluicne are flagstones, lying upon their long sides the length of a man. Normally they are so close that a man's hand can just fit sideways between them. But when a new king is born to the people they are opened, like the thighs of a woman in labour, and he in his chariot comes forth from between them to ride the course and wheel about the pillar-stone at the other end. If he does so correctly and if he is the true king the wheel-boss of his chariot will scrape the stone as he makes the turn and shriek, so that the people and the world will know that the king has been reborn and the heavens have accepted the mystery. Thus, just as the Member of the King of the World superseded our first Stone of Destiny, the ritual of rebirth for king-priests at Tara was to supersede the ceremony I described earlier when Nuada was inaugurated. And I will have more to say about it before I have finished. The ceremony of a king was maintained for inaugurations elsewhere than at the mysterious and holy centre.

Lugh was still a boy, barely twelve, at the time of the battle with the Firbolg. He was distressed and angry at not being allowed to participate, which my mother, Sena'an, expressly forbade. It is an extraordinary thing, but she lavished more indulgence on him, her foster-son who was not of her blood, than she ever did on her own children. This was about the only significant time I ever remember her thwarting his wishes. What is interesting is that she did so, as she saw it, for his own safety (although several boys about his age were present, though they did not take part in the actual fighting) and that his resentment was an indicator of future events.

It was some time before the leaders of the people were able to assemble at Tara. When they did the most urgent matter was that of the kingship.

The meeting to decide the question was held in the Central Hall, which was the only one of the major buildings then standing (apart, that is, from the great banquet hall), within the seven-fold ramparts. The other buildings were built or begun — for example, the Assembly Hall of Ulster which I, myself, have designed and laid out — later on.

Four hundred lords, kings, ollamhs, druids and seers of both sexes, of the noble families of the people were there — two for approximately every three hundred persons — more than might normally assemble for a preliminary examination. But this was no ordinary occasion. Nuada, his good arm resting on his knee, his cloak covering his right shoulder and severed arm, with Maeve beside him, sat where all could see him. He was flanked, as of old, by his retinue, but the Scythian bodyguard of the king remained outside. Everyone expected that he would seek to retain the kingship. We also knew, although there was a body of opinion which would have suspended the law in his favour, that it was impossible. For all my reservations and prejudices about him, he had, without doubt, given ample demonstration during his kingship that he possessed the three kingly virtues. He had been victorious beyond question; under his rule the land had prospered and been fruitful and the people healthy. And, until now, he had shown himself to be just.

Nuada himself opened the proceedings by striking the bells of the Slabhra Éisteachta, or Chain of Attention, with his white cló, or wand of office. Methger, who sat beside him, was of course the first to speak — even in those days the king was required to remain silent until the chief druid first broke that silence. Behind Nuada two trumpeters blew a triad of notes on their curved instruments and the hall went quiet as if an autumn wind had hurried through a beech-wood disturbing the trees and suddenly passed on, leaving the whispering and fallen leaves to rustle into a suspended silence.

'Nuada would address the assembly,' cried Methger.

'What is your pleasure, Lord?' he said, deliberately avoiding the word king.

'The kingship', replied Nuada, his soft voice compelling attention to that flat-planed face, 'is our business today.'

Without pause Ogma's voice was heard — perhaps a little too quickly.

'I nominate the most accomplished of us, the Dagda, to be king in Nuada's place.'

A disturbing pause followed. There was no seconder. Then, sharp as a whetted knife, Maeve's voice cut the atmosphere. 'There is no need for another nomination. Nuada will continue as king.'

This sudden introduction of the hidden issue seemed to take the hall by surprise. Then, very quietly, Fergus said:

'Nuada is not eligible — by law,' he added when he felt that Maeve was about to interrupt.

A murmur of assent rose from the assembly and I was sure she had lost her cause by introducing it so rudely.

'Nuada's blemish is no impediment,' began Maeve. But Methger caught her eye and even she was unable to face down the sardonic depths of his. His thin, twisted face turned to this side and that as he glanced about. He fingered the toe of his upturned right sandal with his left hand and it was clear that his fingers were talking, but too rapidly for me to read ... or, I believe, anyone except perhaps Ogma, who could not see. Methger was calculating. He leaned slightly forward against the spread of his knees on the covered cushions of hay.

'The law is clear. The king of the people must be free of all deformities or blemishes likely to impair his efficiency as leader, or', he went on, 'lessen the respect of the people for him.' He looked at Maeve as he spoke and she had the grace to blush. But she maintained her ground.

'Nuada's arm can be mended,' she said. This brought a gasp from the hall. I could not understand her clumsiness; not then!

'Remember Cian,' cried a voice, and I was grateful to whoever it was.

'Cian broke his geasa,' she snapped. 'But remember Nuada and what he has done for the people. Who brought us safely to Ierne? who made us prosperous? who led us against the Firbolg and defeated them and who gave us wise leadership? Will you throw all that aside ... and for what?' She turned towards the Dagda but did not look at him. 'For what I ask? Don't misunderstand me,' she harried. 'No one respects the Dagda more than me. But he is old. He could be Nuada's father.' A mutter of anger rippled the hall. The Dagda was held in very high regard and all knew what she was.

'Listen,' she said. 'Nuada has lost his hand. But Diancecht has preserved it in wine and special herbs. He will fit it back, make it whole again. Then Nuada will be without the blemish.'

A noisy clamour swept the hall. Through it I heard Diancecht asked if this was true. He tried to answer, but the noise made it impossible to hear him. Finally he unfolded his legs and stood up bringing silence when they recognised him.

'Is what she says true?'

The physician nodded. 'It's true. I have preserved the hand ...'

'And you can refit it?'

Diancecht looked out from under his heavy brows. He ran his tongue over his dry, thick lips before replying. Sweat ran down his forehead, beside his eyes and cheekbones and on the back of his neck.

'I ... think so.'

'Have you ever done the like before?'

The colour of Diancecht's face deepened. 'Not exactly ...'

'Why do you think you can do it now?'

The physician straightened. 'I am the greatest physician in the world. If anyone can do it, I can.'

'That does not mean you will succeed.'

'I will try.'

'If you don't? We must have a king. We can't wait.'

Maeve cut in quickly. It was remarkable, as if she had prearranged it. But I don't think so. She was just a great opportunist.

'Creidne, of all our goldsmiths the greatest and chiefest, will make a hand of silver for Nuada which will be as good, if not better than, one of flesh.' She looked about defiantly. Nuada gave her a warning glance. He, too, realised she wasn't doing him much good.

'An artificial arm?' asked Methger.

She stared at him.

'That will not do,' Methger continued. 'The king must be whole. He is the spouse of the goddess. He can have no impeding blemish. An artificial arm will not suffice.'

Maeve stood and threw her arms upwards in a violent and dramatic gesture so that the attention of the entire hall focused on her.

'Very well; very good! But if Diancecht *can* restore his arm do you want to run the risk of losing Nuada's leadership? Do you want that?'

'The Dagda will lead us well,' growled Ogma. She turned on him furiously.

'In spite of my respect for the Dagda I can see that he is old. What way will the goddess respond to an old spouse?'

Her question was harsh, but none could deny its relevance. When a virile young king marries the goddess, she is young and fair, fruitful and benevolent beyond description. But when he ages or is incapacitated she becomes a hag, the true Cailleach, bloated and obscene, with her barren pudendum, a hanging fright trailing among the long grass. Only with the death of the old king and the mystic birth of the new, is she herself renewed and bountifully rejuvenated.

'Is there another suitable candidate?' Several heads turned towards myself and I knew that someone was about to name me. But I had no desire to be a compromise candidate whose tenure could end in disaster, or worse, in disgrace. But Maeve again intervened.

'I have a suggestion', she went on, 'which will solve the dilemma. If we cannot wait to see if Diancecht's skill will work then something else is called for. But neither do we want to lose the benefit of Nuada's leadership if it does work. Yet if we elect another king that will happen?' She looked round. It was from what she said next that I understood her apparent clumsiness. Recalling the day in the grianaan when I told them about Barnea, I saw it was a plot. I believed that she had been coached and it was pretty clear to all — except perhaps Nuada — who it was that had coached her. But at the same time what she said appeared to offer a sound and practical solution. If her motivation was self-interest that — at the time — seemed to be merely an irrelevant bonus for her.

She went on: 'Perhaps the most important thing for us in the immediate future — besides doing what we are here for — is to improve our relations with the Fomorians.'

She was holding their attention.

'I have a proposal to make which will I think meet both requirements and, also, enable us to benefit from Nuada's leadership and continued kingship if Diancecht is successful.'

No one answered, then Methger said: 'What is your proposal, Maeve?'

'Simple! Let us make Bres regent. It will ensure good relations with the Fomorians, it will keep the kingship open and it will enable us to prosper and develop peacefully and fruitfully.'

A rumble ran through the hall like waves breaking in the hollow of a cave. It got louder and louder until Ogma, staring at Methger, crashed his fist on the table and shouted: 'And what will the goddess do without a king?'

'But', said Maeve sweetly, 'it is not a name the goddess is concerned with but a mate. So long as the kingship is inviolate she will not desert us or harm us. And we will have the kingship for the rightful king when the time comes. In the meantime we will have a regent and a mate for the goddess.'

'And you, you bitch,' I heard Ogma mutter and she must have heard, for she turned ice-cold eyes on him for an instant.

I could see that Nuada had been used in the plot, though he probably thought himself part of it. He stayed silent, without forcing himself to be. Obviously something had been arranged between himself, Maeve and Bres. Yet ... I thought I also detected a doubt in his eyes and a faint, but discernible frown above them which, perhaps, had less to do with his wife's proposal than with a dawning suspicion regarding her enthusiasm for it.

In any case, after much discussion, the suggestion was adopted, supported strongly, perhaps not surprisingly, by a majority of the women of the people, many of whom had lost their menfolk in the recent battle with the Firbolg. Thus began the worst seven years in the history of the people until that time, for if the goddess was stayed from harming the people by the attentions of her new spouse, he, most surely, was not similarly affected by any divine recognitions from her.

First I must tell you about Diancecht's attempt to restore Nuada's hand and what that resulted in.

The attempt did not work and caused Nuada great distress and discomfort. Finally it was abandoned and Creidne, Diancecht's foster-brother, a craftsman of unparalleled skill, was asked to make a silver hand as promised. This took a long time, but it was finished at last and fastened with straps on Nuada's forearm above the wrist. It was cleverly designed to fit over the stump, while the fingers were fixed in a flexed position so he could grasp certain objects. There was a flexible joint at the wrist so that he could set the hand in a number of different positions when it was fitted. Nuada was pleased, but there was no question of his resuming the kingship.

Meantime Bres had become regent and the matter of an alternative king appeared to have gone by default, even though it was through threat of superior force. Bres's relationship with Maeve continued, of course, and she was so successful in fooling Nuada that, although he must at last have guessed, it was by then too late for him to do anything effective without completely losing face.

One of Bres's first actions was to invite a Fomorian mission to Tara to negotiate a new treaty now that the Firbolg were no longer a threat. This move was in accordance with the reason for making him regent and no one raised any objection.

I witnessed little or nothing of what I am now going to tell you, for a very good reason. Neither Keth's family nor my own lived at Cathair Cró Fhind. Instead we moved further south and slightly east; here to this place we call the Black Pool, or Dubh-linn. Our rath stands in a valley above the river Life some miles upstream from a favourite place of mine — where I now sit in my royal pavilion, dictating this. This is the hillock overlooking the wicker ford of the river, Ath Cliath, from where I can see the sloping head of Ben Eadair across the wide bay to the north and, to the south, the high mountains of golden Wicklow. In the valley we built our rath or family home. It consisted of the main house, that is my own — for you must remember that I was of a higher order now than Keth — and those of my followers, which were built both inside and outside

250

the palisaded, circular rampart, and Keth's house which was also within the palisade. In all we numbered a community of about a hundred and fifty people, too small for a settlement but large enough to fend for ourselves. Naturally we visited what is now Tara and Usna and the other sacred places at Samhain and Bealtaine and as occasion demanded, but our own worship and propitiations were conducted more intimately at smaller and more personal shrines.

The effects of the Fomorian visit and the resulting treaty were not long making themselves felt. As I heard it the Fomorian mission arrived, four hundred strong — more like a war-party than emissaries. They visited themselves on Tara for the duration of the negotiations … Negotiations? There were no negotiations!

'They came on horseback, every man,' Ogma told me. 'All accoutred for battle, with shields and helmets and, besides their venomous spears, they carried toothed matana, or maces and warclubs, tuaga.'

They were dressed in the usual hairy skins and squinted with one eye in their customary and hideous fashion. Worst of all, having been welcomed and entertained for three days by the people, they then demanded an unheard-of tribute with the alternative of immediate war. This was a tax on every kneading trough; on every grindstone; on the baking flags for the bread. An annual payment of an ounce of gold for every man who could be stood on the Hill of Usna was also demanded and, if it were not forthcoming, the man in question would forfeit his nose. The first payments to be made immediately.

We were aghast at this news when we heard it: more so when we learned that it had been accepted.

'We had no choice,' said Ogma. 'In the face of the threat Nuada agreed, when Bres said that he would otherwise enforce it, with Fomorian help if necessary.'

'A plot,' said Keth, 'from the beginning.'

Ogma made no answer. There was no need. We were betrayed. I recalled the morning, months ago, when I had warned Nuada against Barnea and realised that even then Bres had been plotting to control the people. Events had helped to place us in his hands. I wondered

251

what might have happened if Nuada hadn't lost his arm. There seemed little doubt that some other disaster would have overtaken him and I inwardly flinched at the extraordinary passion which could make of such a once-loyal woman as Maeve so corrupt a slave and tool of destruction.

Some instinct, perhaps the inherited blood of the seer which my mother referred to from time to time, stirred in me and I persuaded my parents (though I could well have ordered them) to send Lugh with Ogma to the Dagda's rath near Brugh na Boinne, Newgrange, where for some reason I felt he would be better off than isolated here with us. A vaguer, nameless compulsion strengthened my purpose in this and it was curious to see that belief justified in due time.

For seven years the Fomorians bled us with their taxes. As each year went by more were added until they lived off us like the locusts of Egypt, leaving us stripped. They took gold, cattle, clothing, slaves; produce of all kinds; and the once-proud people were brought to their knees under the yoke of Bres, who ruled from Tara, with Maeve as his whore, and countless women — aye, and men — as his bed companions, willing or not.

There was no house in all Ierne not under tribute to the Fomorians and the people were stripped by Bres of all they possessed. Moreover he disgraced the people before the world by forbidding them the mystic and sacred resources of music and poetry, story-telling and riddles, feats of skill and competitiveness. Towards the end of his reign not a harper, or piper, not a trumpeter or musician of any kind was heard in the beleaguered land. The prohibition on music badly affected my father for no one now wanted harps or lutes. So corrupt and parsimonious was Bres that it has been said of him — and has been handed on from one to another, and the saying, I believe, will continue as an ultimate denunciation until the sun is dead — that the knives of his people were not greased by him nor did their breath smell of ale at his table. But at last his cupidity was instrumental in bringing about his deposition.

Finally, when the poet Cairbre visited the Royal Dun, he was shown into a cabin which was dark, had neither fire nor furniture nor bed in it, and he was given three small, dry cakes to eat and nothing else. Next day he made a satire against Bres which showed both the extent of popular feeling against him and the sentiments of the people in general at the ruin and destruction he was bringing them to.

Before that took place something else occurred which I must recount since it is of great importance in this telling. In spite of the fine silver hand Creidne had made for him, Nuada — now known as Nuada Airgead-lamh, or Nuada Silver-hand — continued ill and weak. He burned with an unremitting fever and a fearful stench surrounded him, which not even the finest and most expensive of scented oils could conceal. He was obviously dying by degrees. His eyes retreated into his skull and were rimmed with black; his cheeks were hollow and the once flat planes of his face were sunken. The skin itself was sickly, like the whiteness of a rotting thing that has been kept overlong in the damp and dark.

He still lived in the royal quarters at Tara and it was evident to those around him that Maeve was impatient to see him dead so she could have Bres for her own … a thing, I don't doubt, that did not feature in his plans. After the battle with the Firbolg, Miach, Diancecht's son, did not go to Tara but stayed in the west at Sliabh an Iarann where he devoted himself to study. Thereafter he travelled to Albion and to Europe and, so I believe, as far as the distant empire to study with the magi, before returning again to find his country and his people in the abject state I have described. Seeing what had happened he went to Tara to see Nuada and offer him the benefits of his skill.

When he arrived he was first taken to Nuada's steward or chief-of-staff, Giolla, who was called Suil Amhain or One-eye, because he had lost the other in the battle with the Firbolg. He was left with a festering socket which he kept covered with an eye-cap, not unlike the one that Balor had worn. But, while this was considered a misfortune and while the unpleasantness of it affected his character (for both of which reasons people avoided him when possible), he was not thought to be evil or malevolent since it was not his left eye which was affected.

253

When Miach explained his business Giolla said, 'If you are such a great physician, heal me.'

Accordingly, Miach cleaned the wound, disposed of the old and filthy eye cover and so successfully treated the afflicted steward that at the end of a week the suppuration had stopped and the pain was relieved. When the steward saw how improved he was he brought Miach to the dying Nuada.

Miach was horrified to see the once proud and haughty Nuada reduced to such helplessness, but he hid his feelings and examined him thoroughly.

'Well,' Nuada whispered when Miach was finished, 'what do you think?' He clearly expected Miach to say something vague, not tell him the truth which, he knew, was that he was dying.

'You are being poisoned,' said Miach.

The shock silenced Nuada. But Giolla responded.

'Rubbish,' he cried. 'What do you mean poisoned? Everything the king takes is tasted by a slave first. No slave has shown signs of poisoning.'

'He is poisoning himself', said Miach, 'in the same way that you were poisoning yourself.'

Giolla did not reply.

'What do you mean?' whispered Nuada.

'Nuada,' continued Miach, 'the silver hand must come off.'

Involuntarily Nuada clutched the hand, the visible symbol of his attempt to retain the kingship.

'That is what is poisoning you,' said Miach.

There was a perplexity in the look Nuada gave him — perhaps anxiety. He kept his hand firmly on the silver one as Miach took it again in both hands to examine it and began to unbuckle the straps.

The steward moved to the bedside.

'Let him see, Nuada. He has a great gift.'

'Diancecht, his father, bade me never to remove the hand or I would lose the kingship forever,' said Nuada.

'If you don't let me take it off', said Miach bluntly, 'you'll lose your life, and that will surely be forever. Now ...'

He unbuckled another strap.

'It's all right, Nuada,' said Giolla. 'He cured my eye ...' Nuada did not further resist, but his good hand remained resting on the silver one and he turned his wretched face away. When the straps were undone and Miach tried to draw the silver hand off, Nuada's fingers involuntarily clenched convulsively about it. But Giolla gently loosened them and with great difficulty Miach withdrew the silver arm bringing a gasp of pain from Nuada as he did so.

When it finally came away a dreadful stench filled the room and both Miach and Giolla were horrified to see the swollen, black and red oozing mass of flesh, a whitened bone protruding from it, that lay beneath. The agony must have been appalling. As it was, Nuada had passed into merciful unconsciousness before the stump finally cleared the silver socket of the fabricated hand.

Miach met Giolla's eyes above the recumbent chieftain and both knew what he was about to say.

'I must amputate.'

'What do you need?'

'Hot water. Herbs ... Is my sister Eremed here?' Giolla shook his head.

'Can you get her?'

'She can be here by morning.'

'Send for her.'

And so my wife was summoned to Nuada's bedside and, together with her gifted brother, she laboured to save his life, pouring all her knowledge of herbs into the most potent healing compost she could devise.

Meanwhile Miach severed the corruption from the arm at the elbow joint and applied a poultice of Eremed's herbs for three days to draw the poison from Nuada's veins. With extraordinary skill he left a flap of non-malignant skin below where he cut the arm. When the wound was clean and delicately cauterised, this flap was pulled across the wound and sewn into place with a fine needle made from a piece of Nuada's own bone and which, for some mysterious reason, Miach had first boiled and then dipped in new wine. By the end of a week

Nuada, although extremely weak, was clearly improving and at the end of two weeks was out of bed and on his feet.

When the stump was healed Miach had a padded leather socket made. This fitted comfortably and could easily be removed. It extended from the stump for about two hands' breadth and at the other end was a leather glove which looked very natural. Nuada could do very little with it, but it looked normal when seen from even quite close.

At this success Miach was revered and honoured by everyone – except three: Maeve, Nuada's wife, who never spoke to him and went about in a black cloud of continual anger; Bres, who hid his real feelings behind polite acknowledgement through which one could sense the frustration Miach had generated; and last, and worst, Diancecht, his father, whose mad jealousy brought a tragic sequel.

Diancecht had become more degenerate and was bloated and old looking. His matted hair was streaked with dirty grey. His clothing was as uncared for as his person. His little eyes were continually watery and were sunken within folds of red and choleric flesh. He breathed loudly through his mouth – and that with difficulty – so that one could hear him approaching even through the pillars and passageways of the Teach Micuarta, the huge banquet hall, before ever one saw his grotesque bulk. It was on such an occasion that the tragedy that next occurred happened. Miach was standing in a sunny spot within the hall, in the northern or contentious corridor (for, inasmuch as the north, Ulster, is the province of Battle, the approaches to that quarter are called after the qualities for which Ulster is distinguished, namely contentions, strifes, rough-places, haughtiness, pride, assaults, hardness, unprofitableness, wars and conflicts). Miach was talking to Giolla and another – a warrior whose name I do not know – when Diancecht was heard approaching. Knowing of the old man's injured pride Giolla took Miach by the arm to move him on and avoid the confrontation which had been threatening ever since Nuada had recovered at the expense of the silver hand, but Miach ignored him. He looked blankly at Giolla with that almost inimical expression – expressionlessly is perhaps a better way of putting it — and continued talking to the anonymous warrior. Diancecht came into the pool of sunlight, but did not, as Giolla feared, stop. He shuffled on towards the group, his eyes elsewhere, and it seemed as if he would go, peacefully, wherever it was he was going. But, as he passed the group in the confined space, he stumbled, deliberately or not who knows, and fell against both Miach and the strange warrior, who were sent reeling by his huge bulk. Diancecht neither stopped nor apologised but continued as if nothing had happened. The young warrior leaped to his feet, white with anger, and shouted after him: 'You ...' Then, realising who he was with, and that it was father and son, he quenched his anger, but could not resist converting it into contempt, which was worse.

'Never mind, Diancecht,' he cried, 'what is a push from the past from one-who-was?'

With speed, unbelievable for a man of his age and condition, Diancecht wheeled and ripped a sword from the wall. Before he could be stopped — and it would, I believe, have taken more than those three to halt his bulk — he charged with the upraised sword and with one brutal sweep, cut the throat of his brilliant and unarmed son. A fountain of blood spouted from above Miach's gold collar and drenched the sunlit corridor and everyone in it. When I heard I remembered the powerful magic that Miach had made against his father in the wine house in Spain so many years before and shuddered. I made the sign against the thought.

Miach was buried by Eremed who lovingly planted healing herbs, representing much of the skill and knowledge that she and her brother shared, one for every part of the body, on the grave mound. But Diancecht was so obsessed with hatred for his dead son that he came by night and scattered them and trampled on the site.

He was mad. Nothing else could explain the murder or the speed with which he had committed it, from which it was clear his body had become suddenly light as air. It was thought that the Fomorians had at some time made a dásachtach or madman of him by having a druid throw a dlee, or magic wisp of straw, in his face. He was tried by Nuada but, on account of his madness, no sentence was pronounced and, as it did not seem to greatly affect him except in hatred of his son, and since he was still the greatest physician among the people, it was felt that there was nothing further to be done. To whom would an eric, or honour price, be paid? Diancecht himself maintained he was a victim of his son's malignity and evil; that all his problems and afflictions had been caused maliciously by Miach who, now that he was dead, would trouble him no more. Things were left so. But Diancecht did not live that much longer himself.

Between one thing and another events began to move swiftly. The cloud – whether it was encouraged there or not – lifted from Nuada's eyes. He saw what was going on both in Tara and throughout the land and he took action. First he banished his wife, Maeve, who suddenly became an old woman clinging with pathetic despair to the crumpled vestiges of a once disdainful beauty. Then he assembled his Scythian guard and at their head marched to Bres's quarters and banished him. To give Bres credit, he left without protest when he saw such to be pointless.

Nuada was in doubt as to what to do about the Fomorian tax-gatherers, who were due. To refuse payment would surely bring a Fomorian invasion at once and – perhaps harkening back to the tactics at the first Battle of Moytura nearly seven years earlier – he was anxious to put this off as long as possible so as to give time to prepare. On the other hand if the people paid the tribute there would be nothing left with which to buy arms and men from the Bretani or from Gaul, and without the Gaetanae … But, before the tax-gatherers arrived at the Hill of Usna – which they had renamed Balor's Hill, because it was where the tribute was paid, and as another indication of their contempt for the people (for it was the troops of Balor who collected the taxes) – another and altogether more important visitor came there, this time from the east, from Brugh na Boinne, the Mansion of the Boyne, which is also mystically called the Roof of the World in Enduring Paradise. The newcomer was my foster-brother, Lugh Lamh Fada, or Lugh Long Hand, as Balor had named him. He had adapted well to the name. His skill and ability with the sling – either the teilm, the ordinary sling, or the crann-tabaill, the staff-sling — excelled even that of Ogma or myself, so that his name had grown with him, Long-Handed. I had seen him infrequently since he had gone to live with the Dagda, and I was taken by surprise by the young warrior who now approached. He was mounted on a magnificent horse that he rode with a pride no less than that of the prancing animal, which danced towards us on high-curled legs and with arched neck. He wore body armour and a great sword, which I afterwards learned was called Answerer, Freagartha. On his head a jewelled helmet glittered in the morning sun. The boy who'd cut my fishing line eight — or was it nine? — years ago and who had gone with me to Balor's camp and got named by his grandfather, was gone, and prancing into Nuada's assembly came instead a strong and haughty young warrior.

I ran to where he reined his horse and grasped the bridle. He looked down at me, smiling.

'Well, brother?'

'Well yourself,' I shouted, 'what happened to little Lugh who used to ride on my back?'

The smile on his face didn't change as he turned towards me and swung his leg over the saddle. Kicking the other free of the stirrup he slid down with his back to the animal and stood looking squarely into my face. The smile was still there as he began to speak, but it faded from his eyes a little before he finished.

'He's gone, brother, and the man who has replaced him has things to do.'

He greeted my father and mother who came up behind me and then turned to Nuada to whom he also paid his respects. Nuada, who was sitting on a cushion, raised one knee for him, and Lugh acknowledged the honour by bowing in return. Hardly had the civilities been exchanged when a murmur, like a groan, started among the people assembled on the hillside. We turned and there, far off on the plain, raising dust from the road westwards from where we stood, we saw a cavalcade approaching. At first, because of the dust, we could see only the head, a group of five or six horsemen. But as they came closer we could hear them and were able to pick out other riders and the carts they had brought, with slaves to drive them, in order to carry off the tribute.

When they came closer Nuada and all the people stood to greet them. Lugh watched in astonishment at this remarkable honour offered to the surly, unkempt Fomorians who rode up the hill.

It was clear he had never been at Usna for the tax-gathering before, which had been my intention in sending him to Brugh na Boinne.

'What's all this about?' he asked.

'Why does Nuada stand for these men ...?' he turned from me before he finished.

'Nuada,' he called, loudly, but not unduly so.

'Why do you stand for these savages, but not for me?'

Heads turned towards him, but his eyes remained on Nuada.

'It is the custom ...' began Nuada.

'A shameful one,' replied Lugh, as the first of the Fomorians, of whom there were eighty-one in all excluding slaves and retainers (a significant number, nine times nine), swaggered up and brushed past him to face Nuada. They had evidently not met Bres for they gave no indication that they knew what had happened.

'It is the custom', continued Nuada across the heads of the uncouth newcomers, 'because they have made it clear that if there was but a child of us even a month old sitting before them, they would consider it insult enough to slaughter us.'

The Fomorian heard what Nuada said, as he had been intended to do, and with a growl he turned towards Lugh to see who was being addressed.

'What is it to you?' snarled the Fomorian in his thick accent. Lugh did not answer him. Instead he continued to address Nuada. 'I swear', he said, 'I'll kill them.'

The Fomorian turned back again to Lugh, drawing his sword as he did so, but before it was clear of the man's scabbard, Answerer leaped into Lugh's hand and the Fomorian's head rolled at Nuada's feet. As the trunk swayed before falling, a thick gout of blood shot from its neck and spattered many of those standing nearby, including many of the Fomorians. They at once raised their own weapons, but before they could achieve anything, most of them were overwhelmed. The accumulated rage and frustration of the people exploded and many of the tax-gatherers were literally torn to pieces.

'Stop,' cried Lugh. 'Stop it!'

Nuada saw him trying to restore order and immediately commanded the trumpeters and horn-blowers near him to sound the cease-battle. Instantly the rising notes of the singular call blared from the stoccana, the trumpets and the cornera, the horns, with their deeper and more musical tone. Fifteen Fomorians were left alive when the slaughter ended and these were roughly hustled to where Nuada and Lugh stood in the centre of a small group of whom I was one. Without a word Lugh immediately slew six of the sullen prisoners, so that eight times nine were killed. The other nine were spared, but had their eyes put out with needles.

'You are spared', said Lugh, 'so that you may return to your masters and tell them what has happened here. The next Fomorians we see had best be armed for battle. Now go.'

War with the Fomoire was now inescapable. Nuada assumed the regency and — how strange is the application of justice — the fact of his blemish was overcome by the positive action he proceeded to take and the leadership he gave to the people. He immediately began to prepare for war.

After the blinded Fomorians had gone a meeting of the council, with all thirty-two leaders, including myself and, now, Lugh, met. Mead, who was still alive, though extremely ancient and feeble, counselled delay as he had done seven years before when we fought the Firbolg.

'How can we delay?' asked Nuada. 'They will be down on us like wolves.'

'You must send an ambassador,' said Mead. 'Seek time.'

'An ambassador would go to his death.'

'Perhaps so. Perhaps we all go to our deaths. But if we are to have any chance you need reinforcements and weapons.'

There was a heavy silence, before anyone spoke, and then several did so at once. Nuada held up his hand and struck the slabra estechta, the chain of attention, with his false hand.

'We can do nothing,' he said, 'unless we have order.'

'I realise I cannot be king,' he went on. 'But this is no time for dissention among ourselves. I am prepared to stand aside and hand over leadership. But leadership we must have.'

'The Dagda ...'

I think it was Fergus who started to speak, I'm not certain, for another silence swallowed the words. But they lay on us like a weight.

Nuada looked about him. 'If that is what you want ... I agree.'

'Wait!' Mead's cracked voice had authority.

'If you make the Dagda king, who will you send to the Fomorian?'

Several heads nodded in agreement. And it was hard to see who else could go with the remotest prospect of success. The Dagda could not be both king and ambassador.

It was finally agreed that Nuada would be regent until the Fomorian question was settled. The Dagda was to go to them as ambassador, principally to cause as much delay as possible, and I was to accompany him. There was no question of Lugh accompanying us this time.

It was high summer when we left the royal centre of Ireland for the Fomorian north-west, swiftly, on horseback, with a company of three fifties of men also mounted. They made a brave sight as they rode past the high walls of the city, Nuada, Lugh, Ogma and the other chiefs standing together on the ramparts of the outer barbican, watching. The Dagda and I sat our ponies beside the gate until the end of the mounted column had passed, each man wearing a sea-blue cloak, a helmet of bronze with nodding eagle feathers, his great, oval shield hung behind him by the sciathrach, or shield-strap, round his neck, and a long lance in his right hand, standing in a socket attached to the saddle.

As the last man passed us Nuada gave a signal and the trumpeters and horn-blowers sounded a salute of departure which followed us as we galloped to the head of our company.

It was a dull day, and heavy. The clouds were low and weighty, suffocating the world beneath, so that sweat ran from us and we became easily breathless. Nor was our departure without omen, although we could make no sense of it at the time. But, as we went by the last of the houses where the communal cattle pens separate the fringes of the city from the fields of vegetables and the hazel woods that stood between them and the wide corn-fields, I happened to glance along a mud path between the houses and the fields and saw a large black dog trying to mount a small white bitch. Several other dogs stood round panting eagerly. But when she heard the clatter of the horses and the jingle of harness the bitch took fright and ran from under the dog and away with her, all the others in pursuit. The black dog fell on his forelegs on the ground and, his strength having left him, they buckled under him. From this position he put up his head and howled. I could not help laughing and drawing the Dagda's attention to it and he laughed with me. But the image of the crest-fallen dog remained stubbornly in my mind until I came to believe it was an omen, but of what I did not know for many days.

The hot plain was covered with white and red clover flowers and creamh or wild garlic, which made the sultry air fragrant. As we rode across it, on the broad road from Cathair Cró Fhind, larks leaped at the clouds and sang shrilly to distract us from their nests and, in the distance, I saw two hares sparring and wondered what was wrong with them to be behaving so this late in the year. Moreover, we could not sleep that night for an owl hooting in the trees where we camped. But in the morning I saw against a clear, blue and yellow sky, an eagle circling aloft on motionless wings, and my confidence was restored.

Three nights later we reached the Fomorian stronghold. This time we were not met by any advance party and we rode into their settle-ment with the dominating citadel through menacing crowds of gathering savages. We — that is the Dagda and myself — dismounted before the narrow entrance and instructed the men to ride back and make camp by the river a mile downstream. It was our intention to join them later.

A silence as sullen as the evening was our only greeting from the hostile faces around the gateway and staring down from the walls. Stooping swiftly, the Dagda entered the tunnel-like gateway and I followed, momentarily blinded as his great bulk blocked the light from the other end. We emerged to face a semi-circle of menacing Fomorian warriors, of both sexes, painted and accoutred for battle, many of them standing, woefully, on one leg. In the centre were the Indoch Mac de Donnon, with Delbaeth to one side of him and an evil-visaged man I had not seen before on the other. Beside him stood Balor, glaring at us from his single malevolent eye. No one spoke as we straightened and greeted them. I saw the Dagda swiftly signal me with his fingers to do as he did. But I did more for, involuntarily, when I saw Balor, my own fingers shot out against the evil eye, and I think he noticed.

'Hail, Delbaeth, great king of the Fomoire, peace and prosperity and the favour of the elements be with you,' said the Dagda.

Delbaeth did not answer.

'I bring you greetings from Nuada,' said the Dagda.

Still no answer.

'We come in peace,' said the Dagda.

No one answered him, but, before he could speak again, the Fomorian leaders separated to make a clear space in which stood Bres, a sardonic smile on his lips, and the nine blinded emissaries who had been sent back by Lugh.

'Peace, Dagda?' enquired Bres with a sneer. 'Your notions of peace are strange to us.'

'I did not mean this ...' said the Dagda.

'I'm sure you did not,' replied Bres smoothly.

'I can explain ...'

'To be sure you can,' said Bres. 'Seventy-two of our men dead and you come in peace.'

'Our whole people enslaved and reduced to starvation,' cried the

Dagda, 'cruelty and degradation. What did you expect?'

'We expected you to live by your word and your treaties,' snapped Delbaeth.

'And had we not the right to expect the same from you?' The Dagda's voice was as angry and louder. He did not intend to give an inch, even if it cost him his life. I saw Balor turn to the evil-looking man beside him — whom I, correctly, took to be the third Fomorian king, Tethra — and exchange looks with him. Clearly they would kill him on the spot given the opportunity.

'You have killed and blinded our emissaries,' Delbaeth said. 'Is there any reason why we should not do the same to you?'

'You have that power,' said the Dagda. 'But hear me before you do. We do not come as tax-gatherers or as oppressors. We are here as heralds and representatives of the people`...' and he held aloft the sacred symbols of our office, the wand and the sword, and I did like-wise.

'You can kill us in revenge for what happened to your arrogant and tyrannical tax-enforcers, but if you do you will not perform an act which has justice, honour or honourableness. You will profane our sacred right and betray something far more important than our lives. If you wish to do this and behave like savages, who am I to pre-vent you?'

An angry murmur rose at this and for a moment I thought he had overplayed it. If there is one thing the Fomorians are particularly sen-sitive about it is any reflection on their barbarianism and they resent and bridle at any reference to it. 'Savages' touched them on the raw.

Delbaeth stared at the Dagda for a moment longer, anger mount-ing in his face too. Then with a jerk of his head for us to follow, he turned and stalked towards his great hall, which we remembered from our previous visit.

We were jostled and shoved as we followed, but the other leaders, including Bres, closed around us and we reached the door of the hall in safety, for which I was both surprised and deeply grateful.

Inside the hall was lit with rush lamps and torches fixed to the wooden pillars supporting the roof. A fire blazed in the centre of the hall and it was hot, smoky, stinking and uncomfortable compared with the lofty and airy palace we had left behind. I gagged with nausea as the stench enclosed me in its warm, clammy grasp. And my uneasiness must have shown because I was pushed, hard, in the back by someone who laughed as he did so. I stumbled into the Dagda and, only that he was so enormous, we might both have fallen. As it was a space was cleared for us facing Delbaeth's place, and we were ringed by several hundred of the chief men and women of the Fomoire.

'What is it you really want?' growled Delbaeth.

'An early death,' snarled Tethra, and then laughed which was generally taken up, for the Dagda, though still very active, was an old man. 'Peace,' replied the Dagda with dignity. 'We want peace. We can share this land between us ...'

Delbaeth cut him short.

'Don't try that,' he roared. 'You're not dealing with the Firbolg now. We were in this land before you, or them for that matter. It is for us to say if there will be peace or not.'

He leaned back and glared at the Dagda. Things were not going well and we had been there less than half an hour. I glanced at the Dagda and it was intercepted by Bres.

'The cub looks to his master,' he laughed, 'as always. Why did you not bring Ogma ...? Oh. I see. Of course! You were here before, and if the trappings of your 'sacred office' won't protect you, you're relying on hospitality. Shrewd enough.'

'What do you think should be done with them, Bres?' Indoch Mac de Donnon spoke. Apart from Bres he was the only other elegant figure in that barbaric gathering. He leaned against a carved pillar, beneath a torch, and observed things from under hooded eyes. But appearances were deceptive. I remembered the apple feat and how he had behaved towards his daughter when I defeated him.

'A good question,' replied Bres.

'String them up now,' snarled Tethra, 'by the feet, over the fire, and roast their brains.'

Balor nodded.

'Cut them,' he said, 'and let the women have them for sport.' I shuddered. I knew too well what the Fomorian women did for sport.

Delbaeth shook his head. 'No,' he said, 'we'll sleep on it. Let's think about it. Perhaps they will reveal something to us given time.'

'Meantime,' said Bres, 'the Dagda is famous for his harp playing and for his harp — indeed, if I'm not mistaken, it is one that was made by Cian's father. Right?'

I looked bleakly at him.

'What matter. We can have some entertainment from the Dagda while we wait … he can sing for his supper. His other accomplishment being one of his appetites. Truly phenomenal. Unlike the other which, alas, fell a victim to lies, and deceit and, was it guile? I'm sure he will entertain, and amuse, us.'

There was a wicked lilt to his voice which Delbaeth, his grandfather, caught. I recalled her nickname which, through her passion for Bres, the Dagda's wife had acquired and which Bres now provided, and I glanced at the Dagda. He was visibly restraining himself. Bres grinned maliciously.

'Very well,' said Delbaeth, 'you will play for us, Dagda, I'm sure, won't you?'

The Dagda looked at him for an instant. Then abruptly nodded. 'Good. And you have your harp with you? Good. It shall be fetched. In the meantime you may sit over yonder; beside the hostages,' he added menacingly. We knew well the danger was far from over.

While we waited for the harp to come from our escort's camp where Bres had sent for it, we discussed in whispers what we should do.

'We must delay as long as we can,' said the Dagda. Every day counts. Whatever else we do we must delay their killing us as long as possible.' I agreed wholeheartedly, but from more diverse reasons. That they intended to kill us was not in doubt in his mind.

That night was bad, and worse followed. When the harp was brought, the Dagda was forced to play tune after tune, composition after composition for hour upon hour. If he paused they threw weapons at his harp which he tried to protect with his enormous body, so that by the middle of the night he was wounded – but not severely – in several places and his clothing was ripped and torn so that flesh showed through.

At one stage he tried to trick them by playing a series of Suantraige, or sleep musics. But they are so uncouth that they have no tradition of being lulled to slumber by such sweet sounds and I was the only one affected. I was almost asleep when my head jerked awake, to catch the derisive sneer on Bres's face, who guessed the Dagda's purpose, and its futility. Nonetheless he played on, went from the sleep music to the Gan-traige, or merry music, and from that to the Gol-traige, the sorrowful music, and so round again, with expressive music of his own making as well. But it was all for nothing before these savage brutes.

Meanwhile I had been forced to dig a hole between the Dagda and myself and into it I had to pour slops from their tables; bones, vegetables, meat, porridge, all together, and the dregs of their tankards and drinking horns.

Towards the darkest part of the night, when the hole was full, Delbaeth cried: 'Well, Dagda. There you are. A feast for a king. Let us see you finish it ... all of it!'

We looked at him in disbelief. Delbaeth stared back grimly. 'Eat it,' he went on, 'for it is all you will get while you are here, and so it will remain until you do.'

With that he stood and left, followed by several of the other Fomorian leaders. As he passed us Bres raised one eyebrow in a grimace of whimsical tragedy and I could have killed him then with complete satisfaction. Our legs had been chained to one of the pillars near the hole I had dug, and we were left with a guard of half a dozen men who lounged among the tables by the fire, eating and drinking what their betters had not finished. After a while they fell asleep.

'We must escape,' I whispered.

'No,' growled the Dagda, and I knew hunger must already be gnawing him, for he was certainly a prodigious eater.

'We must stay as long as we can. But we need to drink.'

But we had none that night, nor for most of the next day. Not until we were taken out for natural reasons did the opportunity present itself. I simply and casually asked one of the guards for a drink of water from the well as we passed it and he unthinkingly stopped long enough for us to get it. That night was a repeat of the previous one — with the difference that I managed to conceal a crust and a couple of half-chewed bones with my leg, which we ate after the 'festivities' were over. These were somewhat enlivened from the far end of the hall by the torment of two men by some of the lesser Fomorian chiefs. As they had their backs to us and were surrounded by their tormentors, we could not see who they were.

For the next day, and the one after that, this continued unchanged except that we were not so lucky in getting either food or drink. The Dagda was so far gone that he scooped a bone from the pit at one stage and began to gnaw on it, but the instantaneous and contemptuous laughter from the king's table stopped him in disgust and he threw it back.

'The time will come,' laughed Delbaeth, 'when you will not despise the hospitality of our tables in that fashion.'

This brought further roars of laughter. But when they saw that the Dagda could not be further provoked, they began throwing knives and darts at his harp and he was forced to play for them again. Not that it made any difference to the savages for they didn't listen. But if he stopped they reacted immediately. We both knew that the danger increased as time passed and the novelty wore off. The other Fomorian leaders were under pressure from both Balor and Tethra to kill us and it was only the intervention of Bres with Delbaeth that prevented it.

On the fourth night, and for the first time since we arrived, I saw Matha, Indoch Mac de Donnon's daughter, again. She came into the banquet hall as the Dagda was playing, for the hundredth time since we had arrived, a beautiful lament into which, for some reason on this occasion, he poured his deepest feelings. Perhaps it was the infinite fingers of the goddess resting on his own as he plucked the harp-strings, who knows. But at all events the music gentled the hall and many of the savages seemed calmed by it. Matha approached the table where her father sat and leaned towards him, obviously to tell him something of interest to them both. With an impatient gesture and frown he brushed her away, indicating that she should not trouble him with — what would appear to be — trivialities at that time. She turned and, as she did so, her eye caught mine. I thought I caught a significance in the glance as it passed me by, before she went to a pillar on the other side of the fire and stood there until the Dagda had finished the lament. But try as I would I did not catch her eye again. She kept her head turned from me, almost, it seemed, deliberately.

Later, when stillness had fallen on the citadel, a movement behind me, close to the pillar, awakened me and as I sat up in alarm, a voice whispered, 'Quiet. It is me, Matha.'

'Matha!'

'I can help. You must get away. They will kill you. Perhaps in the night, tomorrow. All your men are dead.'

'What?'

'Did you not hear them being flayed at the other end of the hall these four nights? The others were killed in your camp.'

I said nothing. What could I? She was in great danger herself.

'You must get away. Now come with me.'

'We're chained. Have you anything …?'

I saw the tears start suddenly in her eyes. She shook her head.

'I am so stupid. I did not think …'

'No,' I whispered. 'Hush.' I was afraid she would wake the guards which would mean the end for all of us, Matha included. But she was far stronger than I gave her credit for.

'Why do you want to help us?' I asked. 'You are taking a great risk?' She smiled.

'You were kind to me,' she whispered. Her eyes moved to the sleeping bulk of the Dagda, 'and his music. It was so … so …' she broke off.

'Can you get us food … and drink?'

I looked towards the tables at the far end of the hall from the fire where the guards were sprawled. She nodded and glided away. In a moment she was back with a flagon of water and her skirt full of meat and bread.

'I will come again tomorrow night,' she whispered. 'I will have horses … weapons and something for the chains. You must get away…' Her eyes wandered to the Dagda, and I wondered.

'We'll be here,' I said wryly, 'if you are … if we're any place at all.'

She slipped into the shadows of the quiet hall and I waked the Dagda. I told him what had occurred. We filled our bellies and slaked our thirst quickly and scraped a hole in the floor and hid some of the food and water for the morrow. I thought the dreadful rumbling of his inordinate belly must surely waken and alarm the guards, but they slept on peacefully, as we both did until we were kicked awake ten hours or more later, in full daylight that filtered gloomily into the bedraggled building.

That night the atmosphere was somehow different. I could sense it and it was more violent and threatening. While the Dagda was playing and without preliminary, a knife suddenly flew past my ear and buried itself in the post behind me. The Dagda immediately stopped and I gaped at the knife that had missed my throat. But instead of laughter an ugly growl came from the watching Fomorians. The Dagda nodded and immediately resumed playing. But his music was drowned by shouts and noise which Delbaeth made no effort to stop and, when I looked, I saw Bres's gaze fixed unblinkingly and unfeelingly on me. He gave no sign of recognition.

Suddenly Balor stood up — they do not, of course, observe the courtesy of the Slabra estechta here — and shouted for attention.

'Delbaeth, there has been enough play-acting. Seventy-two of my men are dead in Ireland. These —' he looked at us '— feathers-in-the-wind are alive long enough. Our armies and fleets are ready. Let them sail from the islands and march through the country and rid us of these Tuatha de Danann. And', he roared, 'let these two be the first to die.'

Before he finished he was striding towards us, his one eye glittering in the flickering light, and his arm outstretched for a weapon. Someone handed him a club that he raised as he came on towards us.

A murmur of approval accompanied him. He stopped in front of me and, strangely, what I remember most of that moment is his smell. I know he raised the club to crush my skull. I looked up and he towered over me. The Dagda's shout froze him in that position and sounded loudly above the tumult.

'No! If we must die, let us die a proper death. We may not have many rights. But are you so — so —' I could see him swallowing the word savage that thrust behind his teeth, '— so unfeeling as to deny us the privilege to die with the moon as the goddess comes into her own? Here we are, chained, helpless! What glory is there in killing us like dogs?'

Balor still stood with the club raised and I realised my life hung on what happened next.

'Bres!' called the Dagda, 'Delbaeth, king of the Fomoire, will you deny us the privilege of a sanctified death? I expected more of you.'

Surprisingly he looked not at Bres but at Delbaeth as he said this.

Slowly the king nodded. 'Let them be, Balor. Tomorrow they will die. Ritually,' he added significantly, 'when the sun dies tomorrow, if that is what they prefer.'

Balor looked at me and at the Dagda. A smile gathered his lips. He lowered the club and mockingly brushed its stone face against my head.

'Ha! Very well,' he replied. 'Believe me, you will wish it had been here and now.' Turning he faced down the banquet hall and shouted. 'And when that is done the fleets will sail and the armies will march and you will find and destroy the Tuatha de Danann and this murderer they call Lugh, the Il Dana' — a name I'll explain later — 'and when that is done,' he went on rousing them with his passion, 'let you tie cables to the island of Ierne which has given us so much trouble, and tow it far to the north of Lochlann letting the ocean fill its place and leave it there in the cold abyss where none of the Tuatha de Danann will follow or find it.' These exotic words were greeted with a tremendous roar and he swaggered back to his seat with the air of a man who has achieved a great purpose.

Under cover of the noise the Dagda whispered, 'If your friend doesn't turn up tonight our goose is cooked — and I mean cooked.'

But she did.

This time we were both awake: had been for hours, afraid she might not come. As the minutes passed the fear grew, and it lay heavy in my stomach. Then I saw a shadow slip across the hall near the door and next moment she was whispering in my ear.

'Are you all right?'

'Yes. Have you something to force the locks?'

She slipped into my hand a rod of iron, the kind which can be beaten into a blade. In a moment I had levered the locks open and we were free.

'Quick,' she whispered, 'but be quiet.'

The guards, as usual, were asleep near the fire. They felt quite secure. The roaming dogs, half-savage like their masters, were our main worry. We had to rely on Matha in case of trouble there. Those in the hall, like the sentries, slept. We crept over the filthy floor, keeping low and in the shadows, trying to make as little noise as possible in the scattered rushes. We reached the door without trouble. We stood with our backs to the wall while Matha looked out, only to duck back quickly.

'Someone's coming.'

With one hand, the Dagda moved her effortlessly aside, and peered out. Timing it perfectly he opened the door as the man was within a pace of it, took him by the throat with the other massive hand and lifted him into the air while he gestured to us with his free hand to come out and slip past. When he lowered the body to the ground and followed us, it was a lifeless corpse with a broken neck.

Matha had horses, weapons and food waiting outside the citadel. To reach them we had to negotiate the compound, the huge wall itself and the sprawling hillside settlement outside. Fortune and the goddess favoured us, for the same thick blanket of cloud that hung over us when we started our journey north over a week before hung again between the world and the night sky, so there was no moon. We crossed the compound, from shadow to shadow, following

Matha who led us to a narrow flight of stone steps leading to the ramparts. In a moment we climbed them, crossed the narrow platform, were over the wall and down the sloping outer wall on the blind side of the settlement. Below, a ditch circled the citadel and we had to clamber across it and up the far side. A heavy dew had fallen and our legs were soaked by the time we reached the top. We reached the oak-spinney where Matha had the horses tethered. I was surprised to see three of them. But I immediately realised that she had to come with us or die. We walked the horses through the spinney before mounting and circled east before turning south. We laid up during the day in a cave in a country full of lakes, and it was there that the significance of the omens became clear to me.

I woke before it was dark and went outside while the Dagda and Matha were still sleeping. I saw the clouds darken in the east. Large raindrops smacked and shook the leaves on the trees around me and loudly spattered the grass and boulders. When I raised my face they hit it with considerable force, and they were warm. Thunder troubled the clouds somewhere and a sundered one bellowed and emptied its belly, and darkness hurried on. I turned back into the cave.

As I stood in the entrance lightning flickered behind me and was followed by a sharp cry from the back of the cave. Another brighter flash lit the interior with a simultaneous crash of thunder overhead. In the sudden light I saw a naked Matha shoot from under the similarly naked bulk of the Dagda, and then darkness covered them again. I remembered the dogs we had seen when setting out, and the soaring eagle in the sun, and I smiled, content. Before we resumed our journey we ate the meat and bread Matha had brought. Then we rode through the rain and the night. By morning the rain had stopped. But the world was grey and dripping when we first saw the towers and ramparts of the Crimson City.

A great deal had happened during our absence, though we were away in all for less than two weeks. Some of the first things we saw for example when we entered the turreted gate of Rath Ri, turned right and then left to traverse the double wall, were the frames and wheels of four chariots in front of the king's rath, resting on their rear shafts, the four long, holly poles with dangling yokes attached, pointing to the far horizon. As yet the wicker sides and floors had not been lashed into place. But they were a reassuring surprise and we were impressed to see iron clamps on the protruding ends of the axle to take saw and scythe blades so that they would become carpat serdanna, or scythed battle chariots. The wheels were beautiful. Masterpieces, almost fit in themselves to be roe-rawachs or wheels of divination and symbols of the sun. They were of ash and beech, with types of fine-drawn iron. No wheel was higher than a man's shoulder or thicker at the rim than two fingers, and they turned on well-fitting wheel bosses, fixed on the holly axles by a pair of oaken wheel-pins. Some had six, some eight, spokes, which were fine and straight and were fashioned from the sprung branches of the mysterious rowan.

Later we learned that Keth, my father, was responsible and that, with Lugh, he had persuaded Nuada that they were a necessary weapon of decisive quality in the war with the Fomorians, which he could produce. For the second time the gentle Keth had made a suggestion about war which was to be of vast importance to us. Curiously, in doing so, and in applying his skill in instrument making to making chariots, he advanced a degree in the community, for the chariot artificer, as you know, is of a higher order than the instrument maker. But not so high that Sena'an could sit in the banquet hall. For that she had to wait.

We were at once brought to Nuada and a hastily-assembled council meeting to which we recounted everything that had happened. Matha was made welcome and accepted as a member of the Dagda's household. Indeed, it would have been a cause of more problems if anyone had suggested anything else. But, in due time, because of what happened to the Dagda and the attitude of his termagent

275

wife, she was brought under the protection of the ageing Ogma.

'They will have marched already,' the Dagda told the Council. 'They were preparing to do so as we left. But where, and when, they will first strike I have no idea. If they march directly on us here we have, at best, perhaps four weeks. If they strike in the west it might be anytime.'

'We are not ready,' Nuada mused aloud, 'but we are almost as ready as we will ever be. You saw the chariots?'

'Magnificent.'

'More are in the making. We hope to have nine chariots ... We may thank Keth for them, and Lugh. They will be worth a battalion!'

'If they are ready. What about ponies? Charioteers?'

'Ready and training,' Nuada sounded confident. 'We have been training almost since you left. Thirty ponies are already broken and paired, with more to come, and charioteers are training under our best informed old horse-handlers.'

Later, when we had rested, I heard the full story from Lugh, who spared a moment to eat a bite with me. He was gnawing a venison bone when I asked him. 'After you left with the Dagda,' he mumbled, his attention on the bone, 'I went to pay my respects to our parents.' He paused to rip some meat from the bone, and I don't blame him for it was that time of year when the venison is at its best, with a little fat to give it flavour.

'By the way,' he went on, 'I am going to marry Naas.'

I was about to ask 'Naas who?' when I realised he meant my sister. The idea seemed preposterous. She was still a child ... or ...? I looked at him again and remembered my sister and the subtle change of womanhood that had crept, almost stealthily, over her in the last year, and smiled. He smiled back, and we left it at that for then.

'Keth was fashioning the neck of a harp when I arrived,' he went on, 'curved and delicate and beautiful ...' he mused.

'He is a remarkable man ... I was lucky ... Anyway, without stopping, he said to me, "What we need, Lugh, are chariots." But I was short with him.

' "Where are we going to get them?" I asked. Do you know what he said?'

I thought of Keth, shaving the neck of the harp fine and finer with controlled strokes of a spokeshave, and I smiled again. 'I can guess.'

' "I'll make them," he said. And that was it. We discussed it for the next hour and then went to Nuada. Within another hour a hundred craftsmen were under the direction of your father and a further three hundred or so selecting and rough cutting suitable timber. It was fast dried in pits like cooking pits. They may not be the best chariots in the world, but they'll do us ... and they're all we've got.'

The wheels of course were the problem, but, harnessing all the accumulated skill he brought to bear on the manufacture of harps and lutes, my father made, in all, thirty-six pairs of wheels, four sets for each chariot. Except for the iron tyres and the rough cutting, he did all the work himself.

When I saw him later that day he was working on the ninth pair. He looked tired, but in full command. The remaining chariots were made during the next weeks, fitted with their wheels, and all nine were then equipped with their wicker floors and sides. The pole — the sithbe sheeva — of each was fitted a long, toothed blade projecting ahead. To the twin shafts at the rear were fixed out-curving hooks with deadly points and nails, and sharp projections of iron and bronze were fitted at various points on the frame to do as much harm and damage to an enemy as possible. But the deadly, flying scythes and saws which would be fixed to each end of the axle were not fitted. They were stored in the body of each battle-chariot for use only as they charged the enemy ranks. But, in spite of the Dagda's predictions and our hurried preparations, five weeks were to pass before we had further news of the Fomorians.

A mugh or slave staggered into the Crimson City on a broken-winded pony at the end of September with our first news of the

Fomorian invasion. Like the animal beneath him, he was half dead from wounds and fatigue when he arrived and was ready to collapse. He was brought first before Nuada and the Dagda by two of the Scythian bodyguard and thrown on the woven carpet before them.

'Well?' Methger standing behind Nuada snapped.

'The savages, Lord. . . .'

'What savages?'

'Ollvooraigh do hyaght . . . the Fomorians . . . have come . . .'

'Where? Where are you from?'

'Eas-Dara.'

The Dagda leaped to his feet. Eas Dara, Ballysodare, was the territory of one of his favourite sons, Bodbh Dearg, Bove of the Red.

'And the king?'

'Safe, lord. He withdrew to the mountain with a full battalion of three thousand and many of his people; but the savages have made great slaughter and killing. They burn all before them.'

'How many?' snapped Nuada.

'Legions. They are countless.'

'What direction?'

'They seem to move south and east.'

'How fast?'

'Slowly, Lord, or I wouldn't be here.'

Nuada gestured to the Scythians. 'Take him away. He may have a quick death.'

'Lord . . . mercy, Lord.' The Dagda held up a hand.

'It is my son's land. He is my son's slave. I claim the right to deal with him.'

Nuada was indifferent. 'If you wish. I thought the wretch deserved a quick death for coming even if his news was bad. But do what you like.'

'Take him to my dun,' said the Dagda, 'and let him be fed from my Cauldron. Thanks to him we know where to march. Then let his slave's halter be broken off and let him be raised to the level of a saer-fudir, a free-bondsman.'

Nuada looked at him as if he had lost his senses.

'You will not kill the slave who brought us bad news?' he asked. 'You feed him from the Cauldron of the Dagda?'

'I do!'

'Then on your own head be it.'

That night the council decided that the army, now swelled with a welcome battalion of Gaetanae and another of Bretani from Albion, would march the following night that they might be favoured by the protection of the goddess. And that was done.

It took our army four weeks to reach the eastern shores of Lough Arrow, north-east of where the battle with the Firbolg had taken place seven years before. And it is an interesting and mysterious fact that seven years, twenty-eight quarters, of twenty-seven plus one, the mystic number, passed between what came to be called the First and Second Battles of Moytura.

On the journey we received reports of the depredations of the Fomoire, who for the moment, seemed content to stay where they were and not advance towards us. The council could not decide if this was because they were unable to control their troops, who were satisfied pillaging and looting within a day's march of where they landed, or whether it was a deliberate tactic to draw us to them, tiring us and forcing us to fight on ground of their choosing. We heard nothing to give us a clue to the truth and neither the Dagda nor myself could help. We both knew, if it were a question of Balor's troops only, that it might well be a deliberate tactic since he had the will and the power to control them. But the same could not be said of the undisciplined horde that went under the banners of the other leaders. Accordingly we decided to be safe and made a secure camp on the shores of Lough Arrow where we consolidated, made final preparations for battle and reconnoitred the area.

It was during this period that one of the worst acts of the invaders, with its awful consequences, came home to us in a very personal manner. One of our scouting parties discovered the tortured remains of some people, men, women and children, in a nearby forest glade. All, except two, were of Bove of the Red's people, and were mostly merely slaves. Nevertheless they were surprisingly distressed and, I admit, it was a heart-breaking sight to see the scarlet bodies of young children hanging from trees by their own skin, stripped off the living flesh. What they had done to the women was indescribable. It was clear that it was Fomorian women who had carried out the torture, probably for the benefit of a watching audience of their men. But among the victims were two who were known to all of us, although we were able to recognise them only from their personal jewellery which, of course, the Fomoire would not take for fear of their spirits. Both their heads were gone, presumably to adorn Fomorian door-posts. Otherwise what had been done to Barnea and Creda, Nuada's champion, defies description. We buried them and, as was their due, gave to one a pillar stone and to the other a burial mound.

Barnea had defected, shortly after the Dagda and I had left, to follow his mentor and — by then — lover, Bres. Creda had been reported missing only a short while before his body was found. All our efforts to reconstruct what had happened were inconclusive and to this day I can only guess that Creda stumbled on what was happening to Bove's people, intervened like the champion he was and that, for some reason, Barnea was there without Bres and became involved too. Perhaps Creda recognised and identified him; perhaps he had already been abandoned by Bres; perhaps, as seems most likely, he had never found him and was captured by this band of Fomoire together with the others. We will never know. But, for all that he was a traitor, he was a nobleman and we buried him accordingly.

What was more to the point, our troops were deeply excited by these murders and Nuada and the other leaders, myself included, had to impress on them, very forcibly, that prisoners must be brought to us alive and any man failing in this would die himself. That night one of our patrols brought in three Fomorian prisoners, wounded and beaten, but alive. Their leader had a massive and crooked shoulder, which caused him to stoop towards the ground with one long arm, adding to his already evil and forbidding appearance. The immediate reaction of all those who saw him was to make the sign against the evil eye, and spit. In his twisted way he looked sideways and slightly upwards — for his disfigurement thrust one shoulder up and the warped one down — at all those around when he was escorted into the flickering light of the great battle-camp. His name was Firmly Bent, or Crom Cruach.

He was brought before the council, together with his companions, and from what they eventually told us it was decided to face the Fomorian hosts in battle after two nights had passed, on Samhain Eve. When the interrogation was over they were nearer dead than alive, but, nevertheless, a ceannmilidh or battalion commander asked Nuada what was to happen to them.

'Let them be killed,' he replied.

'The troops want them,' said the commander.

'What for?'

'It will be Samhain', he said, 'and we must celebrate. We cannot do it as we should like. We have none of the appropriate offerings with us. But we must do something, for the goddess and for ourselves and for the outcome of the battle.'

Nuada said nothing. He looked at the commander and nodded, and I believe that he knew, even then, what was to follow.

Next night, the day before Samhain Eve, the appropriate feast of little Samhain was celebrated but without the customary offerings of harvest and with a new and terrible difference. I was unaware of what was being planned until, like the others, I assembled for the ceremonies. At one end of the camp where a temporary sacred circle had been established, I saw that the usual wicker figure had been constructed, but it was very much larger than any I had ever seen before. I could not understand this as it seemed pointless, since we had nothing to put in a normal-sized mannikin, much less this outsize one.

'What's the idea?' I asked Co-en who was beside me, nervous faced with the prospect of his first battle. He didn't answer, but shrugged.

From the other side Dara's voice, hard-edged, said: 'Look!'

I followed his eyes which remained on the distant figure we were approaching, but could still see nothing.

'What?'

He nodded ahead, his face set and eyes still fixed. Again I looked and then, in horror, I saw something I shall never forget. Within the outsize headless wicker figure I discerned a movement. Then, my eyes adjusted, I realised I was looking at people, three of them, locked within the grotesque effigy of themselves which was to be their coffin. Soldiers were piling underbrush about the monstrous feet of the wicker man. I turned to Dara. 'My great goddess, they can't do this. It's blasphemy!'

'Try telling them ... or, better still, don't! Not if you don't want to join them.'

'But they can't ...'

'They can! They are!'

'Nuada must stop it.'

'Nuada will not stop it.' He turned to me. 'Nuada must win a battle with these troops tomorrow. He will not stop it.'

'But he must. Someone must.'

'Who?'

Frantically I thought. 'The Dagda ...' Dara looked at me. 'Lugh ...' I saw coldness, hurt, betrayal, but above all a kind of despair, in his eyes. He shook his head. He turned away to look at what was happening.

'No one will stop it, Cian,' he said. 'No one can stop it. And we must remember,' he turned his eyes to mine again and held them, 'it may be the will of the goddess.'

The tone of contempt with which he spoke these words shook me and I lifted my hand to make the sign, but something in his expression halted me and I paused, dropping my hand again in confusion. But wishing I hadn't, and yet ashamed to do so then.

The rest you know. How the custom originated then and has grown ever since to supplant the tradition we knew and revered so long. I can only hope and pray that it will not last. I believe it to be an abomination and an affront to the goddess and nothing anyone can say will convince me that she willed it, whatever Dara might think.

We heard the screams of the unfortunate creatures within as the flames roared upwards through the wickerwork and one could see a single black figure clinging to the crumbling framework even as it was itself consumed by fire, before the fingers slipped and it fell. Although there was cheering and savage rejoicing while this was going on, the excitement quickly faded afterwards and the troops were herded back to their quarters to prepare for the battle next day. Weapons' sharpening and ritual cleansing and greasing, liming and polishing, occupied a goodly part of the evening and then the men slept. I heard Dara in the night in a corner of our shelter muttering the rituals he had learned from his grandparents and swaying back and forth as he prayed to his god. May he assist us too, I asked, if he has the power. I had no fear that the goddess would be jealous of my simple request, for the enemy we faced was terrible and formidable, and we needed all the help we could get.

The first real skirmish occurred next day and in it I lost one who had been — if not close — very much an influence at significant times in my life. One of our companies was patrolling the northern end of the lough when it was attacked by a reinforced company of Fomorian cichloiste, women warriors and archers. Our men fought — not seriously at first until several of them were killed, then with increasing desperation. They were outnumbered and out-ranged. Luckily they included five Balearic slingers who managed to keep the archers busy as the main body of the troops worked to outflank and gain height on the enemy, who were held in front by one fifty of the company which charged the enemy repeatedly, and withdrew before becoming locked in combat. Then the other two fifties turned the Fomorian flank and the battle closed and ended with a rout. Fourteen of their warriors, all women, were captured. The leader of the people in that engagement was Oran who, in fact, was a battalion commander, but had gone with one of his companies that day to see for himself. You will recall his proud nature!

While they waited for their stragglers and advance scouts to return, they held the women in the nearby and abandoned house of a bo-aire, farmer, who, with his family, had fled or been murdered. The women were locked in the barn, directly opposite the dwelling house which Oran used as his command post. They were fierce and unruly and he was uncertain whether to bring them all back with him or not. To help him decide he went to interrogate them himself, first separating them into two groups. The larger, consisting of the more experienced and harder-looking warriors, he had taken to another building, the calf house. That left five in the barn. Leaving six of his men on guard outside he went in alone. It was gloomy inside and the women were grouped together near one of the roof poles, glaring hostilely at him. He walked to the middle of the barn and stood for a moment looking at them with his hands on his hips. I can see it clearly, although I only have a description from one of the guards who peered through the window, and told me what had happened before his execution.

Oran questioned them, but got only spits and jeers for answers. The guard told it to me like this:

'Then he turned away, sir, with his back to 'um like and walked a few steps. I couldn't see clear what them wimmin was doing, but they seemed to be whispering among theirselves. Then one of 'um — a young one she was — stepped forward a bit, and he must have heard her in the straw 'cos he turned. And there she was. I could see 'er plain. Smiling at 'im. She was holding out her hand to 'im, I could see that, saying something. No, sir, I couldn't hear. But she come on and I seen him reach for his water-bottle. She come right up to 'im then, sir, still smilin' ... you know — like they do when they're going to give it to you an' at the same time want something for it. I knew that wouldn't make no difference to him, sir, knowing 'im like, but she tried it on. Putting 'er 'and up to 'is face. But he just took it with his right hand, sir, gentle like, but firm, and 'eld out the water-bottle with the other ... and ... and, by the goddess, sir, that's when it 'appened. With 'er other 'and she buried a knife in 'im and they were all on 'im before we 'ad time to move. 'Ad his balls off and 'is throat cut before we had the door open, sir. ...'

284

So died Oran. And need I say that the women all died on the spot? Next day, at a place north of Moylurg and the Curlieu Mountains, near the northern tip of Lough Arrow and perhaps sixty miles northeast of where the first battle occurred, the second battle of the plain of the pillar stones took place, on Samhain Eve. In the dawn Lugh made the glam dichenn, the roaring curse, upon the enemy and went corrguineacht at them, with mystic venom; left-handed, on one leg, with one eye covered and with one hand tied. For he was half a Fomorian and the power he summoned against them was awesome. It shrivelled the blood of his hearers in the cold dawn as he made this evil against them.

No one who was there was ever afterwards able to forget that decisive day that opened with Lugh, the Ildanach, Master of all arts as he was called because of his extraordinary proficiency at everything he turned his hand to, calling down malevolent forces on the enemy in the turbulent dawn. Even as we watched a strange thing happened. The strong winds which had swept over us from the great ocean during the darkness of the night now piled tall, grey rain clouds all around, but far off, so that they formed a mighty circle on the surrounding hills leaving us with a clear sky above. It was in this natural amphitheatre that the battle was won and lost.

Thanks to the organisation of the Gobniu and his fellow smiths we had huge stores of supplementary weapons which had been divided between the battalions. There were also additional shafts of ash and holly for spears and javelins, and wagon-loads of sling stones and arrows. These important replacements played a vital part in redressing the balance of the armies for we were heavily outnumbered.

According to the chroniclers who recorded the events of the day there never came to Ireland a host more horrible or fearful than that of the Fomorians, and I believe that to be true. They also said, but on what authority I have no idea, that this Second Battle of Moytura and the destruction of Troy by the Greeks seeking the return of their queen, occurred on the same day, but I am sceptical of that and believe it to be merely a necessary poetic embellishment on a story that needs no such contrivance. Thanks to the Gobniu's store of weapons, when the Fomorians finally did march out of camp in strong, indestructible battalions, we were less dismayed than we might otherwise have been to find that not a chief, nor a man, of them was without a hauberk, helmet or great spear. Each also had a heavy sword and shield and I heard around me whispers such as 'it will be like striking our heads against a cliff ... we're putting our hands into a serpent's nest ... talk about putting your head into the fire ...'

But they were not defeatist remarks so much as grudging recognition of a formidable foe. They formed against us, two or more for every man of ours, about nine hundred paces off, in a ragged line and there was none among us who could tell male from female in these ranks. The trumpets and the curved horns blared — and I remember the startled flight of some bird above the jingling and clinking of arms and the sudden laughs and whispers — and the hosts moved towards one another on the bleak plain. They did so quietly for a sudden silence cupped a great hand over us. Then, with a shout, the hosts came together and the air became hideous with shrieks and embroilment under billowing clouds of dust and coloured lime.

My own battalion, in which I commanded three companies, was in reserve. Some things impressed themselves on my mind so much that morning that I only have to be reminded of any one to recall the whole battle — or, at least, the battle as I saw it. The rattling and jingling of the saiget-bolgs, the arrow-bags, or quivers, with their deadly cargo is a sound forever part of that morning and even now the unmistakable chink of arrow-heads together brings it flooding back in all its mighty and portentous horror. Again the whistle of darts and the distinctive sound of the gablachs, the forked javelins, as they came at you, is another.

There were too many men engaged to be commanded all at once and as the morning passed the battle became groups of smaller battles heaving and struggling in different parts of the plain. My battalion was engaged by Indoch Mac de Donnon's troops and a fearful and bloody encounter it was in which a thing happened that seemed fortuitous, at the time, but which was later to impress me with its strangeness. In the struggling and heaving mass of men and women, with blood and noise flying equally upon the hideous wind, I suddenly came face to face with Indoch himself, ankle-deep in muddy gore, naked and sweat-streaked. He saw me at the same time. I do not know if he recognised me but he was on me with a shout and we fought for minutes, clashing and struggling with weapons, hands and bodies, until I slipped and fell in the unspeakable mire.

With a shriek as mindless as his frenzied eyes he leaped towards me, his crescent blade raised to sever my head from where it had rested all my life. My own sword, the one my grandfather gave me before he was put adrift, had fallen, and I saw the gross visage of death leering at me from behind his shoulder. With an energy and speed that I am certain was more than my own I snatched the obsidian knife from my belt and, with a twist of my body and all the power I could muster, threw it. The effort turned me so that my back was to Indoch and I knew I must surely die. But I did not. The scream that ripped my ears over the noise of the battle was not mine and I rolled again to see. My cast had taken Indoch between the legs and totally unmanned him, just as he was again about to prove his warriorship. He rolled on the stinking ground, blood pouring from between his ten fingers, which clutched his groin in an agony of bewilderment and destruction.

While this was happening, Nuada, too, was killed; by Balor whose troops held the centre against the best efforts of our finest battalions. The Gaetanae were turned when their charge came within range and even the phalanx was stopped before them. Balor's troops hurled flight after flight of arrows and javelins, high and low, so that the air was thick with them, like flights of birds, and they made the same rush with their passage, so loud that it could be heard over the cries and screams of the wounded on the saturated ground.

When Nuada fell the Dagda took the leadership. He was on a hillock in the rear overlooking the plain and, as if by consent, the armies drew apart shortly after the deaths of Nuada and Indoch. Together with Lugh I went to discuss the situation with the Dagda.

287

Strangely he looked suddenly old and yet more in command than I had ever seen him. And he seemed to have shrunk and become less gross and his orders were decisive and crisp.

His first was to direct that the fallen weapons of the Fomoire were gathered and brought in or smashed; his next that all our fighting troops must be fully equipped.

In making his dispositions he required a solid front, like an enlarged phalanx, four battalions across, to be held with connecting links between one battalion and the next. He stationed a reserve battalion, not in the centre where they could neither see nor be seen, but on two hills on the wings. He gave me command for the second reserve, the last battalion. To Lugh he gave the nine chariots.

When the other commanders had returned to their units he looked a long time over the reeking battlefield at the black lines of the enemy. Then, as if he was talking to himself, he said: 'A strange thing. I knew it would be like this ... I know what is going to happen ...'

I felt the familiar shiver between my shoulder blades and I knew that the hair on my neck was straining to quiver under its lime wash.

'I dreamed a dream last night ...' He paused. I saw Lugh's impatience. The Dagda obviously sensed it also. 'Go, Lugh. I'll tell you when to strike,' he said in a completely altered tone. Lugh grunted an acknowledgement and hurried off, glad to be away, but, I thought, a bit resentful that he had been given only the nine chariots and not a battalion to command. 'Let me tell you, Cian.' The Dagda's eyes were still in the distance. 'You will understand and it is right for you to know. Perhaps one day you will have the need to know.'

For a long moment his gaze wandered out to where the armies now showed signs of restiveness before resuming conflict.

'I dreamed I was in Glen Etin through which the River Uinshinn flows. All Sligo was under my gaze and a mighty woman stood with one foot on the north of the river and the other on the south and washed her body from the flowing water. She was a great, wild female with nine loosened tresses of hair on her head. Big as she was I took her in my dream and entered her. But for all my endeavour I could not enliven her.' He paused there and I felt a shiver because I both knew and was uneasy about what he was going to say. 'I know my fate!' he said and looked full at us. I nodded. I could do no more and it was written in the clouds, as I plainly observed through my inherited gift, and reflected in the depths of his sad eyes.

'She was ugly and infertile and I had fruitless congress with her,' he went on, 'and that will be the nature of my kingship. Unspectacular and infertile, but peaceful. The earth mother does not adopt the glory of a young woman for such as myself whose locks are grey. But neither did she come in the aspect of the hag, the Cailleach, and, my years notwithstanding, she welcomed me with powerful thighs and we strove together and she clasped me and spoke to me, telling me what was to happen. She came in the aspect of the Morrigu and she said, which was true, that the Fomoire would attack at Magh Scene. She foretold the death of Indoch Mac de Donnon and that he would be deprived of his kidneys of valour at your hand. And she named this place, where it occurred, the Ford of the Union and of Destruction, which it surely is . . .'

He let go a deep breath like a sigh and I understood that he was thinking of his future as king. Then, suddenly, he snapped alert.

'They are moving!'

I turned. The Fomoire were advancing at a walk at first. As we looked they broke into a trot and then, when the whole black mass of them was moving together towards our stationary ranks, there was an ululant cheer and they started to run headlong at our lines. The clash was terrible. They spread and enveloped our battalions as a surge of the incoming sea does a solitary rock. But the Dagda's orders prevented our front being broken and, though they milled around our forces with noise and destruction, they were repulsed after a time. Again they attacked, and again, until finally they withdrew to regroup for the fourth time. Then the Dagda ordered Lugh's chariots to attack.

From where we stood we watched our lines part and the nine chariots, in an extended line, sweep through the gap at a gallop and on towards the startled enemy. They were magnificent. The charioteers, reins wrapped round their waists, crouched on the butt of the poles and urged on their steeds or, in one or two cases, ran along the poles in the chariot feat and leaped onto the neck-yokes of the horses, from where they hurled darts as they ran the enemy down. The armoured champions standing in the rear (for the usual seats, for obvious reasons, had not been provided) swung their swords and maces, their clubs and lances, but above all, their fearsome, heavy spears, with devastating effect.

When the front ranks of the Fomorians saw the chariots bearing down on them, the flaring nostrils and the flying sods from under the feet of the ponies, heard the rattling and crashing of the chariots, they broke and tried to run. But there were so many pressing forward from behind who could not see, that the result was confusion and panic which contributed enormously to the awful casualties. The chariots tore into the enemy ranks, their wheel scythes and saws mowing them down in bloody heaps. Almost as one they wheeled about where the panic-stricken enemy had drawn back their packed ranks and drove, still at a snorting gallop, across the front of the enemy in staggered formation, so that each chariot cut deeper into the ranks of the Fomorians, like harvesters sowing in a field.

At the end of the front they wheeled and returned. Not one chariot, charioteer or champion had yet been damaged, wounded or hurt so far as we could see. Then one, the last in line, smashed a wheel on a rock. The vehicle foundered. The charioteer was thrown from the pole and dragged between the wreckage and the ponies until they stopped, quivering. When found later, he was mangled and dead, the reins still tied about him. But the warrior leaped clear and landed running as the chariot went over. It was Lugh.

Without pausing he plunged into the routed Fomorians striking them down as they ran. When they saw, the left wing of our army gave a great shout and charged, anyhow, after him, slaying and killing until they were weary and the very ground was an ooze of red mud. The centre phalanx advanced more slowly, driving any resisting remnants before it. The right stood fast for the while. But then the blood-lust became too great to bear and all, right flank, reserves, my own battalion — including myself — charged with a cheer to kill and kill and take what heads as we could in a mindless frenzy of blood letting.

Meantime Lugh searched out Balor who had kept the rout from affecting more than a few of his disciplined troops, who had formed around him and were fighting a rearguard action north to the sea.

Like a madman Lugh burst apart their outer defences, striking right and left, until his frenzy cleared an open path, at the other end of which was Balor, two hundred paces off.

'Bualim sciath,' screamed Lugh, 'I strike my shield, Balor, at you.' But, paradoxically, even as Balor turned, Lugh dropped his weapons from his hands and stood facing his grandfather, his arms held slightly out from his body. Balor looked back at him.

'It is I,' cried Lugh, 'Lugh Lamh Fada that you yourself named; your own grandson! Come to kill you as was foretold.'

An almighty silence fell on that part of the battlefield. Friend and foe alike turned to watch. The hideous and mighty Balor stood at one side of the clearing, surrounded on all sides by his savage Fomorians, the smaller, slighter Lugh was opposite to him, few of his supporters near, but with the afternoon sun glinting and dazzling from the burnished helmet that he wore and, it almost seemed, from the golden hair that flowed from under it. Balor heard him and raised a hand to protect himself against Fate. He shouted.

'Let me see the babbler who is shouting at me. If you are who you are then it is you who will die. First I'll strike you with the terror and power of my Bireach-derc, my Speary-eye.'

So saying he raised the eye-cap he wore over the evil white eye that he might put its fatal curse on Lugh.

Lugh reached back and drew his crann-tabaill, staff-sling, from his belt. In his hand he already had a tathlum, a special, powerful and malignant sling-ball made from the blood of toads, bears and vipers mixed with sea sand that he had specially prepared, and as Balor began to chant his glamdicheann Lugh fitted it to the sling and hurled it at the giant Fomorian. From where we stood we could not see the course of the missile. But Balor's head suddenly jerked and his huge body straightened. He raised both hands towards his head and swayed backwards. We still heard the horrid sound of the curse he had been bellowing which had to travel the distance between us, after it had in fact stopped, and he swayed again forwards now, and fell full length on his face on the battlefield. Lugh's tathlum went straight through his evil eye, through his brain, and out through the skull at the back which — when I saw it — was an open and bloody mass as if it had been hit from the outside by one of his own stone Fomorian warclubs, instead of from within by a magic tathlum. But one of the properties of such a missile is that it spreads on impact.

After that it was a rout and our men pursued the Fomorian stragglers towards their ships. I do not know the real number of Fomorian peasants and rabble who fell in the battle, but of lords, nobles, champions, king's sons and over-kings among them who were killed, the chroniclers computed it as follows: lords, 5063; nobles, 150; champions, 80 045; king's sons, 168; overkings, 42. Of servants, 847 were said to have died, and of half-men, or those chained in pairs so they won't flee, there were so many they were not counted.

Such figures, of course, belong more to the imaginations of the chroniclers and bards who put them together than to the battlefield. Even including peasants and rabble from both sides it is doubtful if the combined armies totally eighty thousand, much less that being alone the number of Fomorian champions slain. In my own view the figures of the chroniclers should be divided by nine or even ten. The only true record is from the stones and they have long since become cairns and mounds among the multitude of pillars that mark this second plain of death.

In any case, the main point is that while our own losses were severe, they were nothing by comparison to those of the Fomorians. But one incident that affected the future occurred when the fighting was all but done and should be noted. When she saw her husband fall, Caitlin, Balor's hideous wife, hid herself among the dead until the rout was past. Then, when the Dagda himself came onto the field to see the destruction, she leaped at him and wounded him in the kidneys before she was cut down.

Before that he had sent the Scythian bodyguard in pursuit of the Fomorian kings to retrieve his harp, which was left behind when he escaped from their northern settlement, and which was used as a trophy to taunt us with during the course of the battle. They succeeded in recovering it and, as well, in putting the settlement to the torch so that nothing was left standing but the stone citadel, which we later occupied and developed as a settlement of our own.

After the battle, in spite of his wound, the Dagda made this poem to the goddess in her aspect of Badbh, the Raven of Battle (much in evidence; the ravens of the battlefield, it might as well be noted, are both black and white. Those of the land being black and those from the sea and the shore being white):

> Peace up to heaven
> And from heaven unto Earth;
> The earth is under Heaven;
> Strength to every birth.

The Dagda, the Accomplished King as he was called, ruled three years and one half; seven halves. As he had foretold, his kingship was peaceful and unspectacular, neither unduly prosperous nor unusually harsh. But he was old and sick from his wound when it began and towards the end of that time he was enfeebled. From time to time he sought me out — for his brother, Ogma, had died and ever since the battle with the Fomoire the Dagda had great faith in my strange, inherited powers. In any case, as Tanist, I was the one he would naturally consult with. In the royal booth in the hall of the king's dun he would whisper to me what the goddess looked like and what she said, and the meaning of both, when she visited him in his troubled dreams.

Ever since his wife, Fuaim — better known as Lies, Deceit and

Disgrace — was executed after Nuada resumed power, he had had no regular wife for a long time. But, even before that, the beautiful Taillte, who had been wife of the Firbolg king, Eochaidh (and a chief of the Firbolg in her own right), went to Brugh na Boinne, the Dagda's private mansion, to be safe from the pillaging Fomorian tax-gatherers when Eochaidh died and a new Firbolg king took his place in Connacht. In spite of her slave origins (and — as Bres pointed out to us before he became corrupt with power and cupidity — they had become a nation in their own right with honour), the Dagda now made her his chief woman in the palace at the Crimson City and Matha again became part of it after Ogma's death. They cared for the old man devotedly, and even provided him with younger women at night from time to time, to keep his old bones warm, for that was all that was now involved.

Ogma's death came as a surprise to us all. It was a great personal sadness to me, who owed so much to that gentle and cultured champion. It was he who taught me the secret language of the druids: finger language; ogham and writing on waxed boards or on cloth with pointed sticks and brushes dipped in black dye. He it was who patiently taught me the rhythms and tones, the pitch and inflections to enable me to memorise the laws and judgements and the traditions of the people, so that I had long since become an ollamh.

He died as tranquilly as he had lived — excepting those wars and battles which were part of our destiny — in his sleep after a night of feasting, story-telling, music, riddles and enjoyment in the great banqueting hall, where he sat beside his brother, the king, and smiled and joked; argued; played a game of fidchell; drank wine and did his favourite sword-feat with Orna — which was to cut a hair floating on a cauldron of water. Before the night was over he excused himself and, accompanied by Matha, went to his sleeping quarters in the king's dun. In the morning he was dead. He lay in his bed, covered to the chin with a blue blanket lined with linen, his eyes shut. His mouth was open, but there was no breath. We buried him with the ceremony that was his due.

First he was ceremonially wrapped in the strofess, the wrapping of birch leaves, and then was sprinkled liberally with the blood of cattle — his own — sacrificed in his honour to propitiate the benign powers of the other world as he journeyed there, and frighten the malevolent ones. The bier of a champion was made for him and carried by two horses, one in front and one behind. With flaming torches we went at night in a long procession from the Crimson City to the burial ground at Brugh, where the bier was smashed against his inscribed pillar-stone to prevent its use against him by spirits after his burial.

The druid, Forgall, took the horrid fé, the aspen rod used for the measurement of the dead, and we averted our eyes while he performed his ominous rite. When he was done Ogma was placed standing in the prepared grave, the cistemhen, which now became the otharlige of Ogma, Ogma's last sick-bed, facing west towards his enemies, the sword Oran in his right hand and his great iron spear in his left. The stone box was built around him and the grave was covered and then the flaming torches were extinguished so that night fell upon us with all its invisible mysteries, and we quickly returned to the city to partake of the fled-cro-lige, the feast of the death bed, and to celebrate the funeral games in his honour. A fine pillar-stone was erected on which was carved: 'This is Ogma lying here: I was a Champion and a Seer.'

Matha, who was his woman though not his wife, visited the principal lords and chieftains throughout the night, but I do not think that many of them did more than pay her the courtesy of a token gesture which, in these modern times, is fulfilled with a mouthful each of mead from the gilded drinking horn she carried for the purpose.

So departed my great friend and teacher and, now, his old brother, the king, the Dagda, tremblingly clutched my hand with his stiffened fingers, and whispered to me in the seclusion of the royal booth in the Teach Micuarta.

When he spoke about the goddess it was with increasing unease. For now she came, more and more frequently, in the hideous aspect of the hag, Cailleach, withered, bloated and obscene all at once, and he knew his kingship was near its end.

It might be thought I was the logical one to succeed him when the time came, but Fate again intervened, and the new king was to be Lugh. With his accession a new and momentous era began in which the mystery of the divine relationship between the king and the goddess who lives forever was further kindled with old mysteries into a new and awesome dimension.

When we came to the Crimson City as I explained, and saw the Cloch Greine, the Stone of the Sun, the Bud Ard Ree, Member of the King of the World, that stands upright on the very navel of Ierne, and learned of the old mysteries of the womb of the goddess, our thinking and rituals were much affected.

The druids and seers examined these profundities and, through their studies, the meaning of the change that occurs in the nature of the goddess (who is also earth and the land of Ierne) from being a young, fertile, beautiful woman, to being the dessicated, obscene, worn-out, mindless hag, became evident. Her change was connected to the change in the living king, who was her spouse among the people. As he aged and became infirm, so did she; so did earth, land, and its produce, and the produce and virility of the people. This was all accepted, of course, from the beginning of the world but now, too, it had a visible reality. When the life-giving essence of the sun penetrated the Womb of the World at Newgrange on the last day of November, there is a birth that is a renewal. Clearly the goddess and the god had caused these earthly images, the Womb and the Member, to be placed where they were for a purpose. What other purpose could it be except the regeneration of the king and his supernatural consort, the goddess, when both had become old, hideous, weak-minded and infertile?

In the Womb of the World at Newgrange the old king is reborn as the sun impregnates and renews the fruitful world; so with men. It can not be less.

Truly Ierne is the Island of the Blessed! Here, on the green plain beside the river, called Boinne (after Boan, one of the Dagda's paramours), are the mysteries of both worlds; the riddles of the stars, and the sun and the moon and the clouds; those of the sea and the land

and all the elements, were made known to human understanding. And we, the people, acknowledged these wonders that were here revealed.

The Dagda was dying and the people knew it. There was a deadness on the land. The hag had been seen by many and there was murmuring against the king. Eventually the discontent reached the city and penetrated the great halls. Men and women could be seen leaning towards one another and muttering among themselves away from the king, to fall silent when his rheumy eye turned in their direction.

At last it was left to me. The leaders and ollamhs had made their selection and chose Lugh, not out of disrespect for me — indeed he beat me by only three votes — but, I think, because his youth and vitality were in stronger contrast to the Dagda's great age, and the mood of the people demanded an extreme change. I, who remained Tanist, was to inform the Dagda of the decision and of his role in the new inauguration rituals and the offering to the queen-goddess.

I did the best I could. But it was not easy.

'So you see, my king,' I finished, 'it will not be your end, but your rebirth. As the goddess ...' I nearly said 'dies', but caught myself just in time, 'changes from being the Cailleach, and is reborn in surpassing beauty as Banba or Fodhla or Eriu, whichever she chooses, so will the king and the kingship be reborn and perpetuated.'

I felt I had overdone it. But what could I do?

For a moment he said nothing, just looked at me. Then he turned his head away, and nodded and sighed into the shadows behind him. I felt sorry for him, but I was glad to get away. I felt I had been right. After all, the mystery is greater than the man. Nevertheless I was uneasy ...

It was to take place one month after Samhain. There was the usual fasting and cleansing and, during that evening, the druids led by the now ancient Methger and Dara my cousin, now called Dara Dearg, Dara the Red, because of his red hair, who in spite of his mother's objections would succeed him, went secretly to Newgrange and into its inner recesses. Do not ask what they do there, or why, for I can

297

not say . . . although I know.

It is enough to know that they commune with and prepare the goddess. Naturally Brigit, sister of that other Brigit who had married Bres, and who was a priestess also and a great mid-wife, was with them, even though the Dagda was her own father. And they were assisted by other priestesses who helped them then and later.

Before midnight the king was driven to Newgrange in the royal chariot, sitting in his seat to the left of the charioteer. He was wrapped in a great cloak and was fully armed, but I, who travelled behind him, noticed that he did not even raise his head as the caval-cade passed his own mansion of Brugh na Boinne where he had lived and been happy for so long. When we reached Newgrange itself he required to be helped from the chariot. In the flickering torch-light then, with a final look round at the faces, at the sculpted stones that flanked the entrance and at the white mound itself on which reflected points of light jumped and wavered, he turned and shuffled through the narrow entrance and disappeared along the passage to the womb within. No trumpets sounded. And of Lugh there was no sign.

We chiefs, ollamhs and leaders of the people, stayed outside and watched. From the opening torchlight spilled into the forecourt like water, to be absorbed quickly by the dark sands of night. After an hour, when midnight was past and labour for the new sun had begun, we drove back to the city. The chariot course, and all around it, was thronged. Everyone from the city was there as well as groups of the people from all over Ierne, besides native peasants, slaves and rabble; freemen, chieftains, lords, champions, sons of kings, under kings; bards, seers, druids, ollamhs, men, women and children. Tents and shelters that had grown around the city had expanded it to twice its width. Open places and passageways were covered in mud, which had been strewn with wicker panels to provide a surface. The cattle pens were surrounded by dwellings now and the home pastures had vanished. But none of this could be seen. What was visible as we drove from Newgrange was a multitude of lights so powerful that the scudding clouds reflected a red glow as if from a far-off fire.

Stewards kept open a broad passage from Newgrange along which we drove through a cheering and cheerful throng, waiting the rebirth that would spell prosperity. This avenue led directly to the chariot course which was also clear. We drove straight to the city end, behind the Cloch Greine, and dismounted. Our charioteers took horses and vehicles to the stables and we took our places in open-fronted pavilions which had been erected for the occasion. There was nothing then to do but wait.

We were looking east. I remember how cold it suddenly became in the still darkness before the dawn. I don't think I had ever noticed that particular cold before, although the darkness and stillness were not new to me. I wrapped myself more tightly in my cloak and stamped my feet slightly. Then in the distance a line formed between a darkness and a lighter emptiness and the two worlds began to separate; the earth and the sky moved apart. A blackbird called. The sky paled and an expectant rustle scurried through the crowd when it became evident the sky was cloudless. Then it was dawn and the first, fine ray of the sun lipped above the rim of the world and shone on us. A cry that was a groan and a welcome and an emptying of the spirit in humility before unimaginable majesty rose from the assembly, most of whom fell on their faces and on their knees facing to the east. We all knew that that same shaft of light was even then piercing the aperture that was the hymen of the goddess of the World; penetrating the fertile passage of the earth and lodging its life-giving warmth in the profoundest depths of the Womb of the mother. And so it was. (Later I was to learn how, as the life-bearing beam of sunlight flooded the passage and the interior, the Dagda died under a sacrificial knife wielded by Brigit and how during the day his body was burned in a massive and sacred carved-stone urn, placed there for that purpose.) A cry, I was told, came from the mound and Lugh, naked, his body splashed and streaked with the blood of the Dagda, symbolising both power and the blood of parturition, burst from the inner chamber where he had been concealed, down the passage and out into the forecourt where the royal chariot stood waiting behind a pair of horses, now, responsive to the atmosphere of the moment, champing and stamping on the cobble-stones.

Lugh hurdled the distance between the entrance to the womb and the chariot in a bound, grasped the curved handle of the brightly-coloured chariot and swung himself over the rear shafts and onto the platform all in one movement. The charioteer kept the reins tight on the prancing ponies and, still taut, handed them to Lugh before jumping from the chariot so lightly he seemed to disappear, according to Methger, who stood in front of the entrance and struck a craebh-cuill, a musical branch, which hung from a wrought bronze stand beside him. Instantly, from the top of the mound, a triumphant salute of trumpets sounded, and Lugh loosened the reins and was off towards the city with a crash of iron-shod wheels.

We heard those trumpets and the rumbling of the crowds lining the route from where we were seated. Before long we heard the creaking and rattling of the chariot as it thundered on the road, the wheels striking sparks from the stones and the clods and lumps of mud and clay flying from beneath the ponies' hooves high in the air so that it seemed as if he was accompanied by a flock of flying birds as the king reborn galloped to his royal city.

Bloc and Bluicne, the thighs of the earth, had been moved in the night so that they were apart with a passage between them just wide enough to take the chariot. We heard his coming amid the swelling roar of the multitude and then he was with us, guiding — rather, it seemed, propelling — the horses between the thigh-stones with that sureness in all he did which earned him the name Ildanach, the consummate Master.

We sat at the far end of the chariot course under a scarlet awning with blue side walls behind the Cloch Greine, and he bore down on us with frightful speed. I saw the distended nostrils of the ponies and the rolling eyes in their straining heads. I saw the froth fly from the bronze bits chafing their mouths and their blurred hooves that never seemed to touch the ground, but nevertheless drummed the hard surface of the course like a monstrous sounding board. The whirling iron-shod wheels crashed on the pebbled surface and the cracking and flying of small stones resembled the sound of sling-balls smiting

300

strong shields, and shattering on iron greaves. And as we watched the naked, blood-stained figure of the king ran along the leaping chariot pole, between the racing flanks of the ponies, and, holding the shortened reins in his hands, jumped on the yoke between them so that he came at us like the god he is named for, with the sun behind him, standing astride the backs of both racing animals.

'The goddess save him,' I thought. 'He can't wheel the pillar like that. He'll be killed . . .'

But that is exactly what he did do. Without slackening the pace he urged the ponies at the pillar. Then, when it seemed he must crash, overshoot — into us, I might add — or capsize as he attempted the turn, he pulled on the right rein with immense strength so that he leaned backwards from the ponies' shoulders, almost parallel to their backs. He loosened the left rein and in one almighty sweep hauled the chariot round the pillar on one wheel, the inner one stuck to the ground as if with glue, its metal boss screaming off the standing member and scoring it so deeply that the burnt smell of fresh limestone filled the air and clouds of it mingled with the flurry of his passing, to bring us all to our feet cheering.

That cheer from the huge assembly lasted many, many minutes: long after he slowed his ponies to a trot, then to a walk, and disappeared from the far end of the course. We knew he would circle the city outside the throng and we could mark his passage from the moving sound that accompanied him.

Much later, he emerged, resplendent in a purple cloak, folded five times between his neck and ankles over a gold-embroidered tunic. He wore a shoulder-cape of red and blue and white wool and triubhas, or trousers, of yellow with silver patterns. On his fingers and arms and ankles were rings and clasps of wrought gold, and round his neck a beautiful, heavy torc stretched from shoulder to shoulder to end in front with a pair of exquisitely-carved horse heads facing one another.

The cheering was renewed and lasted a great while. Thereafter we sat down to the wedding feast of the king and the rejuvenated goddess, now named Eriu, who was seen all about us. A poet at the feast

301

(when he had sufficient wine) described the earth-queen-goddess in her new and beautiful aspect of Eriu in these rather extravagant words: 'Her cheeks are as rosy as the lichen-crimson on the crags of Leinster: her hair is as golden as the buttercup of the pastures of Bregia or the blazing furze of the hillsides, and her matchless green mantle is everywhere to be seen.' The rejoicing lasted nine nights.

Thus we acquired our first king under the new dispensation and I was doubly glad because he was my foster-brother and because he married my sister, Naas, who became his first mortal wife.

Ever since he announced his intention of marrying her, young Naas had been watched and guarded closely by our mother, Sena'an, to whom the marriage plans gave particular satisfaction since they were foster-brother and sister and, thus, provided a lingering echo of royal practice among her own Egyptian ancestors. Because of the mystery involved — they being both clean and unclean, holy and unholy, not of this world nor of the other — girls at this time (as also at their time of the month and in childbirth) are a source of possible great harm to themselves and to the community, unless the power in them is controlled and converted to beneficial uses. Therefore at such times they must be kept apart and not associate with ordinary people. They must be confined and contained so that the power may make them fruitful, as the seed is confined and contained in the belly of the mother-goddess. They may not touch the sacred earth nor experience the rays of the sun, lest they contaminate the one ànd profane the other.

Therefore Naas, when her puberty was close, was put in a small cabin in my father's grianaan, where the sun would be about her but not on her. The cabin was raised on pillars so that its floor was well above ground and it had to be reached by a flight of steps. She was attended by one of the priestesses whose function it is. Here she spent a month and, thereafter, five days whenever it became necessary. This cabin is called the single-pillared tower for reasons I do not know.

In spite of our great expectations, due to circumstances which none of us celebrating the wedding-feast of the king to my sister could foresee, Lugh's reign was a short one. I will recount those circumstances in a moment. First I must tell about a thing he did which was more significant long after his death than anything he did while king, or anything at all he had done when he was alive, save, perhaps, the killing of the Fomorian tax-gatherers and of his grandfather, Balor.

That was the inauguration of the games at Taillte, called after the Dagda's consort, who with the Dagda had fostered Lugh for part of the seven years he lived away from us. She influenced him greatly, and in the privacy of her own rath had initiated him in the rite of the Arch of Anann, and he never overcame his deep affection for her on that account.

Before his kingship was a year old, a Tauv, or plague came down on Albion and the Island of Mananann, whither it travelled in boats. Many of the Bretani on the south-east coast died in agony after they refused to stop trading with Albion in spite of Lugh's instructions, and many of their duns and raths were burned. But the Tauv escaped and some of our own people were also affected as the Duinebeth, man-death, skulked from place to place. But we defeated it in the end by ruthlessly burning everything at the first signs of his presence. These were a kind of speckling on the body, which we called galar-breac, the speckled disease. When it became worse, we called it bolgach, the bag, or pustule, disease. Taillte fell to it.

After a suitable period of mourning Lugh buried his chieftainess, his foster-mother to whom he owed so much, near the dun he had given her and where she died, some miles north of the city. In her honour he celebrated the greatest funeral games that were ever held and, moreover, ordered that they be held each year on the anniversary of her death. Now this raised an interesting point, because Taillte had died on Lughnasa, the feast of the very god for whom Lugh himself was unwittingly named. It was also the date of an older festival celebrated by those who dealt with the gods who conceived Newgrange and who appealed to those gods for a fruitful harvest. It was called Bron Trogaire and the name is itself a propitiation, meaning the Festival of the Poor Grinding, that, by druidical inversion of course, implores the gods to prevent any such thing.

303

Lugh now decreed that Lughnasa and Bron Trogaire be jointly celebrated by the great games of Tailltean. They were similar in thought to the games created by our forefathers in Ionia (which, I'm told, the Greeks have now also taken up at some place on the Corinthian Isthmus). They included, among other important things, horse-back races, which were his own invention, ball-games and feats of skill; running, javelin throwing and wrestling. It was his wish that the games be held every year and this has been done up until now and, I have no doubt, from what has occurred, that they will continue to be held long after I am gone.

There are music and dancing competitions and contests of every conceivable sort, and it has become a celebrated centre for match-making and marriages as the people assemble there on the first day of August from all parts of the land; from Albion, from Prydein north of it, and from Spain and Gaul as well.

The first horse-race held at Taillte was an exciting contest. None of us had ever seen any organised race of the kind attempted before and it was fitting that the winner should be Lugh himself, riding his favourite steed, a chestnut mare, that carried him to victory before all comers (though I sometimes wonder at it and suspect that some 'co-operation' might have been involved).

It was at the first Tailltean Games that he met Blanaid of the Flowers, daughter of a Munster King, who was to be his destruction. Although she was little more than a child and barely out of her first housing in the single-pillared-house, he became infatuated with her. When one spoke to him it was plain to see. His eyes would wander inwards after a minute and a foolish smile soften his mouth when it should be sharp and direct. He would jerk back after a moment, say 'Eh?' and listen for a while. But soon the glaze would enter his eyes again and his mouth would curl. Moreover he was impatient when she was not near him, and idiotic when she was. Finally he made her his second wife, and at a great bride-price. Her father was content. But the same could not be said for the Flower that Lugh plucked. She was as vain as she was empty-headed and nothing would content her but to flaunt her breasts and her thighs for every man in the city.

There was one in particular who lost his senses over her. Cermaid, son of the Dagda — and foster-brother to Lugh — found her irresistible, as had Lugh.

Cermaid was a large, dark man, with fine blue eyes and black hair that curled to his ears and was stiffened behind with lime to a white wave. He loved to wear gold and he showered Blanaid with it, unknown to Lugh. Flattered by his obsessive attention she went too far, enticed him and lay with him. Then she became frightened of what she had done and lied to Lugh that Cermaid had taken her by force. Lugh killed Cermaid.

But Cermaid's son, Macuil, swore revenge and would accept no eric fine, saying it was geasa on him to avenge his father. Thus he became an outcast. Nevertheless within a short time he speared Lugh with a spear of iron while the king was one day hunting on the plains of Meath, and Lugh died.

So I became king. Because there was no old king to be reborn I did not emerge in blood from the Womb of the World, but was inaugurated in the old style by the Cloch Greine, which shrieked satisfactorily as I wheeled my chariot about it. I took the white wand and turned three times about facing the world and swore by the elements what the druid, my cousin Dara Dearg, bade me swear. And I was king. And I never had but one human consort, who was Eremed, and she was my queen.

I reigned forty-five years and my kingship was peaceful and prosperous until the end. The people founded settlements everywhere in Ierne and, aided by the aboriginal inhabitants, developed the natural resources as well as farming and pasturage. Trade was extended. The great timber of the forests was used for all kinds of building, for road-making, for ship-building, and was also exported for these purposes. Surplus wool, wolfhounds and cattle were produced for trade with Albion, Gaul and Spain, and tin and copper were mined extensively and also exported. Our produce was known and sought after as far away as the Federation and the Empire. But our principal export was worked gold. This trade grew so much that — although there was no shortage of it in our own rivers and mines — we imported great quantities of gold from the continent to be worked and re-exported as jewellery, ornaments or decoration.

In return we got wine, silk and other precious fabrics, iron, pottery, leather, slaves ... whatever the market would bear.

Ports were established in several places around the coast to cater for the ships that travelled regularly to and from these countries ... at Waterford and Wexford, south of Wicklow, where the crossing to Albion was fast and safe; in the great harbour of Cork in the southwest to trade with Spain, and near my own family rath at Dubhlinn, below the ford called the Wicker Ford, or B'la Cliath.

Of course, between natural births and immigrants the population increased very much and prosperity in many forms pleasured the land and the people. We had two minor plagues during my reign, but nothing unusual, and our cattle were infected no more than was to be expected.

During this time also I performed for the first — and only — time the full ceremony of the goddess as Ishtar at a quinquennial ceremony. There is no need to describe the ceremony in detail, only to say that this was to be the most lavish we ever celebrated. Although I had reigned nearly fifteen years I had not taken the leading part before. The first time the occasion arose after I became king I was ill of a fever, and it was considered unpropitious that I should perform the ceremony, so Dara Dearg did so instead.

On the second occasion I was in far Gaul fighting with the Etruscans — or Turseni — with whom we had ties from the days of our ancestors, when both they and the people lived in Asia Minor. They were having difficulties with a subject people south of them, from a city in Latium called Rome, and we, together with many of our cousins, had responded to their call for help.

It was on this expedition that I discovered the ideas which greatly troubled me and influenced my thinking and ruling in the years ahead. My father has often been the decisive instrument of many important times in my life — and, strange as it may be, it was through Keth that the first of these ideas, which altered my life, came to my attention.

One afternoon we were resting from the heat of the sun in a fig grove near Veii. All round us were the pastures and fruit trees of fertile Etruria and, in the distance, the equally rich lands of north Latium. Some of the farms were burnt out as a result of the recent fighting, but there was no smoke now and all was peaceful. I had brought a company, three fifties, of warriors, and there were many more contingents from the two Gauls and from Albion and Spain. The Romans were tough and capable fighters and I had lost thirty men. They were contained that time, but I wondered about the future.

The fighting was over now, however, and the harvest was ripening. We were on our way home with plunder, gold, wine and some of the coins that one could use in exchange for goods. I had decided to examine the possibility of using these in Ierne, and I'll explain why presently.

As we rested in the shade Keth took out a harp and began to play, idly allowing his fingers to follow his thoughts across the strings.

'That's a tune I've not heard before.'

The voice was old and it was with difficulty I understood the speaker, who spoke a variety of Celtic, but with a dreadful accent. He leaned on the tumbled wall of the field, looking at us. We were too relaxed to hear his approach and some of my men jumped up belligerently, to hide their shame, but I waved them back. Even had the fighting not been over, this old man offered no threat. I beckoned him in and offered him meat, bread and wine with a gesture which he declined, but asked for water which he sipped while chewing a handful of figs. Keth, meanwhile, said nothing. But now, as if nothing had occurred in the interim, he answered the other's question of five minutes ago.

'You did not. It's the first time anyone heard it.'

'A nice tune. A sad tune. May I see the instrument?'

307

Without hesitation Keth handed the harp to the old man, who was bearded and cloaked in some sort of loose garment. He ran his fingers over the strings and produced a strange sound, unmusical, yet regular.

'Yours?'

Keth nodded. 'I am an instrument maker — and a chariot maker,' he said, but, surprisingly, without pride.

'Ah! A fine instrument.'

'You are Greek?'

'From Magna Graecia south of Latium.'

'May one ask your profession?'

'I am a philosopher?'

I interrupted.

'A philosopher? You are a magus, then?'

For several hours, until my men became restive and it was past time to go, we talked to the old man — rather, listened to him, for he asked us few questions except when we told him that the people originally came from Miletus. He became quite excited and asked in his queer mixture of Tursenian, Greek and rude Celtic, if I had heard of Thales and Anaximander of Miletus, and I had to say that I had not. But Keth had. They were Hellenic teachers — philosophers — from whom the people, through the power of the goddess, had derived part of their own understanding of life and the universe. Thales taught that all things were related to water (and is not the goddess queen of rivers and of the river of heaven itself?). Anaximander taught that the principle of the world is infinite, which is also true. But Keth did not know what happened to them after the sacking of the city. Yet, strangely, we were to have further reminders of Miletus — the old Miletus as I will now call it — before my reign was over. Indeed the very forces that were to affect us profoundly were already on the march even as we sat under the shady fig trees talking to this fascinating old man, whose name was Pythagoras. A good deal of what he said I have forgotten but he had travelled much and knew Ionia well and, naturally, I asked him about it. He'd also spent considerable time in Egypt and both my father and myself were interested in that because of my mother. Among other things he told us of huge stone animals on the western bank of the mighty river and pointed buildings of unimaginable size, built so long ago that, as he said, their origins are in doubt.

'No, they were built by man,' he said in answer to my suggestion that, like Newgrange, they had been built by the gods, 'the records clearly show that.'

'With the help of gods, then,' I said. For how else could it have been, I thought.

'Perhaps,' he smiled. 'Look.' He picked up the harp again. 'There must be order in all things. It is the first cause.' He plucked a group of strings. 'Listen!' The notes hung upon the heavy air, until they diminished and vanished. 'Now listen again.' He plucked another group, producing a different sound and we waited until it, too, faded.

'Did you notice anything?' He asked. We looked silently at him.

'Listen again.' He repeated what he had done and then, when Keth said the only difference was that one sound was higher than the other and lasted longer, he replied, 'Exactly!'

I looked at Keth, who shrugged slightly. Perhaps the old man was loose in the head after all. He went on. 'Why does one sound last longer? Why is it more intense? What are the differences between one group of sounds and another?'

I shrugged.

'Well,' he said, 'the difference can be measured and determined. The notes you play by instinct can be given a precise mathematical value which can be measured and learned and which, one day, will enrich music beyond all knowing.' He plucked the strings again and, this time, I listened with a new ear. And, suddenly, I understood what he meant when he said there is order in all things. The thought grew and spread outwards from music to encompass all I could see and feel and, for a moment, I felt dizzy. When I looked at him again the old man was nodding as if in sympathy with my feelings.

'You understand,' he said. 'I am glad. Not everyone grasps the thought so quickly. But now consider this; if you believe — as I think you do — that you possess a soul, a spirit, that does not die when your body dies.'

He paused and now I was hoping he would continue. He did.

'I also believe that,' he said, 'and that if order extends to and is in everything, then', he went on, 'when we die our souls live on, and must do so in another order of things. Perhaps a higher one, who knows?'

It was a strange, even extraordinary idea, the more so to have heard it beneath a fig tree in a strange land. Then Pythagoras said something almost as extraordinary. It was almost as if he read my mind.

'The whole world is stirring with new ideas,' he announced. 'Ideas that will change it and affect it till the end of time.' His voice changed slightly and he looked directly at me as he said:

'I believe that in mathematics lies the key to the truth. It is the highest form of human order. In order to see and understand truth we must be pure — I don't mean those horrible rites, I'm sorry, but they are offensive to me and I do not mean to offend you — I mean personal purification of the mind and of the body by moral thinking and by abstinence. I have a school dedicated to the seeking of truth and where such disciplines are practised.'

'And have you found it? Truth?'

He smiled and it was a toothless old man's smile, but in him it was beautiful. He spread his hands.

'Who knows?' he said. 'We can only keep looking.'

We listened to him for a long time, and we exchanged a great deal of information. But what he had given to us — to me anyhow — I believed was more valuable than all the gold and booty we had with us, or had ever taken. It was with real sadness that we parted, he to the south and we to continue north.

That was five years earlier than the time I speak of. Now the five-year festival had come again and this time I must perform it. In the interval I had achieved some of the things I wanted to do and had been able to put into practice some of the ideas I had learned in Etruria and from traders and merchants, ambassadors, wanderers,

310

teachers, thinkers and bands of our own young nobles and warriors returning from service with lords and kings in other lands, from the kinglets of Albion to the Emperor Darius.

For one thing I made a start at introducing some sort of standard in currency instead of relying on the arbitrary value of cattle, which fluctuated. I based it on three things since I discovered that to make coins, while acceptable as foreign currency — provided they were either gold or silver (such as came from Massilia) — was almost impossible because of problems of standardizing them throughout the country. Struggling with this problem I remembered the buinne-d'at which Ogma (may his soul be at peace) wagered with me so many years ago and how I had dedicated it to the goddess, and it occurred to me that here there was a ready-made basis for a common standard.

Accordingly I introduced what we now call buinne, without the do-ats, instead of coins. These are small lunula-shaped rings of much the same size and weight. I also standardized the value of cumals, female slaves, as being roughly equivalent to three milch cows or six heifers, so that external trade was also regularized, and to reinforce this I attached a staple value to iron currency-bars, which had to be imported also. They were the raw material for swords and spear-heads and were pinched at one end to make a tang or socket. The thinking behind these changes were simple. When trading took place at the great fairs and aonaighs which I caused to be held at Tara, Taillte, Usna and other places, such as Carmun in the south — and I'll explain my reason for these also — it was noticeably difficult, and often a cause of trouble, for the buyers and sellers to have to weigh the gold and silver ingots on scales, to say nothing of having to carry them — and bought and sold produce — about with them. Where the transaction was in cattle it was simpler, but it still created difficulties. Moreover there was also the problem of faulty weighing scales and adulterated metal. But while this was difficult for the wealthy, they could manage. Freeman and skilled slaves were much worse off. How could they trade with merchants and travelling salesmen? More to the point, if they did how could they avoid being cheated? I had

311

seen how these problems had been solved in other countries — in Greece, I'm told, they even use copper coins — and was determined to see what I could do here. Hence the three standards which could, as the occasion required, be modified ... even by cutting the iron currency bar, the pieces of which still had a value proportionate to the standard size. In all of this, as I later discovered, I was following the example of the Lydian king, Croesus, whom the Great Kurus defeated, and who first produced standard exchange talents of a fixed shape, quality and weight.

My doing so, however, had at least as much to do with the political and economic condition of the whole of the island of Ierne as with providing a means of exchange other than barter which would benefit the less well off. My motives were not, naturally, entirely philanthropic. I had the welfare of the people as a whole in mind although what Pythagoras said to me in the fig grove in far-off Etruria was nurtured in my mind and made me increasingly restless and uneasy as the years passed. I could no longer so easily accept that I was right just because it happened to be the way I felt. Especially at night, the importance of men, and of their souls, stalked me; the significance of order and the place of man in an ordered state, haunted me; and the idea that all men, in some way, were part of a greater order pursued not far behind. And again came the idea that, if this is so, then the role of one man in that order is just as significant as the role of another. These were difficult ideas to struggle with and I reasoned, to myself of course, that if I brought material order then what I did must be of benefit to more people.

Therefore I built roads between the settlements and between the settlements and Tara, Usna and Taillte, and to the ports. Ever since the great Assyrian wars of previous generations — what the Persians and the Greeks (of all people) refer to as the barbarian invasions — the old order had been disrupted and was not, I'm told, restored until the time of Kurus. I had seen with my own eyes the benefits that this brought about. I had also seen in Etruria and Latium the effects of isolationism, where valley competed with valley, village with village, territory with territory, and where this competition is not merely

312

physical, but extends also to produce and even to values, so that there is no commonwealth between them. I did not want that to happen in Ierne. Therefore the great trading centres were established and the fairs and aonaigh lasted days and sometimes weeks at these centres, where marriages and peace, laws and lawgiving, policy and trade were the prime considerations of importance, and sport and feats the prime ones of relaxation.

Above all I wanted to ensure balanced exchange between settlements, towns and cities so that commerce would develop. I was well aware that growing populations, and subsistence levels of agriculture and fishing, could provide temptation to raid and steal land from neighbours as the Fomorians did, and I wanted to prevent that if possible.

I persuaded the druids (who were very hostile at first, since it trespassed on what they considered their private mysteries) to permit the writing signs called the Alphabet, invented at Ugarit and Byblos by the Phoenicians, to be used for educational purposes among the nobles. I succeeded in this only by agreeing that Ogham would be retained as the mystic writing of the druids. But my great triumph was in persuading the people not to celebrate our victory over the Fomorians at Samhain with the commemoration ceremony they called Crom Cruach after the captive who was burned alive in the wicker effigy at the time. Each year the horrible performance was repeated using captured enemies or slaves. The offering was dedicated to the fruitfulness of the earth, and also to the god of battle, Neit. Dara, as I have said, was long since Chief Druid, but he had neither forgotten nor abandoned the particular beliefs in a single all-powerful god that he derived from his parents (an idea that had begun to interest me also). In any case I used this to convince him and, somehow, in spite of the years of peace and prosperity we enjoyed, we persuaded the other druids and ollamhs that it was an affront to the goddess and the god as well as to human dignity, and to such effect, that it was agreed not to include it in the celebrations for the forthcoming quinquennial festival. Far more important for me, personally, is the fact that the chief priestess, with whom I was to

313

perform the rite, was my own beloved consort, Eremed. And so we assembled at the great Fair of the Crimson City to hold the first five-year festival at which I officiated.

I need not dwell overmuch on it. I have already described the essential ceremony and those of you who may hear my chronicle and remember will be familiar with such festivals, which differ little from one another wherever in the world they are held. The principal law of the fair was that it be peaceful. Any man breaking this rule, for whatever reason, was subject to severe penalty, even death. Whatever quarrels or grudges that existed between individuals or families or clans, were bound to be put aside at the great fairs. Any action that might give rise to a dispute was forbidden. Even a debtor, no matter how great the charge upon him, was safe from arrest. All was patterned on the common knowledge and regulations that had been handed on to us as remembered from Ionia.

While the buying, selling and trading was going on, the meeting of the principal men, the kings and ollamhs, also took place. This was the Dáil, where laws and regulations relating to the kingdoms and the land were discussed, enacted and learned. The leading women also held Aireachts, or councils, to decide matters concerning them-selves. But the greater part of the day was devoted to games and con-tests for men and women of all degrees. They did not, of course, compete with one another, either the men with the women or those of high degree with the common people.

All kinds of entertainment was a feature of the evenings; music, poetry and story-telling claiming much of our attention. While for the masses there were showmen, jugglers and clowns wearing comical masks to keep the crowds amused. There were skilled per-formers who gave exciting displays of horsemanship and, of course, craftsmen and tradesmen of all kinds, making, buying and selling from the thousands of booths that sprang up for the duration of the fair. Each trade or craft had its own area, so that you could buy or sell livestock here, clothing and food there, gold and silver yonder, weapons and embroidered cloths over beyond. And there were kitchens and eating houses with food of all kinds for sale everywhere.

On the evening, before the sun went down, all the lights and fires of the land were extinguished and silent crowds of the people everywhere gathered before the sacred circles, the largest in the city. Just as my grandfather had while I watched from the roof of a hut when I was a boy in far-off Tartessia, I, too, now welcomed the symbol of the goddess as it rose from beneath the world to rest for a moment on the pillar-stone before ascending the broad heavens. But instead of the cape of feathers he had worn, I, and those celebrating with me, wore capes of feathers of heron and eagle and kingfisher that reached to our ankles. I sang the song and was answered by Eremed, my wife and priestess: singing it I thought I sensed something stir in my bosom as I implored the goddess, on behalf of the people, to join with me for their prosperity and the fertility of the land. I felt some hesitance, but not so much as at my initiation and I was also excited by the thought that the goddess, as Ishtar (as I sometimes thought of her in my mind), might indeed come to me in a real sense in the night as I believed she had to my grandfather so long before. With the beautiful bow used by my grandfather, and selected pieces of timber and tinder, such as he had also used, I conjured fire out of nothing as evidence of her eternal and mysterious presence and bounty. Again I sang and was again answered by Eremed and now the refrain echoed from the multitude — or from the druids and priestesses around me — I was by no means certain. The great moment of what was taking place, the building of a sacred cone of power, coupled with the effects of the secret infusion that Dara had given me beforehand to release my inner awareness, also confused my hither world senses slightly. I was part, the instrument, of a preponderant event of which the majesty was awesome. When my fire was glowing, then blazing, and my part of these events over and as the long column of people — which would not finish until past daybreak — began to file in and out, I slipped away to keep my tryst with the goddess. Pausing only to exchange my feathered cloak in the palace I ran on foot to her. I knew exactly where to go although I had not been told. There was but one place. The womb! Or rather the belly above the womb, where a single stone, similar to the Cloch

315

Greine, but smaller, stood upright to mark the navel of the earth-queen. When I reached where I could see the foot of the mound, lustrous in the fitful light from a lambent moon that welcomed me between flying clouds, I slowed to see how the belly above the womb glowed in the night. It was wonderful with a touch of fear in it. Around the base stood the great retaining slabs, marked with old, old symbols. Outside them again, the greater circle beyond which the common people could not go. From the shadow of the oak-grove that separated my path from the road I absorbed the atmosphere a while. While there I heard a muffled clatter, like that of a single-ponied chariot, on the hidden road. But somehow different. It did not remind me of the brave, iron-shod approach of other chariots, but was as if it had wheels of many spokes shod with light wood like Egyptian chariots; and as if the pony's hooves were muffled. The strange sound troubled me further and I shuddered. I went on but when, close to the outer rim of boulders, I could see the road, it was pale and empty. I cleared my mind and concentrated on my purpose. Not wishing to profane the holy entrance to the womb, I circled to the side and climbed the flank of the white hill, careful to avoid disturbing any of the shining stones that covered it. When I reached the top with its shallow, grassy grove I was covered in sweat. The moon's pale light came now from an uncluttered sky bathing the hollow and its slender pillar-stone with silver effulgence. My heart beat; my temples pounded. I passed the ring of stones and stepped into the tufted hollow, the only green place on that glistering mound of quartz.

As I did so the miracle occurred. Nor, as I have said, do I, to this day, know how or why (whatever I may suspect), for it was concealed from me as it was also on the first occasion. Then it was due to my eating the magic mushrooms I stole from my grandfather's pouch. Now, in the intoxication of urgency, my hurrying foot plunged in a cleft provided to carry off water where I thought there was firm ground, and I fell striking my head on a small boulder as I did so. If I was unconscious it was not for long. But when I sat up, I was dizzy and could not see clearly. There was a haze about everything, particularly the moon, which, as long ago, had a nimbus round it that rushed upon me as I looked. I shook my head to clear it and shut my eyes. When I opened them a woman, naked, beautiful, walked from the shadow of the pillar. She was tall and lissom and the moonlight was behind her. She stood and held her hands towards me, and I stood as best I could and reached for them. ....

There is no more that I will tell of the remainder of that night. It is part of the mystery and is of no interest to any but myself, and, perhaps ... well! I do not know! When I woke in the morning, wrapped in my king's cloak, I lay alone in the grassy navel of the world and my head was bandaged. As I stirred a voice said: 'Well, it's about time.'

And Dara, now the principal druid of the people since the death of Methger, stood up from where he had been sitting on one of the small boundary rocks.

'Dara! Are you alone?'

'Who did you expect? You are alone yourself?'

He said it as a question, not a statement. 'How's your head? I bandaged it while you slept.'

'So it was you ...'

He nodded.

'Come, Cian. Let's go. You can tell me about it on the way.'

But there was little I could – or would – tell. When I got back to the palace I asked a slave to fetch the queen. But he returned after a while to say that she was indisposed and was resting. I drew my blood and purified myself in a sweat house before eating a meal. Then I rested, myself.

The next twenty-five years of my reign was peaceful. The country continued to prosper and the people to multiply. I lost some old friends and made new. My mother's death was the first serious personal loss following the deaths of Ogma and Lugh. But I was pleased that before she died she had the satisfaction of sitting in the highest seat of honour for a woman at many banquets in the Teach Micuarta when Eremed was not available. To my great grief her death was shortly followed by that of Eremed herself from a fishbone lodging in her throat. From that day it was geasa for fish — even honey-coated salmon — to be served at my table. But there were joys as well, especially in my three daughters, Banba, Eriu and Fodhla, named in honour of the goddess.

As the years accumulated I grew older and greyer and stiffer from my wounds. I began to be troubled by dreams and visions which — perhaps because I did not want to — I at first failed to understand. A woman I did not recognise would appear to me when I was by myself or asleep. I saw her once on a wind-swept hill one winter's afternoon, scattered raindrops flying horizontally. She pointed a long finger at me, then at the barren winter earth. Her black rags streamed upon the wind and she looked like a crow. Another time I woke and she stood beside my bed looking down at me. But all I saw were her eyes. Each time her face was hidden. When at last I saw it it was ugly and old. Thereafter she came more often in my dreams, each time older and uglier than before: each time wearing less clothes until she was naked but for a filthy shift, in hideous obscenity, and offered herself to me with both hands. My own cry woke me and I was sweating. I had long acknowledged that it was the goddess, as the Cailleach, telling me that my kingship was coming to an end. But she revealed no more; who the successor was to be, nor was there any hint from the people that she had been seen abroad in the land, and the land itself was prosperous. I was worried.

Then, one Bealtaine, a thing — rather two things which at first I did not connect — happened that alarmed me more than anything. Keth, my father, was now an old man, more than ninety, and I had the habit of visiting him at dawn to see if he was all right for, as you know, it is geasa for the king to be abroad before the dawn. As I crossed my grianaan I could see the distant light between gaps in dark clouds. I was thinking about the ceremony at Usna later, when I felt drops of wet on my head. They were large and scattered, and I looked up and held out my hands. Even in the faint light I could see the drops were dark. When I reached my father's quarters, I found my face was spattered red as if by blood. I hurriedly returned to the palace and purified myself; slaughtering a mare and ritually washing in its blood mixed with water. I drank some drops of the blood in water and then had a sweat-bath attended by priestesses, but I was troubled.

Later that day warriors from a settlement near my own dun at Dubhlinn arrived, bringing the body of a foreigner who, they said, was the leader of a warrior ship that had sailed up-river and landed near the settlement. They were evasive as to why they had killed the visitors, saying only that they had been insulted and that their druid had advised it. They killed them, buried them without taking their heads and brought the body of the leader to me. I was not unduly disturbed until I learned that this leader, whose name was Ith, and all his men spoke a dialect very similar to our own.

I discussed this and the occurrence of the red rain with Dara and the ollamhs. But they were little help. Dara read the clouds and the entrails, the roth-ramach or rowing-wheel, and the four rods of ogham, but could only tell me that the readings were confused. We summoned the leader of the settlement for an explanation as to why the foreigners had been killed and, after some persuasion, he told us that it was because they had violated the laws of hospitality, having made it clear that they expected to be treated as conquerors, not guests.

'How', he was asked, 'could they expect that: one ship?'

He shrugged. 'They did! They were the forerunners and were to return with news of Ierne to their brothers in Spain.'

I looked about the circle of faces, recalling why we ourselves came to Ierne to avenge Nemed more than fifty years ago.

'Very well,' I said. 'There was little you could do.' We sacrificed to the goddess for twenty-seven nights thereafter. One evening while I was at a banquet in the great hall a herald from the south-east came to say that a great fleet was seen off the coast two nights before. Scarcely had he finished than another arrived from the south with news of another fleet off the Munster coast four moons ago.

I immediately sent couriers to gather accurate information, to find the invaders and parley with them and discover if they were one group or two.

When the news came it was as bad as it could be and enabled me to begin to fit the meaning of the visitations from the Cailleach, the blood-like rain, the tumultuous clouds at dawn, the obscure portents, together in an ominous pattern. These newcomers were our cousins, not just in name. They were so close they called themselves Milesians, from their leader, Mil, named from their city of origin – the very Miletus from whence our own forefathers (and the Firbolg) had come.

Their fleets had landed, one at Bantry, the other two days later north of the city near the mouth of the Boinne. Quickly I arranged to meet their leaders, the sons of Mil, Eber and Eremon, who led the fleets, and their brother, and poet and chief ollamh, Amergin of the White Knee.

They came to the city with simplicity and power. Their weapons all of grey iron; their horses large and swift. There were, perhaps, two thousand and five hundred of them, without, so far as we knew, a woman among them. Only the leaders and an escort came to the city and I, with my court, went out to greet them. The Firbolg had already told us that they would not join us against them, but they would not fight with Milesians against us either. 'For', they had told my ambassadors, 'we are all of the same origin.' The Bretani simply said – 'settle your own affairs.' There was no time to summon any Gaetanae and we were disconcerted, later, to see a full company of them with the Milesians.

If I could I wanted to avoid battle. But the invaders were just as determined to have vengeance and, it seemed, to take our island from us.

They joined forces south of us and approached on horseback at a canter. Their haughty, purposeful bearing did nothing to reassure me. They were tall, fair men, dressed for war, and all were young. Each man looked like a nobleman, and there were six fifties of them

320

coming towards us. Each fifty wore a different coloured cloak and — a remarkable and impressive thing — they advanced in a regular column, six horsemen abreast. It was the seventeenth of the moon and in front rode Eber, Eremon and Amergin.

When they reached the chariot-course where we waited they stopped and formed up, facing us across its broad reach. Then one — whom I quickly discovered was Amergin — rode to the centre, beyond the Cloch Greine, and, ignoring us, dismounted and declared this poem. As I listened I felt cold and clammy and my forehead was damp. I heard my grandfather's voice again celebrating the ceremony of Ishtar, and his poem, that began 'I am the Wind on the Sea; I am the Wave; I am the Roar of the Breakers; I am the Bull ...' and I shuddered. But not from the recollection, nor from the cold sweat that covered my body, but because the marvellous voice of Amergin sang a song that was the same; a song that echoed my grandfather's down the years, and yet did not; a song that had the power of my grandfather's ... and much more besides!

In the trained tones of a high druid Amergin sang:

> I am the Wind of the Sea,
> The Wave of the mighty Ocean;
>
> I am the Roar of the Tide,
> The Bull of Seven Combats;
>
> I am the Hawk on the cliff,
> The sacred Dew on the grass;
>
> I am the loveliest flower,
> The bold Boar of valour;
>
> I am the speckled salmon
> The lake in the plain;
>
> I am Poetry and Wisdom,
> The deadly edge of weapons;
>
> I am He who makes Fire for a king.

Who will soften the mountainous crags?

Who tell the ages of the moon?

Who knows the resting place of the Sun?

Who the god that makes limitless boundaries?

Mystery in Deaths! Mystery in the Moving Wind.

I!

As he finished he threw his arms upwards and stood still in the centre of the course, a seemingly small figure — that dominated the silent concourses on either hand. I knew then what was not clear before.

Although they were kings, Amergin and his brothers wore the robes and carried the symbols of heralds. This too was unusual. The signs and the auguries began to have meaning. Samhain was only three months off. Was not their coming — from first Miletus and then Spain, just as the people had done before them — a re-coming? Was this the meaning of Amergin's poem? With sudden and great clarity I saw that a re-birth of an immeasurable nature was imminent. Amergin still stood in the centre of the course. I stood up on the dais where I had been waiting to receive them and throwing my arms wide, and contrary to all custom, I walked towards him across the expanse of the chariot course, clasped him in my arms and kissed him three times. At this a gasp of awe and astonishment ran like a whisper through the throng of onlookers.

We brought them to the Teach Micuarta and gave them a royal banquet. Eber and Eremon sat on either side of me, Amergin oppo-site, in the appropriate place for a great poet. Clustered at his feet were my three daughters, as if drawn there by some powerful force. When we had eaten and been entertained with music I asked why they had come to Ierne. Eremon answered, his reply short and pointed.

'For vengeance and the country.'

'We deeply regret the death of Ith and his comrades. We will pay an appropriate eric.'

'The eric we require is the island of Ierne; the fealty of the people; the marriage of the goddess.'

Whatever I answered, I thought, would be questioned and criticised. I thought for a moment and said:

'You seek justice. All of us here seek justice. That is what brought us to this land and now it brings you here. We would feel justified in meeting you in battle, or in meeting you in peace. You have invaded our island with vengeance in your hearts. Is there justice in your demand? I put it on you that you leave Ierne in peace.'

'Do you mean we should leave?' Eber asked incredulously.

'I do.'

He started to laugh, but I stopped him.

'Let Amergin judge. And I put it on him,' I said, looking directly across the room to where he sat behind the far table so that our looks intermingled, 'by the wind and the waves and the air and the fire and the earth and all the elements, to judge truly, on pain of death.'

There was a shocked silence. While it lasted Amergin and myself stared at each other. Someone, I think it was Eremon, started to say something but Amergin stopped him.

'Let it be so,' he said. 'I pronounce it. Let this island of Ierne be left to them in peace … for three days. And let justice be done.'

He stood up and his brothers and then all their people along with them. I had done my best.

'How far shall we go?' asked Eber.

'Past just nine waves,' replied the poet, still locking glances with me. Then he turned and led his brothers and their following from the hall. They left for their respective fleets that night, that which had landed at Bantry, now just to the south of the River Boinne where it had been brought by the Milesian king, Donn, who died as they approached the shore.

When they were gone I assembled the council, twenty-seven besides myself, which is the correct number. Looking at the well-known faces, a few older than my own, a few with the strength of fresh manhood, mostly men and women of middle years, I saw that they were simultaneously puzzled and aware … as if they guessed,

323

but did not want to acknowledge the meaning of what was happening.

The lights in the council chamber were strong. Torches projected outwards from the pillars, three to each, and there were many candles on the table and lamps here and there on stands. The smoke rose to the high roof, well above our heads, and I could see clearly. Nevertheless I could sense an additional, unseen presence. I sensed the others also felt it and that this, at least partly, accounted for their uneasiness.

'What do you suggest?' Dara's voice was quiet.

'We must fight!' One of the younger ones, a chieftain called Fiachna of the Clan Ruari. To my surprise there was no support for him as he looked round. One of the older ollamhs, for whom I had much respect, asked: 'Your opinion, my king?'

I looked round again before answering, trying to put my mind and my heart into some kind of order.

'Samhain is close,' I began. They were all looking at me.

'We will be invoking the renewed year; the renewed sun.' I paused. 'It is many years since we invoked a renewed queen.'

I saw from their expressions that they caught my thought. Having planted it, I deliberately turned away from it again.

'Yes, we can meet them in battle. And if we do what will be the outcome? In the whole land they are fewer than we, but they are here, together, not twenty miles away. Even in the three days can we field a force powerful enough to defeat them?'

I saw hesitation where, if they believed we could, there should have been resolve.

'Perhaps there is another way,' I said. 'Listen.'

I outlined and we discussed what was in my mind — or as much of it as I felt was necessary at that time before dawn stole on us many hours later. The council continued the next night and part of the next and on the day of the third moon my ambassadors went to greet the leaders of the Milesians with this proposal.

The Tailltean Games were due to begin in four days. Instead of war and combat I proposed that the Milesian nobles and ourselves should compete at the games, the victors to rule the land.

In the meantime I made certain preparations of my own. In case they refused I had assembled what troops I could, but still had managed to bring together only one fighting battalion and perhaps four or five of rabble. Even though the Milesians had only about one battalion themselves, I wondered if the rabble might not be more of a hindrance than a help in battle. I bivouacked my troops outside the city. But I was not encouraged by what I saw. We had had no serious fighting for years and the only action any of them had seen was against bandits and cattle-raiders and, if they were lucky and in place, in one of the sporadic raids by small bands of Fomorians. But battle . . .!

I had also summoned the leaders who did not belong to the council and held a day-long meeting after the ambassadors went to the Milesians. When that meeting ended there was no rejoicing and each leader, man and woman, sent heralds to their cities and settlements telling the people not to come to Tailltean, or to turn back if they had already started. When all that was done I waited.

On the third night my ambassadors returned to tell me the Milesians had accepted and would meet us at Tailltean two days hence. The victors were to rule the country and the people, the vanquished to depart. I was much relieved. I knew then that, in any event, it was preordained, but I was relieved to know I had interpreted the wishes of the goddess correctly. It was a personal gratification also to know that she shared my reluctance for unnecessary bloodshed and, as became clear, sacrifice on the scale of pointless battle did her no honour. I understood that. I arranged to honour her fittingly and in keeping with the magnitude of the occasion should we be defeated, and I was content.

There is little left now to do but describe the outcome of the games. I had myself driven there in the fine, crimson and gold, four-wheeled

chariot with the purple awning and curtains, drawn back so the
people could see, that I used on ceremonial journeys. The people
were largely silent as we passed. In spite of my warnings rumour had
spread through the city like a plague and the quiet crowds knew
what depended on these games. If they were disappointed at not
being allowed to take part with their fellows from all over the country, that was buried under their sense of the occasion. Yet there was
some cheering as I passed and I waved from my cushioned seat at the
head of the royal entourage on the way to Taillte. The other nobles
were already there, and Tailltean looked bright and gay that
morning. Overhead large white clouds hung nearly motionless in a
blue sky, and it promised to be a golden day. The Milesians were on
the other side of the plain, across from the tents and booths of the
people. There was little colour about them. They were just an armed
mass, from which, from time to time, came a flash of sunlight
glancing off iron or bronze. Where we were, flags and banners
clustered thick. Every king and chieftain was determined to show his
standard, the less important he was, it seemed, the more flags he
showed and I could not help smiling and being proud. Thousands of
people from in and around the city came to watch and, with the
slaves and attendants of the chiefs, and the silent ranks of the
Milesian troops, made a respectable enough audience.

I greeted Eber, Eremon and Amergin in the centre of the field
while the trumpets and horns played a fanfare. I invited them to my
pavilion to watch the progress of the games but they refused on the
grounds that they intended to take part themselves, in the wrestling.
(I am glad to say that, while Eber won his bout, Eremon was beaten
by the champion of the people.)

I am weary of the telling now, and perhaps it shows. Indeed what
more is there to tell? There was foot racing, competitions for spear
and javelin casting, for wrestling, chariot racing, horsemanship, feats
with the sword, with the sling and with the bow. Towards the end of
that long day, when we all knew the tally by heart and victory rested
on a footprint, the honours were even, and it looked as if it was to be
war after all. I called a respite and again asked the three Milesian

326

leaders to join Dara and myself for wine and fruit, which they did. After some awkward conversation I casually commented:

'What a pity you have no women with you. We might match one of them against my daughter, Eriu, who is a fine horsewoman, to decide the issue.'

They looked up, suddenly alert.

'But we have a woman with us,' they declared, 'our sister Scota. She is considered the finest horsewoman among us.'

Thus was the final and decisive competition arranged almost by accident. Scota was one of the most beautiful women I ever saw. In some ways she reminded me of my lovely Eremed — but where Eremed's head was of red gold, Scota's was yellow. But she was even more beautiful, though the beauty of her nature did not glow on her skin as it had with my dead love. Like Eremed she was tall and lissom, but where Eremed's eyes were hazel-green, hers were brown. She had a beautiful, open smile which captured all those, including myself, on whom it was turned. Whether as a horse rider she was a match for my daughter, Eriu, remained to be seen. Eriu was like her grandmother, my mother Sena'an, dark haired and dark skinned, with high cheekbones, and she had a full and generous mouth that matched her fine, arched eyebrows. She was smaller than Scota, and looked more muscular, but unless she stood beside someone a good deal taller than herself, she seemed tall. She was well proportioned and she moved with the economic grace of a cat. She rode a horse better than any woman I ever saw and better than most men. Now on these two women rested the fate of our peoples and of all who lived in Ierne. As a matter of honour we offered the Milesians first choice of my stables if they were so inclined, but they refused saying that Scota would ride Amergin's horse — a large, white animal, its ears dyed red and its flowing mane and tail a kingly purple. Each nostril was ringed with red, too, so that when it pranced, threw back its head and flared them, it looked a royal steed indeed. Eriu's pony, Dearg-Donn or Red-Brown, was much smaller and lighter and was not coloured at all, except the ears, which were blue. The course was four times round the chariot course at Taillte and it was agreed that I would start the race. For the occasion I put on my feathered cloak of kingship and druidism, which brought exclamations of admiration from the Milesian nobles. Each woman, stripped to the waist and wearing only a leather kilt about her waist, stood on the left of her steed. Each wore a band about her forehead, similar to the saffron band of a charioteer, to keep the hair from her eyes. Scota's was scarlet and Eriu wore one that I had given her, of white with a thread of gold in it.

It was a beautiful evening, the clouds that hung in the sky in the morning had drifted off in the direction of Albion. Now, as the sun declined towards the west, touching the edges of the world here and there with red and gold, the sky was blue and cloudless and a milky moon sailed above.

The girls grasped the manes of their mounts with their left hands. I gave a signal to the trumpeters and they instantly blew the gallop. Simultaneously each woman sprang from the ground in a graceful ech-léim, or steed-leap, and they were off at a gallop towards the turn at the far end of the course. Each had only an echlasc, or horse-rod, Scota one of yew ornamented with silver and having a bronze boccan, or goad, at the end, while Eriu's was of ash and was ornamented in bronze throughout. Her smaller animal was quicker away and she was half a length ahead before they were half way to the turn, but as soon as he found his stride the size and speed of the other horse told and Scota passed her on the outside and was ahead when they reached it. But on the turn the big horse had to swing wide to take the corner. Eriu swung the pony round almost on one leg and they were neck and neck half-way back towards us. Again the horse edged in front and again Dearg-Donn took him on the turn. As they passed my pavilion — where we were all on our feet shouting and being drowned out by the cheering from the onlookers outside — I could see the strain on the girls' faces and in their eyes, as they sought and fought for position on the course. Above the cheering and the shouting one could hear the smacks of the echlascs as they lashed their mounts, and see the sun glance from the ornamentations as the women wielded them deftly to guide their steeds this way or that over the uneven track, which had been badly cut up by chariot racing earlier in the day.

Round again and two things were very clear: Scota was as good a rider as Eriu in nearly all respects, and although the pony was putting up an amazing performance, the size and strength of the horse was beginning to tell. At the end of the third circuit the larger animal was in front and drawing away with every stride. Eriu's face as she passed was a bleak mask of determination. Her blazing eyes were fixed on her rival's black and the echlasc rose and fell like a sword on the flank of Dearg-Donn. Froth flew from the pony's mouth and I plainly saw his eyes roll. Much more and I knew he'd drop. But although she loved him above anything, I think, Eriu urged him to that extra effort ... With a man's length between them they thundered past for the last turn and Amergin turned to me unable to hide the satisfaction in his eyes. His brothers were openly smiling. But even as they smiled my head snapped up, for the big horse stumbled and Scota lurched forward on his neck almost losing her seat. She recovered quickly, but the horse had broken its stride and Dearg-Donn was on them, coming fast and inside. Scota lashed her beautiful horse with her echlasc and we could hear her swearing even from that distance, but it was no use and Eriu and the pony rounded the last bend ahead of them and were away towards the finish, a length ahead. How she did it I don't know, but Scota wheeled the big horse, almost as Eriu did with her pony, round the pillar, and had lashed him to a gallop all in the one movement. She leaned far forward over the horse's ears and shouted at him, lashing with her echlasc all the while. The gap between her and Dearg-Donn was closing, closing ... but yet, the pony might do it. Eriu must have sensed something, or heard her, and she glanced back across her shoulder, and then urged her little mount with one hand, voice and heel until they seemed to be one beast, intent only on reaching the finish before the great white animal thundering down on them from behind, lashed to a riot of splendid speed.

As they passed us on the far side it seemed certain that Eriu on Dearg-Donn must win. My heart was already rejoicing. Eriu was a full half length ahead with less than three-quarters of a forrach — fifty yeards — to go. But then, by some supreme effort, even as the smile came to my lips and the pounding of my heart began to subside, Scota stretched herself full length along the back and flank of her steed and stabbed him with her goad. The animal responded with reserves I would not have believed possible. Neck outstretched, red-painted nostrils flaring, purple tail and mane flying in the wind of his passage, he seemed to swoop on Eriu and Dearg-Donn and pass the finishing line a stride in front. Eber, Eremon and Amergin were on their feet cheering as were all the Milesians grouped at the finishing post. From our own people, so magnificent was the win, a spontaneous shout rose up — only to be instantly checked with realisation of what the win meant. In response, Scota leaped to her feet on the back of her steed and galloped towards us, her smile lighting her lovely face, guiding the horse with her echlasc. But its heart was broken with the effort. As it passed the pillar-stone it stumbled to its knees, flinging Scota across the painted ears. Horse and rider fell together, the one to die of exertion, the other when she struck her beautiful head against the pillar-stone and dashed her brains in a bloody mass across its base. The silence that halted the cheering as the horse fell turned to groan and a great wail as Scota's body folded, lifeless into the ground. The first to reach her was Eriu who sprang from Dearg-Donn and who was cradling Scota's broken head against her naked breast when we reached her, the tears streaming down her cheeks. Wordlessly she looked at me and sobbed.

'She ... she ... was great ... she ... it was ... my ... fault ... she ...'

The Milesian kings took the body of their sister from Eriu and carried her away in silence while my daughter buried her head in my shoulder and sobbed as if the world had ended, as, perhaps, it had. In that way we lost our land and the Milesians gained it, but lost their beautiful queen, Scota.

That was three months ago. Afterwards they came to me and I told them how sad I was that their joy at winning was marred by such a tragedy.

'It was the will of the goddess,' said Amergin, and again I looked at his eyes and again felt he knew and understood more of what was taking place about us than anyone else.

'You have seen the goddess?' I asked. He nodded.

'Once. But not since coming to Ierne. But I feel her presence all round us here.'

'She has been coming to me recently,' I said and I think he understood, because he said no more.

That was in the Royal House at the Crimson City, Cathair Cró Fhind.

'We will not be harsh,' said Eber — though Eremon looked over my head and I wondered if he agreed. That Amergin did, I already knew.

'If you will ... we would share the land with you.'

I shook my head. 'That would not be just.'

'You have been just with us and, I think, we with you,' replied Amergin. 'We feel there is a contribution we can all make for the future. Let us marry your women; we will rule the people guided by your wisdom, and, in time, they will benefit from the best from both of us.'

'It was agreed that the vanquished would leave.'

'We no longer require that,' said Eber. And then, with certainty, I knew and understood what was to be done, not only by me, but by my fellow nobles whom I had already instructed to prepare for the possibility of migration, perhaps to Albion or further north.

'I appreciate your offer,' I told them, even as my mind considered the profound message I had received from the goddess. 'It is a generous, noble offer. I must consult the lords of the people. All I ask at this time is that you give us until Samhain. By then all that is to take place will have taken place and the new year and all that it foretells will be re-born.'

I looked directly at Amergin and he understood instantly.

'Of course.'

'Meantime,' said Eremon, who up until then had not spoken,' we require you to vacate this place, which we shall rename Teamhair, or Tara. From here we will rule, as you have. But we will not share it with you.'

I looked at him, and at the others, who appeared a little uneasy at the brutal manner in which he had said this, but they were in apparent agreement.

'Very well,' I said, 'we shall be gone within one week.'

'Two days,' said Eremon.

'We must hold a council meeting ... make arrangements ...'

'Hold it elsewhere ...'

'Will three days be sufficient?' Amergin's voice was low, but firm. It was little, but I would make it do. I would not get more. I nodded.

'We will rule the country between us, Eber and myself. We will divide it in two,' went on Eremon, 'I shall take the northern half and Eber the southern.'

'That would seem appropriate,' I said, but I think only Amergin understood my thrust, for I was referring to the nature of the poles. North, that of Battle, contentions, strifes, haughtiness, pride, hardness, wars, conflicts; and south, that of Music, fairs, nobles, knowledge, subtlety, wisdom, honour, learning, warriorship, fierceness, modesty and fertility.

They left soon after and I summoned the council and instructed the nobility not to return to their towns and settlements. We sat for two of the three nights and on the third moon were ready to leave the city which had been so generous to us and which we had built and extended and developed so that the number of tall and noble buildings, some of them higher than fifty feet from floor to ceiling and many with two and even three stories, was now more than three times what it had been when we arrived. They could be seen crowning the hilltop from all quarters of the plain. The whole population — many of whom wanted to come with us, but were prevented by the Milesian troops — lined the streets and cried and lamented as we left for our raths. It was a sad leave-taking, but I did not look back, nor have I visited it since in spite of the pride I took in developing it and watching it grow. It is my city no longer; it is no longer the Crimson City, Cathair Cró Fhind of the Tuatha de Danann, but Tara of the Milesians.

Now, to my sorrow, I heard that some of the common people

have told them about celebrating at Samhain our defeat of the Fomorians with Crom Cruach, the very practice I hoped to stamp out. And I am told that they have made not one but several wicker figures for tomorrow night's ceremonies, and have a number of fettered prisoners, criminals and law-breakers, held in stone forts for the purpose.

As for us, we are ready. When tomorrow's dawn breaks the nobles, kings, lords and chieftains of the people, more than two thousand men, women and children, will have at once accepted the generous offer of Amergin and his brothers to stay and share the land with them, and simultaneously will have made the greatest and most important offering for renewal and rebirth that has ever been made to the goddess as earth mother.

My story is over. I am sitting here, in my favourite place on this small hill above the wicker weir of B'la Cliath, dictating to you, Dara, and your scribes. Look out there with me. Over there, north, is the Womb of the World. Just across the broad bay is Ben Eadair, Howth, coloured by the declining sun of winter. The sun that will rise tomorrow will be a new sun. When we rise tomorrow we will be a new people. You, in your raths and duns, you will lie and remain there forever. I …? I thought, and my mind wanders. The thoughts are bigger than I can easily express! Now, suddenly, I am conscious of the awareness of things expanding outwards from the point that is myself. I comprehend that it is exactly that same for every one, as if the world is simultaneously experienced by a numberless multitude of spreading fans, each ending in an acute speck. When you get right down to it, perception and knowledge belong exclusively between each individual and — and — what was it Pythagoras said? The soul is infinite? Well, then, to that infinity! Of which the goddess, too, must be part.

If I have any sadness it is that I have no son to leave behind … and even if I had he, too, would lie tonight in my rath with his sisters, Fodhla, Banba and my little Eriu, as the nobles will lie in every rath in the country, having drunk the fairy mead, the miodh sidhe, mee shee, from the druid's cup and it would make no matter. But I would dearly have loved to pass to a son the knife my father gave me, and his to him, and so on, until its beginnings are lost in the beginnings of our family, even if he slept with it in his hand for eternity. So, since I have none I wrapped it in doe-skin, and buried it here, on this hillock sheltered from the wind, with the sea on my right hand and the dying sun on my left.

It is time for me to go. My chariot is below at the ford and I must be at Newgrange and enter the Womb of the World before the middle of the night. For I am still king. And I have seen the Cailleach in her most hideous aspect. She waits there for me. Tomorrow the king will be reborn, the goddess will be reborn in youth and the land, with its new rulers, will be reborn. That is the end of my story. So be it.

Select Bibliography

Coon, Carlton S., *The Hunting Peoples*, Jonathan Cape.

Clark, Graham and Piggott, Stuart, *Prehistoric Societies*, Hutchinson.

Fraser, J., *The First Battle of Moytura*, ed. and trans., Eriu VIII.

Fuller, J.F.C., *The Decisive Battles of the Western World*, 2 vols., Eyre and Spottiswoode.

Herodotus, *The Histories*.

Joyce, P.W., *Old Celtic Romances*, Talbot Press.

——, *A Social History of Ancient Ireland*, 2 vols, M.H. Gill & Son.

Leahy, A.H., *Heroic Romances of Ireland*, A.H. Nutt, 2 vols.

Levi-Strauss, Claude, *Structural Anthropology*, Allan Lane.

Lissnar, Ivar, *The Living Past*, Jonathan Cape.

Neeson, Eoin, *The First Book of Irish Myths and Legends*, Mercier.

——, *The Second Book of Irish Myths and Legends*, Mercier.

Nylander, Carl, *The Deep Well*, Allen and Unwin.

O'Duffy, Richard, J., *The Fate of the Children of Tuireann*, ed. and trans. with notes, Society for the Preservation of the Irish language.

Powell, T.G.E., *The Celts*, Thames and Hudson.

Rees, Alwyn and Brinley, *The Celtic Heritage*, Thames and Hudson.

Sharkey, John, *Celtic Mysteries*, Thames and Hudson.

Stokes, Whitley, *The Second Battle of Moytura*, Revue Celtique.

Wright, Thomas, *History of Ireland*, 7 vols, The London Printing and Publishing Company.

Xenophon, *The Persian Expedition*.

Yadin, Yigael, *The Art of Warfare in Biblical Lands*, Weidenfeld and Nicholson.

Eigse.

Eriu.